LAVENDER

LAVENDER

THE MIDNIGHT PEACE RUNNERS SAGA #1

CHRISTINA KING

First Edition
Copyright © 2025 Christina King
All rights reserved.

This is a work of fiction. Names, characters, businesses, places, events, and incidents are either the product of the author's imagination or used in a fictitious manner. Any resemblance to actual persons, living or dead, or actual events is purely coincidental.

No part of this book may be reproduced, stored in a retrieval system, or transmitted in any form or by any means, electronic, mechanical, photocopying, recording, or otherwise, without the prior written permission of the publisher.

Published by Crown and Keys Press
ISBN-13: 979-8-218-68881-3
Cover design by Barbara Morrissey
Learn more at www.christinakingbooks.com

For Dad.
My #1 Fan.
♡

And for everyone who feels out of tune.
You just haven't found the right song yet.

ONE

HIGH SCHOOL relationships should have an expiration date.

At the very least, a renewal date. Like hey, time to check in. We've been together a year now and you're a bit of a jerk these days, which makes the fact that your toes hang over the front of your sandals even harder to overlook. And also, if you feel the need to kiss someone that's not me, let's just call it. Cause, *really*?

"Hey, Siri. Am I more likely to die from social humiliation or this insane heatwave?"

"I can't help you with that."

"Course not."

Brandon's eyes stare back at me from the framed selfie on my desk. His bronzed arm drapes over my ghostly white shoulders while I gaze up at him with a naïve, love-drunk smile. *Ugh.* I slam it down—the splinter of breaking glass cutting through the silence of my bedroom. My knuckles sting from the impact, and I instinctively bring them to my lips. "Fuckanutter."

My phone buzzes and I brace myself for Brandon's name to pop up again—but it's just my best friend. I let out a long breath.

Emma: You okay?

"No," I mutter to the destroyed frame. Of course, admitting that to Emma is not an option; she'd be over here in minutes. Suffering in solitude feels more fitting for this particular catastrophe.

My gaze drifts to the mountains outside. Despite the ninety-degree heat, the peak of Mount Snettles holds onto patches of snow, though now it's more cookies and cream than vanilla. The forest below stretches out below, crowded with evergreens and aspens.

I push the window open, and a blaze of summer air floods the room. *Nope.* I quickly shut it and flip on the small fan beside me, but the soft whirring does little to ease the heat clinging to my skin.

At an elevation of 9,300 feet, we've never needed air conditioning until this summer. Dad refuses to get it, insisting it's just a "weird year." Right. And global warming is just a bedtime story.

My shaking thumbs fumble across the digital keyboard as I respond to Emma: **Why did he have to make out with Paige? Feckin Paige.**

I know the answer, of course. She's beautiful and popular. Confident and "normal." Everything I'm not.

My chest feels heavy as I slide the shattered frame into the small white trash can beside my desk, careful not to let any glass slice through my skin—the buzzing of my phone syncs with the clink of glass meeting metal.

Emma: Cause he's an ass. You CAN swear though. Say it out loud. Right now. Fu-king.

I hate this day.

My mouth feels coated in Elmer's glue. I open and close it, disgusted by the sticky sensation, and grab my pink Stanley only to suck in air. Shaking the empty tumbler, I push to my feet, heading for a refill as Brandon's excuses circle in my mind. *He was drunk. Since when does he drink? He's always preaching about sober living.*

And how convenient that Paige, who is weirdly obsessed with him, shows up at "guys only" night.

What's next? Did he trip, and his lips accidentally land on hers?

As my thoughts spiral into chaos, a faint strumming of an acoustic guitar seeps into my ears. I pause, holding my breath to hear better. The quiet notes float through the air, carrying a hint of melancholy— as if God himself is composing my life's soundtrack.

I hold my phone to my ear then cross the room to inspect the pink Bluetooth speaker on my nightstand. It's off.

Doubling back to my desk, I open my MacBook to the same result. Nothing's playing, and besides, the melody sounds too far away.

Weird.

"Jake? Kalendar?" My voice carries through the upstairs hallway as I wander barefoot, the warm wood floors sticky beneath my feet. The only response is the mysterious guitar riff drifting through the house. Passing my older brothers' rooms, I glance inside. Kalendar's bed is a mess of clothes and empty water bottles, while Jake's room is, as usual, spotless.

A buzz in my back pocket makes me flinch, and against my better judgement, I pull out the phone. *Brandon.* I press decline for the third time, trying to ignore the sour churn in my stomach.

The music grows louder as I creep downstairs to the kitchen. It's haunting and moody, like a lost Lorde track. Sunlight spills through the picture window, making the white marble countertops gleam. I am drawn to the mountains again, but they look almost too perfect now, majestic against the bluebird sky. Something feels different— dream-like.

I poke my head into Dad's music room at the end of the house. Hundreds of albums sit neatly on bookshelves and the record player sits idle on his desk. The sound is fainter here. Still, "Dad?" No answer. *Hmm.*

The living and dining rooms are empty, and only my Bronco rests in the detached garage, the three bays wide open like a mechanic's shop.

Cranky and sweltering, I return to the kitchen and collapse into the breakfast nook, shoving aside one of the ten thousand throw pillows Mom insists on cramming onto the bench. A bead of sweat drips down my neck, and I lift my hair to fan myself.

Bruce, our German Shepherd, trots in through the dog door. He pads over and rests his head in my lap, his wiry fur radiating the outdoor heat.

"Where's the music coming from, buddy?" His big brown eyes search mine with curiosity.

A flash of orange through the window catches my eye as Bruce whines and darts back outside, the plastic dog door flapping behind him. I follow him onto the porch, and the music swells, the notes filling the air while the heat wraps around me like a cocoon. The melody seems as if it's coming from the woods, but I can't make out anything through the tightly packed trees. *Maybe campers?*

Bruce sniffs at a planter, where a cluster of butterflies has settled. I've never seen anything like them. They're no bigger than a quarter and there are so many, at least fifty, their orange-and-black wings dance over the lavender blooms. Bruce loses interest and bounds down the porch stairs. He flops onto his back and wriggles in the grass. A welcome breeze picks up, blowing my long hair across my bare shoulders.

The tune suddenly shifts from haunting folk to an energetic country-rock riff, and the butterflies take flight, spiraling toward the forest. Bruce barks and takes off after them, barreling through the invisible fence line.

"Bruce!" I sprint after him barefoot, wincing as tiny pebbles dig into my soles like dull thorns poking through the rough dirt of the driveway. "Bruce, come here!" My foot catches in a dip, and I slide through the dust, my body skimming the ground. Bruce's tail disappears through the ranch archway and into the road. I mutter a fake curse, picking myself up and brushing the dirt off.

The music cuts out the moment I reach the county road, leaving a quiet so profound it's as if the melody never existed. Bruce sits in the dry sagebrush outside our gate and lifts his nose, sniffing the air as the last of the butterflies vanish into the trees. Sweat drips down my temple as I brace my hands on my knees.

"Bad boy, come here." I call to him, my breath unsteady.

Bruce slinks over, his head lowered. I grab his collar while my eyes drift to the darkened tree line steps away. The familiar 10 MPH snowmobile sign, tacked to a weathered pine, marks the entrance of the trail to the National Forest, where I'm certain the melody was coming from.

My breath slows, and the air hums with the memory of the music; an inexplicable need to uncover the source pulls me toward the trees.

I glance at my feet, now dusted in cocoa-brown dirt, regretting my lack of shoes—not that I had a choice. Swallowing hard and tightening my grip on Bruce's collar, I step toward the woods just as a child's whine breaks the new silence, snapping me back to reality.

"Mom, are we there yet? My legs hurt."

A woman and a little boy emerge from the forest trail. The boy's Denver Broncos cap sits low over his eyes while the woman, dressed as if she walked straight from a Lululemon photoshoot, exhales a heavy sigh. "Yes, bud, we're almost there."

"Hi there," I say gently, careful not to scare them as Bruce slips from my grip.

The woman startles, her gaze meeting mine. "Oh, hello! Beautiful day, isn't it?" Her smile widens as her focus shifts to Bruce, now sitting at her feet. "May we pet him?"

"Oh yes, he loves attention."

She kneels and starts rubbing behind his ears. Bruce's tail kicks up a cloud of dust as it wags. A speaker dangles from her backpack.

"Was that music coming from you?"

"Huh?" She glances up at me, then follows my gaze to the backpack. "Oh, I forgot that was there." She laughs. "No, we weren't listening to anything."

"Really?" My eyes sweep over the trees again. "Do you know where that music was coming from then?"

Her manicured eyebrows lift. "Music?"

Before she can answer, a small voice cuts in.

"Are your eyes purple?"

My cheeks flush as I try but fail to push my oldest insecurity aside. The little boy's big eyes lock on mine.

"Theo! That's not polite." His mom stands and pulls him close with an apologetic grin.

My lips twitch into a grin. "It's okay, I'm used to it." Lowering myself to his level, I meet his curious gaze. "Yep, they're purple."

Theo stares, then tilts his head. "But they're *really* purple."

I nod. "Like neon purple." *Yup, I'm a freak.*

Theo scratches his cheek. "But, why?"

My voice drops to a whisper as I deliver the rehearsed, totally made-up response I came up with years ago, hoping to add a cool factor to my lack of melanin. "It's called Alexandria's Genesis. I can see better than anyone and live to be 150."

His eyes go wide. "No way."

"I'm kidding," I laugh. "But it sounds cool, right?"

Theo giggles.

"Okay, that's enough, Theo." His mom smiles, taking his hand. "We'd better keep moving. Have a nice day."

"You too."

As they continue down the road, Mom's car approaches. Her white SUV slows to a stop beside me, the mountains reflecting off its windshield. The window rolls down, revealing her smiling face. Graying hair sits in a low bun at the base of her neck, and she wears a purple tank top with her yoga studio logo across the front, a simple lavender flower, with a small crescent moon cradled beneath it.

"Hey, Mom." The car radiates warmth as I fold my arms on the window.

Her eyes flicker to my bare feet. "Lavender, what are you doing down here?"

Bruce sprawls out on the dirt beside me; I nod at him. "He ran through the invisible fence."

She raises an eyebrow, poking her head out. "Really? He never does that."

"I know." I gesture toward the mountains. "But I can't blame him. It was…weird. There were all these butterflies, and this, like, music playing…."

"Oh, yeah?" Mom's expression changes, her eyes filling with worry.

I put my hands on my hips. "Why are you looking at me like that?"

She shifts into park, her gaze locking onto mine. "Emma called me," she whispers.

"Seriously?" *C'mon Emma.*

"Oh, honey. I'm so sorry about Brandon." She steps out, wrapping me in a hug. "He doesn't deserve you, my beautiful girl."

My arms hang limply at my sides as she buries my head into her chest. "I *literally* found out, like, an hour ago. I can't believe Emma already called you."

"She cares about you." Mom pulls away and pushes a strand of hair behind my ear. "Have you talked to him?"

I nod, rolling my eyes to the sky. "He's not denying it, and tried making excuses, so I hung up on him. He keeps calling, though."

She lowers my chin to meet her gaze. "How did you find out?" The little crow's feet at the corners of her chestnut eyes deepen.

"Paige told me herself. Sent me a DM on Instagram." I cross my arms. "Nice, huh?"

"Oh, honey." She squeezes my shoulder. "I think it's for the best. Not that he cheated on you," she quickly adds. "But I never thought he was good for you."

The trees blur at the edges as tears threaten to spill. I blink hard, but it's no use—everything's gone watercolor.

Mom takes a deep breath, and I glance at her as a lone tear slips down my cheek. She brushes it away. Her lips curl into a smile that I recognize immediately—the one she gets when she's about to drop some yoga-inspired wisdom. I wish she would save it for her clients at the studio, but I brace myself for the inevitable.

"You and Brandon were never right for each other," she says, her voice steady with certainty. "You are a special soul. Don't settle for someone who doesn't recognize that."

I start to roll my eyes, but she catches it. "I'm serious," she insists. "Even after a year together, Brandon never really saw you—not the real you. He's in love with himself, if we're being honest."

"And you? I always felt you were more in love with the idea of him than who he actually is. You always did the things he wanted to do, and he never reciprocated. Remember last week? He was mad when you volunteered at the food pantry and missed his soccer game—even though you've been to every other one. You deserve better, sweetheart."

"Mom, I don't want to talk about this." I uncross my arms, then wipe at my eyes, eager to move on. "What are you doing tonight?"

Her gaze lingers on mine before she answers. "I'm meeting Dad and Jake at the Mason rodeo. Do you want to come?"

"Can't, I have plans." I twist my lips, feigning disappointment. "I promised Emma I'd go to the concert on the green."

"Well, that'll be fun." She shoots me a sidelong glance. "Ya know, Kalendar's going to the concert, too."

I run a hand down my face. "Great," I grumble.

Mom clicks her tongue. "I'm not sure what's going on with you two, but you haven't been all that nice to him lately."

Avoiding her gaze, I slide my phone from my pocket to check the time and ignore the two more missed calls from Brandon. *5:15.* "I should get ready. The concert starts at six thirty."

She sighs. "Okay, grab Bruce and hop in. I'll drive us up." As she opens her door, she adds, "And don't forget to take off his collar—last thing he needs is another zap."

Mom's phone rings as we reach the house. Aunt Mia's name crosses the display panel.

"Why don't you go inside? I'm going to take this."

"Sure. Tell Aunt Mia I say, hey." I reach for the door handle and climb out of the car, Bruce following at my heels. Aunt Mia's sing-song voice fills the space as I close the door behind us.

A hawk swoops low over my head, gliding toward the barn before vanishing into the woods. My eyes track its flight, but then something catches my attention—something out of place. I squint, straining to make it out. Halfway down the mountain, nestled among the thick evergreens and aspens, hundreds of tiny lights flicker—like fairies dancing in the trees.

"What's that?" I whisper.

Beside me, Bruce perks up, ears twitching.

As I turn to ask Mom about it, the guitar riff returns, stopping me mid-step.

The original haunting melody weaves through the airwaves and the fairy lights appear to glimmer in rhythm with the phantom tune. Then, a man's voice, low and soulful, melds into the song.

The lyrics are barely audible, but one word cuts through, unmistakable, like a whisper in the dark: *Lavender.*

TWO

I'M NOT GOING. I puff my cheeks and cross my eyes at my reflection in the floor-length mirror. *Definitely not.*

A text message ping pulls me from my drama.

Emma: You HAVE to come tonight. I'm 99% sure you're talking yourself out of it right now. I promise we'll have fun.

"Emma," I moan.

I glance back at the mirror. My light brown hair falls in loose waves over my shoulders, and a sleeveless ivory maxi dress hugs my waist, cinched with a braided brown belt. I pose with my hands on my hips, turning side to side, before trying the foot-flip I've seen influencers do. But my toes catch on the hem, and I stumble forward, barely catching the desk before a full-on face plant.

I straighten, laughing at myself.

Everyone has 1000% heard about the Brandon and Paige fiasco by now. Word spreads fast in Rosewood, Colorado—population 948. I certainly don't want *any* attention. But … at least I look cute—kind of. "Fine, I'm going."

I step over to the row of windows and press my palm against the warm glass. The mountain range glows in the early evening light, no longer overshadowed by the blazing sun. Its details stand out—the deep crevices, the sharp ridges, and the peak that has always reminded me of a boob. My gaze drifts below the tree line where the light fades, focusing on the cluster of twinkling lights I'd spotted earlier.

I should have mentioned it to Mom—the phantom song, the way it whispered my name. And I *definitely* should feel weirded out. Anyone that's normal would. But something's holding me back.

Of course, I've cycled through every possibility in the last hour since hearing it. A brain tumor? Psychosis? Don't vampires have bionic hearing or something? *Maybe I'm a vampire!* No, that's ridiculous. But maybe it could explain my purple eyes. Kidding. I think.

"Ender! Hey, Sis." Kalendar bounds into my room, throws an arm around my neck, and kisses my head.

"Kal, seriously, stop calling me that." I duck out from under his arm.

"It's your name, though. Been calling you that since you were born." He flops onto my bed, grabs my favorite childhood stuffed bear, Sammy, and mindlessly tosses him between his hands. "Anyway, Ma says you're headed to the concert tonight, too. Charlie is picking me up. Want a ride?"

Glaring at him, I snatch Sammy from his hold. "No, I'm taking the Bronco. Not sure how long I'll stay." Setting Sammy on the oversize pink velvet chair in the corner, I let out an annoyed sigh. I simply cannot be trapped in a car with Kalendar and Charlie. The conversation would inevitably turn to Brandon, and I can't handle that right now. Gosh, I wish I could erase minds or something. Pretend the whole thing with Paige never happened. Better yet. Pretend my relationship with Brandon never happened. Isn't there an old Will Smith movie where he has a mind eraser pen or something? How can I get my hands on one of those?

The fairy lights twinkle outside the window. Are they brighter now? Or is it my imagination? I blink hard, then open my eyes again, searching for any change.

"I see. Want to make a quick getaway if Brandon shows up, huh?" Kalendar's voice drips with sarcasm.

I whip around. "No, Kal, thanks for your *concern*." With a huff, I turn away from him.

His reflection fills my mirror. Kalendar's smile fades, and his large blue eyes fill with worry as he removes his cap, revealing his tousled, dirty-blond hair. He walks over and wraps his arms around my shoulders. "I'm sorry. Are you doing okay? For real?"

I shrug his hug away. "I'm fine, Kal. You better get going. Charlie's here."

He follows my gaze out the window; Charlie's red truck bounces along our dusty driveway. The stereo blares, and a smile pulls at my lips—"Paint It, Black" by the Rolling Stones. Charlie and I share a deep love for classic rock. Any genre of rock, really.

"Okay. See you there, then." Kalendar lingers before leaving.

I wait a few minutes before slipping on my brown strappy sandals. Grabbing my favorite sweater from the closet, I peek out the window as Kalendar hops into Charlie's idling truck, then head downstairs.

Outside, the air smells sweet of pine needles and wild roses. Before reaching the garage, I listen for the guitar again. A symphony of chirping magpies and clicking band-winged grasshoppers echoes around me, but nothing else. I push my disappointment aside and continue on.

"Hey, girl." I pat Betty, my 1968 Ford Bronco, before hoisting myself inside. Dad's obsessed with restoring old cars and recently painted her bubblegum pink just for me.

I toss my sweater in the back seat, roll the windows down, and hook up my phone. As I ride into town, my Greta Van Fleet playlist blasts through the speakers. The warm breeze tangles my hair as the music momentarily drowns out the looping echoes of a cheating loser and a ghostly melody in my mind.

THREE

THE TOWN GREEN swarms with people. Little kids run barefoot and giggling. The smell of freshly cut grass and fried dough fills the air. Everything is lit in a twilight glow, with the sun hiding behind the mountains.

I weave through blankets and lawn chairs toward the right of the stage, where I'm supposed to meet Emma. My eyes focus on the destination, desperately hoping to avoid unwelcome run-ins. But of course …

"Lavender!"

Shoot. I recognize the voice instantly: Billy Beauford, one of Brandon's closest friends. Billy slides his arm around my waist, catching me off guard. His striking green eyes lock onto mine.

Billy is hot. Like movie star hot. And charming. He's the boy most girls swoon over with his quick wit and curly brown hair. While I've been friendly enough because of my connection to Brandon, he's never been my favorite person. Brandon *always* finds himself in trouble when he's with Billy. It was Billy's house where the Brandon and Paige make out sesh went down, so case in point.

"Billy, what're you doing?" I cross my arms, unintentionally striking a genie pose. *Wonderful.*

"I hear you might be back on the market." He tightens his grip. "I bet Brandon wouldn't mind if I took you out for din—"

"Dude, back off! I get first dibs," interrupts Micah, another of Brandon's friends. "Choose me, Lavender." He bows dramatically and plants a kiss on my hand.

My pulse spikes as I yank my hand free from Micah and step away from Billy.

"Oh, please, Micah. Like she'd ever go out with you." Billy grins, shaking his head.

"I don't think she'd go out with either of us." Micah nudges Billy with his elbow. "Those witch eyes are only for Brandon."

Billy doubles over in laughter.

My face turns crimson as I look around. Sure enough, they have caught the attention of everyone in our vicinity—my worst nightmare.

Billy straightens and then sets his eyes on me. "Oh—yeah. Sorry about what happened at my place. But you know Paige. When she wants something, she gets it." He shrugs like it's totally fine that she KISSED MY BOYFRIEND.

My fingers dig into my palms.

"Guys, leave her alone," Brandon interjects as he materializes from the crowd.

My stomach clenches at seeing Brandon for the first time since Paige slid into my DM. His blonde hair is perfectly in place, his bright blue eyes glow in the waning light, and his white T-shirt is *just* tight enough to show off his muscles. He's Rosewood's very own Ken doll. I'm surprised he's never tried to play his guitar *at* me. But something is different now. The spark I once felt at the sight of him is gone. He seems almost... pathetic.

Brandon steps closer, his face inches from mine, brows drawn together in frustration. "Why haven't you been answering my calls? I need to explain." His familiar scent—soap and berries—fills the space between us.

I hold his gaze, hoping the hurt and betrayal in my eyes will answer for me.

"Look, I know I messed up, but can you just… forgive me? The thing with Paige…it meant nothing. Let's move past this. It's really not a big deal." He reaches out to rub my arm, and I flinch, pulling away from his touch.

"You *cheated* on me, Brandon." My tone is sharp as I glare at him. "That *is* a big deal."

He pulls back, glancing around to see how big of a crowd we're drawing. His hand rises to the back of his neck—his discomfort obvious. Heaven forbid anyone witnesses a crack in his flawless facade.

"So no, I can't forgive you. And I don't want to. We're done." I'm so pissed the words land louder than intended. People are watching, whispering. My heart pounds as I scan the crowd. I just need Emma. *Where is she?*

Billy's obnoxious laugh cuts through the tension. "Damn, man. You got dumped!"

My eyes flick to Brandon.

His face hardens, and a sneer curls on his lips. "Whatever. I shouldn't be with some purple-eyed freak, anyway," he says, his voice booming.

The words hit like a slap, stealing my breath.

"Lavender! Over here!"

Thank goodness, Em.

"Assafrass," I say, turning on my heel.

Brandon's mocking laughter follows me. "And learn how to swear!"

Emma's perched on Kalendar's shoulders, waving frantically to get my attention, and for a moment, my shoulders relax. Until I catch sight of Kalendar's group of friends behind them, chatting and laughing. *Great.*

I wave back at her, my smile stretched thin as I make my way toward them.

Emma gets down and hugs me longer than usual.

"How are you doing?" She releases me and cups my face in her hands.

"Okay."

"Really?"

"Yeah," I say with a sigh. "But he's a dick; wish I had known it sooner."

"What did he say to you just now? You look upset." Emma's dark eyes sweep my face.

"I don't want to talk about it." I purse my lips. "And next time, can you *not* call my mom?"

"Oh, *fine,*" she says, exhaling heavily. "But you needed support, and I know you wouldn't have told her right away."

"I mean, you're right. But, still—"

"Message received," Emma cuts in. "Now let's focus on what really matters—having fun! This is our last summer before senior year!" She squeals, yanking my hand and dragging me toward Kalendar and his friends.

I pull on her hand.

"What is it?" she asks, eyebrows raised as she turns to me.

"Can we not hang with them tonight?" I whisper. "Where's Aly and Sofia?"

"They're not here. Aly's dad took them camping; I think they get back tomorrow." Emma leans in close. "And it's only Kalendar's friends. I don't think Paige and her minions are here. C'mon." She tugs at my arm and I reluctantly follow.

Emma steps confidently into the circle, seamlessly joining the conversation with the recent high school graduates. I linger behind her, shifting awkwardly before pulling my phone from my bag. I open a new text thread and begin typing manically to no one. If I appear busy, I'm unapproachable. Right?

"Hey, you." Charlie towers above me.

Wrong.

"Oh, hey, Charlie." I throw my phone in my bag and meet his eyes briefly before feigning interest in the surrounding crowd.

Still feeling his presence hovering, I meet his gaze again.

Charlie's eyes grow soft. "Do you need a hug? I know you've had a day."

A lump rises in my throat. I tilt my head up, focusing on the pink and purple clouds streaking the sky, trying to keep my emotions in check. "I'd actually love a hug," I admit, my voice shaking.

Charlie wraps his massive arms around me, and I bury my face in his warm, broad chest. He's been Kalendar's best friend since preschool and feels like another brother. The lump in my throat disappears.

Speaking of Kalendar…I glance around the group, scanning the faces of his friends, but he's nowhere to be seen.

I pull back from Charlie. "Do you know where Kal went?"

"Yeah, he answered his phone and then walked away. I think he was having a hard time hearing." Charlie squeezes my arm. "Do you feel like talking about Brandon? He sucks. You deserve better."

"Not tonight."

"But—"

"Charlie, please. I don't want to talk about it." I hold his gaze.

He bites his bottom lip. "Okay."

Mick Jagger's voice suddenly filters into my ear. My eyes drop to Charlie's phone.

"Ya know, at a concert, you don't need to play your own music," I say with a laugh.

"Ah, my dear Lavender, you might assume so, but can you hear any music now?" His voice booms in a comically terrible British accent, instantly grabbing the attention of the friend group. He raises his index finger beside his ear. "Nope, didn't think so. And so, you're welcome for the delightful interim tunes, which will keep you entertained as we await the bands who will grace the stage."

"Well, thank you then, Sir Charlie." I match his ridiculous accent, tucking a strand of hair behind my ear.

Charlie winks, then leans in so he's close, his tone shifting to a whisper, "You sure you're okay?"

I nod, and he smiles, then straightens, clearing his throat. "Alas, the loo is calling me. I better go before the *real* music starts." With a bow, he walks to the line of porta-potties.

I can't help but laugh as I watch him stop occasionally to tip his hat to a stranger.

"Ready for some music?" Emma shouts, throwing her arm around my shoulders.

"Always." I rest my head against her arm. "So, who's playing tonight?"

A man and woman in matching cowboy hats set up guitars and microphones on the stage.

"It's two bands. This country duo." Emma swings her arm toward the couple. "They're married; how sweet is that! And the other band is a mystery. I hear they're rock with a folk twist; you'll love them,

I'm sure." Emma knocks her elbow into mine. "They don't have a band name, though." She shrugs.

"Weird." I try to sneak a look backstage for the mysterious band, but I can't get a clear view.

As soon as the music begins, Emma shimmies to the front of the stage and starts line dancing with the older folks. She waves for me to join, but I shake my head. *No way.* Most of Kalendar's friends follow her, while the rest head to the food trucks.

Alone again, I take a slow breath, letting my gaze wander across the green. Couples are holding hands, kids are laughing while they chase each other, and the line-dancing group has tripled since the song started. Everyone here is so happy, so carefree. So *connected.*

I instinctively reach for my phone, desperate for anything to distract me from my loneliness spiral.

Billy's scent invades the air before he comes into view—the rich, overpowering mix of tobacco and clove cologne.

"Hey, again," he says, with an annoyingly confident tone.

"Oh, um, I was just leaving to grab dinner," I stammer, stepping to move away, but he blocks me and wraps his arm over my shoulders.

"Hold on a sec. I was serious about what I said earlier. I want to take you out."

Reluctantly, I meet his eyes. Something dangerous flickers behind them. The air suddenly feels thick, suffocating.

"No thanks." I try to pull away, but his grip tightens.

"C'mon. Just one date." His breath, minty with peppermint, warms my ear as he leans closer. "It's not like I'm asking you to marry me." His fingers dig into the flesh on my upper arm.

"You're hurting me," I whisper, panic rising in my chest.

"Don't be ridiculous," he murmurs.

"Billy, get off of me." I shove against him, but the harder I move, the tighter his hold becomes. The familiar sting of a bruise spreads across my arm.

"Hey!"

I turn at the sound of Kalendar's voice, my heart reeling with relief.

"Let her go, Billy!" His voice thunders.

"Dude, chill. I was joking." Billy lets go and eyes me up and down. "Like I'd ever want to go out with a witch, anyway. She'd probably put a hex on me or whatever."

Kalendar's jaw tightens. He steps forward, his face inches from Billy's. "Don't you *ever* come near my sister again."

Billy raises his hands in mock surrender, rolling his eyes as he turns and stalks away.

Kalendar waits until he's out of sight before turning to me. "You okay?"

I swallow hard. "Yeah."

"Don't listen to him, Ender. He's a loser." His breathing slows. "I'm so glad he—and that asshole boyfriend—are out of your life."

I lean into Kalendar's chest; the steady beat of his heart is comforting. "Thanks, Kal."

He wraps an arm around me. "Of course. You sure you're good?"

I nod against him.

"Charlie said you were on a call. Who was it?"

Kalendar pulls away, shifting uncomfortably. "My new roommate." He rubs his jawline. "You know, we need to talk about the fact I'm leaving for college next month."

I look away. "Yeah, but not now."

"Ender, it's just Montana. It's not like I'm going—"

"Not now, Kal," I snap, my eyes narrowing.

"Alright," he says, frustration slipping into his voice. "But there's something else I need to tell you…"

A familiar sound pulls me from the conversation—a male voice, singing. Where have I heard that before?

"Ender? Where'd you go?" Kalendar waves his hand in front of my face.

"Sorry. I thought I heard a guy singing …"

"You did. The other band started." He points to the stage, where three shapes move in rhythm to the music. "You all right?"

"Yeah, sorry. A little distracted. What do you want to tell me?" My focus shifts back to him briefly before returning to the band.

"Let's talk about it another time. I can tell you're itchin' to see these guys."

"You sure? You saved my life, after all. The least I can do is listen."

"That's a little dramatic," Kalendar laughs. "But yes, I'm sure. Let's go."

As we approach the concert, Emma breaks through the sea of maxi dresses and jorts to meet us.

"Where were you? Are you okay?" she asks, her eyes scanning my face before shifting to Kalendar.

I clear my throat. "Um—"

"I don't want you girls anywhere near Billy Beauford," Kalendar interrupts, his tone firm.

"Why? What happened?" she presses, her eyes narrowing.

"I'll fill you in later. Let's see this band." I grab her hand, and we make our way through the crowd.

The band comes into focus as we near the front. I zero in on the girl behind the drums. Golden dreadlocks frame her face, and her nose ring sparkles in the lights. She's wearing a white tee paired with ripped jeans. She bops along to the beat with a confidence that makes me jealous.

Next to her, the bassist appears younger. A rolled bandanna holds back his long blond hair, exposing his baby face. He sways with the music, eyes closed and seemingly lost in his own world, while his fingers glide over the strings.

The lead guitarist scans the crowd like he's in on a juicy secret as he strums his guitar with ease. Shoulder-length brown hair falls from beneath a weathered cowboy hat and a dusting of stubble shadows his jaw. Our eyes meet, and for a moment, he holds my gaze. Something unspoken sparks between us.

"Yikes, he's hot," Emma whispers. "And he can't stop looking at you!"

I feel the heat rising to my face. He smiles at my obvious embarrassment and then shifts his eyes to the rest of the crowd; they return to mine briefly with curiosity.

He sings; his voice is raspy and deep, with a slight twang. I'd guess he's from somewhere in the South. Their sound is unique—rock and roll meets folk.

I move in rhythm with the music; the lyrics are about a simple life in Tennessee, spending time with his grandmother on the porch and watching the stars shine above. His gaze locks with mine as his voice rises in the song.

"Grandmom says there are those who seek out the good

in this universal neighborhood

Sweet gifts like these are rare. It's up to you to make them aware."

His stare is intense, his brows drawn together, and my stomach flips. I run a hand through my hair and glance behind me. Maybe there's someone here he knows? An older couple grins back. *Unlikely.* I turn back, and now all three band members are staring, their focus razor-sharp, as if they know something about me I don't. My pulse speeds. What is *happening*?

Forever a flight-over-fight kind of girl; I lean in close to Emma. "Em, I'm heading out."

"Why? This band is the best."

"They are." I shift uncomfortably, casting a glance at the stage. "But they keep staring at me."

"Yeah. Because he obviously loves you. Love at first sight." Emma giggles.

I shoot her a deadpan look. "I don't think so. But you have fun. Have you seen Kal?"

"Yeah, he's at the back. Said he didn't want his height to block anyone's view—always so thoughtful."

"Sure. Call me tomorrow?" I squeeze her hand in a goodbye.

"Uh, huh. Love you."

As I break away from the crowd, the band launches into a new song.

Kalendar stands by the lemonade cart, nodding along to the music.

"Hey, I'm heading home. Are you going back with Charlie?"

"What? Why? This band is awesome."

"I just want to get home." I shrug. "You should stay, though."

"Nah, I'll come. I don't know where Charlie wandered off to, anyway."

Kalendar moves to leave, and I trail behind, but I can't resist sneaking one final glance at the lead singer. His eyes meet mine, still carrying that same curious gaze. Not sure what else to do, I flash him a smile and—totally out of character—a wink. At least I'll give him something to remember me by. Chances are, I'll never see him again.

FOUR

THE FULL MOON bathes the winding dirt road in silver light, making it feel like we're bumping across the lunar surface.

Kalendar grips the steering wheel with one hand, cranks up the volume with the other, and the latest Noah Kahan track blasts through Betty's speakers, shattering the silence of the night.

As is typical Colorado weather, the temperature has dropped significantly since late afternoon, and I reach for my sweater in the back seat. I pull the cozy cotton around my shoulders, then rest my arms on the open window, my gaze drawn to the stars, locking onto my favorite constellation—Orion. His iconic belt and brilliant sword usually ground me when my thoughts spiral, but tonight, my mind keeps returning to the band's singer. The way his eyes kept finding mine. The deep, soulful sound of his voice—rich and raw, like Chris Stapleton's. And he and his band had watched me so intensely. *Why?*

A sudden flicker at the edge of my vision startles me. My breath catches as tiny lights sparkle in the trees.

"Kal! Can you stop?" I reach for his free arm.

"Why? What's happening?"

"Just … please?"

He slows the car and turns to me, eyebrows raised.

"I thought I saw something," I say, glancing at the road behind us. "Small blinking lights, like fireflies."

"What? Ender, those don't even live here."

"I know, but I swear there's something. Can you back up a bit?"

Kalendar sighs as he reverses Betty.

We scan the trees, my eyes narrowing as if squinting will somehow summon them.

"Is anyone there?" I call, straining to hear, but the only response is the rustle of aspen leaves in the wind, thrumming like distant rainfall.

"There's nothing there, Ender. Maybe it was our headlights reflecting off the mile marker." Kalendar nods at the white number five, glowing against the darkened forest.

"Maybe," I mutter, scratching my nose. "Let's just go."

Minutes later, we pull into our driveway. Kalendar drives up to the house and eases Betty into the garage. "Thanks for driving," I say as I jump from the passenger seat.

"Sure thing. Why don't you head inside? I'll close up."

As I near the house, a glimmer draws my eye. A cluster of fireflies dance in the field beside our home, and suddenly I'm back at Aunt Mia's in Rhode Island—barefoot in the grass, knees streaked green, chasing lightning bugs with a mason jar. I rub my eyes, blinking once. Twice. Yep, definitely fireflies.

"Kal! Over here!"

"What now?" he asks, closing the garage door behind him.

A smile spreads across my face as I prepare to prove my point. I *was* right. But as I look back at the field, my grin falters. The fireflies are gone. *What the?*

"Giddy up!" Jake's voice echoes from the front door. My oldest brother wears a cowboy hat, boots, and a belt buckle that's practically the size of a dinner plate.

He smiles wide before jogging down the stone steps, then shifts into full cowboy mode the second he hits the ground. His expression turns serious, and he strolls toward us with an exaggerated swagger. When he reaches me, he tips his hat like we're in an old Western.

"Ma'am," he says with a straight face.

I laugh and nudge him with my elbow. "Hey Jake, how was the rodeo?"

He breaks character, returning to a smile. "Fun. Lots of horses, lassos, pretty ladies, and beer." He puts his arms around our shoulders and steers us toward the front door. "More importantly, though, how are you, Lavender?" He stops walking and drops his arms, turning to face me. "Ma told me about Brandon. Are you doing okay?"

Jake and I have an age gap of five years, which means I'm lucky enough to have not two but *three* very concerned and overprotective grown-ups constantly worried about me.

"He's a loser. She's better off without him," Kalendar says, pushing past us to the stairs.

Jake raises his eyebrows at me. "What happened?"

"Um, let's say I'm glad to be rid of Brandon and his friends." I glance at Kalendar. "And Kal is a pretty good brother."

"Huh." Jake clicks his tongue. "So, does this mean you guys are friends again? No offense, Lavender, but you've been kind of an ass to him lately."

Kalendar swings around. "Ah-ha! I knew it wasn't just in my head." He laughs as he retraces his steps, throwing an arm over Jake's shoulders.

Sighing, I cross my arms tight over my chest. "Okay, fine. I've been a jerk. I'm just mad you guys are leaving me for college."

"Sure have," Kalendar says, his tone teasing. "But I'm glad you're finally being honest. Ready to talk about it?" He wiggles his eyebrows.

"Nope. I'd like to live in a world where my brothers never leave me, thanks." I unfold my arms and smile. "But anyway, I love you two dummies."

"Ah, didn't quite hear that. What'd you say?" Jake says.

"I love you guys," I say, louder this time.

"Jakey, is Ender saying something? I swear her lips are moving, but no sound is coming out." Kalendar smirks.

"I LOVE YOU GUYS!"

"Well, shoot, Lavender. There's no need to yell." Jake grins.

Kalendar laughs and I roll my eyes.

"Who wants to sit outside by the firepit?" Jake asks.

"I'm in," Kalendar says, leading Jake up the stairs. My gaze flicks to the empty field.

Kalendar turns at the top. "You coming, Ender?"

"No thanks. I'm exhausted. I'm going to bed. Love you guys."

"LOVE YOU, TOO!" they shout in unison.

Fresh from a warm shower, I step onto the balcony outside my bedroom, tightening a thick fleece robe around my silk PJ set. Kalendar and Jake sit by the firepit, their heads huddled in deep conversation, faces illuminated by the twisting flames. Beyond them, the lawn fades into darkness—where the hill's edge vanishes into a black abyss.

The crisp mountain air fills my lungs as I fixate on our backyard and the mountains, searching for the fireflies. I know I saw them. Twice. Surely, there's a reason they're here. Maybe someone brought them in from the humid states and set them free?

The twinkling lights I spotted before the concert still glow in the mountain, faint but steady. No one else seems to have noticed—or if they have, they're not talking about it. A chill creeps down my spine. Those lights have to be connected to the music and I *know* I heard my name earlier. There's no way I imagined it.

The emotional weight of the day settles heavy on my shoulders. I step inside, flicking on the Himalayan salt lamp that Mom has placed in every room—'It cleans the air,' she insists. I slip beneath the summer quilt, feeling the cool breeze that flows in through the window kiss my face. Within seconds, I'm asleep.

FIVE

A SOFT TAPPING noise pulls me from sleep, and a quick glance at my phone shows it's only midnight. I groan and bury my head into the pillow, but the sound persists. With one eye cracked open, I'm immediately struck by patterns of yellow dancing across my walls.

I snap upright, scanning the room. Light seeps in through the windows, casting a dreamlike aura over my bedroom furniture. I push the blankets off and climb out of bed. My skin prickles with goosebumps as I move closer to the balcony door.

Stopping suddenly, I gasp.

Hundreds of fireflies flutter against the glass, their wings creating a soft, rhythmic drumming.

My first instinct is to run for Mom and Dad, but a familiar sound stops me. That same acoustic tune from earlier—folk again, but brighter now. Playful. Like bluegrass came to crash the party.

The luminous insects glide to the rhythm of the music, and my initial anxiety melts away as I watch them; they don't seem threatening. I step closer to the balcony door, pressing my forehead against the glass, mesmerized by their soft glow. Slowly, I push it open and walk onto the deck, the wood cool against my feet. All at once, the fireflies swirl around me, their delicate wings brushing against my skin like a thousand tiny feathers. I feel weightless as they move together, a stream of light enveloping me. They float down into the backyard and pause, hovering as if waiting for me to follow.

Without hesitation, I grab a sweater from my room and slip on my shearling-lined Birkenstocks, then creep downstairs and step outside. The door clicks shut behind me.

Wrapping the sweater around my arms, I watch as the fireflies move together, a circle of light bouncing through the night sky. They're headed toward the forest.

I hesitate for a moment, glancing back at my house. *What am I even doing?* But before my rational mind can catch up, my feet are already in motion, jogging after the glowing swarm. They take me up into the woods. This trail is familiar, and their light, combined with the full moon, makes it easy to avoid tripping over fallen branches or rocks.

The forest at night feels different—magical. Maybe it's the moonlight, but the trees seem to glitter and as I wander through them, faint whispers pass in the air.

We're getting close to the twinkling lights I saw from my house, and as we near, I realize they're lanterns hanging from branches. Hundreds of them flicker in a soft cadence, illuminating the leaves and pine needles.

The music grows louder, and my stomach hitches a rollercoaster ride somewhere between the whispering trees and the whimsical lanterns.

The swarm halts and each bug flies individually toward the sky, making a vast circle that illuminates the ground beneath them. I know this place. My brothers and I spent many afternoons in this meadow when we were younger, building stick teepees and playing hide-and-seek.

The music stops.

"Lavender?"

A man's voice calls my name from across the meadow. I squint, spotting three figures gathered around a campfire. My heart thuds in my chest, but the familiar crackle of flames brings a sense of calm. The smoke rises in twisting ribbons, dancing through the atmosphere before vanishing into the stars. The aroma of burning wood hangs in the air as I take cautious steps in their direction.

"We weren't sure you'd come," the voice says as I draw near. It's warm, with a touch of amusement—and unmistakably familiar.

Reaching the group, I gaze into the same eyes I'd locked with earlier that evening. The lead singer casually puts down his guitar and rises from a tree stump.

"My name is Campion. But most folks call me *Camp*," he says, extending his hand to mine. My breath catches. Up close, he's even more gorgeous. His smile reaches his eyes, which twinkle in the campfire's flickering light. An electric pulse runs through my body when our hands touch, and his smile deepens. *Did he feel it too?*

"*Ahem*," someone interrupts.

Camp glances at the others—his bandmates from the concert.

"Lavender, I'd like you to meet Anna and Nate," Camp says, gesturing to them.

Anna bounces over and hugs me. I awkwardly return her embrace with one arm.

"It's so great to meet you finally!" exclaims Anna.

Finally?

Nate keeps his focus on the ground as he walks toward me, eventually glancing up and offering his hand. "Hey," he mumbles.

Our hands brush before he pulls away and resumes his place by the fire.

I survey my surroundings. Three teepees are near the campfire; beyond them sits a canopy with a set of drums, three microphones, and two speakers. String lights entwine throughout, and a blank banner stretches across the back.

"You're the band from the concert." I find my voice.

"We sure are." Anna grins.

There's an uncomfortable pause, and I fidget with my sweater as they stare at me like I'm some kind of alien creature.

Anna and Nate glance at Camp; he has his eyes on me and motions for me to sit. "Please?"

I eye him cautiously, then lower myself onto the tree stump furthest from Nate. The fire lights up my face, the warmth wrapping around me. Camp sits on the ground beside me, his elbows propped on his knees, eyes on the fire. Anna joins us.

"I'm sure you're wondering why we're here," Camp chuckles, his deep Southern drawl stretching through the night.

Anna and Nate watch me, anticipation in their eyes. I shift on the log; the rough bark bites into my bare thigh. But that's the least of my worries because WHAT IN THE H-E-DOUBLE TOOTHPICKS IS THIS?

Camp removes his cowboy hat, letting it dangle from his fingers like he's about to say something important. His gaze meets mine, and his smile falters.

"Your eyes," he whispers. "They're—"

"Beautiful," Anna cuts in, her voice floaty.

Camp smiles, not taking his eyes off me. "Exactly that."

A blush creeps up my cheeks and I glance away, flustered.

"Sorry. I'll get right to the point," Camp says, his voice gentle. "Lavender, you have a gift. We all do." He waves his hat toward Anna and Nate. "I know it sounds insane. Believe me, it took a while for me to… well, nevermind."

My stomach tightens, and I flex my legs, subtly shifting my weight—just in case I need to get the ef out of here *fast*.

"Gift?" I say, narrowing my eyes at him.

He nods. "You heard my music this afternoon, right?"

I arch a brow. "At the concert?"

"No, before that. Here, in the woods."

I blink at him, waiting for more information. But then—of course.

The phantom music. My whispered name. The random firefly show on our way home from the concert. Well. At least I'm not losing my mind. Or am I?

My fear fades as curiosity takes over.

"I thought I heard something." The words come out more like a question than an answer.

"And no one else heard it except you, right?"

I tilt my head. "Oh, I don't know. I was by myself. I'm sure someone else heard it, too."

"Maybe." Camp laughs, but it's hesitant. His smile wavers as he glances at Anna, who nods encouragingly at him.

Camp rubs his forehead, exhaling a slow sigh before his eyes meet mine again. "Nate, Anna, and I—we've been chosen, in a way." He lifts a hand, making air quotes around *chosen.*

"I know it sounds cliché, but it's true. Each of us has a unique talent that makes this band more than just another rock band."

Nate snorts.

Camp shoots him a side-eye before adding, "Or folk band. That's an argument for another day." He winks, the moment light but fleeting. His voice steadies again. "The point is, we're here for something bigger—something that could actually change the world for the better. But…" His gaze sharpens, fixing on mine. "We're incomplete."

The weight of his words lingers, the silence stretching as he waits for me to fill it.

"Um… are you saying I'm supposed to be part of,"—I gesture vaguely around us—"whatever *this* is?"

Camp nods.

I stare at him unblinkingly.

"And…you're the only human who can hear the music I was playing just now. Well, I mean, besides us." He gestures toward his bandmates before continuing, "It's played at a frequency most humans can't hear. But creatures can—animals, plants, even insects." He looks at the sky, where fireflies drift like floating embers. "That's how we brought them with us from Tennessee. We speak to them through music, and they speak back." His grin deepens. "If you haven't noticed, fireflies are natural-born dancers." He chuckles.

Noticing my unamused expression, he clears his throat and glances away briefly.

"Everything is interconnected—people, animals, plants. But most humans don't think about life in that way. Our mission is to restore harmony among all living things—to reclaim peace. These guys are ready for a change." He motions at the surrounding trees. "Now we just gotta get humankind on board."

I blink. I blink again. Three times.

"Ah, okay. I know what's happening here." I rise from the tree stump and walk to the nearest aspens. "Kal! I know you're here," I yell. "You can come out now, Kalendar. You got me!"

This has to be a prank. Kalendar's obviously behind it. I've seen him watching hidden camera reels on YouTube lately. And, of course, he would find the hottest guy on the planet to play Camp—if that's even his real name.

Camp looks at Anna and Nate and shrugs.

"Who is Kalendar?"

I ignore him while frantically peeking into the teepees and searching behind trees and rocks. He's *got* to be here somewhere. I have to admit, though, the instrument setup is a clever touch—he's going all in on this. I peer behind the drum set, expecting to catch his smug face, but he's not there.

"Kalendar!" I call out again, my voice echoing into the night. Defeated, I plop myself onto a nearby rock and shiver as the cold stone seeps through my silk shorts.

Camp puts his hat back on, walks to me, and squats down. "I know this is hard to wrap your head around. Do you want to take a few days to digest all this? We'll be here nearly every night. You can come back when you're ready."

Anna and Nate watch me from beside the fire, their expressions masked, the flickering flames casting shadows on their faces.

"What exactly do you mean by change the world for the better?" I ask, raising a brow. "Are you guys like, supernatural or something?"

"We're not werewolves, if that's what you're thinking." Nate jumps in, deadpan. "I know girls are into that tortured bad-boy vibe. Don't get any ideas."

Camp shoots him a look. "Wow. Thank you, Nate." He turns back to me with a pained smile and lowers his voice. "What I meant was… the world's a mess. People are angry, lonely—it's like we've forgotten how to be human. We're unkind to each other, to nature. We want to change that—to rekindle connection, joy, community— to spark a peace revolution…"

He trails off, and I realize he's watching my reaction closely. I'm sure he can see that I'm one second away from asking if he's high on something.

I clear my throat. "Well, there's definitely been a mix-up. *Even* if this is real and what you're saying *is* true, I have *zero* talent." I nod toward his guitar. "I'm talking Phoebe Buffay level here. Trust me, you don't want to hear me play."

Camp laughs. "I hate to tell you, but you're wrong. You have a beautiful voice and are creative; you'll help us write our songs, even if it's a rendition of 'Smelly Cat.'"

"How do you know that? Are you stalking me?" I bite the tip of my thumb, choosing to ignore his clever knowledge of my favorite nineties show.

He fixes his gaze on mine, his expression serious. "We aren't stalking you. Why don't you take some time to think about this? We can discuss it more next time. I don't want to overwhelm you on our first night together."

Our first night together. My cheeks flush at these words. And also, I'm annoyed.

How dare this guy—this ridiculously handsome guy with flawless hair and a face that should be illegal—wake me up in the dead of night, claiming I'm meant to join a mysterious band with no explanation. Why should I trust him? For all I know, they could be scam artists, but... something tells me they aren't.

"I need more info. Camp? Is it?" I press my palms together, trying to keep my composure. "That sounds like a made-up name, by the way."

He chuckles. "You'd have to take that up with my mom." His smile falters. "But yeah, of course—what do you wanna know?"

"I still don't understand. Why me?"

He takes a deep breath, eyes flicking to the stars above us. "Some things can't be explained logically. They just are." His gaze shifts back to me, a smirk tugging at his lips. "I know. It's not the answer you want, but it's the truth."

I give him a skeptical side-eye.

Camp drops his gaze for a second, like he's recalibrating, then straightens. "Okay, let me try this another way," he says, his tone softer now. "Have you ever felt like you don't quite fit? Like no matter how hard you try, people just don't get you? Or like… maybe you're meant for something more than this?"

My jaw tightens. *How does he know?*

Something in his face relaxes, like he knows he's hit the mark. "Because we get it. We've all felt that way, too. And this band? It's the first thing that's ever made sense. Ya know, after you can get past the supernatural elements." His lips twitch into a smile.

He clasps his hands together and leans in closer. "Look, none of us asked for this at first. But once you realize that you can make a difference by doing one of the greatest things on earth—making music—it's like the best kind of high." His eyes meet mine. "So I'm asking you to think about it. Whatever questions you have, I promise I'll answer them now, or whenever the time is right. But we can't do this without you."

He holds my gaze, steady and sincere, like he needs me to understand how real this is.

"I have one more question."

"Shoot."

"How did you find me?"

He smiles wider, something enigmatic about it. "Let's just say you've got someone looking out for you. A guardian angel, of sorts. You'll meet her soon, and when you do, everything will become clear."

Guardian angel? This whole thing feels more like a riddle than an explanation and a wave of sudden exhaustion crashes over me, as if my body can't keep up with the mind games.

"Okay." I roll my eyes and stand, making my way toward the trail I arrived on.

"I need time to process this," I say loudly, then turn on my heel to face the three of them. "Anyway… have a good night. Or, uh, morning. Whatever."

"Wait!" Anna shouts as she runs over to me. She puts something in my hand: a little crystal heart figurine. It's a simple shade of rose, muted and dusty, but it seems to glimmer in a way I've never seen before. "Take this."

I wrap my fingers around the stone. It's warm and smooth, reminding me of the beach glass I've collected near my grandparents' house in California.

"Um, thanks?"

"I know, it's weird. This is all weird. Just trust me, okay?" Anna breathes.

"Sure …" I place the heart in my sweater pocket.

I descend the trail with the fireflies lighting my way home. The strumming of the guitar returns once again. It's the theme song to *Friends* and I can't help but smile.

The aroma of bacon wakes me and there's a distant sound of pots and pans at work. I tap my phone on the nightstand, *8:18*, before turning over to rest my head back on my pillow. The silky fabric feels lovely against my cheek. The mountain air has chilled my room, but I'm warm and cozy in bed until memories from last night jolt me awake. Sitting up, I search for lanterns outside my window, but find none.

What a crazy, beautiful dream. I smile to myself, recalling Camp's captivating eyes and intoxicating grin.

I stretch my arms overhead, roll my neck, and swing my legs out of bed, toes fumbling for my Birkenstocks. As I slip them on and head toward the bathroom, something catches my eye. I freeze. There, on the desk, bathed in the morning light, sits the crystal heart.

SIX

THE SUN SITS HIGH in the sky, which means I've spent hours fixated on the forest. I must appear nuts to anyone caring to notice, a violet-eyed zombie sitting on a balcony staring into the abyss. And judging by the blazing rays, I'm certain my fair skin is lobster red. This is what I am now: a lobster zombie.

Bruce sprawls across the sun-warmed deck at my feet. My rocking chair creaks with each slow sway, the crystal heart resting in my hand, its cool surface mingles with the warmth of my palm.

The wind swirls through our ranch, its gusts mimicking the whistle of an old steam train. It's a haunting replacement of Camp's guitar. I'd assume last night was a dream if it wasn't for this heart. None of it seems possible. But I *can not* explain this crystal. I turn it over, tracing the edges with my thumb. Unless it's one of Mom's strange talismans that somehow ended up in my room. Or Kalendar's. Who knows with those two.

Emma's ringtone drifts from my bedroom—a snippet of "Lavender Haze"; she's the ultimate Swiftie. I run inside to answer it.

"Hey, Em."

"Hey. How was the rest of your night? Did you dream of that sexy lead singer?"

I swallow hard. "I think maybe yes?"

"Wait. For real? Tell me everything."

"It's long and weird. Forget it." I run a hand through my hair. "What're you up to today?"

"Want to grab lunch? I'm meeting Aly and Sofia at that new Mexican place in an hour."

"Uh." I've spent all morning debating whether to go back to the campsite. I mean, how insane would it be if I—Lavender Flynn—actually had a purpose in this life? And in a band, no less. Camp seems to think I have some kind of mus—.

Wait.

His name is Camp.

And I saw him at a *camp*site.

I laugh out loud.

"What?"

"Oh, nothing. Just losing my mind." Definitely a dream. "Yeah, I'll come."

"Great, meet you there." Emma hangs up before I can respond.

Settling into a white plastic chair on the patio of El Pijama del Gato, I slip off my sandals and let my feet glide over the AstroTurf, the fake grass tickling my toes.

"What does this mean?" Sofia points to the restaurant's name on the menu.

"Do you not pay attention in Spanish? It means 'the cat's pajamas,'" Aly answers, shaking her head.

Sofia's eyes widen. "What a weird name for a restaurant."

Across the street, a few guys in neon orange vests are disassembling the stage from last night. Another man tugs at the "Rosewood Concert Series" sign tacked on the massive town bulletin board. He rolls it and tucks it under his arm.

"Why was the concert series so short this year?" I ask, watching the sign disappear. "We had, what? Three concerts?"

"Something with budget cuts," Aly says, her nose buried in the menu.

"Oh." I glance around at my friends, all absorbed in their food choices, and take the crystal heart from my pocket. Rolling it between my fingers under the table, I clear my throat. "Do you guys ever have, like… freakishly realistic dreams?"

"Yup, all the time." Sofia replies before taking a sip of her ice water.

"Really? Like what?"

She leans in, her voice dropping to a conspiratorial whisper. "Just last week, I had this one dream where I made out with Charlie. Like, we were really going at it." She grins, clearly amused by the memory. "The next day I was so embarrassed. I thought for sure Charlie would somehow know."

"Like Charlie, Kal's best friend?"

She nods, her grin widening.

"Gross, he's like my brother." I laugh, shaking my head.

"Why do you ask, Lavender?" Emma looks up from her menu, suddenly curious. "Is this about that hot singer?"

Heat rushes to my cheeks as images of Camp's smile return.

"From last night's concert?" Aly asks, lowering her menu.

Emma nods. "He was gorgeous. And *totally* into Lavender." She wiggles her brows.

"Of course." Aly sighs. "I always miss the good-looking ones, shouldn't have gone camping with my dad."

"Stop, Aly. It was fun." Sophia says then turns to me, eyes bright. "So tell us about this dream, Lavender."

"Well," I say, my grip tightening around the crystal heart. "These fireflies led me into the forest and—"

My phone buzzes on the tempered glass table. Emma glances at it, lifting her sunglasses.

"Why is Brandon texting you?"

I slip the heart back into my pocket and read the text out loud to the girls. "Hey. Sorry for the eye comment last night. You're right, we should probably end it. Good luck."

"We should probably end it?" Emma scoffs, swatting the air. "Don't respond. You broke up with *him*; he's just trying to save face."

"What's the eye comment?" asks Sofia.

I slide my sunglasses from the top of my head, covering my eyes. "It's nothing. He was just being a jerk."

"I'm with Em on this," Aly agrees. "Ignore him—he *cheated* on you, Lavender. He doesn't deserve any more of your time."

I sigh, resting my chin in my hand. "It's so humiliating. My first real boyfriend, and this is how it ends? I wish he had just broken up with me instead of cheating with Paige."

"Let me ask you something." Emma lowers her sunglasses to the tip of her nose, fixing me with a pointed look. "First off, I love you, so I'm saying this because I care, but… did you even like Brandon? Because, honestly, you seem more embarrassed than heartbroken. I'm not getting any 'devastated ex' vibes here." She twirls a finger in the air for emphasis.

Sofia and Aly stare at me, waiting. Heat creeps up my neck. I hate being the center of attention—getting called out is even worse. But even Mom said something similar. Was I that blind to my own feelings? Dating one of the 'popular' guys felt good, sure. But had I felt anything beyond that? Now, I don't know.

"I mean, I liked him. But… maybe you're right." I drop my gaze to the menu, hoping to steer the conversation elsewhere. "What's everyone getting?"

"I'm getting the quesadilla, but who's Camp?" Sofia asks.

My heart stutters at the name. I skim the menu until I find *Camp's Quesadilla*, printed halfway down the page. I slam the menu on the table.

"Are the food options that bad?" Aly laughs.

"Yeah, what the hell was that?" Emma frowns.

"There was a spider," I say quickly, glancing around the restaurant.

"So finish telling us about your dream! Is it X rated?" Emma smirks, crossing her arms on the table.

"Oh, um—" I laugh nervously and wave a hand. "Never mind. It was nothing."

SEVEN

THE MOMENT I STEP into the mudroom, Camp's—er, that singer's—voice floods the air. I freeze, my quesadilla leftovers slip from my hands, hitting the tiled floor with a thud. Bruce materializes out of nowhere, pouncing on the to-go container.

"No, Bruce!" I lunge to rescue the mangled box, but the damage is done. My heart kicks into overdrive as I follow the music into the living room, where Jake sits on the couch, his laptop open on the coffee table.

Over his shoulder, the band glows on the screen, bathed in pink and purple stage lights. They're performing outdoors somewhere unfamiliar; the crowd pulses with energy. The camera zooms in on Camp's face, and my breath catches. His eyes—I know them too well now. There's no way I imagined what happened last night. Unless my memory of the concert on the green is really *that* good.

"Hey," I say, keeping my voice as casual as I can manage while walking around the brown leather couch to sit next to Jake. "Who's that?"

He glances at me before returning his attention to the computer. "It's this new band; they're good, actually." He nods at the screen. "They're opening for Dave at Red Rocks tonight." *Dave* as in the Dave Matthews Band, Jake's absolute favorite.

"The Red Rocks in Denver, right?"

Jake turns to face me, his expression serious. "The one and only. The acoustics that bounce off those rocks are unreal. Every concert I've been to there feels… spiritual. I can't believe you've never been. It's only five hours away, and you're as much of a music freak as me." I cringe at his use of "freak," but he doesn't notice, already focused back on the screen. "I'm going to see Dave there tomorrow, but this band's not opening for him. Bummer. They're awesome."

I scratch my arm. "Do you know this band?"

"No, first time I'm hearing them." His foot taps in rhythm with the music. "Ya know what's crazy? They don't have a band name." He laughs. "I've never heard of such a thing."

"Crazy," I mutter.

The band wraps up their set, and Camp (lead singer or whatever) grabs the mic. "Goodnight, y'all. Thanks for making this evening so special." My skin prickles at the sound of his familiar drawl.

"Hey, guys." Mom's voice drifts in behind us. Jake lowers the volume and glances up at her.

"Hey, Ma."

"What are you looking at?" She squints at Jake's laptop.

"Dave Matthews is performing tonight at Red Rocks, just watching the livestream."

She crosses her arms and arches a brow. "I thought you were going to his concert tomorrow?"

"I am. He's playing a two-night stand."

Mom chuckles. "You certainly are quite the fan." Her voice softens. "How are you doing today, Lavender? Did you have fun with the girls?"

"Mm-hmm," I hum distractedly, my attention drawn to the screen. The band is exiting the stage—Anna (?) blows kisses at the crowd, Nate (?) swings the bass around his neck.

"Where's Kalendar?" Jake's deep voice cuts through the air.

"He just left for the movies," Mom replies.

The lights on the stage go dark, and I glance up at her. "Oh yeah? With who?"

"He didn't say. Probably Charlie."

"Fun." I stretch my arms overhead, stifling a fake yawn. "Well, I'm gonna read for a bit."

Back in my room, I beeline to my MacBook. Last night might have been a dream, but this band is real. They've got to be somewhere on the internet.

My hands hover over the keys. Where to begin? I type "Bands at Rosewood Concert Colorado" into the search bar. The summer concert series for our town pops up as the first result. I click the link and scroll until my eyes land on the lineup section and lock on yesterday's date: July 19.

Opening Band: The Sweet Eyed Moonies — Country Duo from Boulder, Colorado. Main Set: Unknown Indie Rock / Folk Band from Chattanooga, Tennessee. Emma and Jake were right; they don't have a name. Is that even legal?

Frustrated, I close my laptop, my gaze drifting to the crystal heart on the bedside table. It pulls me in, like a magnet. Unable to resist, I rise from my desk chair and cross the room to hold it, running my fingers over its smooth surface.

A sudden jolt of electricity surges through me, so strong it knocks me backward onto the bed. My body hums with energy as my eyes flutter shut, and a strange scene floods my mind.

I'm on the stage of Red Rocks, surrounded by a sea of cheering fans, their fists pumping in the air. Rainbow bracelets wrap around their wrists, each one vibrant in the sunshine. My fingers clutch a microphone as I scan the stage—and there he is. Camp. His guitar is slung over his shoulder, he's flashing that swoon-worthy smile.

But wait.

Something's wrong.

Someone's missing.

Kalendar.

Where is he?

Panic surges through me as I search through the audience, desperately calling his name into the microphone. The cheers fade into silence, and the crowd stares back at me, their faces streaked with oversize bubble-tears. Camp's eyes are red-rimmed, and he pulls me into a comforting hug. "Kalendar!" I scream, collapsing to my knees.

"Ender, I'm here. Wake up." His voice finally breaks through, though it sounds distant, muffled. Someone is shaking my arm, pulling me out of the dream world.

Kalendar sits beside me, his hand resting on my shoulder.

"Hey," I mumble, eyes rolling toward the ceiling. They feel wet; had I been crying?

"Crazy dream, huh?" he says, his eyes fixed on me.

"Yeah." A croak escapes my lips in reply.

I sit up and notice the world outside is black.

"Where have you been? Where is everyone?" My head is foggy, a wave of shame creeping in. How long have I been asleep?

Kalendar looks away and swiftly stands up as he answers, "I've been out—went for a hike." He rubs his jawline.

I narrow my eyes on him. "Mom said you were at the movies."

He glances toward the hallway, shifting on his feet. "We were gonna go, but ended up hiking instead."

"Who'd you go with?"

Kalendar clears his throat just as Jake pops his head into my room.

"Hey, guys. Anyone up for a movie?"

"Definitely," Kalendar says, flashing me a half-smile before heading out.

"Lavender, we'll be in the living room if you want to join," Jake's voice carries from the hall.

I drop my head into my hands, rubbing my eyes with my palms. *What was that dream?*

Then I remember the crystal heart.

Turning on all fours, I dig through the folds of my quilt before spotting it on the faux sheepskin rug beside my bed.

A flutter stirs in my chest as I reach down to grab it, rolling it in between my fingers. The moment my hand closes around it, heat surges through my skin—so hot I gasp and fling it onto the rug, bringing my palm to my lips.

I stare at it from the safety of my bed, heart pounding.

Sweet Jesus, what have I gotten myself into?

EIGHT

SUPPOSEDLY, AIR-DRYING naked after a shower is better for your skin—something about locking in moisture. But that advice definitely didn't come from someone living in a place where the nights dip below fifty. I snatch my fleece robe, throwing it on as fast as humanly possible before digging through my closet for work clothes. With the outside world still wrapped in darkness, the harsh glare of my closet light feels blinding. These early mornings at the coffee shop are brutal.

Dressed and ready, I look in the mirror. The glimmering crystal heart reflecting on the mirror's surface immediately catches my eye. It's still nestled in the folds of my rug, right where I left it.

I'm hugging the wall as I leave, trying to keep that mysterious stone as far away as possible. I release a slow breath in the hallway and start toward the stairs. But something pulls me back. I retrace my steps, grab the heart, and jam it into my jeans pocket. *Whatever.*

The coffee shop is a beacon of light in the twilight shadows. I pull into the spot designated for employees and jump down from Betty. The scent of fresh pastries and coffee fills the air. Aly's round face is visible through the screen door. Her family owns the coffee shop and market in town.

"Morning, Al." I say, entering the shop. Aly glances up from the espresso machine.

"Hey." Her eyes are half closed. "I need four shots in my latte this morning—do you want one?"

"Two for me, thanks." I grab a black apron from a hook behind the counter.

My mouth waters as I remove muffins from the industrial-size oven in the kitchen. Aly's mom wakes at the absurd hour of 3:00 a.m. daily to guarantee a supply of fresh baked goods for her customers. Bakers deserve a national holiday, though they probably already have one. I found out recently there's a Dance Like a Chicken Day. May 14. You're welcome.

"Here you go." Aly joins me in the kitchen and hands me a mug with their coffee shop's name and logo: So, You Need Some Joe? Joe, Aly's grandfather, started the business decades ago. A cartoon image of his smiling face appears next to the handwritten font. I've always thought he resembles Tony from *The Sopranos*.

"Thanks. How was the rest of your night?" I take the mug from her.

"Mellow. I laid low, prepping for the week. You know me, I need to be in bed early for these mornings. You'd think I'd be used to it by now," she says with a roll of her eyes. Aly helps her family in the shop five days a week, even when school is in session, a fact that Mom often brings up when I complain about helping her at the yoga studio. "Did you do anything fun?"

"Um." *I watched a mysterious band play at Red Rocks via livestream, and apparently, the universe chose them to change the world. Oh, and I'm meant to sing with them? Which I guess means I'm also among the chosen. So that's cool. But honestly, I could have dreamt the whole thing. And a crystal heart nearly electrocuted me. Yup, a heart made of crystal that was nowhere near any source of electricity. Then I had this awful dream where Kalendar just... wasn't there. But…* "Nope, not really."

The antique grandfather clock in the corner strikes six. Aly jumps. "Ugh. It gets me every time."

I laugh. "Opening time." I walk to the door and flip the sign from *Closed* to *Open*.

Minutes later, a couple walks in wearing athletic attire. They appear to be in their late thirties, maybe forties? Anyone over twenty-five seems old to me. I don't recognize them as locals.

The woman moves toward the counter; he, a corner table. Her gaze drifts up to the chalkboard menu above my head.

"Good morning. What can I get for you?" I ask, my tone bright.

"Morning," she says, her eyes lowering to meet mine. She pauses, her thin brows lift.

"My goodness! Your eyes! Are they …"

"Purple? Sure are," I interrupt. Heat rises to my face. *Here we go …*

"Erik, come here! This girl has purple eyes! They must be contacts, right?" she asks me.

"Nope, they're real," I reply sheepishly.

"Well, I'll be. That is some sort of gift you have—I've never seen it before!"

Her partner—Erik?—joins her and stares at me.

"Wow, cool. Congratulations," he says deadpan, then returns to the table.

I cough into my hand, hiding a laugh at his nonchalance.

As I prepare their order—one black coffee and one caramel macchiato with oat milk and a double shot, er, make it four—the woman speaks quietly to her companion. The words "purple" float through the air at least twice, but I can't make out the rest. My hands shake slightly as I bring it over.

"Thank you, hun," replies the lady. "Do you mind if I take a quick photo of you? I want to show my friends at home."

"Nelly! No way, that's rude," Erik says.

She turns to him. "It's not. She should be proud. I'd want to show the world if I were her." She returns her gaze to me and raises her eyebrows.

"Um, well …" I tug at my apron.

"Lavender, can you come here, please?" Aly shouts from the kitchen.

"Er, sorry. I gotta go." I retreat from their table.

Aly stands in the kitchen, arms crossed over her large chest, an annoyed expression on her face. Her hair is in a messy bun beneath a hairnet. I glance at the counter; she is knee-deep in the breakfast burrito assembly line.

"Geez, that lady was completely out of line. Are you okay?"

"I'm kinda used to it, but I appreciate you rescuing me, Al."

The door chimes, and I swallow hard, making a move for the register.

"Hold on. Why don't you finish these burritos? I'll cover the front. At least until that lady leaves."

"Really? Thanks so much."

"Of course." Aly walks toward the front, then pauses to face me. "She was right about something, though."

"Oh yeah? What's that?"

"Those eyes are a gift. I know you've had a hard time with them. But I've always been jealous. You may not see it now, but one day you will."

The hours roll on, and it's already past one; my shift is nearly done. Aly clocked out after the morning rush, leaving me to run the register solo. The shop is empty for the first time, and I seize the rare silence to turn up the volume on the wall-mounted TV.

"Wildfires rage this morning in California…" The news anchor's voice is muffled as she attempts to shout through a mask and gesture at the hills blazing behind her.

"Not again," I say, my stomach twisting.

Reaching for my phone, I open the Notes app and scroll until I find my to-do list.

"Talk to the Fire Department about wildfire prevention," I murmur as I type, adding it to the bottom. My eyes linger on the line above: *Start a CheddarUp for Hoosier at Hi Five Organic Farms.* Our eighty-year-old neighbor's tractor finally gave out last week, and I know there's no way he can afford a new one.

I'm navigating the fundraising website when the bells over the door jingle, and in strolls Charlie. I mute the TV.

His sunglasses are still on, his truck key dangles from his index finger, and Led Zeppelin blares in his ears. I can't understand how he isn't deaf—every word of "Black Dog" blasts across the room.

"Hey, Lavender!" Charlie yells too loudly as he reaches for his phone to pause the song.

I laugh. "Hey, Charlie. You have a great song on today."

"Only the best for a Monday." He grins. "I'll be right there to relieve you."

"Take your time."

The summer heat lingers in the air from Charlie's entrance. Outside the window, cars cruise along Main Street like ants marching under the cloudless sky. A Jeep Wrangler passes by with its top down, and my body jolts with recognition.

It can't be.

I steady myself against the counter, then rush outside, glancing up the street toward the Jeep. A pair of eyes meet mine in the rearview mirror—Camp's eyes. He extends his arm out of the window and waves. I freeze, rooted to the spot, staring at the rear of the Jeep until it disappears, the Tennessee license plate fading into the distance.

A warm sensation spreads over my thigh and I reach into my pocket, pulling out the heart. I hadn't thought about it since this morning, but it's warming in my hand, and the crystal is … glowing. My breath catches as the dusty rose hue shifts, turning neon pink.

"Hey, all good out here?" Charlie nearly gives me a heart attack.

"Ah, yes. I just thought I saw someone." I dodge his eyes and head back inside, thrusting the heart into my pocket. The grandfather clock shows me it's 1:20—just ten more minutes until I can get out of here. My face is hot, and my hands are visibly shaking. I fold my arms across my chest to disguise them.

Charlie hovers next to me at the counter. "You sure you're okay?"

"I'm good, honestly," I say, scratching my nose. "So, how was the hike with Kalendar last night?"

Charlie's eyes narrow. "I wasn't with Kalendar yesterday. Emma was. I thought you were going too?" He whispers the last word, his gaze dropping to the floor.

What? Beads of sweat trickle down my back. *Kalendar and Emma together without me?* My stomach flip-flops as the realization sinks in.

I glance at Charlie just as the world appears to tilt. "You know, I'm actually not feeling great. Can you take over?"

"Lavender, I'm sorry. I assumed Kalendar was with Emma *and* you. I had no idea …"

"It's not your fault," I assure him with a faint smile.

I grab my bag from the kitchen, hang up my apron, and wave goodbye to Charlie before stepping out the door. By the time I reach my truck, my hands are trembling.

How did I miss this? Sure, they've been a little close lately, but Emma never keeps secrets from me. Never.

My cheeks burn as I fumble with the key, finally hopping into the driver's seat. I pull out my phone and call Emma.

She picks up on the second ring. "Hey! Are you done with …"

"We need to talk. Where are you?" I interrupt her.

"Um, I'm home. Want to come here?" she responds tentatively.

"I'll be right there."

Emma is sitting cross-legged on a bench her dad fashioned from an old snowboard. Her lips twitch with a slight smile as I park in front of her garage.

My phone buzzes—Kalendar again. I silence his call for the third time and climb out of the truck. Charlie must've called Kalendar as soon as I left. I couldn't blame him; I'd do the same.

Emma stands, slides on her flip-flops, and walks over to greet me. She tugs at her ponytail, a nervous tick from childhood.

"How long have you and Kalendar been sneaking around behind my back?" I demand.

"How did you—" Emma stares at her hands, tugging at her tank top. When she looks up, her eyes are shining. "We didn't plan for this. It started off as harmless flirting. Kalendar's always been like a brother to me—" she falters, "—until he wasn't." Her voice softens. "We were going to tell you."

"How *long*, Emma?" I demand again.

"About a month," she whispers.

"A month?" My fists clench. "You've been seeing each other for *a month*, and neither of you thought telling me was a good idea?"

I'm in total disbelief as my mind races through memories, searching for any hint of betrayal, but finds none. They're practically siblings. How could they do this? It teeters on incest. And now, what would the future hold? Would they push me aside, forgetting me in their newfound romance? Is it not enough that I just lost Brandon?

"Kalendar wanted to make sure we were serious before coming to you. He tried telling you at the concert, but … I don't know …" A tear slips down her cheek. "I'm so sorry."

A sudden rush of dizziness washes over me, and I lock my knees to steady myself. I meet Emma's eyes, trying to hold her gaze even as the hurt churns inside.

"You're supposed to be my best friend, Emma," I whisper as I turn on my heel, my heart splintering with each step.

"Lavender. Please, let's talk," Emma shouts behind me.

I ignore her and climb into Betty. With a twist of the key, the engine hums, and Taylor Swift's voice cuts through the tension. The volume's cranked up high, and "Cruel Summer" thunders through the empty streets as I drive off.

I take off my sneakers in the mudroom. Dry tears stain my cheeks. I'm not ready to confront Kalendar, but I know it's inevitable—his truck is in the driveway. At least my parents aren't home. They'd want to have a family meeting. *No thanks.*

Kalendar sits on a stool in the kitchen, his sad eyes fix on me as I walk in. I meet his gaze with a sharp glare.

"Emma? Kalendar, how could you both do this to me? Dating is one thing, but not telling me about it? She's my best friend …" A lump forms in my throat.

He stands, reaching to put a hand on my shoulder. I flinch, and he pulls away. "Ender, this isn't how I wanted you to find out. I'm so sorry. I don't know what to say. We messed up; keeping this from you was wrong." He shakes his head. "What can I do to make it right?"

I break away from his gaze, my attention shifting toward the mountain peaks. The snow has melted a lot since Saturday, only small patches of white remain. "I need space. I can't be around you right now," I say, my voice steady.

Kalendar nods. "When you're ready, then." He sighs and hands me a sealed envelope with *Lavender* written in rushed cursive on the front.

"I found this wedged in the door. I guess it's from whoever you were with the other night," he adds, his voice calm but curious. "Seems I'm not the only one with secrets."

"What are you talking about?" My stomach lurches.

"Saturday night, after the concert. I heard you sneak out around midnight."

"Impossible," I reply, my heart quickening.

He looks at me, his expression serious. "I know what I saw, Ender. You weren't in your bed. And then you came home like an hour later."

Without another word, he turns and walks out of the kitchen.

The envelope trembles in sync with my hands as my thoughts return to the Jeep I saw earlier—*Camp*.

Taking the stairs two at a time, I rush to my bedroom, step out onto the balcony, and close the door behind me. Easing into the rocking chair, I tear open the envelope. Inside is a folded piece of paper. My breath hitches as I read the handwritten note:

Believe in the unknown. Midnight tonight. Same spot. Xo Camp, Anna, Nate.

I glance toward the forest. The lanterns flicker again at the campsite, like they're calling me back.

NINE

IT'S SEVEN P.M. *Only* seven.

I've thought about showing up early, but there must be a reason they chose midnight. Maybe they're out? Nate made it clear they're not werewolves. *But* maybe vampires? Or another fantastical creature I don't know about? *Great.*

As the wind picks up, the creak of our windmill echoes in the waning sunlight. I tighten my oversize scarf around my shoulders.

Since reading the letter, I've been sitting on my balcony, scanning the woods for any sign of them. Yet, aside from a group of passing hikers, the evening remains eerily quiet.

"Believe in the unknown," their message had said.

Ugh. Could they *be* any more cryptic?

Still… the other night actually *happened.* That's kind of exciting. Terrifying. Completely weird. But also, really feckin cool.

I want to understand more about what it all means and where I fit in. Plus, me rocking out with a band would make a killer Instagram story. And okay, I can just imagine Brandon's face when he sees me with Camp. Now, if time would move faster. I glance at my phone: *7:01. Come on.*

A movement in the valley catches my eye. I rise to my feet, leaning against the wooden railing as I zero in on it. A fox inches close to our chicken coop.

"Nope. Not today, sir." I step toward the open balcony door, ready to rescue my poultry friends, when Bruce's barking stops me. He races to the barn, swiftly handling the situation for me.

"Good boy, Bruce!" I cheer as the fox darts in the opposite direction.

The rich aroma of butter and garlic drifts from the kitchen, and my stomach twists with hunger. All I've had today is a 6 a.m. latte—no wonder I'm starving.

I step inside and pause at my bedroom door, listening for any sign of Kalendar. Once I figure it's safe, I tiptoe downstairs.

Mom stands at the stove, stirring a pot.

"Smells great," I offer.

She turns, concern etched on her face. "Hey, babe," she says. "How are you feeling?"

I brought Mom up to speed a little while ago. She tried to stay neutral, but I could see it—disappointment in Kalendar and Emma flickering behind her eyes.

"I'm fine," I say, looking past her to the stove. "What are you making?"

"Grandma's spaghetti and meatballs. I hope you're hungry."

"I am." I pause, glancing into the entryway off the kitchen.

"Kalendar's not here," she says, reading my mind. "Dad took him for a drive to have a 'man-to-man talk.'"

"Hmm," I murmur, strolling to the window to peek in the driveway just to make sure.

"Sit. You need to eat something." She pulls out a stool, the metal scratching against the tile floor. My mouth waters as I watch her plate my dinner.

"What are your plans for tonight? Want to escape for a bit? Take a mother-daughter trip?" Mom presents a heaping dish of spaghetti, meatballs, and garlic bread.

I'm already diving in before she can finish setting it down.

"Goodness, Lavender, and here I was worried you wouldn't eat." She laughs, reaching for the napkin to dab sauce from my cheek.

The fork clinks as I place it on my plate for a breather.

"Thanks, Mom. Tonight feels rushed. Maybe tomorrow?" For a moment, I consider divulging my evening plans, but I'm not sure how she'll react. This is completely unfamiliar territory for "Lavender, the rule follower."

"I have the perfect place in mind," she says, her eyes sparkling with excitement.

Preparing for a midnight rendezvous in the woods, surrounded by magical fireflies and Hogwarts-esque lanterns, poses a wardrobe dilemma. A clothing explosion has detonated in my room by the time I settle on my favorite jeans and a cozy purple sweater. With my hair braided loosely on one side and a delicate gold necklace around my neck, I'm ready to go. I glance at my watch. *11:38 p.m.* Peering out the window, the lanterns twinkle in the distance, and my pulse speeds in anticipation. I toss the blue shirt I borrowed from Emma in the trash on my way out the door (sorry, not sorry).

Stepping into the hallway, I hold my breath and listen. It's silent. Jake had called earlier to say he was spending another night in Denver—one less person to worry about.

Bruce greets me in the kitchen, his tail wagging. I contemplate bringing him, but no. His absence would raise suspicions if anyone awoke. "Sorry, buddy, not this time," I whisper, nuzzling his ear.

I slip into my Converse sneakers and grab a flashlight. The crisp air sends shivers of excitement down my spine. I creep the length of the driveway; the gravel crunching underfoot. Blinking to adjust my eyes to the darkness, I resist the urge to flick on my flashlight until I've safely cleared the house.

As I near the road, a glowing orb rushes toward me. *Ah, the fireflies.* They greet me with a swirling dance around my body. "Hey, guys." I laugh. They flicker in place for a moment before ascending the trail.

I stumble behind them, my steps much less graceful than last time, as my nerves spike.

Soon, the lights from the campsite appear and I pause, tuning into my surroundings. There's no music tonight to greet me, but the murmur of voices fills the air. Though I can't make out their words, the conversation sounds easy and cheerful. I press on, allowing the fireflies to guide me forward.

They come to a gradual stop. We're here. Goosebumps rise on my skin.

The fireflies drift individually toward the sky, making a circle like last time. Below, I catch sight of Camp, Anna, and Nate gathered around the campfire, their laughter loud and contagious. Nate is bent over, laughing hysterically, while Camp, perched on a tree stump, gestures wildly in the middle of what must be a hilarious story.

Anna spots me first. Her face lights up as she rushes over, pulling me into a tight hug. "I'm so glad you're here," she whispers as her scent—a calming blend of lavender and frankincense—wraps around me.

"Me too," I say. Everything appears draped in a soft pink glow, creating the sensation of living in a dream. I pinch my arm to reassure myself I'm not. *Ouch.*

"Guys, Lavender came back." Anna shouts over her shoulder.

Nate lifts his head and half-smiles, then returns to his conversation.

Camp taps Nate's shoulder, quieting him without a word. His gaze finds mine, and a slow grin spreads as he rises from the stump. His cowboy hat sits low over his brow, a strand of brown hair slipping free near his eye.

"Evening, Lavender." Camp approaches with an easy stride.

"Hey, Camp," I say, feeling the heat rise to my cheeks, thankful for the cover of darkness.

"Thanks for coming." He extends his hand to mine.

I hesitate for a moment, expecting a hug instead, but I push aside my disappointment and grip his hand firmly. His rough, calloused fingers swallow mine. I can't help but wonder if he feels the million little fireworks going off in my fingertips.

"I had to. You guys are so mysterious. Thought maybe you're vampires or something." A nervous laugh bubbles up before I can stop it.

"Vampires, huh?" Camp's eyes twinkle with amusement. "And yet, here you are."

"Call me crazy, I guess," I reply, matching his playful tone.

"Well, all right then." He chuckles.

My heart races as my hand lingers in his.

"Group hug!" Anna announces, waving Nate over. I reluctantly let go of Camp's hand.

"Nah, I'm not a good hugger." Nate calls from his place by the fire. "I'm good right here." He raises his water bottle in a mock toast.

"Nate! Don't be like that," Anna groans.

Camp leans in close, his voice lowering. "You'll have to excuse Nate. He lacks social skills."

"Heard that!" Nate yells in response.

"Anyway, let me give you a tour of the campground." Anna takes my hand, throwing Nate a sharp look.

We make the rounds to everyone's teepee; Camp's is last. My heart flips when she takes me inside. An enchanting scent of sandalwood and rose fills the space. A wooden chair is in the corner with an acoustic guitar leaning against it. String lights hang from the top of the teepee, cascading like a waterfall. A black Patagonia duffle lies on the floor next to his bed, and resting atop his faded blue-and-white checkered quilt sits a well-loved journal.

"Camp clearly wins with ambience." Anna laughs. "Okay, follow me to the good stuff." She pats my arm as she exits the tent, and I steal one last glance at his space before backing out.

Anna stands in front of the canopy housing the musical gear that is set up just as before. I gesture toward the blank sign hanging along the back. "I notice you don't have a band name. Why's that?"

"We've been waiting for you," Anna smiles.

"Me?"

"Yes! Trust me, we've tried. They've been *terrible*." She looks at me earnestly. "Camp's intuition tells him you'll be the one to name us, so we've been waiting."

"Oh, um, I'll give it some thought." I run my hand down my braid and glance around the campsite again. "Do you pack up every time you leave? It seems like a lot of work."

"It's not so bad. The beds are inflatable, and the teepees are easy to disassemble. We're not swimming in money, so we bring our gear everywhere. We only stay in a hotel when the weather's bad."

I nod, impressed. "You guys were in Denver, right? Playing at Red Rocks?"

"We were. How'd you know?"

"My brother Jake was watching the concert online. He's a huge Dave Matthews fan."

"Ah, yes. Nice guy, Dave."

I can almost feel my eyes popping out of my skull. Unbelievable. Jake would flip if he met Dave Matthews, yet Anna appears unfazed. Another day in the life, I guess?

As we circle back to the fire, I glance at Camp and Nate. They huddle together and Camp strums the guitar, stopping occasionally to ask Nate a question.

"What are they doing?" I ask Anna.

"Writing a new song. They always craft the music together; it's pretty cute."

"That's sweet," I murmur, my gaze fixed on Camp—his long-sleeve Henley clings to his muscular frame, accentuating his broad shoulders in the firelight. Dimples appear when he smiles, a detail I hadn't noticed until now. He flicks his gaze at me. *Shoot.* I look away.

"So, how did you get involved in the band?" I rub my forehead as I peek back at Camp; his eyes are still on me. My blush returns, and I swing my gaze around the campsite like I'm searching for something. *Pathetic.*

"Camp and Nate came to a concert at a local bar I performed at in Seattle, my hometown," Anna adds, her voice carrying the nostalgia of the memory. "I was the drummer for a girls' alternative rock group then. We were awesome." She winks. "Anyway, they told me about a band they were putting together to revolutionize the world. I couldn't understand it at first either." She smiles. "But they kept coming back, every night. Finally, they mentioned the phantom music that only I could hear. That's when I believed them."

"So you heard the music, too?"

"Yep, same as you. I thought I was losing my mind until I met Camp and Nate. We're like a family now."

I lean close to her and lower my voice. "I get the feeling Nate doesn't like me."

She snorts. "Nate? He's moody. And well, he's kind of on a deadline."

"Deadline?"

"His dad has given him an ultimatum." Anna's voice drops. "If our band isn't successful by the end of the year, he needs to quit and work at his family's law firm in Utah. Get a 'proper job.'" She air quotes with exaggerated fingers.

"That's rough," I say, suddenly grateful for my supportive parents. "But he seems nice to *you*," I murmur, my eyes flicking back to him.

"We've been searching for you a long time. He's just ready to get on with this," Anna says with a shrug. "Don't worry. The trick is not taking him too seriously. Give it time. He'll warm up."

"How long have you been looking for me?"

"Exactly one year. Touring without a band name—" she laughs "—looking for you."

"Wow..."

"Well, not you specifically. A girl with violet eyes—at least that's what she told us at first. Came to her in meditation. Eventually, your name came up."

"Who told you that?"

"Maggie."

"Who's Maggie?" I ask, surprised. Nobody mentioned her the first night. Unless, is she the guardian angel Camp was referring to?

"She's the vision behind this band. Totally cool, completely confident. Very mysterious." Anna wiggles her brows. "You'll meet her one day."

"Camp mentioned I had a guardian angel of sorts the first night. Do you think Maggie is who he was talking about?"

"Oh, definitely." Anna nods. "She's like an earthside angel."

Before I can press Anna for more details, Camp walks toward us, guitar in hand. He lifts it slightly. "Do you want to hear a song, Lavender?"

"Oh—um, yeah." I sweep the area, double-checking for any overlooked teepees or traces of this elusive Maggie.

Camp chuckles. "You sure? I was hoping for more enthusiasm." He tilts his head, watching me.

"Yes! Definitely. Sorry, I'm just… distracted." I exhale and settle onto a patch of grass near the makeshift stage, tucking my legs beneath me as the band gathers.

Anna sits behind the drums while Nate grabs the bass. Camp steps up to the microphone with his guitar, his eyes meeting mine.

The track they perform carries a haunting, folksy vibe. Its lyrics narrate the journey of a woman who found her life's purpose while strolling the streets of New York City.

As Camp sings, his Tennessee drawl echoes through the song, and each lyric pulls at my heartstrings. But, it's the last verse that gets me:

Neon signs light up her path
As she walks this city's aftermath,
Her dreams close in with each step she takes
New York City
Where her spirit wakes

A tear slides down my cheek, and I don't bother brushing it away. The words seem deeply personal. I can't help wondering who they're about.

"Guys! That was incredible." I clap.

"We're good, huh?" Anna says.

With his guitar still slung around his neck, Camp approaches me and offers his hand; I'm quick to take it. He guides me to the microphone, positioning me beside him.

"Do you want to sing?" His eyes smile down at me.

My heart pounds and a sheen of sweat coats my palms. Singing in front of anyone besides Bruce has *never* been high on my bucket list. Sure, I'll belt it out in the car and sometimes in the shower, where *no one* else can hear.

"Camp, I'm honestly not a good singer."

That's it, they're sending me home.

"Huh. Can you prove that?" Camp raises his eyebrows.

"Well, it's just, I've never sung in front of anyone before, so ..."

Camp laughs. "Okay, okay. Maybe next time? You have a better voice than you give yourself credit for."

"I'm not so sure about that, but yes, next time. I promise—guess I'll have to practice or whatever."

"Or whatever," Camp repeats. *Gosh, those dimples.*

Anna takes me aside as Camp and Nate continue on to the campfire.

"You have an incredible voice. You know that, right?" she asks.

"What? How do you even know?"

"Maggie."

"How the heck wou—"

"Anna—can you come over here? Camp doesn't believe my story of our run-in with Olivia Rodrigo," Nate calls from the fire pit.

"Coming!" Anna grabs my hand. "You'll *love* this. Nate totally embarrassed himself in front of her."

Am I stuck in a reality TV show?

We hang out by the fire for the rest of the early morning hours, swapping stories and listening to Camp play his guitar. Laughing with them is easy, and my worries about Kalendar and Emma fade.

I settle onto a log beside Camp. He's actually very funny, and his laugh is infectious—dropping unexpectedly and loudly. I catch myself stealing glances at him more often than I should.

As the night sky transitions into twilight, our conversation mellows with the onset of sleepiness. The bonfire scent lingers in my hair, and the air grows colder as the embers dwindle. Realizing it's time to head home before my family wakes, I rise.

"I better get going," I say, stifling a yawn.

Nate stands and meets my gaze with an intensity that makes my stomach flip. "You're coming back, right?"

I shift my weight, tucking my hands into my pockets. "Um, yeah. That's the plan."

"You have to. We need to make a difference and…" his voice falters. "We've just been at this for so long. It's time."

My chest tightens as I sense more behind his words than just a deadline from his dad. "But you all have been playing just fine without me…"

"No." He interrupts, stepping closer. "It doesn't work like that. We need you; your gift. Your lyrics most importantly. This band, this—this thing we're doing? It's more than just playing good music. It's everything."

I nod, unable to find the right words to match his intensity.

"Good." He exhales sharply, like he's relieved. "I'm headed to bed." He turns, strolling toward his teepee, the morning breeze tousling his long hair.

"When can I see you all again?" My eyes rest on Camp.

"We're leaving tomorrow to play a festival in Utah," Anna replies.

Camp jumps in: "We'll be back on Sunday. Can you come by around three? Let's meet in daylight next time and prove to you we're not, in fact, vampires."

"Oh, Sunday?" My voice drips with disappointment.

"It'll go by fast, and soon, you'll join us at these concerts," Anna says. "If you ever need to feel connected to us while we're away, hold that heart I gave you."

"I've been meaning to ask you about that actually, the heart is magic. Literally. Where's it from?"

"That's a story for another day. You better get home." She hugs me. "Goodbye, Lavender."

"Oh, okay." *Another dang mystery.* "Bye, Anna."

"I'll walk you home," Camp says with a grin.

"Th-thanks," I stutter, face-palming as Camp turns to grab my flashlight on a nearby rock.

We walk silently beside each other, the forest floor crunching with every step. Birds serenade us as we pass by, perched on the branches of the evergreens. I sneak glances at him occasionally, noticing the faint smile on his lips as he walks confidently beside me.

I press my lips together before speaking. "How did you come to join the band?"

Camp's smile fades. He stops mid-step, his gaze dropping to the ground before he slowly turns to face me. There's something heavy in his eyes.

"I had a rough go of it for a while. I was in a dark place." He looks away. "Didn't really want to go on living if I'm being honest." He squints at the sky. "One morning, I woke up to the most beautiful melody I'd ever heard. I followed the music without thinking, wanting to know where it was coming from. That was the morning I met Maggie." He resumes his stride.

I watch him walk away, unable to move. His pain feels heavy. I want to know more about his "rough years." But more importantly, who is this Maggie? I have to know.

Jogging to catch up, I count to one-two-three-four-five before asking, "Anna mentioned Maggie earlier. She said Maggie started the band?"

"Yeah, it's Maggie's vision," he began. "She's had a hell of a life. She believes our music can save the world. We need to send messages through our songs—let people know they're not alone. Give them hope for a better future. Encourage them to take care of each other and the environment." He stops walking to look at me again. "She can see it happening. She sees us making a change. The universe speaks to her."

I arch an eyebrow.

Camp laughs. "I understand how insane this seems. Trust me, though, it's in you." He gently taps my forehead. "Believe it, and you'll see."

"When can I meet Maggie? Where is she?"

His eyes twinkle. "She's a bit... elusive. Always on a mission. But don't worry—you'll cross paths soon."

We continue on in silence, but his words keep echoing in my head: *It's in you.* What does that mean? What's so special about me? Nate mentioned lyrics, but I've never even written a song. And why am I so drawn to them? It feels like there's something bigger at play here, something beyond explanation.

As we near my driveway, I stop and cast a glance at my home, nestled on the hill. There are no signs of life yet. *Phew.*

"I should walk the rest of the way myself, just in case ..."

"Of course. I'm glad we got you home safely."

"Thanks for walking me."

"Any time." He holds up his hand for a high-five.

I meekly bring my hand to meet his.

"What was that? That's not a high-five," he chuckles, holding out his hand again.

I hit his hand harder this time.

"Better." He laughs.

"See you Sunday, then," I say.

"I'll be counting the days." He takes his hat off and bows.

Walking away, I sense his eyes on me. I steal glances back, finding him rooted in place, his gaze unwavering until I disappear around the corner of my driveway, out of sight.

Slipping inside my house, I tiptoe up to my bedroom. As I change into my nightgown, I catch my reflection in the mirror. I haven't smiled this big in a long time.

Before shimmying under the covers, I pull Emma's shirt from the trash bin.

TEN

"LAVENDER?" A VOICE from another world swirls into my unconscious, echoing through my mind's hazy sky. "Sweetheart, wake up." I open one eye to find Mom hovering over me, a smile on her face. "Morning, sleepyhead."

I rub my eyes. "What time is it?" My words are raspy and deep.

"It's eleven—late for you. Are you feeling okay?"

"Eleven?" I sit up, blinking in surprise. Sunlight streams into my room, thick and warm, drawing a sheen of sweat on my forehead. The distant hum of tractors from the nearby ranch floats in through the open window.

"I'm fine," I murmur, wiping the dew from my head.

Mom stares at me, her eyebrows raised.

Shitza. Does she know I snuck out? My heart speeds in my chest.

"What's up, Mom?" I nervous-laugh, tucking a strand of hair behind my ear.

"Still interested in that mother-daughter trip?" Her eyes shine.

My heart slows.

"Oh … yeah. Where are we headed?"

"Well, my first thought was a yoga retreat, but don't worry; I know my audience," she laughs before continuing "so instead, I was thinking …" she claps her hands, eyes wide "… a trip to Aspen!" she shrieks.

"That sounds perfect," I reply with a wide smile. Mom's enthusiasm is unobtainable, and I've long since given up trying to match it.

Wait, the coffee shop. "Shoot. I need to work on Thursday." My voice drips with disappointment as I mentally try to resolve the snafu. *I wonder if Charlie …*

"That's taken care of. I called Charlie this morning to see if he could cover for you. He said he's happy to."

Of course she did. "Thanks, Mom. You're the best." I lean in to hug her.

"Absolutely, sweetheart. Okay, so I was thinking we could leave around one. Let's see where your suitcase is …" she rummages through my closet. "Oh no. This closet is a hoarder's haven. Hun, you need to sort through this when we get back."

"All right, all right. Please get out now." I get up from bed and take her by the arm. "I can find my suitcase."

"Fine. Start packing and come downstairs when you're ready. I'll make you breakfast. Or perhaps, lunch?" She arches an eyebrow.

"Breakfast will be just fine." I laugh.

"Breakfast, then," she says, kissing my head. She clicks shut my bedroom door behind her. "And clean that closet!" her muffled voice reminds me.

Leaning against the door, I breathe a sigh of relief. She doesn't know.

We arrived at the hotel in Aspen near dinnertime. After a quick check-in to our suite, we bolt for the closest restaurant, our stomachs rumbling.

The rich aroma of grilled meat and herbs swirls through the mountain air as Mom and I sit across from each other at a trendy Italian restaurant. String lights shine above us like stars, and a warm breeze swirls in and out of the outdoor seating area, which has proven to be a prime spot for celebrity sightings.

"There's Kate Hudson." I whisper to Mom.

"Oh, and her brother, Oliver, is with her. He's quite funny, you know." Mom waves her hand in the air. "Kate! Olly! Hi, dears!"

My face turns as red as the tomato bruschetta in front of me, and I try to shield myself with my hand as I sneak a look at their reaction. To my horror, they wave back. "Have a nice dinner!" Kate calls out, and Oliver throws up a peace sign.

"Mom! What the heck? You can't just do that."

"Why not? They're people too. So nice, those kids. Goldie raised them well."

"You know they're only like five years younger than you, right?"

Mom picks up the menu. "Hmm, really? Maybe I should be friends with them." She winks as she puts on her oversized reading glasses, which rest on the tip of her nose. "They make their own pasta here; did you know that?" She peeks over her glasses, then suddenly freezes, her gaze fixed on something beyond me.

"What is it?" I ask, turning to look behind me.

"Shh. No, no. Turn back around." She grips my forearm.

"What? What's happening? Who are you hiding from?"

Mom holds the menu in front of her and glances over the top.

"Seriously, Mom. Who?" I turn around again.

"Lavender, don't stare. It's Josephine Dunton."

"Who?"

"Josephine Dunton! You know, the meditation guru?" She lowers the menu and nods toward a woman walking on the street.

I pretend-scratch my nose as I follow her gaze. My eyes land on Josephine.

Her ebony skin appears to glow in the twilight sky. She has long braided hair which sits in a low ponytail. She wears a Southwestern sweater over a relaxed white tank with a music festival logo. Paired with high-waisted black joggers and chestnut Birkenstock clogs, her outfit is effortlessly cool. I make a mental note to replicate it for myself.

"I mean, she looks awesome. But really? *Now,* you're acting shy?" I raise an eyebrow.

"She's a true spiritual goddess." Mom exclaims. "I'm so inspired by her. I've always wanted to meet her."

"Why don't you introduce yourself, then?"

"Oh, I couldn't! I don't want to bother her."

I shake my head in disbelief. "You didn't think saying hello to Kate and Oliver bothered them?"

Mom swats the air with her hand. "This is different."

I roll my eyes. "Okay, well, I'm sure Josephine would be honored to meet such a fan." Josephine continues down the block, her back to us now. She walks with such grace and confidence, I can understand Mom's admiration.

"Maybe we'll see her again," Mom says as she watches her walk away.

"What's her story? I've never seen you so starstruck."

She looks at me, her eyes wide.

"I don't know the details of her younger years, but from what I've heard, it wasn't easy. There's talk that she went through a profound 'dark night of the soul' experience several years back, during which she had a spiritual awakening. Since then, her meditation practice has become incredibly powerful. She's literally changed people's lives. Some even say the universe speaks through her." Mom pauses and looks up the street, where Josephine last was.

She lowers her voice. "She's also quite mysterious, traveling the world and making spontaneous appearances to conduct meditation workshops. I've always hoped she'd visit our studio in Rosewood one day."

"Well, she came to Aspen. Who knows, Rosewood could be next."

"One can wish." Mom sighs.

The busboy arrives with our drinks.

"Thank you, Bobby." Mom pats his arm.

Bobby's eyebrows shoot up before he looks at his name tag and grins. "Of course. Let me know if you need anything else." His eyes sparkle.

After dinner, back in the hotel suite, I'm tempted to tell Mom about the band. The ease of the evening has me feeling refreshed, happy, and closer to her than I've felt in a while. Maybe she'd be excited for me. The whole *universe-is-speaking-to-me* is exactly her kind of thing. And apparently, Josephine's too—her idol.

"Mom, I—"

"Hold that thought; I need to use the restroom. I'll be right out," Mom says as she closes the bathroom door.

I sink into the oversized chair, instinctively grab my phone, and open Instagram. A post from the Utah music festival—cleverly named Harmony on the Rocks—catches my eye. I've been following their page ever since Anna said they'd be performing there. I swipe through photos of bands I've never seen, red arches, and cool outfits;

my heart stops at the fourth image. Camp is onstage with a tall, gorgeous blonde. Her hair is in a high ponytail, and she's perfectly in shape—a (very) short skirt shows toned legs. Her eyes gaze into Camp's as she clutches a microphone. He smiles warmly at her. My stomach churns. I fling my phone on the coffee table and cross my arms over my chest.

"What's wrong?" Mom asks as she returns to the living room.

"Nothing. I'm just tired." I rub my eyes. "That was fun, thanks. I'm going to bed if that's okay."

"Sure, okay. Did you want to tell me something?" Her eyes soften with worry.

"Umm, I forget—it couldn't have been important. Love you." I blow her a kiss as I close the door to the bedroom and throw myself onto the bed.

What the actual f? Did they find someone new?

I visit the Harmony on the Rocks Instagram page again, psychotically scrolling through every post and story, but there are no more pictures of the band. I return to the photo of Camp and Concert Barbie and zoom in. *Yep, they're in love.*

I throw my phone on the carpeted floor and bury my head in the pillow.

How can they replace me so quickly? I mean, they've been living behind my house! Who does that? And Camp, *of course*, he'd fall for someone like that.

Maybe it's a misunderstanding. Maybe it's just a fellow musician? Or a friend? Maybe, maybe, maybe, *BLAH*.

Curling into a ball, I pull the quilt over my head.

The next morning, Mom and I set out for a hike and I'm, admittedly, an ogre to be around with visions of Camp and his new girlfriend swirling through my mind.

I'm holding a wooden hiking stick so hard my knuckles are turning white. I glance back to find Mom stopped again, bent over a blueberry-looking plant. "What is it now, Mom?" I ask, not bothering to hide the annoyance in my voice.

"These are bilberry bushes; they're delicious in jams. They taste just like blueberries." She picks a few and offers them to me.

"No. Can we keep going? We're nearly at Maroon Bells."

"Sure, hun."

I pick up the pace, counting my steps like it'll somehow stop my brain from spiraling: 2,022; 2,023 …

Mom clears her throat.

What now?

"Lavender, we need to talk about Kalendar and Emma," she begins with hesitation. My jaw clenches. "I've spoken to both of them separately, and they feel terrible. Kalendar even told me he'd call it off with Emma if it'd make you happy, but the thing is … I can see they care for each other. It doesn't seem to be just a fling." She pauses, waiting for a reaction from me. When I don't give her one, she continues: "Anyway, I understand why you're hurt, and I'm disappointed with the way it unfolded, but I'm asking you to consider that this relationship might be more than we initially thought."

I stop, sigh loudly, and face her. "I appreciate what you're saying, but I'm not ready to forgive them, let alone be okay with them dating. Emma and Kalendar are … were … the most important people in my life and I'm hurt they kept this from me. I don't understand why; I would've been cool with it." Mom raises her eyebrows. "Well, maybe not cool, but I would've eventually come around."

I take a sip of water before continuing. "It's going to take a long time for this to be okay for me … if it ever will. Even if they have actual feelings for each other, it doesn't make sense. Kalendar leaves for Montana State next month. There's no way they can keep a relationship during that, so this will have been for nothing. Anyway, they hurt me, and that's all I can focus on right now."

Mom nods. "Okay, sweetheart. But holding onto a grudge is never healthy. I'll leave it at that."

Ignoring her last comment, I plop onto a bench.

We've finally reached Maroon Lake. The turquoise water mirrors the Maroon Bell Mountains like a painting, its surface as still as glass. Several fellow hikers take photos and stare at the majestic scene.

I chew on my lip until it breaks the skin.

ELEVEN

IT'S OUR LAST FULL day in Aspen, and I've reluctantly agreed to a group meditation tonight with Mom—my peace offering for being in a terrible mood. There's supposed to be a "special guest" leading it and Mom's hoping it's Josephine.

The streets buzz with tourists as I head to the juice bar in town to grab a smoothie for Mom and me. Pristine cowboy boots *click-clack* on the brick walkway as expensive Western hats bob through the pedestrian mall. A string quartet plays a beautiful rendition of Journey's "Don't Stop Believin'."

I round the bend and spot Josephine Dunton stepping out of a black SUV in front of Hotel Jerome. My stomach knots. I pivot on my heel—ready to go tell Mom. But no. I can handle this. She's Mom's favorite, and she'll probably be gone before Mom even makes it here.

I take a breath, push my shyness aside, and head toward her.

"Um, Josephine?" My voice cracks. *Great.*

She pauses, turning to me with warm eyes. Warm *purple* eyes.

"Hi there," she says, her voice even and confident.

A wave of dizziness washes over me, and I blink hard to steady myself. This can't be happening. I thought I was the only one with eyes like these. My doctor had mentioned something about there being others, but I never really believed him. Anyone can fake purple eyes with contacts. I've seen them. But hers? Hers are real. There's a difference.

Swallowing hard, I thrust my hand out. "I'm Lavender. It's nice to meet you."

Her handshake is gentle.

"So you are," she replies with a smile, her gaze steady but kind.

I glance at my Converse and then back to her. "Your eyes…I…Have you…Are they…" Words fail me as I'm drawn into her violet irises, glowing like embers against her smooth ebony skin.

Josephine chuckles, a look of amusement spreading across her face. "Yes, they're real," she fans her eyes playfully with a manicured hand. "I imagine you get that question a lot, too?"

My voice seems to have vanished, so I nod instead.

She winks. "We're a special bunch, aren't we?"

I shift uncomfortably as the sun beams into my eyes, forcing me to pull my sunglasses from the top of my head. "So, you've met others?"

"I have, yes. Two others, sisters. They live in Costa Rica. Special souls, those two." Her smile deepens.

"Sisters?" I repeat, trying to process this new information. I try to picture them—these purple-eyed sisters. Do they look like me? Or like Josephine? Is it possible there are others?

Josephine's face softens. "Yes, sisters. They soak up the attention, though I can't really relate. I've had my own journey with my eye color—just like you, I'm sure. We don't exactly go unnoticed, do we?" She laughs, a knowing glint in her eye.

A car beeps as it passes by us on the street and I jump, startled.

Josephine gives a quick wave toward the car, then turns back to me.

I clear my throat. "So, are you leading meditation tonight? My mom's a big fan and has wanted to meet you for so long." My words stumble out.

She searches my face before answering. "Is that so? Well, I look forward to meeting her. And yes, I'm teaching at the meditation center. Will you be joining us?" There's a hint of anticipation in her tone, almost as if she's hoping I'll say …

"Y-y-yes," I stutter, my face turning red.

Her lips press together in amusement. "I'll see you then," she says before walking away.

Returning to our suite, I find it empty. I set Mom's smoothie on the coffee table and drop onto the overstuffed couch, the cushions swallowing me whole. My fingers hover over my phone before unlocking it and opening Instagram. The Harmony on the Rocks page loads instantly.

Another photo of Camp and concert Barbie fills the screen. My stomach twists into a knot. This time, it's the whole gang—Camp, Anna, Nate, and Barbie—on stage, arms wrapped around each other, grinning down at the crowd.

I stare at the image, my thumb frozen mid-scroll. My eyes sting with unexpected tears.

Tapping on the photo, I zoom in on their faces. Barbie's smile is radiant, her eyes locked on Camp. Anna leans into her, their heads nearly touching. Nate's arm is across Anna's shoulder. One big happy family. *Ugh.*

The screen blurs and I lean back, closing my eyes, but the image is burned into my mind.

I've been replaced.

Stomach rolling, I head into the bathroom and turn on the shower. As the water warms, an undeniable pull toward the crystal heart takes hold of me again.

I grab my vanity case and take it out, gripping it tightly as warmth spreads through my palm. The moment my eyes shut, a vision floods in—just as vivid as before.

I'm again onstage at Red Rocks, standing next to Camp. Someone begins to scream, and I quickly find the source.

A woman in the crowd is pointing at the sky. I track her finger to see Kalendar dangling from one of the infamous Red Rocks. He must be nearly three hundred feet in the air, holding on with his fingers.

"Kalendar!" I scream. He turns to look at me, causing him to lose his grip and fall, gravity pulling him faster and faster to the ground.

"Lavender? Lavender! What's wrong?" Mom's pounding on the bathroom door.

I snap back to reality, tears flowing down my cheeks. My throat feels hoarse, as if I'd been screaming. Opening the door, I fall into Mom's arms, sobbing.

We arrive at the meditation room twenty minutes early. Mom insisted we get here first to secure space at the front, as close to Josephine as possible.

My breakdown in the bathroom rattled her, but I passed it off as a post-traumatic reaction to the whole Kalendar and Emma fling. I can't believe she believed me, but I also can't bring myself to reveal my crazy vision. It was, after all, only that—a vision. Still, I feel an urgency to mend things with Kalendar when we get home.

Mom was thrilled when I told her about my run-in with the magical, mystical goddess that is Josephine Dunton. And swears she did not know Josephine had purple eyes too, which I find to be very strange. Maybe she wears colored contacts sometimes to cover them. I'd totally do it—if Mom didn't think it was "blasphemy to cover up the gift God gave me."

Short, thick candles cast dancing shadows across the studio walls, and the aroma of frankincense fills the air. I follow Mom's lead and grab a floor pillow from the corner of the room. We are indeed the first ones to arrive. Mom sets her pillow up at the front, and I sit beside her.

The room fills up quickly. It's crowded; word must have gotten out that the special guest is Josephine Dunton. I glance at Mom often while waiting for practice to begin. Her eyes are closed as if she's already in a deep meditation. Meanwhile, here I sit—taking up coveted space at the front and not knowing how to pass the time until the class begins. I kneel on the mat and sit on my heels, extending my arms in front of me—defaulting to child's pose in yoga.

Suddenly, hushed whispers fill the room. I lift my head and turn toward the rear of the studio. Josephine steps gracefully to the front, a serene smile playing on her lips. She winks at me as she settles in front of us, and my ears flush warm.

The meditation was nothing like I expected. Josephine spent a lot of time on breathwork at the start, which helped me calm my racing mind and shove aside my usual feeling of inadequacy. Even Concert Barbie got pushed to the backburner. I sank so deep into the meditation that I nearly jumped when the bell rang and Josephine asked us to bring our palms to the heart center. The whole hour flew by like ten minutes. She definitely lived up to the hype.

Mom approaches Josephine when the class ends, and the lights come on. I trail behind her, peeking sheepishly over Mom's shoulder while she speaks. "It's such a pleasure to meet you. I love your work. I've been following you for a long time."

"The pleasure is mine. I can assure you," Josephine responds with such warmth that I smile. "Where are you from?"

"We live in Rosewood, Colorado. It's a three-hour drive from here. This is my daughter, Lavender. I believe you met her earlier today." Mom steps to the side, destroying my pathetic attempt to appear invisible.

"Ah, yes. Hello again, Lavender," she says, gazing at me with the same endearing intensity as before.

"Hi," I squeak out. I don't know why this woman makes me so nervous. Maybe it's her unwavering confidence. The way she dresses. Her ability to transport me to another universe …

"So you live in Rosewood?" She returns her attention to Mom.

"Yes. I own a yoga studio in town. We'd be honored if you made a trip there one day."

Josephine taps her fingers against her chin, briefly locking eyes with me before returning her attention to Mom.

"Okay, then. I'll come."

Mom looks at Josephine incredulously. "You will?"

"Yes." She smiles. "I'll come by on Saturday. Will you help me arrange a class for Saturday evening? Let's say 7:00 p.m.?"

Mom's speechless; she hesitates for a bit too long and I poke her from behind.

"Y-y-yes, yes, of course. The whole town will want to come," Mom stammers.

"I hope you have a big space, then." Josephine laughs. "Will I see you there, Lavender?" She looks at me, her eyebrows raised.

"Yes, of course."

"Wonderful. I'd love to talk about your life experience, particularly when it comes to your purple eyes."

I flush.

"Oh that would be incredible." Mom answers for me. "She's always been a little self-conscious. I think they're absolutely beautiful. A divine gift. You two are lucky."

Lord, please make her stop.

"We sure are." Josephine smiles. "All right then, I'll see you ladies in a couple of days." She gives each of us a quick hug and turns to the line of people behind us, eagerly waiting to speak with her.

The next morning, Mom could hardly contain her excitement about Josephine the entire drive home. She spent half the ride on the phone with her Rosewood friends, hyping up Josephine's spontaneous class tomorrow night. Each time she retold the story, I could practically feel her beaming with pride.

As we round the bend in our driveway, Mom stomps on the brake, her grip tightening the wheel. "I have to call you back," she murmurs into the phone before shifting into park.

My stomach clenches as I spot Emma's car sitting out front.

TWELVE

EMMA DASHES OUT of the door, furiously wiping her eyes with her hand. Stumbling at the bottom of the steps, she picks herself up and flees to her Subaru.

Mom creeps past her and parks in front of a garage bay to avoid blocking the driveway. Dust billows in Emma's wake as she speeds down it.

Mom and I exchange glances. Her eyes drift to the porch, and I follow her gaze. Kalendar stands at the front door, his shoulders slumped and his hand lingering on the handle as he watches Emma's dust settle. His expression brightens when he spots us and he descends the stone steps with a slow, hesitant stride.

I roll down my window.

"Hey, Ma; hey, Ender," he says as he approaches us, smiling. "Glad you're home."

"Hey, sweetheart. Everything okay?" Mom nods down the driveway.

"It's fine. Sorry you had to see that." He runs a hand through his shaggy hair, then rests his arm on the roof of the car. "How was your trip?"

"It was nice." I wiggle my brows. "Mom met her girl crush."

Kalendar laughs. "Oh, yeah?"

Mom's eyes glimmer. "Sure did. Josephine Dunton."

"What! No way!"

"Yup. And she's coming *here.* Tomorrow!"

Kalendar whoops with joy. "Is she teaching?"

"Yup." Mom replies smugly.

"Wait. Kal, you know who Josephine is?" I grip the edge of the open window with one hand, shading my eyes from the sun with the other as I gaze up at him.

"Doesn't everyone?"

"Apparently." I arch an eyebrow. "And did you know she has purple eyes?"

"Really? That's awesome." Kalendar elbows me through the window. "See, Ender? You're not the only one."

"Guess not. Anyway, it's good to see you, Kal." I've missed him. My bizarre visions, Concert Barbie—everything has me wanting to retreat to the comfort of my brother. And I suspect Emma won't interfere anymore, considering what I just saw.

"Good to see you, too." He messes my hair with his hand. "Y'all coming inside, or hanging in the car?"

Mom laughs. "Inside sounds better."

Kalendar opens the trunk to grab our suitcases while Mom and I gather empty coffee cups and our purses from the front seats.

The moment Kalendar drops our bags in the mudroom, I rush at him, burying my head against his chest and wrapping my arms tightly around him.

"Whoa." Kalendar chuckles but returns the hug. The soft fabric of his T-shirt feels warm against my cheek. The familiar scent of outdoors and our family laundry detergent makes me smile. I catch Mom watching us. Although her lips curve into a grin, a trace of sadness lingers in her gaze, though I can't imagine why.

Later that night, Kalendar asks me to sit with him outside after dinner.

He kindles the wood in our firepit before settling into one of the Adirondack chairs. I join him, and for a while, we stare at the flames.

Even though the fire is warm, an inexplicable chill runs through me. I pull a flannel blanket from the storage box and wrap it tightly around myself, grateful the sweltering heat has lifted, even if just for today.

The crackling fire transports me to my time with Camp and the band a few nights ago. But then thoughts of Concert Barbie intrude, and my stomach twists uncomfortably.

Needing a distraction from the chaos in my brain, I look at Kalendar. He wears his trucker hat backward and sizable blue crescents frame the skin under his eyes. The image of him falling at Red Rocks flashes in my mind, causing my throat to tighten. I can't begin to imagine life without him.

"Ender." Kalendar says, breaking the silence. "I'm sorry for how things went down with Emma. She's your best friend, and I shouldn't have gotten in the middle of that. I was being selfish." His eyes shift from the fire to meet mine, filled with regret. But there's something else there too, something I can't quite decipher. "I love you and I'm sorry I messed up like that."

My eyes wander to the twilight sky. I appreciate the apology, but a big part of me was hoping we could just pretend it never happened. Ya know, sweep things under the proverbial carpet. But fine, here we go...

"I guess I can understand why it would be hard for you to tell me about you and …" I can't bring myself to say her name. "It just hasn't been easy for me to accept the fact that you're leaving for college soon. And then I find out about this." I wave my arm in his general direction. "It's like I'm losing you in more ways than one." Tears prick at my eyes as I pull the blanket tighter.

Kalendar rests a hand on my knee. "Hey, you're stuck with me, alright? I'm always here, Ender—even if it's over the phone."

"Thanks, Kal." I smile, tilting my head. "So, what's the deal with you two? Are you actually into her, or is this just a fling?"

Kalendar rubs his chin and sighs.

"It isn't going to work," he finally says. "You're too important to me, and you're right; I'll be leaving for Montana soon, anyway." He looks away. "I broke the news to her this afternoon."

I can sense the pain behind his words, but selfishly, I'm happy to hear this.

"I know you're mad and you've got every right to be, but can you find it in your heart to forgive Emma? She's been wrecked since you confronted her. I'd feel a whole lot better knowing you have Emma when I'm away."

"I can't." My voice comes out sharper than I expect, but I don't care. Forgiving Kalendar is one thing but Emma? She should've known better. Sisterhood and all that.

His shoulders sag, and his gaze falls to the ground.

"Let's focus on repairing you and me for now, okay? I need more time with Emma," I say, gently this time.

Kalendar looks up again and smiles, "Okay, then."

Rising to his feet, he stretches out his arms, and I find myself wrapping mine around him.

"Okay if I join you two?" Jake calls from the kitchen window.

I giggle. "Wonder how long they've been watching us."

"Oh, definitely the entire time." Kalendar laughs.

"Of course, you fool. C'mon out, Jakey!" he shouts in reply.

Jake joins us with two beers and holds one out to Kalendar.

"Glad you two made up. Trying to figure out whose side I should take has been exhausting," he says.

"Obviously, Lavender's —"

"Obviously, mine —"

Laughing, we sit around the fire.

"So Jake, tell us about the concert," I say. I haven't seen Jake since he returned from Red Rocks.

"Dave crushed it, obviously," he says. "Red Rocks is hands down the best place to see him live. Oh, and—" he lifts his brows, "I met the booking manager of Red Rocks, Jim Baker. He's my friend's dad. We got to talking, and when I mentioned I'm studying music production at UCLA, he started asking me all these questions about what I want to do when I graduate. He might even offer me a job!" Jake's expression shifts to something more serious. "At least, that's what my friend told me afterwards. How cool would that be?"

"Jake!" I squeal, tapping his foot with mine. "That's like your dream job."

"Congratulations, Jakey, that's huge news!" Kalendar pats Jake on the back.

"I'm so proud of you! Does this mean you'll stay in Colorado?" I ask.

Jake chuckles. "Well, hold on, I don't have a job yet. But if it works out then, yes. I'll be back in Colorado just as you leave."

I cross my arms. "Who knows where I'll end up going to college."

"Yeah, right. You're off to the East Coast, Ender. That's always been your dream," Kalendar says.

"You've been talking about going to college in New England since you were little," Jake adds.

"Well, things could change …" The band pops into my head.

"Whatever you decide, we support you." Jake squeezes my arm.

"We'll always support you, Ender. Just promise you won't run off to Australia or something. That's, like, twelve time zones too far."

"Not Australia but maybe New Zealand, though," I tease.

"Very funny." Kalendar rolls his eyes.

Jake shakes his head, "Anyway, this guy was the coolest. Dude knows so many bands personally—makes me jealous."

My heart flutters. I wonder if… "Did he mention the band from the first night? The one that opened for Dave?" I try to sound casual, but it's so forced I internally cringe.

"I actually asked him," Jake says. "Apparently, they were a last-minute addition, and he didn't know much about them."

Jake and Kalendar shift to a new topic, but my mind drifts back to the band—and Concert Barbie. I've been so caught up in the idea of her replacing me that I never stopped to consider the possibility that I'm wrong.

But why would she show up in *two* photos with them?

Still, Camp and Anna were so insistent that I was the missing piece. Maybe I shouldn't be so quick to assume. There's only one way to find out.

THIRTEEN

AFTER HOURS OF online stalking and Instagram doom-scrolling, I've finally uncovered Concert Barbie's identity. Her name is Brooke, and she's the lead singer of The Gnarlettes—an all-girl punk rock band, according to their website. Unfortunately, she's insanely talented and even better looking than those stupid Instagram photos. So, yeah. There's a very real chance the band has replaced me before I even got a shot.

I pull up The Gnarlettess' Instagram page for the fifth time when Mom walks into my room.

"You ready, hun? Thanks for helping today," she says, brushing back my hair.

"Of course." I grin up at her. "I mean, it's not every day a *celebrity* leads meditation at your studio."

She clicks her tongue. "Laugh all you want, but she *is* a big deal."

"I know, I'm kidding. I'll grab the extra candles and cushions and meet you at the car."

"Sounds good, thanks, hun. I'll get us coffee," she says, giving my shoulder a quick squeeze before heading out.

Half an hour later, we arrive at the yoga center. Mom's best friend, Suzy, waits for us on the bench in front.

"Josephine Dunton!" she exclaims as we slide out of the car. "How on earth did you pull this one off?"

Mom smiles at Suzy and nods in my direction. "It's all thanks to Lavender. Josephine took a real liking to her."

I roll my eyes. "No. She's just a kind lady, that's all."

"Sweetheart, take the compliment. It's an honor for Josephine to take an interest in you. Maybe she wants to take you under her wing. You both know what it's like to go through life with a unique eye color. You *really* should talk to her about it."

"Maybe." I shrug. "So, what do we need to do?"

"Suzy and I will start getting the room ready. Do you mind taking the sidewalk chalkboard down the street to Lacey? She said she'd create a welcome sign for Josephine."

"Sure." I walk inside the studio and grab the A-frame chalkboard leaning against the reception desk. A laugh escapes my lips as I peer at Mom's delicate cursive. *If you fall, don't worry, I got you. XOXO Your Mat*

The nostalgic scent of paint and clay fills the air of Lacey's art studio. I grew up taking her art classes; they're a cornerstone for children growing up in Rosewood.

"Hey Lacey, it's Lavender," I call out.

Lacey appears from behind a curtain. She's wearing a smock full of paint splatters. Her gray hair sits in a bun, and tendrils frame her face. She puts on a warm smile when she sees me. "Lavender, sweetheart. How are you?"

"Great, thanks." I hug her with my free arm. "Mom wanted me to bring this by." I hand her the chalkboard.

Lacey takes it from me and laughs at the faded sentence written on the board. Turning it to me, she says, "This is too good. I'm not sure I want to write over it."

I laugh. "I know. Mom can be funny sometimes."

"She sure can. So, Josephine Dunton is in town, huh? Your mom said you were behind it. That's impressive. She's world renowned, ya know? I can't believe she's coming here."

I wave off the compliment. "I can't take the credit. Josephine knows how big a fan Mom is. It's great she's coming to town. Mom is so happy."

"That's wonderful, dear." She smiles. "Give me twenty minutes, and I'll have this ready. You're welcome to stay here and wait."

"Thanks. It's so nice out; I think I'm gonna go for a walk."

"Sounds good, hun."

Stepping out of the art studio, I wander toward the park. The brutal heat has returned, and after a few steps, I tug off my long-sleeve shirt, leaving only a tank top.

Sitting on my favorite bench near the swings, I shift my thoughts back to the band. They're coming home tomorrow, and I have no idea what to do. I can't just disappear without an explanation. Still, I'd rather eat a toad than confront them about concert Barbie.

A shadow falls across the bench.

"Hi, Lavender," a calm voice says from behind me.

I look up and into Josephine's purple eyes. She's effortlessly cool (again)—wearing a knee-length silk kimono over black jeans. Her hair is down today; perfect box braids hang around her shoulders.

"Hi, Josephine," I say with as much confidence as I can muster. "It's great to see you. When did you get here?"

"Oh, about an hour ago. I've been admiring your lovely town. The mountains are gorgeous, and everyone is so friendly."

"They are friendly, yes, and many people have been expecting your arrival, so I'm sure they're on their best behavior." I laugh. "Mom did a great job spreading the word."

"I knew she would." Josephine smiles. "May I?" She gestures at the empty spot next to me.

"Y-y-yes, of course." I scoot over to give her room.

She slides gracefully into the seat beside me, a scent of lemongrass trailing behind her. A grin sweeps her lips as she watches kids playing on the swings. She says nothing, just sits there, cool, calm, and collected.

"Are you looking forward to the class this evening?" I ask, unable to sit in silence.

"I am. Very much so." She adjusts the sleeve of her kimono. "How about you?"

"Oh yes, *really* excited. I never understood the point of meditation until recently. My mom was always pushing it on me. Sitting still and clearing my mind seemed impossible. This past week, though, I've loved it. Your class in Aspen really opened my mind."

"I'm glad you enjoyed it. It took me a long time to begin daily practice. How old are you, sixteen?"

"Seventeen. I'll be eighteen on September 28."

"Ah, nearly eighteen. You have so much life to live. You should be proud that you're discovering meditation so young. I have no regrets; everything happened to me for a reason, ultimately bringing me here." She pauses and looks at the mountains in the distance. "But if I had learned mediation earlier, I may have fared better during hard times."

I nod, my chest puffing up a little with pride.

"How is life for you, Lavender? Are you happy?"

I blink, caught off guard by the question. No one has ever asked me that before—at least, not outside of my parents. I'm finding it difficult to respond as I swallow the lump building in my throat.

She studies me and a look of concern washes over her face. "Sorry, I didn't mean to—"

"No, it's okay," I interrupt. "I'm not sure what's come over me." I sit up straight and wipe my eyes.

"Breathe in for four seconds, and breathe out for six seconds. Close your eyes. Keep repeating that breathwork," Josephine says calmly.

Following her advice, my anxiety diminishes.

"Thank you," I murmur. "Sorry."

"Never apologize for your feelings. It's healthy to express them."

I turn my gaze to the mountains, looking for a distraction—the shades of green stand in striking contrast to the clear blue sky. This juxtaposition has always been beautiful, but today, it hits differently. A fresh set of tears fill my eyes at its beauty. *What's wrong with me?*

"I'm going through a bit of a hard time right now," I admit, my voice cracking.

Josephine's lips press into a knowing smile. "Sometimes we push aside feelings because we don't think we have the right to feel a certain way. But we're all human, and while some have it worse than others, that doesn't mean that any sadness you feel isn't valid."

I let her words sink in. "Yes, but there are so many horrible things happening in the world—wars, poverty, natural disasters. Who am I to complain when I live here?" I raise a hand, the gesture as limp as my thoughts. "I don't know. It's just hard to be human."

Josephine laughs. "It can be." She squeezes my hand. "You have a big heart, Lavender. I recognized it from the moment we met. You have a gift. Other than the color of your eyes, of course." She laughs.

My heart quickens. Lately, everyone seems to be talking about this supposed "gift" of mine. But what does that even mean?

"A gift?" I echo, uncertain.

"Yes. You care deeply for others, though I sense you have a hard time letting people in to reciprocate." She tilts her head.

My body heats and I start fanning myself like the sun is the cause of my instant sweating, muttering something about the sun being *weirdly aggressive today*. Lord, I hate when people call me out.

"I can see you care deeply because I'm the same way. Why do you think I travel the world? It's exhausting, and I'm not a spring chicken anymore." She laughs. "But my life's purpose is to serve others. I can do that through my gift of meditation."

"What do you think my gift is?"

She smiles, then looks at the sky. "I'm sure it'll reveal itself in time."

Ugh. Why is everyone I've been speaking to lately so frustratingly vague?

My thoughts drift back to Camp. He thinks my so-called gift is singing—even though he's never actually heard me sing. And Nate? He's convinced I'm the next Meghan Trainor thanks to my *apparent* songwriting skills. Pretty sure this elusive Maggie is the one feeding them these wild ideas. But none of it matters now, not with Concert Barbie in the picture. Did Maggie's mysterious visions include *her*, too?

"I need to prepare for this evening. Why don't we meet for tea tomorrow morning? We can talk more then." Josephine smiles warmly.

"I'd like that, thanks. I'll see you tonight."

She nods and stands.

A quick glance at my watch shows that over twenty minutes have passed since dropping off the chalkboard with Lacey. Standing, I tie my shirt around my waist and make my way back to the art studio along the sidewalk.

A red truck zooms past and I recognize it as Charlie's. His music blares, deafening as ever, windows vibrating with the beat.

I freeze in place as Camp's voice fills the Rosewood streets. It's the same song they performed on the town green: *Grandmom says there are those who seek out the good …*

Charlie waves from the driver's side window. "Hey, Lavender!"

The song fades as he recedes along the street and I can't help but wonder if it's the universe talking to me, a sign of my gift—the band. Or if I'm just looking for meaning in something that was never mine to begin with.

FOURTEEN

IT'S SUNDAY. *Bleh.*

That's negative thinking. *Maybe* everything will be fine? *Maybe* I'll find out Concert Barbie is Camp's sister? *Sure.* At least I've finally decided to meet them. I deserve an explanation, even if it hurts.

As I descend into town to see Josephine, the wind swirls my hair. The air is dry, and the sky is robin's-egg blue. Cartoonish puffy clouds dot the horizon.

Last night was flawless. Josephine stole the spotlight, but Mom wasn't far behind. They were the center of attention after class, and I smoothly faded into the background. I'd had plenty of time with Josephine, and I didn't want to be greedy.

I'm sad to see her go, but excited about our morning tea.

Tea, eh.

The hot debate of the morning has been whether I should order tea or coffee. In my opinion, tea is gross. Hot, lightly flavored water? No, thanks. *But* I'd hate for Josephine to think less of me. After all, aren't spiritual people supposed to drink tea? And according to her, I'm *way* ahead of time with the one week of meditation under my belt. Mom rolled her eyes and told me to stop overthinking it and just order what I want.

Josephine sits outside *So You Need Some Joe?* at a green café table; two steaming mugs are in front of her. In a slight panic, I look at my dashboard clock. *Phew, three minutes early.*

Hopping out of Betty, I weave through the tables on the red brick patio, tossing a friendly wave to some locals as I approach.

"Good morning, Lavender," Josephine says as she stands up to hug me.

"Morning," I return her hug.

My gaze slides over her shoulder to a few of my neighbors whispering and nodding their heads approvingly in my direction.

She gestures toward the coffee mug on the table. "I asked inside if they knew your favorite drink, and they gave me a latte. Our drinks were on the house; they insisted. They love you here."

"They're great people." I run a hand through my hair.

Sitting, I reach for my latte. Josephine's organic tea bag label dangles along the side of her mug, and I'm immediately ashamed.

"You know, I love a good latte. I almost got one myself," she says, as if sensing my insecurity. I choose to believe her.

With a sip from the mug, I close my eyes and allow the delicious blend of vanilla, espresso, and milk to linger a moment before swallowing.

I set my latte down and glance at Josephine. "Last night's class was absolutely amazing. I can't thank you enough for making the trip to Rosewood. It meant everything to us, especially Mom." I lift my mug again for a larger sip.

"You're very welcome. Like I said, it was my pleasure. I love this town. I'm considering staying around for a bit."

A coffee volcano erupts from my mouth, spewing in every direction. "I'm so sorry," I say, reaching for napkins to clean up my mess while fighting the urge to bolt. "Did any get on you?" My face is on fire.

Josephine laughs. "Not at all. Here, let me help you." She gathers more napkins from the dispenser on the table to our left.

"Thank you. Gosh, anyway … Why stay in Rosewood? For how long?" Coffee-soaked napkins sit in a pile in front of me. I quickly grab them and thrust them under the table as if that will make the evidence of my fumble disappear. They're soggy and sticky and 1,000 percent leaking onto my bright white shorts.

"I get the sense I'm needed here. Let's just say my intuition is nagging." She winks.

"Wow, Mom's going to be so excited." A trickle of coffee runs the length of my leg. "Of course, I'm thrilled you're staying too." I wipe at it with my free hand.

"Thank you," she says. "Should you throw away those napkins?" She peeks under the table at my mortifying mess.

"Uh, yeah, one sec." I dispose of them in the nearby trash can, along with whatever shreds of dignity I have left.

"So, can you tell me about the rest of your family?" Josephine asks when I return, hands covering my stained shorts.

"Well, there's my dad. He's pretty great and totally into music, which is where I get it from. My love of music, that is. I don't know why you need to know th—Anyway, him and my mom are a true love story. I have two brothers, and they are both older than me. This year, Jake will be a college senior, Kalendar a freshman."

"Two brothers, that's wonderful. You're lucky. I had a brother; it's a special relationship between a sister and a brother. Are you close with them?"

"Oh yes, very. Jake is my protector, and Kalendar and I are only thirteen months apart, so he's always been my best friend." I smile. I *am* lucky; having someone remind me of that is nice.

"How are you feeling about Kalendar leaving? That must be hard on you." Josephine asks, her eyes soft.

"It's hard," I squeak out, but it's more than that. Kalendar leaving feels like losing a part of me. Like a limb or something. A tear slips down my cheek. Gosh. Why am I so emotional around her? This "tea" experience has been nothing short of humiliating.

"Do you want to talk about it?"

I dig my nails into my thigh as if the pain can ground me, refusing to allow any more tears. "Yes, one day... not now."

I turn my attention to the road, watching the cars as they pass. Many have bikes strapped to their trunks or fishing poles on the roof. The license plates are from all over: California, Texas, New Mexico, Utah … I silently pray that a certain Tennessee plate won't appear—my coffee stained shorts are undoubtedly visible from space, let alone the street.

Josephine's eyes are closed as she sits next to me, face tilted toward the sun, with that serene smile resting on her lips. It's so permanent, I'm starting to wonder if it's actually a tattoo.

Now feels like the right time to ask what's been circling my mind.

"Josephine, we were talking about gifts yesterday. You seem to think I have one."

She opens her eyes and turns to me. "Yes, I do," she replies, her voice unwavering.

"Well, how am I supposed to figure out what my gift is? I know you said it'll reveal itself in time, but I'm not exactly the patient type. And it can't be these ridiculous eyes." I gesture vaguely, then wince. "Er, sorry. I'm just used to being the only one with this color—I can get a little self deprecating."

Josephine furrows her brows, her expression thoughtful. "Why is that? Sounds like a defense mechanism to me."

I shrug, avoiding her gaze. "Guess it is." I take a slow sip from my mug. "It's just, I was made fun of as a kid—especially by this one group of girls. They were ruthless. For a while, the entire school thought I was a witch." My eyes go wide. "Like, they truly believed it. It got so bad the principal and my teachers had to get involved. It was so embarrassing."

"Ah." Josephine nods slightly and crosses her arms on the table. "Ya know, kids made fun of me, too."

My eyes snap to hers. "Really?"

"Mm-hmm. I think it's par for the course when you have something that is unique." Josephine smirks. "Or that people are jealous of."

A snort escapes my nose before I can stop it. "I don't know about jealous." I shake my head. "But what'd you do?"

"You learn to see it for what it is—some people are just unhappy. It's easier for them to tear you down than face their own struggles." Her lips press into a thin line before she laughs. "Trust me, I know it's easier said than done."

Mom gave me similar advice before, but coming from Josephine, it feels more believable. She's been in my shoes and has felt the pain. I breathe in deeply and my shoulders lighten.

"So…about this gift…"

Josephine laughs, her voice like a melody. "Okay, okay, we can put the eye conversation to rest for now."

"As for your gift." She continues, her tone serious. "I can't tell you exactly how or when it will come to you, but I can tell you it will come in signs. When you regularly see and hear something, it's the universe communicating with you." She straightens in her seat. "For example, I kept seeing signs of meditation everywhere I went when I opened my mind to discovering my life's purpose. I never once thought of meditation in my early years; suddenly, it was everywhere:

on billboards, bumper stickers, the radio. I couldn't ignore it anymore. Finally, I signed up for an immersive meditation leadership class. It's been my whole life since."

"Wow," I whisper. I'm again thinking of the band. Charlie listened to one of their songs as he passed by in his truck. Jake happened to stumble upon them on the Red Rocks livestream. I had joked about it yesterday, but could these be the signs Josephine speaks of? I consider telling her about it all, but it's a moot point—they're probably christening Concert Barbie into the band as we speak.

"Having heard all of that, does anything sound familiar to you? Do you think you've been receiving any signs?" she asks, her eyes searching mine.

I avert my eyes to the road. "No."

I walk into the house after returning from my tea—*ahem*, coffee—disaster. Mom's preparing lunch in the kitchen.

"Lavender! How was your conversation with Josephine, sweetheart? Did you succumb to drinking tea?"

"It was good-ish, and no, I ended up with coffee that I basically spit all over her."

"Oh, my." Mom frowns. "Want to tell me what happened?"

"Please, no." I look at her, a grin spreading across my face.

"What is it?" She chuckles.

"Josephine filled me in on some exciting news." I take her hand in mine.

"Okay …" Mom says, her eyebrows raised.

"Well … she has decided to stay longer in Rosewood! She said she'd call you to discuss scheduling another meditation class."

"What in the world? Did she say why?"

"She mentioned something about her intuition telling her she should stay."

"This is incredible news! I'll have to call the ladies." Mom wriggles her hips from side to side.

"Oh boy. We need to work on those dance moves." I laugh, turning to leave.

"Wait, are you hungry? I'm fixing lunch for your brothers."

"No, thanks. I'll grab something soon." I glance at the oven clock. It's nearly noon; my heart thuds in my chest. There is no way I can eat; the butterflies in my stomach have taken up all the space.

I climb the stairs to my bedroom and fling my bag on the bed just as my phone pings.

Emma: I miss you. Can we talk?

"Nope," I say to the walls, tossing my phone on the dresser.

Swapping out my café clothes for hiking gear, I make sure not to raise any suspicions before heading out. I tuck the crystal heart into my small backpack, ready to return it. I wonder if it'll have the same effect on Concert Barbie. *Ugh.*

I search the house to let someone know I'm leaving. Jake's bent over his computer in the living room.

"Hey, Jake, I'm heading out for a hike. I'll be back in a couple of hours."

He looks up from his laptop. "Sounds good. Do you want company?"

"Oh no, that's okay. It looks like you're in the middle of something, and I was planning on getting caught up with some of my favorite podcasts." I motion toward the earbuds nestled in my ears.

"You sure?"

"Yeah, totally. Why don't we spend time together tomorrow after my shift at the coffee shop? Will you be around?"

"I will; that sounds awesome. Please take Bruce with you."

"Yes, *Dad*." I roll my eyes.

"We all have to look out for you." He winks. "Make sure you're back for dinner and have your phone on you."

"Mm-hmm."

"And taking bear spray is a good idea," his muffled voice lectures.

"All right, all right," I shout as I walk toward the mudroom.

"Bruce!" Bruce's paws click along the wood floor before he comes into sight. He jumps up on me, his tail wagging. "Okay, down, boy." I laugh.

After rummaging through the cabinet for bear spray, I finish packing and head out the door.

As I near the end of our driveway, the gentle strumming of Camp's guitar drifts from the campsite. The *Friends* theme song. "Seriously? Don't even try to charm me now," I mutter as I pick up my pace toward the forest.

FIFTEEN

THE MOMENT WE step into the forest, the melody switches from the upbeat *Friends* tune to the dramatic *Game of Thrones* theme song.

"Very funny!" I yell into the woods, half-hoping Camp can hear me. The air is chilly beneath the towering aspens, so I stop to pull on the Rosewood High sweatshirt from my backpack. Bruce darts ahead on the trail. As I smooth my hair to tame the static cling, he halts mid-run. His ears prick up, and his tail stiffens, a series of barks escaping him as he locks onto something in front of us.

"Bruce, it's okay bud," I call out, trying to calm him while my nerves kick into high gear. He has a near perfect track record for sniffing out trouble—wild animals, strangers, vacuum cleaners—he's on it.

"What's going on, boy?" Softening my tone, I walk up to him and rub his ear.

A soft thudding in the distance surrounds us, and his barks intensify as the sound approaches.

I scramble to retrieve the bear spray from my bag, my only other line of defense. The slick metal bottle slides from my fingers and tumbles to the ground. *Shiitake.*

"Bruce, let's go home!" My voice carries through the trees as I move toward our house. He follows the noise instead.

"Bruce!"

His hind legs are the last thing I see as he disappears into the bramble.

Then—silence.

It's so thick it presses against my eardrums. My breathing becomes ragged as I snatch the bear spray from the ground and inch up the trail, using my backpack as a shield in front of me.

"Bruce?" I call his name quieter now.

A solitary bark reverberates through the woods. I lift my sunglasses, squinting as I peer off the trail through the dense thicket of evergreens.

The rustling of leaves fills the eerie silence, and Bruce bounds over a fallen aspen, tail wagging.

"Thank God." I drop to my knees and wrap my arms around him, nuzzling my face in his wiry fur. He lets out a soft bark, still fixated on the bramble he just emerged from.

Fear blooms in my chest. I swallow hard, and lift my eyes.

Dozens of deer stand in his wake, their wide, unblinking eyes fixed on us. The largest among them—a stag with towering antlers—edges forward. The others follow, their steps careful, nearly soundless against the forest floor.

A whisper brushes against my ear. "Don't be afraid."

What the—? Bruce licks my face before turning back to the deer, his tail wagging.

"Hello?" I scan the forest. "Anyone there?"

There's no answer as the deer gracefully circle us, their eyes gentle.

Holding Bruce by the collar, I rise, turning in place to meet each watchful stare.

Tentatively, I extend my hand toward a doe, her breath warm against my fingertips. But before I can touch her, a surge of melody cuts through the stillness. Camp's guitar returns, the tune of "Do You Want to Build a Snowman." I can't help but laugh at the absurdness of it all. Bruce must feel the same way because he lets out a happy woof and starts doing laps around me like we've entered some kind of enchanted musical.

The deer part ways, creating a path along the trail, inviting us to continue.

Without hesitation, I sprint past them, with Bruce running alongside me. I glance over my shoulder to see the deer matching our pace perfectly, prancing in a straight line. Magpies flit in the trees above us and I'm seriously wondering if they'll start braiding my hair.

Bruce runs ahead as we approach the campsite. The deer stop, letting us move on without them.

Camp's laughter filters through the trees. Then a beat later: "Hey, boy."

Butterflies and nerves swirl through my stomach as I step into the clearing. Bruce wriggles on his back, his tongue lolling to the side as Camp rubs his belly. *Traitor.*

"Hi, friend," Anna says, bounding over as usual. I ignore her, my eyes locked on Camp.

He rises and saunters over, the brim of his cowboy hat casting shadows across his eyes. His dimples deepen as he greets me with a simple "Lavender."

But the warmth in his gaze falters the longer he looks at me. I cross my arms and lower my eyes to a patch of dandelions pushing through the dirt.

How can he pretend everything is fine?

Camp's scuffed brown boots enter my line of sight. He lifts my chin. "Everything all right?" His hazel eyes search mine.

I pull back, letting his hand fall from my face.

Scanning the area for Nate, I find no sign of him. "Where's Nate?" I mumble.

"He's with his family in Utah for a few days," Anna replies, frowning. "What's wrong? Did something happen?" Her brows pinch together as she takes a step closer.

"Isn't there something you need to tell me?" I say, the words slipping out more sharply than intended. There's no concert Barbie in sight, but that doesn't mean she isn't stashed away somewhere.

Camp and Anna share a glance.

"Uh, it's good to see you?" Camp says, his smile uncertain, questioning.

Unbelievable. I let out a huff, scanning the campground for Bruce, thoroughly convinced they're pulling a fast one on me. "Forget it. I'm leaving. I shouldn't have come."

"Hey, now. Don't go. What's going on, Lavender?" Camp walks toward me and rests his hand on my shoulder.

Sighing, I squeeze my eyes shut before opening them.

"I saw photos of you with a girl at the concert." I cross my arms tighter. "I don't get why you even bothered looking for me for *a year* if you were just gonna replace me."

"Huh?" Camp's mouth falls open, his eyes wide with confusion.

Anna bursts out laughing. She's bent at the waist, hand over her mouth, shoulders shaking with every giggle.

"Why's she laughing?" I ask Camp, uncrossing my arms.

"I don't—oh." Camp's frown shifts into a grin; his eyes brighten. "I think there's been a misunderstanding." He shakes his head, his smile widening. "Was her hair blonde? And was she singing with me on stage?"

"Yeah …"

Anna's standing now, laughter still bubbling from her petite frame.

I let out an annoyed sigh. "She's obviously very talented and, well, gorgeous, so I know why you'd choose her, but—"

"Ah, Lavender," Camp interrupts and scratches his eyebrow. "Anna, can you please explain who that lady was?" He puts one hand in the back pocket of his jeans as he pivots on his heel to face her.

Anna pulls herself together, then skips to me and places her hands on my shoulders. Her amber eyes lock on mine. "That blonde you saw on stage is my ex-girlfriend. Remember that band I told you I was in? She was our lead singer, Brooke. She was at the festival with her new band, The Gnarlettes, and joined us for a couple of songs." Anna squeezes my arms.

Wait. What? Girlfriend? My face relaxes and a blush creeps up my cheeks. Feeling Camp's gaze on me, I look in his direction. Smug doesn't even begin to describe his expression. He's the cowboy Elon Musk.

My mood shifts instantly, and I glance at Anna with a smirk. "Well, damn, Anna. She's hot! Why'd you let her go?"

Anna's giggles begin again. "Lord, don't I know it. She's high maintenance, though. Couldn't deal."

I laugh, shaking my head. "Ah, I'm sorry, guys. I saw those photos on Instagram and thought for sure you'd found someone else." I run a hand down my face, feeling the last of my embarrassment fade.

Anna cups my cheeks dramatically. "We could never replace you, silly! Damn, we JUST found you!"

"I even summoned my deer friends to greet you; I wouldn't do that for just anyone." Camp laughs, draping his arm around my shoulders. My heart races as his familiar scent surrounds me.

"Oh yeah, about that … you nearly gave me a heart attack," I tease, attempting to keep my composure as I notice his hand hovering near my breast.

He withdraws his arm. "Shoot, I was worried I'd scare you. 'Course I didn't think of it until after the fact," he admits, his eyes filling with worry.

"They were actually pretty sweet." I laugh. "But, and believe me, I know how crazy this sounds—I swear I heard a voice. It told me not to be afraid, but I have no idea where it came from."

"The trees, obviously." Anna smirks.

I blink at her. "The trees?"

"Yup, they're always looking out for us. Another perk of joining the band," she says with a wink. "Anyway, gotta pee." Anna dances off into the woods.

I side-eye Camp. "So … the trees talk to us?"

"Sometimes." He grins. "You'll get used to it … eventually."

"Right." I take a deep breath, scanning the campsite. In the daylight, everything looks different. The teepees seem tiny compared to the towering aspens surrounding the meadow. The lanterns that hang from the branches of the younger aspens and evergreens are brass and they appear to be antique. The dark blue oriental rug beneath the band's equipment is plush with gold accents, and Anna's red drum set sparkles as if dusted with glitter. I walk over to it.

"I was so mad at you guys. And now I feel stupid," I admit, unlacing my hiking boots and stepping onto the luxurious carpet. My fingers trail over the drums, their surface cool and smooth beneath my touch.

"Don't feel stupid. I can understand why you thought that," Camp says, stepping closer. He takes my hands, his fingers weaving through mine, and meets my gaze. "We'd never do that to you. Promise."

A warm tingle spreads through me as Camp's words linger in the air. I glance at our entwined hands, suddenly feeling nervous. I pull them away and tuck a strand of hair behind my ear. Needing a distraction, I move toward the microphones and lower myself onto a stool. I pull a microphone to my lips and tap it twice. "Is this thing on?"

Anna reappears and flips a switch on an amp. "Now it is." She winks.

I lean into the microphone again. "So, how was the festival?" My voice echoes through the woods, and I wince at the sound. There's really no reason for my voice to be amplified like this.

"Fun. The crowd was great. Amazing musicians." Camp picks up his guitar.

"Yeah, it was cool. We missed you, though." A mischievous glint sparkles in Anna's eyes. "Which brings me to ask you something." She grins. "Will you please sing for us, Lavender?"

Crap. I knew this was coming, but with Nate absent, I foolishly thought I'd be off the hook. I shouldn't have sat in front of the microphone.

Camp's eyes meet mine, a flicker of amusement dancing in them.

"Sing a duet with me?" he asks, rescuing me from the prospect of going solo.

I swallow hard. "Um, I'm not sure."

"Please?" His brows come together.

My stomach flutters. "I guess—okay." I try to smile. "But if I'm terrible, don't laugh."

"Promise." Camp chuckles as he steps up next to me. Slipping the guitar strap over his shoulder, he strums a song I recognize instantly. My breath catches. Is it a coincidence that he's playing one of my favorite songs, or does he somehow know? At this point, it wouldn't surprise me if he did.

A gust of wind sweeps through the meadow, shimmering the aspen leaves. The warm breeze against my skin fills me with energy. Gripping the microphone tightly, I glance at Camp, hoping he'll kick us off on the vocals.

He leans into the microphone, dimples deepening as he looks at me. His throaty twang fills the air as he sings of fast cars.

Lost in his performance, I almost miss my turn. His voice is hypnotizing, giving the classic song a touch of country and a little rock and roll. Tracy Chapman would be proud.

Camp turns to me and nods slightly. I inhale as my fingers wrap tighter around the microphone and my eyes drift shut.

I leave my body as my voice rises from the speakers, and it sounds like I'm listening to someone else entirely. How could this angelic voice be coming from me?

Our eyes meet when it's time for the chorus. The words flow effortlessly from my lips. *"So I remember when…"* Our voices harmonize perfectly, the synchronized notes lighting my soul on fire.

As the last chord fades, Anna bounces up and down, clapping, and Camp releases a loud "Whoop!" Setting his guitar aside, he wraps me in a hug, squeezing me tight.

"I knew you'd be amazing," he shouts. He opens an arm so Anna can join in.

"Incredible!" she exclaims. "You're incredible, Lavender!"

I tilt my head up, spotting a hawk soaring overhead. What is this feeling? This glowy, heart-pounding, confident feeling? It's almost … spiritual. *Maybe I have a gift, after all.*

SIXTEEN

I'M STILL FLOATING from our duet.

I sit cross-legged on the oriental rug, feeling its softness beneath me. Anna sprawls out, her head resting in my lap. Camp is next to us, legs stretched out and arms propped behind him. Bruce is curled up beside him.

"Ladies, we need to make new music. Maggie signed us up for a concert at Red Rocks on October 5," Camp announces, like it's no big deal.

"October 5!" I exclaim. "Camp, that's only two months away."

"I know it's a tight deadline, but we can do it. We already have a bunch of songs. But what we *really* need is our single."

"And a band name," Anna says as she sits up quickly. "I mean it, guys; it's time." She turns to me. "Lavender, can you come up with a few ideas? According to Camp's meditation brain, you're supposed to name us." She closes one eye and points at me.

I laugh. "I'll give it some thought. How do we write a song, though? I wouldn't even know where to begin."

"We need lyrics that will make people feel again," Camp says, getting to his feet and absently strumming a warm chord. "Lavender, this is where you will shine. When Nate gets back, you'll lead us in songwriting."

I gulp. *And how, exactly, am I supposed to do that?*

Thankfully, Camp doesn't seem to notice my self-doubt episode. His gaze is distant, lost in thought. I can almost see the wheels turning.

"Everyone forgets how much good is still out in the world. How much beauty." His eyes meet mine and linger; a flush creeps up my cheeks.

"We're all so distracted—our attention pulled in a thousand directions, always staring at screens. It's like we're slaves to our phones, unable to feel anything real. But this song… it can be the reset everyone needs. A reminder that there's still good out there. Something simple, but something that breaks through the numbness."

Then, with a playful grin, he eases into the opening riff of "Come Together."

"Let's give them something worth coming together for."

"Yes!" I laugh-shout.

"Heck yeah, Camp!" Anna yells.

Camp grins then drops his guitar on the rug before sitting.

"Let's keep this enthusiasm going." Anna turns to me. "Can you meet with us every day?"

"Uh …" I'm unsure how to answer. I certainly can't keep disappearing into the woods for hours. Now that things are good with the band again, maybe it's time to fill Mom in. Actually, Josephine. Yes, I'll chat with her first. She'll know what to do. "Tomorrow is tricky because I have to work; how about Tuesday?" At least I can buy myself a day to connect with her.

"Works for us," Camp says.

"Can you hang for a bit longer? Or do you need to go home?" Anna asks.

I look at my watch. "About twenty minutes."

Her eyes light up. "Great! Let's play a game!"

I raise a brow, lips twisting. "Should I be worried?"

"Absolutely." She winks. "Truth or dare."

I moan.

"C'mon, it'll be fun. Lavender, you go first." Anna sits up straighter, eyes sparkling.

"Fine," I say with a laugh. "Anna, truth or dare?"

"Dare."

"I dare you to sing me your favorite song."

Camp laughs out loud.

I glare at him. "What's so funny?"

"Anna is one of the best drummers I've ever known, but with singing, well, she can't carry a tune." He chuckles.

I narrow my eyes on him. "Camp! That's a horrible thing to say."

"No, no, it's okay, Lavender—Camp's right. I'm honestly terrible, but I'll prove it to you. I never deny a dare."

Anna strides up to the microphone and begins singing "Shake It Off" by Taylor Swift. Her voice is flat and entirely out of tune, and she's *really* trying. Oh man, she's awful. After a few lyrics, she takes a bow.

Camp and I jump to our feet, clapping and laughing.

"See? Terrible." She laughs.

"Well, it wasn't so bad." I say.

Anna pulls me into a hug. "You're sweet, but don't even bother. I can't sing, and I've made my peace with it—because, let's be real, none of you could drum like I do." She runs over to her drum set and performs an extended solo.

Camp leans close to me, eyes smiling. "Best damn drummer there is."

Anna walks back, and Camp gives her a high five.

"Anna. That was incredible." I actually mean it this time.

"Yes, I'm quite good." She winks. "Okay, my turn. Camp, truth or dare?" Anna says.

Camp's eyes sparkle. "Dare."

Anna puts her hand to her chin and looks up at the trees. "Okay, Camp, I dare you to do your most ridiculous dance for us."

With a groan, Camp stands. "Fine, but no laughing," he warns as he winks at me. Then he moves, wriggling his hips and taking short, jerky steps. His arms sway from side to side while maintaining the most serious expression.

I'm struggling to catch my breath while tears of laughter stream down my cheeks. Camp shimmies over to me, holding out his hand. I gulp a million giggles and join him, mimicking his every move.

"Okay, okay, please stop," Anna cries, covering her eyes with her hand.

Camp laughs and crashes back onto the ground.

"Yikes. Okay, Camp, your turn," Anna says.

"Well, okay then. Lavender, truth or dare?"

I sit next to him and wipe the tears from my eyes, still recovering. "Truth." I laugh.

Camp grins, removes his hat, and scratches his head. After replacing it, he locks eyes with me, and my body warms at his intense stare.

"Well...I was wonderin'..." He looks at the ground, then back at me, his perfect Southern drawl fills the air around us. "I mean... that is... do you like pizza?"

"Really?" Anna lets out a groan and hurls her sandal at him. "Pizza, Camp? That's all you got?"

Camp catches her sandal mid-air and tosses it back to her. "What? I'm honestly curious." He says, feigning innocence. "We're a pizza-loving group, and I need to make sure she'll fit in."

I let out a small laugh, unsure what I'd been expecting.

"Of course. Pepperoni's my favorite." I shoot him a side glance.

Camp's eyes crinkle at the corners. "All right then."

I glance at my watch; it's getting close to dinner, and I promised Jake I'd be home.

"Do you need to head back? I can walk you," Camp says.

"Yeah, I told my brother I'd be home soon, but I can walk by myself. Thanks, Camp. I want to introduce you guys but in the right way. They wouldn't be thrilled if I walked out of the forest with a random guy." I laugh nervously.

"I can understand that." He chuckles.

We all stand. Anna hugs me quickly. "See you soon. Don't forget to think about a band name. It's time we have one."

"I will," I say, returning her hug.

Camp gives me a high-five, his fingers brushing mine a beat longer than necessary, then crouches beside Bruce, who leans into him with his whole body, nearly toppling him. "That's a good boy." Camp laughs as he regains his balance.

Bruce and I head home, and I can't stop smiling. I'd built that whole Concert Barbie drama up in my head for nothing.

As we walk, I watch the moon rising, serene and slow, while the sun melts beneath the horizon, a puddle of rainbow sherbert. The contrast between them is stunning. It's amazing how they work together to light up our world. It's like they've got this cosmic partnership, never failing the other—a perfect celestial peace pact.

Wait.

Celestial Peace.

That's it!

I sprint back to the campsite with Bruce right behind me. Anna's at the drums; Camp's starting a fire in the stone pit. They both look up as I arrive.

"I've got the name! For the band!" I shout, breathless.

Camp rises to his feet, a wide grin spreading across his face.

I place my hands on my hips and square my shoulders. "Celestial Peace Runners."

Camp's dimples deepen while Anna looks at the ground with a frown. My heart sinks. I thought for sure …

"Not Celestial but Midnight. That's when we first met you, Lavender. The midnight hour is good luck for us. Midnight Peace Runners," Anna says, her eyes finding mine.

Camp's eyebrows raise. "Lavender?"

"It's perfect."

He nods. "'Course we need to run it by Nate, but it feels right. Midnight Peace Runners," he repeats slowly. "Well, ladies, we got ourselves a band name."

SEVENTEEN

I'VE UNLOCKED A new level of joy.

Enlightenment achieved.

Henceforth, I shall respond only to "Zen Master Lavender."

I swing open the mudroom door. "Hello! I'm home, my beautiful family!"

Kicking off my boots, I fling my backpack onto the bench and pirouette into the kitchen, humming *Fast Car.*

Mom sits at the counter, head in her hands, shoulders shaking with silent sobs. Jake and Kalendar hover beside her, whispering.

My stomach drops. "What's wrong?" My eyes dart around, searching for Dad.

His sunglasses sit askew beside the mail, which is scattered across the kitchen desk. But he's nowhere.

Bruce whines at my feet.

Jake looks up. His eyes are rimmed red. He steps toward me and rests a hand on my shoulder.

"Grandpa's home was broken into last night." He winces as if struck by an invisible slap before continuing. "He must have heard them and, knowing Grandpa, tried to stop them. Because they—" He swallows hard. "They hurt him. Bad."

Tears blur my vision as my breathing turns ragged.

"His housekeeper found him unconscious about an hour ago. We're not sure how long he was like that, but… I think it's been several hours. He's at the hospital now. Dad got the call and left for the airport right away—I'm surprised you didn't see him pulling out." Jake's voice stays steady, but his free hand trembles at his side.

"How bad is it?" My chest tightens.

"It's bad, Lavender. Really bad. They hit Grandpa in the head with a baseball bat. More than once." Jake's voice catches. "He's in critical condition."

My head spins, and my knees no longer seem to exist. I thrust my arm against the wall as involuntary shivers ripple through me. "How's Dad?"

"He's obviously scared. I think he feels responsible because he wasn't there." Jake says, shifting his gaze to the floor.

Since Grandma passed away a few years ago, Dad has pestered Grandpa to move in with us. But Grandpa, stubborn as they come, refuses to leave the home he shared with Grandma, the same house Dad grew up in. And honestly, I could never blame him.

I grip the edge of the desk, grounding myself. "How can I help?

"Just pray for now. Dad's going to keep us updated. I'm planning to fly out tomorrow once Mom's stable," he says, turning to her.

I follow his gaze. Mom shakes her head while Kalendar mutters something in her ear. She takes a fistful of her graying hair and groans.

Mom and Grandpa are close. Very close. Mom lost her dad in a motorcycle accident when she was five years old. Ever since Mom married Dad, Grandpa—without a daughter of his own—has filled that role for her. Their love runs deep.

"Can I come?"

"Dad thinks you guys should stay here until we have more information. The doctors are evaluating Grandpa right now."

I hang my head and nod silently, anger boiling inside me.

In my grandpa's suburban neighborhood, there have been a string of robberies over the past year. Teens are always doing the dirty work and being pushed into it by older criminals who know the young guys will get off easy if caught. I'd written to the local paper more than once, pleading for more police presence. If they'd listened, this whole thing could've been avoided.

"Ugh, if only the town had responded to my articles …"

"I've been thinking the same, but we can't do anything about it now, and placing blame is unfair. I'm proud of you for trying, though," Jake says, hugging me.

I wrap my arms around his thin frame, feeling my anger fade into sadness. I bury my face in his shoulder. "Please keep me updated every minute you learn something new."

Jake nods, kissing my head and handing me a tissue from his pocket.

I clear the tears before stepping toward Mom. Moving slowly; I reach her and Kalendar and rest my palm on Kalendar's back. He turns, squeezes my hand, and lets go of Mom. Her bloodshot eyes land on me.

"Oh, Lavender!" she exclaims, sinking into my arms. A fresh set of tears falls from her eyes as I hold her tight.

Later that evening, I trudge up the stairs, each step feeling heavier than the last until I finally collapse onto my bed. My head throbs as I scream into my pillow. Rolling over, I stare at the ceiling, tracing the pattern of the knotted wood with my eyes.

Eventually, I sit up and pull the crystal heart from my backpack. I walk over to the window, looking out at the lanterns twinkling above Camp and Anna. "We need you guys now more than ever," I whisper, my hand drifting to my throat as memories of tonight's performance return.

Suddenly, doubt creeps in, thick and suffocating.

Maybe tonight was a fluke—some weird twist of luck or adrenaline. I've never sung like that before, and the likelihood that I could do it again, in front of *thousands* of people, just does not seem like a reality.

And now with Grandpa… everything feels different. Urgent.

The whole thing with the band has been fun and kind of… magical. Tonight especially; I felt good. Like maybe I actually belonged with them. But I think I got caught up in it. Forgot the bigger picture.

Camp's right. The world's a mess. And maybe music really *can* do something. Maybe *they* can do something.

But I'm not sure I'm good enough. And if I'm the reason they don't succeed, I don't know how I'd ever forgive myself.

I drag a hand down my face, my eyes drifting to the phone.

Josephine.

She's the only one who'll understand this crazy magical band and what they're trying to accomplish. She'll know what to do.

I pick up my phone and text her. "Hey, can you meet me tomorrow? One thirty at the lake to paddleboard?"

Anticipation knots my stomach as the minutes drag by, waiting for Josephine. Though really, arriving thirty minutes early might've been a mistake.

Yet again, I'm living on the surface of Venus. It must be 385 degrees, and my crankiness has definitely set in. Following Josephine's advice, I focus on my breathing techniques. *Breathe in, one, two, three, four, and breathe out …*

Gradually, my body relaxes and I settle into the shade of a cluster of aspen trees. The grass feels soft beneath me, and the air is thick with the scent of summer.

The lake is peaceful; its surface is as smooth as glass. My eyes move to my pink paddleboard resting against a nearby tree. I almost don't want to break the stillness by taking it into the water.

Gravel crunches behind me, and Josephine pulls into the parking spot beside Betty. I wave to her, then look at my phone for the one-millionth time—still no news from Dad or Jake.

Jake flew out early this morning. I'd arrived at work earlier than usual to make him a coffee for his drive to the airport. Since then, I've anxiously waited to receive updates on Grandpa.

"Hey, Lavender!" Josephine says as she emerges from her Jeep. I do a double take at her vehicle—there's something strangely familiar about it.

She walks over to me, stopping abruptly when her eyes meet mine.

"What's happened?" she asks, her tone suggesting we've known each other for years, or perhaps my it's-the-end-of-the-world face is that obvious.

"My grandpa, he's in the hospital. His house got broken into, and when he went to check things out, well …" My throat tightens.

Josephine kneels beside me and takes my chin in her hand. "I'm so sorry, Lavender."

I offer her a weak smile before turning back to the lake.

"Is he okay?" she asks.

"We don't know yet. He got beat up pretty badly. My dad and Jake are at the hospital with him. He lives in California, so it's not like I can stop by and check in. The not knowing is killing me," I say, wiping a tear from my cheek.

She wraps an arm around me and I rest my head on her shoulder.

"Are you up for this?" she asks, gesturing to my paddleboard.

"Yeah, I need to keep busy. Jake said he'd update me when he knows more." I glance at my phone again; still nothing.

"Okay, shall we, then?"

I nod.

"If you want to talk about your grandpa, I'm here. If you prefer to paddle out and sit on the lake silently, I'm game for that too. Whatever you need," she says, squeezing my arm.

"Thanks," I say, rising from the grass and brushing off the dirt.

An hour later, we're cross-legged on a tiny island in the middle of the lake. The paddle out felt endless, and I'm beyond relieved to rest—my arms are basically noodles. Meanwhile, Josephine looks like she could row to the moon and back without breaking a sweat. Figures. She's in way better shape.

Our paddleboards lap against the shore as a breeze dances across the water, relieving my sticky skin. I glance at Josephine, marveling at how the scorching heat doesn't seem to faze her. Her ebony skin remains dry.

My stomach grumbles, so I dig into my backpack and pull out an apple. I hand one to Josephine, and she takes it with a grateful smile. We sit in easy silence for a minute; the only sound is the soft crunch of bites.

I need to ask her about the Midnight Peace Runners; it's now or never.

My heart pounds; *here we go.*

"Josephine, there's something I want to talk to you about." I start, my gaze fixed on the lake, afraid I'll lose my nerve if I meet her eyes.

"Of course. What is it?"

I suck in a ragged breath and shift my eyes to her. "I think…I might've found my gift. Maybe?"

Her eyes grow into full moons and she clasps her hands together. "Tell me more!"

I exhale, relieved at her enthusiasm. "Okay, this might sound crazy, but a band has been camping in the woods behind my house. They say they're on a mission to change the world through their music. I'm still unclear on exactly how, but the thing is, I believe them." Josephine's smile remains.

"Anyway, they've been looking for me for like a year, saying I'm the missing link to their whole thing. According to them, I've got this special gift—I'm meant to sing with Camp, the lead singer, and write songs."

Josephine nods, fueling my confidence.

I lean in close. "The weirdest part? Apparently, Camp can play his guitar on this frequency that only certain humans can hear."

My eyes widen. "Oh, wait. Actually, animals, plants, and insects *can* hear it too, so I shouldn't say…" I shut up, cheeks hot with embarrassment as the realization of what I'm saying out loud sinks in. I take a bite of my apple.

Josephine's smile fades, replaced by a quiet intensity in her eyes.

"Sorry, I don't know if I'm making sense. Does this sound crazy to you?" A piece of apple comes spewing out of my mouth and lands on my shorts. *Nice.*

"Go on," she responds.

I swallow the apple. "I don't get it. Why me? They said this woman, Maggie, had some vision that I was meant to be in the band, but… what if they made a mistake? It's not like I'm some sort of musical prodigy."

Josephine takes a deep breath and closes her eyes.

I shift to sit on my shins, glancing at the lake and then back at her. Her eyes remain shut, and with each passing moment, my anxiety grows.

Yup. She one-thousand percent thinks I'm crazy. She's probably just searching for the right words. *Lavender, there's this really great mental hospital in Mason…* I can see it now.

After what feels like three years—but is probably just a minute—Josephine opens her eyes and turns to me. Confidence shines in her gaze.

"It's your gift, Lavender. It's what you were born to do."

Her voice is so calm, so certain, it almost makes me believe her.

I exhale.

"Do you really think so? But what do you think of this band? Most people would think that everything I told you is bananas. Like I was losing my mind."

She laughs. "I'm not like most people. This feels right to me. I knew there was a reason the universe brought us together. I'd like to help you navigate this new world if you'll let me." Her gaze meets mine, and within it, I glimpse something I wasn't expecting … hope?

"I'd love nothing more, but I'm not a great singer, and this whole Maggie person is throwing me off. Do you believe in guardian angels?"

"I'm sure you're a brilliant singer. You need to believe in yourself." She looks at the water, focusing on a section near a wall of Red Rocks. Turning back to me, a mischievous glint sparks in her eye.

"Come," she says as she gets up and walks toward her paddleboard.

Did she not hear me ask about Maggie?

I dutifully follow her onto the lake. We paddle near the rocks she was looking at just minutes ago. *What's she up to?*

"Sing for me, Lavender!" Josephine shouts as we near the wall of rocks. Her voice echoes off the aged red stone. I gulp. *Great.*

"I can't," I reply quietly enough so my voice *does not* echo off the rocks.

"What was that? I can't hear you!" Josephine shouts again.

"I can't!" I shout, my voice echoing this time. *Wonderful.*

There's one other car in the parking lot, and the lake is dead quiet—no spectators except the trees and maybe a few bored fish. My shoulders relax.

"Can't? Or won't?" Josephine replies.

Ugh. I take a deep breath and kneel on my board, reaching for the crystal heart in my shorts pocket. It's warm to the touch. Gathering courage, I look at Josephine, who stares back at me with the same broad smile.

"Okay, fine," I mutter.

I sing the opening lyrics to "Let It Be." My voice is soft and I stop to clear it.

Josephine sits cross-legged on her paddleboard, giving me an encouraging nod.

I clutch the heart tighter and continue.

Josephine joins in when I get to the chorus. Her voice is loud, confident and, no surprise, gorgeous.

I laugh before straining my vocal chords to match her. My voice rebounds off the walls. It sounds hauntingly beautiful, echoing in the surrounding space.

Cheering and loud whoops erupt from the shore. A small group of kayakers watch us. *Fantastic. Where were they a moment ago?*

Josephine claps and shouts, "Yes! Keep it going!"

Surprising even myself, I keep on.

"Let it be …" Josephine and the group from the shore join in with me. Our voices blend in-sync (ish). It's more shouting than singing from the folks on the shore, but at least I'm not the focus anymore.

People whistle and cheer out of their car windows as they pass the lake.

I laugh out loud, then press my hand across my mouth.

"See? Music can change the world. And YOU can lead that change, Lavender!" Josephine yells as she places her hands on her heart.

The sun's warmth feels wonderful rather than suffocating. Excitement bubbles up inside me, pulsing through every inch of my body. Suddenly, I *can't wait* to meet up with the Midnight Peace Runners again.

My board hums beneath me as I sit, the faint ringing of my phone cutting through the ripples of the water. I dig it out of my backpack, seeing Jake's name flash on the screen.

"Jake?" I pick up, my heart racing from what just unfolded and the terrifying uncertainty of what this call could mean.

"Lavender. You guys gotta get here and quick." Jake breathes into the phone, his voice cracking. "They don't think he's going to make it through the night."

EIGHTEEN

"*THIS* IS THE HOSPITAL?"

The streaked window squeaks as it rolls down. I stick my head out and glance up at the gorgeous white building. It appears to be Spanish colonial, which I only know because we just covered architecture styles in art class. Palm trees line the entrance, and a fountain that could double as an Olympic swimming pool takes up most of the patio.

"It looks more like a luxury resort than a hospital, don't ya think?"

"Yeah, I guess." Kalendar's voice cuts through the stuffy air of our Uber XL. I pop my head back inside. "Thanks, man." He hands the driver something, then looks at me and nods. "Let's go."

Clutching the handle tight, I take a deep breath and swing open the back-seat door, stepping onto the white concrete. The salty ocean air hits me, instantly transporting me to summer days with my grandparents.

Grandparents.

I'll never be able to spend time with them again. Not in this lifetime.

The thought knocks the wind out of me, and I grab my knees, struggling to force oxygen into my lungs.

"Hey, hey. You're okay, Ender." Kalendar pats my shoulder.

The sound of approaching footsteps forces me to straighten.

"Lavender?"

Jake's wearing the same clothes as yesterday. His flannel shirt is untucked, his khakis wrinkled. His brown eyes appear dull, missing their signature spark.

"Hey, Jake."

"You okay?"

I nod and manage a smile. "Mom's in the car."

Jake bends into the SUV and guides Mom out. She leans heavily on him. Her dark sunglasses hide her red eyes, but her posture hints at her devastation. Her shoulders are slumped, hands gripping a tissue.

Grandpa died last night, sustaining too many injuries for his advanced age. The hospital had tried to do "everything they could," according to Jake. He had delivered the news to us a few minutes before midnight; it shattered Mom. She's usually so emotionally steady, it's jarring to see her this upset.

"Where's Dad?" I ask Jake.

"He's inside talking to the police. They believe they've identified the guys who attacked Grandpa, thanks to a neighbor's surveillance camera." He shrugs. "Doesn't matter now if you ask me, it won't change anything. Grandpa's gone." Jake's voice cracks and he crumples to the ground, his shoulders tremble with tears. Mom transforms into herself again and kneels beside him, holding his head in her arms.

"Damn it!" Kalendar shouts, his face pointed to the sky. I flinch at the outburst and glance around to see if we're drawing an audience. Thankfully, the patio is mostly empty.

"Hey, guys." I look up at the sound of Dad's voice. Jake wipes his cheeks with his thumb and stands.

Dad holds Mom, his head bent toward hers as he whispers something in her ear. She nods in response and kisses him. He walks over to us.

"How are you doing, Dad?" I ask him as he hugs me. His eyes are puffy, but he's a rock. Strong, solid, unwavering. Same as when Grandma passed.

"I'm sad." He pauses for a moment before continuing. "I know Grandpa's happy to be reunited with Grandma, though. And that's what I'm holding on to."

I rise with the sun and slip into the same little black dress I wore to Grandma's funeral. Checking my reflection in the mirror, a glaring deodorant stain screams at me halfway down the dress. *Great.* I splash water on it and rub it with a towel—knowing full well this never works. The smudge stares at me, faded but stubborn. Sighing, I reach for my curling iron, only to burn my knuckle on the tip of the wand.

I already hate today.

We drive in a limousine to the memorial service. The past few days have been exhausting. Sorting through Grandpa's belongings and making arrangements for his funeral has kept us busy, leaving little room to process the fact that he's really gone.

Dad decided not to host a wake with Grandpa. His injuries are too much for an open casket, and anyway, Grandpa had explicitly told him after Grandma's funeral he wanted a memorial service by the sea when it was his "turn to fly" (his words).

Despite the heaviness in my heart, a small sense of peace settles in when I think of Grandma and Grandpa finally reunited. I imagine them slow dancing on an eternal beach—white sand, white doves, perfect sky. They were so in love.

As we pull up to the beach, a wave of emotion crashes over me. Hundreds of Grandpa's friends stand barefoot in the sand, flower necklaces draped around their necks. Our limo slows to a stop at the curb and they all turn toward us—some holding up peace signs in silent greeting.

"I didn't know Grandpa knew so many people." My voice cracks.

"He got really active after Grandma passed. Joined all sorts of clubs. Did you know he even learned how to surf?" Mom says, staring out the window. "The younger surfers adored him. Explains the peace signs." She chuckles.

"Wow," I say, my voice trailing off. A tear slips down my cheek as regret settles deep in my chest. How could there be an entire side of Grandpa's life I never knew? All that time wasted with Brandon— when I could've been here with him. I don't even remember the last time I came here for a visit. I glance over at Dad, who's dabbing his eyes with a handkerchief. Mom reaches over and holds his hand.

She catches my eye and mouths, *I love you*. I grin back, happy that she isn't a mess today. Maybe this is good for her, a closure of sorts. She leans her head on Dad's shoulder and breathes in deeply.

"Ready?" she asks us.

We all look at Dad.

He nods as he opens the limo door. "Let's celebrate Grandpa's life."

As far as memorials go, it was beautiful. Dad invited Grandpa's closest friends to offer heartfelt words and cherished memories. Dad delivered a lengthy eulogy—I doubt there was a dry eye on the beach afterward. The gathering overflowed with love, causing the sadness of losing Grandpa to fade a bit. His long and beautiful life was the focus, not his death. I don't understand why every end-of-life service can't be this way. When I go—music and dancing on the mountain, please.

After the speeches, we gather as a family to send off Grandpa. Standing by the ocean, we pass around his biodegradable urn, each saying our goodbye. Dad takes it last and wades into the sea up to his waist. He kisses the urn and releases it into the waves, watching it float away for several minutes before returning to us. His black pants are soaked and cling tight to his toned calves. Tears run down his face, but his eyes are love as he looks at us, his family.

A seagull swoops down so close, the rush of air from its wings blows my hair back. It circles above us, and we laugh—just for a second, the sadness lifting. Grandpa was the one person I knew who actually liked seagulls. A single feather drifts down, and I catch it, tucking it into my bag. "Hi, Grandpa," I whisper.

Stepping into the restaurant Dad reserved for the "after-party" (again, Grandpa's words on his death wish list), I glance around the large, sunlit room, recognizing several faces from all the years of visiting my grandparents. Many look up to make eye contact; I give them a small smile.

A man dressed in a form-fitting gray suit and John Lennon eyeglasses greets us.

"Hello, Flynn family. I'm so sorry for your loss," he bows slightly. "My name is Derek, the restaurant manager. I'll be looking after you today." He offers a warm grin and looks each of us in the eye. I like him immediately.

"Typically, with these events, the family gathers toward the back of the restaurant so your guests can come and offer their condolences. It's up to you, though, of course." He looks at Dad, eyebrows raised.

"Thank you, Derek, that sounds nice," Dad replies graciously.

"Okay, great. Please follow me this way, and we'll get you set up. A server will assist you with drinks."

Derek leads us to a row of window seats facing the ocean.

"Please make yourself comfortable," he motions toward the cushions.

I eagerly sit and melt into the luxurious, sun-soaked fabric.

"Why don't you take a few moments to settle in, and I'll begin circulating to inform your guests they're welcome to come and offer their sympathies to the family," Derek says.

"Wonderful, thanks, Derek." Mom's eyes are bright with gratitude.

The following couple of hours pass at a sluggish pace. My cheeks burn as I keep a forced smile. My only relief is Derek. He stays close by our side, pausing the line of people when needed to give us a moment to collect ourselves.

Thankfully, the line's beginning to dwindle. I shift my gaze to the end, and my heart leaps as familiar hazel eyes lock onto mine.

Camp's smile is soft, almost private, like it's meant just for me. His gaze lingers, studying my face, as if he's checking to see if I'm okay.

The line moves and he takes a slow step forward, one hand slipping into the pocket of his perfectly tailored black suit, the other lifting in a quiet wave.

I forget how to breathe.

What's he doing here?

Anna and Nate stand by his side. Anna has her palm over her heart. "I'm sorry," her lips form as she looks at me, her eyes glisten with tears. Beside her, Nate stares out the window.

"Wait a minute, isn't that the singer from the band that played with Dave?" Jake whispers in my ear.

Shoot. How am I ever going to explain this?

"Uh, yes. It is, isn't it? How strange that they're here." I mumble, eyes still fixed on my new friends.

"They act as if they know you," he prods.

"Yes, well, they do, actually. I ran into them a week ago in Rosewood. and I've been meaning to tell you. They must be performing nearby." I stumble over my words, unable to meet his eyes.

"Huh." Jake clicks his tongue. "Did you tell them about Grandpa?"

"No." At least that's the truth. I'm assuming word must have made its way around town? But why travel all this way? I chew on my lip.

"Are you, like, close with them?"

"No," I say. My guilt intensifies as my lies stack like the too-many pancakes I had for lunch. My stomach churns.

"Huh," he says again.

I tug at my dress as I watch Camp approaching Mom and Dad. He holds out his hand, and his lips move quietly. Their weary expressions hint at exhaustion, apparently too drained to ask about Camp's connection to Grandpa. *Thank goodness.*

When he reaches Jake and me, he takes my hand, and my fingers spark at his touch.

"I'm very sorry, Lavender," he says, squeezing before letting go.

He extends his hand to Jake next. "I'm sorry for your loss."

Jake accepts his handshake, then says, "Hey, I saw you perform at Red Rocks. You guys were amazing."

"Thank you," Camp replies modestly. "Those are my bandmates, Anna and Nate." He nods toward them as they give their condolences to my parents. Anna looks over when she hears her name and smiles at Jake.

"It's nice to meet you. How do you know Lavender?" Jake asks.

Camp doesn't hesitate. "We ran into her last week at the town park on our way back from a gig in Utah. She'd seen us perform in

Rosewood a couple of weeks ago, and we got to talking. She's quite something, your sister." Camp glances at me, his dimples deepening.

"How did you guys know to come here?"

Jake's persistent; he must know something's up. This is the big brother side of him that's annoying, always meddling in my business.

"We're performing at a venue in LA. We heard about your grandpa through a friend and took a detour to pay our respects. Of course, we don't know y'all too well, but we know what it's like to lose someone we love," Camp responds again without missing a beat.

Who is this friend?

Jake appears to loosen up. "Well, thanks for coming. We appreciate it. Did you guys come up with a name for your band yet? Lavender and I have been trying to find you online."

"Yes. Just recently, actually. Midnight Peace Runners," Camp says, stealing a glance in my direction.

I turn my attention to Nate, who wasn't there when we came up with the band name. He gives me a nod—the most I've ever gotten from him. It's something, I suppose.

"That's a great name," Jake exclaims. "We head back to Rosewood tomorrow; otherwise, we'd try to see your show."

"Oh, no worries, y'all must be exhausted." Camp looks at me with concern.

"Anyway, we like Rosewood and may hang out there for a couple of weeks between gigs."

"No way! Well, if you come by, look us up. We're the last home before Mount Snettles, right on up the county road. We'd love to hang with you guys." Jake shakes Camp's hand again.

"Jake's really into music," I explain, looking Camp in the eye.

"My kind of guy." He smiles at Jake. "We'll see you soon, then. And again, I'm sorry about your grandfather. Grandparents are always a hard loss." Camp nods once before leaving the line.

Anna gives Jake and me a hug, and Nate offers a handshake.

I watch them make their way to the door. Camp turns around to look at me before leaving.

Thank you, I mouth.

He winks, and then they disappear.

"Hey, guys. Sorry, I needed a minute." Kalendar straightens his tie as he approaches us from the restrooms.

"You'll never believe who was just here," Jake says excitedly. "Remember that band you and Lavender saw in Rosewood a few weeks ago?"

"The band with no name?" Kalendar asks me.

"Yes, that one." I laugh.

"They were here? Why?" Kalendar's eyes narrow.

"Lavender bumped into them last week in town and got to know them. They have a show in LA and heard about Grandpa, so they swung by on their way."

"Yeah?" Kalendar tilts his head at me.

"Yup! They're so nice!" I overreact, avoiding Kalendar's suspicious eyes.

"Uh-huh. It sure is nice for someone you barely know to go out of their way to come to Grandpa's funeral," Kalendar's voice drips with sarcasm.

I look him in the eye. "Sure is," I say with a smile so wide it hurts.

NINETEEN

YUP, SHE'S STILL here, yogis! The universe is blessing us. Josephine Dunton meditation class: 7:00 p.m. tonight!

Lacey's handwriting fills the A-frame chalkboard in front of Mom's yoga studio. I tap my phone for the time: *6:37.*

The door chimes as I push it open. Suzy is sitting at the reception desk. Her warm eyes greet me as she clasps her tattooed hands together.

"Lavender, I'm so sorry about the loss of your grandpa. How are you holding up, sweetie?"

"Hey, Suzy. I'm okay, thanks. It's been hard, but he's with my grandma now, and that's all he wanted, anyway."

"That's a great way to look at it." She tilts her head and smiles. "Are you here for the class?"

I nod. "I was hoping to chat with Josephine before, though. Is she here?"

"Yes, in the back."

"Great, thanks." I head toward the changing rooms.

"Josephine? Are you here?" I call out as I enter the space.

"Lavender, hi! One minute, I'm just about changed." Her voice rings out from behind a curtain.

Several yoga mats are neatly rolled in a basket in the corner, and a watercooler sits near the door. Lavender fills the air—the signature scent of the studio since its conception. Mom's choice. Obviously.

"It's wonderful to see you," Josephine exclaims as she pulls aside the purple-and-white tie-dye dressing room curtain. She walks over and hugs me tight.

It's hard to believe I haven't known Josephine for longer. The word soulmate has crossed my mind more than once.

"How are you doing, girl?"

"I'm okay. Thanks for holding down the studio while Mom was gone."

She shakes her head. "Don't think twice about it. How are your parents?"

"They're fine. Sad, but I think they have some closure now."

"I'm glad," she replies with a warm smile. "What brings you here? Didn't you just get back?"

"Yeah, about an hour ago, but I had to see you. I'm hoping I can get advice."

"What's going on?" She asks, taking me by the elbow to a row of wooden benches along the wall. We sit and Josephine folds her hands in her lap, looking at me expectantly.

"Well, you'll never believe this, but my bandmates came to the funeral."

Josephine nods.

"Don't you think that's strange? Don't get me wrong—I'm flattered—but we're still only getting to know each other."

"Not at all. You're a team now. You'll support each other through all of life's events. It's a special connection you have with them. I know it's still new to you, but it seems they have been working on their bond for much longer, so it comes more naturally."

I twist my lips. "It makes sense when you put it that way," I say. "And they *did* have a concert nearby—well, in the same state at least," I reason.

Josephine smiles. "Is there anything else?"

"Yes. Kalendar's suspicious they were at the funeral. He thinks we only met once before in the park. I hate lying to him, but I'm afraid of how he'll react when I tell him the full story. I don't think he'll understand. What do you think I should do?"

She narrows her eyes. "Why don't you think Kalendar would understand?"

"Well… I know he won't be thrilled about me hanging out with people he doesn't know. We're from a small town, so he's very familiar with my *three*"—I roll my eyes—"friends. I'm guessing he'd see my new friends as people he can't trust or something. Plus, two of them are guys. He's just protective. And, well, he might think this whole thing is crazy."

Josephine looks at the ground before returning her gaze to meet mine.

"Lies are never a good thing to hold on to, especially with the people you love. Kalendar loves you. I think he will support you if you're honest with him," she says.

Bleh. She's right. I have to tell him the truth. But how? I need him to get to know the band before making a judgment without ever meeting them. Maybe I'll plan a get-together with all of us. I know Jake will be game. I'm sure Kalendar will come if Jake does. Then, everything will unfold more organically. Fingers crossed.

After class, I leave the studio and step out into the summer evening. The street lights flicker on, casting a magical glow over the quiet town. A sense of peace settles over me. That is, until I spot

Emma leaning against the side of Betty. Heat rises through my body as I slow my pace and eye her.

"Hey, Lavender." She straightens as I approach.

"What do you want, Emma?"

"I'm really sorry about your grandpa," she says.

"Thanks." I reach for my door handle, refusing to look her in the eye.

She moves closer.

"That's not all. I miss you. Can we grab coffee sometime?" Her eyes search mine. "I owe you a major apology."

She looks smaller somehow; her thick black hair is thrown into a messy bun. She wears baggy sweatpants and a stained fitted T-shirt, a drastic change from her usual polished appearance. Is that old mascara under her eyes? *Yikes.*

Guilt sparks in my chest, but it's quickly drowned by images of her with Kalendar.

"No, thanks," I passive-aggressively reply, sliding into my seat and starting the Bronco. Reversing, I glimpse Emma in the mirror. She stands, arms crossed over her chest, watching me drive away.

Needing a mental distraction, I feel around the passenger seat for my phone but come up empty. I fumble with the car radio knob instead, and the static finally gives way to a DJ's booming voice.

"Good evening, you're tuned in to Z104.1 alternative rock radio. Here's a cover of the classic 'The Boys of Summer' with a rock twist. You can thank me later."

Our song, the one Emma and I have claimed as ours, blasts through Betty's speakers and fills the Rosewood streets. I squeeze the steering wheel.

"Ugh, Em!" I slam on the brakes and whip a U-turn.

Emma's sitting on the curb as I pull back into the parking spot. My truck lights shine on her, revealing tear-stained cheeks. She looks up with owl eyes.

Turning off the truck, I jump down from Betty, my keys clinking as I walk over to her.

"Listen. It won't be this way forever. Just give me more time, okay?"

Emma smiles through her tears and nods.

"Okay, then." I smooth my hair, walk back to the truck, and climb in. A gust sweeps through the street, sending the nearby trees into a violent shiver. In between the wind and rustling leaves, I swear I hear it: *forgive her.*

TWENTY

I'VE BEEN SINGING with the Midnight Peace Runners for two weeks now. That's fourteen days of pushing through self-doubt, and eventually finding my voice. Not that I'm the next Adele or anything. 336 hours of bonding with Anna, the big sister I always wished for, and 20,160 minutes of trying (and failing) not to fall for Camp.

I mean, you probably saw this coming. I tried to be indifferent, really. But in the end, there's no denying that he's kind of perfect. That is, if you're into the whole mysterious, cowboy thing. Though, come to think of it, I'm not even sure he's a cowboy, but you get it. The problem is, I doubt he feels the same. We flirt and exchange lingering glances, but it never goes beyond that. And let's be real—he's way out of my league.

Oh wait, and 1,209,600 seconds of trying to get Nate to hate me a *little* less. I think I'm making progress on that front. Maybe.

Today, I'm extra nervous because it's the day my two worlds collide.

The band is excited to meet my brothers, but the feeling isn't mutual. Eh, that's a half-truth—it's Kalendar who doesn't seem thrilled. He hasn't said it outright, but I know him. His not-so-subtle comments every time I leave to meet up with my new friends "again?" haven't slipped past me.

He doesn't know we're a band yet—that's the big reveal today or maybe tomorrow. I'm praying to every god, spiritual being, and angel on high that Kalendar likes them. It'll make explaining the whole "we're-saving-the-world-through-our-music" thing much easier if he actually does.

We're meeting at the rodeo, which seems like a safe place. If things go south, at least we'll have horses and bulls to focus on—no space for awkward silences there. Ah, but it's NOT going to go bad. *Positive thinking, Lavender.*

My reflection stares back at me in the full-length mirror—brown cowboy boots, ripped blue jeans, and Mom's vintage leather jacket with fringe sleeves and floral embroidery on the back. My braided hair falls down my left shoulder, and I'm wearing the beige felt cowboy hat Kalendar gave me at Christmas. A purple feather peeks out the side.

Well, I'm certainly dressed the part.

"Ready, Ender?" Kalendar's voice echoes from downstairs.

"Coming!"

Jake's waiting for us in Betty. Kalendar hops into the back, and I slide into the passenger seat. Jake's wearing the same outfit he wore to the rodeo a few weeks ago, his colossal belt buckle glimmers in the sun. A toothpick sits between his teeth, and he gives me a wink.

"Should we do this thing?" he asks.

I suck in a breath and nod.

"Yeehaw, let's go!" Jake bellows, shifting into drive. His excitement is contagious, and I can't help but laugh as I clutch my hat against the wind, the rush of the moment pushing my worries aside.

The rodeo is in the nearby town of Mason. We park at the venue lot and begin the short walk to the stadium.

"Hey, there's Sofia and Aly," Kalendar says before letting out a sharp whistle. "Hey, ladies!"

They both spin around from several feet ahead on the sidewalk. Sofia's face brightens with a wide grin, while Aly pauses, narrowing her eyes for a moment before putting on a plastic smile.

Great.

Okay, I may have been turning down their requests to hang these last two weeks. It's just…well, I've been busy. You know, band life and all.

"Hey, Flynns!" Sofia exclaims. She waves energetically before bounding over and pulling me into a hug. "I feel like I haven't seen you this summer, Lavender. I miss you!"

"I know. It's been busy. I miss you too, Sof."

"If it weren't for the coffee shop, I'd never see you," Aly says, her voice *way* too high. Ah, yes—there it is, her signature brand of passive-aggression. It's been a while.

"Yeah, thank goodness for that …" I wince at my own fake laugh.

"Do you want to get together tomorrow? We could meet at the lake or shop in town. I'm in desperate need of new clothes." Sofia threads her arm through mine.

Tomorrow, I have plans with the band. We're diving into songwriting—something I haven't tried before but am somehow expected to be brilliant at. No pressure. And Camp will be there, so…

"Shoot, I can't tomorrow," I reply, my face dropping in faux-disappointment.

"Why not?" Kalendar asks.

Ugh. I resist the urge to roll my eyes.

"Oh, I promised Mom we'd spend time together," I lie.

"What about Monday then, after work?" Aly asks.

I'm supposed to meet with Josephine on Monday.

"Yeah, maybe. I'll let you know." I glance at my watch, then look at my brothers. "We better get going, guys. I told the band we'd meet them soon."

"Band?" Sofia raises her eyebrows.

Jake grins wide, his eyes lighting up as he leans toward Sofia. "Lavender here has gotten to know a rad band. You guys should meet them too. They're called the Midnight Peace Runners."

"You didn't tell me that, Lavender. That's awesome." Aly's voice comes off as sweet, but the sharp edge isn't lost on me.

"So cool! Rubbing shoulders with celebrities, huh? We don't want to keep you, then. Don't forget to text me about Monday, Lavender. Bye, Flynns!" Sofia untangles herself from me and swings her arm around Aly. They pick up their pace in front of us and Aly leans in to whisper something to Sofia. *Double ugh.*

"Why haven't you been hanging out with your friends, Ender? That's not like you." Kalendar searches my eyes, his eyebrows slanting with concern. "I can understand Emma—" he looks away uncomfortably before continuing "—but Sofia and Aly?"

"I've just been busy." I shrug. "I'll start making time for them again."

"I hope you do. No friendship compares to your childhood friends." Jake chimes in. "Even if that friendship happens to be an incredible band." He smirks.

"Totally," I say flatly, lifting the corners of my lips but not attempting to hide the annoyance in my eyes.

"All right, let's go meet these guys," Kalendar says, continuing along the sidewalk.

"And girl," I say, correcting him.

"Sorry, and girl." He side-eyes me.

As soon as we step into the stadium, I spot the trio. Unfamiliar faces surround them, probably fans. The air smells of cow manure, stale beer and hot dogs. *Yum.* Food vendors have set up carts in the lobby, and the double doors to the seating area are open, the doors propped wide and held in place by horseshoes. People are funneling through them; a mob of cowboy hats, big hair, and Carhartt.

Camp looks up mid-conversation, his smile deepening when our eyes meet. My heart flutters, but I force my gaze on the ground, pretending to study a stray pebble until the feeling fades. When I look again, he's excusing himself from his fans, exchanging a few words with Anna and Nate, and walking over with that signature swagger of his, slow and confident.

It's not lost on me that most of the fans are female. They watch him walk away, their mouths hanging open. *Settle down, ladies.*

"Hey," Camp says as he approaches. He extends his hand to Jake and Kalendar, and they shake it. He tips his cowboy hat at me. "Lavender." His dimples alone might stop all the wars and bring peace and love to all. Amen.

I swallow. "Hi, Camp."

Anna glides over with Nate in tow. After a round of introductions, hugs, handshakes, and—*thank you, Jesus, this is going well so far*—we head to the bleachers.

We somehow get first-row seats. I settle between Camp and Kalendar. The metal railing of the bleachers is in my line of sight. Right. This explains the available seating. I glance at everyone else—Jake's on the end next to Anna, and Nate's sitting between Anna and Kalendar. No one else seems bothered, and it's going *freaking wonderful.* I guess I don't really need to watch this thing, anyway.

I mentally give myself a dozen pats on the back as the minutes tick by. Anna and Jake are in constant fits of laughter, and even though I have no idea what they're talking about, I can't help but giggle every time I glance over and see them cracking up.

Nate, Kalendar, and Camp are bonding over the rodeo. I guess they *can* see—the difference a few inches makes. They're super into it, cheering on the cowboys and booing when one gets thrown off a bull. Listening to them talk about the bulls is quickly becoming the highlight of my life. They comment on the color and size of each as if they're fashion critics at a runway show.

"Check out the horns on that one," Nate says.

"That's a beauty—look at those white spots," Kalendar adds.

Camp nods appreciatively. "That bull's got some serious swagger."

Camp shares stories about his bull riding days when he was younger.

So he *is* a cowboy.

Kalendar, instantly captivated, fires off a thousand questions. My insides glow, picturing Camp on top of one of those massive bulls. Strong, rugged, masculine. *Is it suddenly warm in here?*

At a break in the event, Camp stands. "Anyone want anything to eat or drink?"

"I'd love water and maybe popcorn. Thanks, Camp," I say.

"You got it." Camp grins.

"I'll come with you," Kalendar offers.

"Jakey, Anna, Nate—do you guys want anything?" Kalendar asks.

"I'm good," Nate answers.

"Diet Coke, please. Thank you!" Anna responds in her singsong voice.

"I'll have a beer, thanks, guys. Do you need me to come with you?" Jake raises his eyebrows at Camp.

"Yeah. I have a year to go, just turned twenty," Camp answers in his Southern drawl.

Wait. What? "When was your birthday?" I squint up at him.

"Yesterday, actually." Camp chuckles.

"What?" I can't hide my surprise. We spent several hours together yesterday. How could he not say something? Anna shrugs, wide-eyed.

Jake and Kalendar slide past me and the boys walk off toward the concessions. Kalendar puts his arm around Camp's shoulder—an excellent sign. I can tell he likes him. I'd be more pleased with this newfound bromance if I weren't so miffed that Camp didn't tell me about his birthday.

I scoot closer to Nate as soon as they're out of earshot. "Hey, did you know that yesterday was Camp's birthday?"

"Yup, he didn't want me to say anything to you and Anna."

"Why?" This comes out harsher than intended. "I mean, sorry. I'm just surprised he wouldn't want us to know. We would've done something special for him."

"I think that's why." Nate rubs his jaw. "Camp doesn't like to be the center of attention. Funny, I know, with him being the lead singer."

Before I can bug him again, a burst of laughter ripples through the crowd. Curious, I rise to my feet and glance toward the arena—right in the middle, a man in a clown suit is awkwardly trying to cram himself into a barrel. It's ridiculous. And honestly, hilarious. I drop back onto the bench, fishing my phone from my bag to record it for Instagram.

Suddenly, the atmosphere shifts, a strange energy prickling at my skin. I look up to find Camp heading back from the concessions, a bucket of popcorn cradled in one arm, my brothers trailing behind. He's just a few steps away when his eyes meet mine—then shift past me.

A commotion flares behind me. Voices rise. One cuts through, clear and unmistakable.

Billy Bea—

In an instant, I'm shoved face-first into the railing. My nose collides with the metal, and the salty tang of blood fills my mouth. Crumpling to the ground, I clutch my head, pain exploding like fireworks. Dizziness washes over me, nausea settles in, and then Kalendar's frantic shouts fill the stadium.

Anna's by my side instantly, holding me in her arms. "Lavender! Are you okay?"

I groan. "Kalendar."

Anna turns to look behind us. My head's pressed against her chest, and her heart's in overdrive. A killer headache forms, threatening a black out. Making sense of what just happened seems impossible. Kalendar's shouts intensify. My world is spinning, but I'm clearheaded enough to understand he's on the verge of a fight. I try to lift my head from Anna.

"Lavender, don't move. You're bleeding. Can you hear me?"

"Please don't let him fight," I plead, opening my eyes enough to meet hers.

"They won't. Nate won't let them."

Sure enough, Nate's stern voice rises. "Camp, guys, it isn't worth it. Lavender will be okay; let's just walk away."

Kalendar drops a few swear words, and Jake's talking to someone in harsh tones, but I can't make out the words. My eyes squeeze shut as the pain becomes unbearable.

Billy Beauford's voice fills the air. "It was a fucking accident, dude, chill. She should've moved. Don't witches have a sixth sense or something?"

Uh-oh.

"Are you FUCKING kidding me?" Kalendar screams, followed by grunts and shuffling of feet.

Suddenly, I'm weightless. *Did I die?*

I blink and see Camp hovering above me, cradling me in his arms like a baby. His eyes are fixed ahead, and his grip tightens around me.

"Please don't let Kal fight," I repeat, my words barely audible.

"Anna's got Kalendar, don't worry. We need to get you to the hospital," he says, his breathing ragged. Each step feels like a dagger to my head.

"Kalendar, LET'S GO! Lavender is begging you to step away," Anna shouts, though she sounds far away.

"You WILL pay, Billy. You better watch your back!" Kalendar yells.

The stadium lights pass by with intensely bright streaks of yellow and orange. I close my eyes again; the dizziness overpowering.

"Ender?" I force my eyes open and find Kalendar, his face flushed with concern.

And then I descend into darkness.

TWENTY-ONE

"LAVENDER, SWEETHEART?" Mom's soft voice pulls me from the dark. I blink my eyes open to see her hovering over me, tears glistening.

I take a moment to absorb my surroundings, noting the sterile white walls and the rhythmic beeping of machines. From a chair in the corner, Dad rushes over, concern consumes his face. "Lavender! Oh, thank you!" He clasps his hands in prayer and shakes them at the ceiling.

My head pounds, and my face hurts. There's something stiff and huge on my nose, a bandage of sorts.

"Where's Kalendar?" I whisper as the memory of him yelling at someone returns.

"He's with Jake and your friends at the sheriff's office. They're giving their accounts of the fight at the rodeo." Mom pauses and turns her attention to Dad. "Hun, can you please call the boys? I promised we'd call them as soon as Lavender woke."

"Of course, love." Dad kisses my forehead. "I'll be right back," he whispers.

I watch Dad leave the room.

"Mom?" I twist my head, and stars burst before my eyes. Pressing my IV hand to my forehead, I focus on my breathing to steady myself.

"Take it easy, babe." She rests her hand on my arm.

The stars fade, and I lower my hand, meeting her gaze. "What happened?"

"Oh, honey. Do you remember being at the rodeo?" Her eyes search mine frantically.

"Yes. I remember getting pushed. The rest is kind of a blur."

Relief flickers over her face and she nods. "Yes. There was an argument between two guys sitting behind you. Over something ridiculous—a baseball game, I believe your friend, Nate, said. Anyway, it became physical, and one of them pushed the other into you." She pauses and sighs. "It was Billy Beauford who did the pushing, by the way." Her lips press together tight. "Kalendar said you flew into a metal railing. The doctor says you have a broken nose and a concussion. How are you feeling?"

I pause, absorbing her words. *Of course. Billy.*

"It hurts, but it's manageable," I finally answer.

She holds my hand as I strain to remember anything beyond the shoving—Kalendar yelling, bright lights, and... I think Camp carrying me? My cheeks flush at the thought.

"You know," Mom says, as if reading my mind, "that Campion, he was very worried. He was by your side until he had to leave for the sheriff's office, and even then, his friend had to pull him away." She arches an eyebrow.

"Oh, yeah?"

"Yup. He appears to really care for you. I'm surprised you haven't mentioned him." She crosses her arms, a playful smirk tugging at her lips.

"Well, we're still getting to know each other," I reply. I know she wants more, but that's all I have energy for. I'm certainly not going to tell her everything right now. But a warm glow at this new information starts in my stomach and spreads through my body, slightly balancing out the relentless jackhammer in my head.

Oh my gosh, his birthday! Our conversation at the rodeo comes back to me. I still can't understand why he wouldn't tell me about it. Nate said he didn't want the attention, and I guess I can relate. Even so, I need to do something.

What would Camp want?

I carefully turn my head to look at Mom. "I have a favor. Can you ask Lacey if she can make glass beads that look like the crystal heart I have? And can she add a musical note in the center? Maybe in a shade of gray?"

"Crystal heart? What are you talking about, hun?" She leans in closer.

Oh, right. She doesn't know.

I glance around the room. "Um, where are my jeans?"

Mom walks over to a chair in the corner and pulls the jeans from a white plastic bag. She holds them up.

"Check my front pocket," I say, straightening.

She takes the heart from my pocket and brings it up to her eye, studying it with a curious tilt of her head. "This is beautiful, hun," she says, her expression shifting. "It reminds me of… well, never mind."

"Reminds you of what?"

"There was this class I took while getting my yoga certification— one on crystals and the energy they hold." She nods toward the heart. "This stone represents love and harmony, which explains why it's shaped like a heart. But my teacher said it can be even more powerful than that in certain cases."

"Oh, yeah? How?"

"According to her, some believe this crystal connects not just to the universe, but to the spiritual world within it. But only in the right hands." She squints at the crystal. "Where did you get it?"

My heart stutters. That would explain… a lot.

But what does it all mean?

"Uh, Anna. My new friend gave it to me."

"Huh." Mom clicks her tongue thoughtfully. "Well, I'm sure Lacey can make a bead like this. What do you want it for?"

"I want to make bracelets."

Mom's gaze lingers on me, waiting for some kind of explanation. As the silence stretches, she shakes her head and smiles.

"Bracelets? How wonderful! I'll swing by her art studio tomorrow morning," she says.

A sharp, searing pain bursts through my skull, and I can't hold back a pained groan.

"What's wrong, love? Are you in pain?" Mom's voice wavers as she runs to my side.

I manage a weak nod.

"The meds must be wearing off. I'll get the nurse, okay? Hang on." She leaves swiftly.

Shutting my eyes, I focus on the darkness behind my lids, silently willing the pain to fade, though it feels like it's just beginning.

TWENTY-TWO

I'M POSSIBLY THE worst patient in existence.

Being stuck at home has been awful. AWFUL. I understand the need to rest, but I'm losing my mind here. With the way my family hovers over me, you'd think I was on death's door. Don't get me wrong—I know how lucky I am to have them—but *come on*. I can't even get up to pee without someone barging into my room. They must have a hidden camera in here.

Seriously, I wonder if they do.

Lifting my head from the pillow, I squint at the dresser and carefully get out of bed. Shuffling over, I peer down at the picture frames. One photo is of Mom and me skiing in Telluride. Another of our family after a hike to the peak of Mount Snettles. The frame of Emma and me lies face down. Yes, mature.

In the movies, hidden cameras are always in picture frames. I lift the skiing photo to examine it, catching my reflection in the mirror.

Oh, man.

The skin under my eyes is swollen and bruised, nearly matching my purple irises. *Cute.* I shake my head. At least there's a bandage covering my nose because without it, it's a flattened mess of black-and-blue flesh. Which *no one* wants to see. My doctor thinks I might avoid reconstructive surgery. To which I asked which type of drug he's high on, because I wouldn't mind partaking a little. He wasn't amused.

The door to my room swings open. "Hun, what are you doing?" I glance at Mom in the mirror, her hand on her hip.

I sigh so loudly that the neighbors two miles away surely hear.

"I'm checking to see where you've hidden a camera." I pick up the other frame.

"Camera?"

"Yeah, you just proved my point that you guys are keeping track of me somehow. I *literally* just got out of bed, and here you are." I swing my arm around dramatically for emphasis.

She laughs, walks over to me, and rests her hand on my back. "There's no camera. Promise."

She clears her throat. "Hey, so, I just got off the phone with Rufus Hoosier. He's over the moon that you set up that CheddarUp for his new tractor. We've already raised $500! I'm really proud of you, sweetie."

I wave her off. "It's not a big deal. I'm happy to help."

Mom smiles, lifting the bracelets off my dresser. "These turned out beautifully."

I look at the colorful bracelets in her hand. Lacey delivered on the beads. They're gorgeous. Each one, shaped like a heart, is a dusty-rose color with a dark gray musical note engraved in the middle. They shimmer when the sunlight hits them as if they hold magical energy. It wouldn't surprise me at this point if they did.

Making the bracelets was the saving grace of an otherwise pathetic week. Braiding the colorful twine and affixing the bead in the center brought back memories of my childhood spent in the art studio with Lacey. I crafted a bracelet for each of us—Camp, Anna, Nate, and me.

When they were done, I snapped a photo of them and sent it to Josephine. She replied immediately, "Love it! What a great gift for everyone. And bonus: your band has a logo now!"

I hadn't even considered that, but I kind of love it. I think the others might too.

"When's Campion getting here?" Mom asks, sweeping my unshowered hair back.

"Two." I grimace at my reflection again.

"Stop that. You're beautiful," she insists, raising her eyebrows. "Are you excited to see him?"

"Uh, yeah," I mutter.

The truth is, I'm nervous about seeing him. I've honestly never looked worse in my life. I tried to keep him away for as long as possible, but he's persistent. Anna's been showing up at my door daily with flowers and cookies, pleading with me to let Camp visit. "You look great; he really wants to see you," she'd always say. I finally gave in.

Two o'clock rolls around, and the doorbell rings.

I've decided to wear the kimono that Grandma gave me years ago after one of her trips to Japan with Grandpa. The silk drapes nicely on my petite frame, and the bright floral patterns whisper "recovering chic." I'm hoping it will offset the disaster that is my face.

"I'll get it. You stay here," Mom insists.

I don't bother arguing and instead sink deeper into the leather couch in our family room. Camp's twang echoes through the hallway, causing butterflies to take flight in my stomach.

His cowboy boots click against our cherrywood floors as he approaches and abruptly halts. I swallow before lifting my eyes to meet his.

He rubs his jaw, gaze dropping to the floor before finding mine again. "You look beautiful," he says, his dimples deepening.

Blushing, I mumble a quick "Thanks" as I instinctively move my hand to cover my nose.

He sits beside me and lowers it to my lap. "Don't."

We spend an hour together, easily the best hour of my life. Camp shares hilarious band stories that make me laugh so hard I'm glad it wasn't a rib I bruised. It turns out Nate is famously clumsy, which gives me a soft spot for him. I've decided he's really just a cranky teddy bear. Camp avoids mentioning the rodeo, except for asking me a million times if I'm okay.

Before he leaves, he gives my hand a gentle squeeze, then traces his thumb along my chin. My lower abdomen buzzes.

"Your mom invited us over for a barbecue on Friday. Do you think you'll be up to it?"

"Definitely," I reply, my heart doing backflips.

He gazes into my eyes, his grin accentuating the stubble on his chin. "See you in a few days, then." He stands to leave.

"Oh, and Lavender?"

"Yeah?"

"Thanks for letting me see you. I've sure missed lookin' into those violet eyes."

I stop breathing as I watch him walk away.

"Hey, man," Kalendar's voice drifts in from the hallway, lowering into a whisper that makes it hard to catch their conversation. I hold my breath, straining to listen. "Get him" are the only words that stand out clearly. Then, "Anyway, it was good seeing you. I'll catch you Friday."

The front door clicks shut.

Kalendar walks into the family room.

"What was that about?" I cross my arms.

"Nothing. Just catching up. He's a good dude, Camp."

"Yeah." I narrow my eyes on him. "Kal, please let it be. I don't know what you and Camp were discussing, but—"

"Ender, don't worry. The past is the past," he interrupts me.

There's a knock at the door.

"On it," Mom shouts from the kitchen.

I look at Kalendar, and he shrugs. "Maybe your boyfriend's back."

"He's not my boyfriend," I say, unable to stop the smile that starts to form.

"Lavender, Emma's here for you," Mom peeks from the hallway, her eyebrows arched.

Kalendar straightens and rubs the back of his neck.

I clear my throat. "You can let her in."

"I have laundry to do," Kalendar says as he sprints up the stairs. He's never done laundry in the seventeen years I've known him.

Seconds later, Emma taps on the entryway to the family room. "Hey," she says, her voice quiet as she grips the wood frame tightly. "Can I join you?"

I nod and smile, making room next to me on the couch.

Emma sits and peeks at me. She clasps her hands together, squeezing them tight. "So, how are you feeling? I was so worried when I heard …" Her voice trails off as her eyes sweep my face.

"I'm fine. It looks worse than it feels," I sigh.

"Oh, it's not that bad."

I give her a sidelong glance, and we both laugh.

"I mean, at least it's not forever. And you're still beautiful," she says.

"Thanks, Em." I put my arm around her. Her eyes light up, and she smiles wide, resting her head on my shoulder.

"I've missed you," she says.

"I've missed you too."

"Lavender, I'm so sorry about Kalendar. I—"

"Don't. Let's put that behind us," I interrupt.

Camp's guitar suddenly drifts in through the window, carrying the "With a Little Help from My Friends" melody by The Beatles. I try to swallow my laugh. Unsuccessfully.

"What's funny?" Emma giggles.

"You can't hear any music right now, can you?"

She glances around the room, eyes narrowing. "No, should I?"

I laugh, "No, never mind."

She cocks her head, amusement sparkling in her eyes. "So, what's this I hear about you and the hot singer of that band? I saw him leaving on my way in."

I look at her, startled. *How does she know?* Maybe Aly and Sofia? I saw them eyeing us at the rodeo before the incident. Anyway, I don't care. I'm excited to talk to someone about him finally.

"Eek! Oh my gosh, Em. I think he might like me."

"Tell me more!" Her eyes are stars. "I *knew* he was into you when he couldn't stop staring at you during the concert."

I fill Emma in on everything: the band, the midnight gatherings, the fireflies, the deer, Josephine, and, of course, Camp. She listens intently, asking questions here and there. When I finish, she jumps up from the couch and starts pacing.

"Lavender, this is incredible! You're going to save the world! I always knew there was something special about you."

"Oh gosh, I don't know about saving the world," I reply. "At least I'd like to make it a little better, and I actually think it might be possible." I meet her gaze. "So you don't think this is crazy?"

"Oh, it's totally crazy," Emma says without hesitation.

I laugh.

She giggles too, then her face softens. "But you're meant for this. Have you told your family yet?"

"No. You're the only one who knows other than Josephine. I'm not sure how they'll take it. I *will* tell them. Maybe leave out the fireflies."

"That's the best part!" Emma laughs. "Really, though, I think everyone will be supportive. I'm not sure they'll love you leaving the house in the middle of the night. Maybe don't do that anymore." She grips her elbows. "The last thing we need is you getting mauled by a bear."

"Yeah, the midnight rendezvous might not go over well." I pause, glancing out the window at the forest. "Though I wonder if the bears are as friendly as the deer." Emma glares at me. "Kidding." *Kind of.*

After hours of catching up, I realize how much I've missed Emma. Regret tightens my stomach as I think about all the summer memories we could've made if I hadn't clung to the silly grudge.

Kalendar enters the room as if on cue and freezes. "Sorry, I didn't know you were still here."

Emma bolts upright and tugs at her ponytail. "Well, I better go," she says, glancing in his direction.

"Emma, no. You don't have to," I say, my eyes darting between them.

"Trust me, it's for the best," she says, leaning down to wrap me in a hug. "Thanks for hanging out today and sharing your story. Can we do this again soon?" Her eyes sparkle with hope.

"Yes, of course. Thanks for visiting me. Sorry, I've been a jerk."

"No. No. I deserved it," she says quickly, stealing another glance at Kalendar.

I smile at her. "I'll walk you out."

"Thanks." She picks up her bag from the coffee table and moves toward the front of the house.

Kalendar follows us into the foyer. "It sure is good to see the two of you back together." His smile falters.

Emma half-grins in response, then leans in to kiss my cheek. "Let me know if you need anything," she whispers.

"Thanks, Em."

She walks past Kalendar to open the door, and I can't help but watch his reaction. His eyes glisten as he bites his lip, clearly struggling with something.

Maybe I misjudged them. Whatever this is, it's clearly more than a passing thing.

TWENTY-THREE

IT'S ONE OF THOSE rare mornings where I wake up smiling, a soft, buzzy warmth humming beneath my skin.

I step onto my balcony. The mountains glow in the early morning light.

The barbecue is this evening, and thankfully, the swelling in my face is nearly gone. After my doctor's visit yesterday, I might even avoid reconstructive surgery; guess he wasn't on drugs after all.

Breathing in the sweet August air, I feel so alive, like *really freaking happy* to be alive. I reach up, my fingers spreading wide as I stretch my palms toward the sky. The temperature is perfect. Cool, breezy, and not a cloud in sight.

I bounce downstairs to the kitchen. Mom and Kalendar are sitting outside on the porch; they look deep in conversation. I make myself a coffee.

Dad walks in and kisses my forehead.

"Good morning." He rests his hand on my shoulder. "You look fantastic, sweetie. Your swelling is nearly gone."

"Finally, right?" I stroke the bandage covering my nose.

Leaning against the counter, I clutch my mug with both hands; the warmth seeping into my fingers.

"What do you think they're talking about? It looks so serious." I nod toward Mom and Kalendar.

Dad turns to look at them.

"I'm not sure, honey. Kalendar's been worried about leaving you, especially since the accident. I imagine it has something to do with that."

I plunk my mug on the counter, coffee sloshing over the sides. "Why is he worried? I'm not helpless. It was just Billy Beauford being an idiot. I didn't ask to get slammed into a metal railing," I mumble, grabbing a dish rag to clean up the mess.

"Of course, you're not helpless, sweetheart. No one thinks that. Kalendar just feels like he's always been around to keep an eye on you, and since he's leaving for college next week, he wants to make sure you'll be okay."

My throat tightens. "He's leaving next week?" *How is that possible?*

"Yup, can you believe it? Freshman orientation begins on the twenty-first. The summer flew by, huh?"

"Oh," I say, lifting my mug again. With everything going on, I'd totally forgotten that Kalendar was heading off to college soon. Or maybe my subconscious had intentionally buried it.

Something doesn't feel right about him leaving. It isn't only that he's starting school and won't be living at home anymore. There's more … My thoughts drift back to the recurring dreams. I pull my phone from my pocket and search for Josephine's number.

Hey, Josephine, my fingers hover over the screen. **Could we grab coffee tomorrow? I need your take on a dream I keep having.** If anyone could untangle the cryptic threads of these nightmares, it's her.

I arrange the plates and utensils on our outdoor table, fighting the wind that's been picking up since morning. The blue-and-white checkered tablecloth flaps wildly, threatening to take off at any moment. Nearby, Jake crouches by the cooler, ice crackling as he packs it with water, seltzer, and beer.

"Shoot!" Mom says from the kitchen.

"What's wrong?" I ask her, stepping inside.

"I meant to get more ketchup." She pulls a nearly empty bottle from the fridge and gives it a shake. "I hope everyone likes mustard."

"I'll run into town and grab some," Kalendar offers, his voice traveling from the family room. He's been on his laptop all day, doing orientation stuff for college. *Ugh.*

"Would you? Thanks so much, sweetheart." Mom walks over to her purse and pulls out cash.

"No worries. Need anything else?" Kalendar strolls into the kitchen and plucks the money from her hand.

"No, that's all. Thanks again." She gives him a quick kiss. "Don't take too long; our guests will be here soon."

"Yup, be right back." He shoots me a wink, then heads out the door.

Minutes later, the doorbell chimes.

"They're here!" I check the mirror, grimacing at the huge bandage. Whatever. It'll have to do. Taking a deep breath, I hurry to the front door.

The latch clicks as I turn the knob. Anna beams at me, front and center, holding an enormous pie like a trophy. Beside her, Nate and

Camp stand with their arms full—root beer bottles clinking together, a bouquet of vibrant pink dahlias spilling over Camp's hands.

"Hey, guys!" I step aside, motioning them to come in.

Mom, Dad, and Jake materialize behind me.

"Campion, these flowers. They're gorgeous!" Mom exclaims. "And Anna, this pie … I love peach pie! And look, hun." She turns to Dad, waving at Nate. "They brought your favorite soda. Nate, how did you know?"

"Just a guess." Nate's cheeks flush.

"Thanks everyone, you shouldn't have!" Mom beams, linking arms with Anna as if they've been lifelong friends. "Come on, let's enjoy this beautiful evening outside." She leads everyone through the hallway, pausing by the floor-length windows to point something out to Anna, her tone light and bubbling.

Camp strolls beside Dad, his dimples flashing as he laughs at something Dad said. Then his gaze catches mine, and his smile deepens, sending a flutter through my chest.

"You're looking good, Lavender," Nate says, falling into step beside me.

I blink. Did Nate—compliment me? Maybe the apocalypse is coming.

Jake smirks. "You should've seen her a few days ago."

I quickly recover. "He's not wrong. This is a major improvement." I circle my nose with my finger. "But hey, thanks, Nate."

Nate is the last to step outside, sliding the screen door shut behind him, his chuckle fading into a more serious tone. "Honestly, I'm just glad you're okay."

Yup, the world must be ending.

I chat with Jake and Nate for a bit, letting their easy back-and-forth fill the space, but my mind keeps drifting toward tonight. The wind's finally settled, and I can't stop picturing how cozy a fire would feel—especially if I happened to be sitting next to a certain someone. As if he can hear the daydream buzzing in my brain, Camp glances over. His eyes meet mine and linger for a moment.

Yup, a fire it is.

Excusing myself, I gather a bundle of split aspen logs stacked neatly under the porch and walk over to the firepit on the lawn. The wood lands with a hollow thud as I drop them into the stone circle. I'm about to light the starter when my phone pings from my sweater pocket.

Josephine: Of course, we can talk about those dreams. Noon?

Noon works great, thanks. See you tomorrow. I set my phone on the arm of an Adirondack chair.

"Hey there, need a hand?" comes Camp's drawl from behind me. My heart cartwheels as I turn to face him.

"I'm almost finished, but thanks," I say, nodding toward the chairs. "Want to sit?"

"I'd love to—if you're joining me," he replies with a grin, waiting patiently as I light the fire before settling into the chair beside me.

On the porch, Jake and Nate are still talking, while Anna has my parents laughing so hard they're nearly in tears, and I can't help but giggle.

Camp joins in my amusement. "What's got you laughing?"

"Just Anna working her charm on my parents." I smile.

Camp chuckles, eyes dancing as he watches Anna wave her hands mid-story. "She's got a way with words," he says, then glances at me. His thumb brushes my jaw, slow and careful. "Your bruise is fading."

My face sparks where his touch lingers and I'm certain oxygen has suddenly abandoned the atmosphere because my lungs refuse to work.

"I think I might dodge surgery after all." I giggle-snort. *What the heck was that?* I swing my eyes away from his as heat rushes to my face.

Camp's smile slips away, replaced by a shadow of concern. "It never should've happened," he breathes.

"I'm okay. Really." I rest my hand on his knee, trying to pull him back to me.

But his stare is distant, like he's looking through me rather than at me.

I pull my hand away, running it through my hair. "Camp, what was your childhood like? I barely know anything about you." My voice is soft, curious.

That seems to bring him back. His lips twitch into a smirk. "That's on purpose." He winks before dropping his gaze to his hands.

"But really, it was great," he says with a small smile. "My parents were amazing—always loving us unconditionally. We grew up on a farm in Tennessee, me and my little sister."

"You have a sister? I love that!" I say, my mind instantly filling with images of a girl version of Camp—brown hair, hazel eyes, and a down-to-earth cowgirl energy. I wonder if she'd like me.

Camp's smile falters as he focuses on the mountains, his hands rubbing together as if he's trying to shake off a sudden chill. *Crap. What did I say wrong?*

"Had a sister," he finally says. "Her name was Jane. She and my parents were killed in a car accident a couple of years ago."

Gasping, I quickly bite my bottom lip and look up at the sky, trying to hold it together.

"Drunk driver." His voice is tight. "They were on their way home from a high school football game—my sister cheered that night." He pauses, swallowing hard. "They died instantly. If there's any comfort in it, I guess it's that they didn't feel a thing."

"I had turned eighteen and was living on my own when it happened. It wrecked me. I moved in with my grandma for six months, though most of that time is a haze. Not because I was drinking or anything—after the accident, I swore I'd never touch the stuff—but I was… numb. A ghost of myself. The only thing I remember clearly is sitting on the porch with her at night, looking up at the stars. She'd tell me the universe had a plan for me. She's always been big on that kind of thing. You'll meet her one day, she's great; refuses to leave Tenneesse, though." Camp's chuckles, sadness flickering behind his smile. "You remind me of her, my sister, Jane. You have the same spirit: passionate, funny, kind …" He trails off as he returns his gaze to the mountains.

We sit in silence, time stretching unbearably. I'm frozen—body and mind—trapped in a moment where words feel useless.

"Don't feel sorry for me. This is exactly why I didn't tell you," he says, smiling, though it never quite reaches his eyes. "I miss them every day, but I know they're together, up there in Heaven."

He fixes his gaze on me. "Until it's my time to be with them again, I'm committed to making this world better." His voice is steady. "There are so many people battling addiction, anxiety, and depression. There's always a reason behind tragedies like theirs." He tents his fingers and presses them to his lips.

"The drunk driver who killed them … his stepdad sexually assaulted him the day before the crash." Camp's face is heavy with a mix of anger and empathy. "He was just a kid, barely sixteen. I can't excuse what he did, but it's a reminder that everyone's carrying something." He pauses, his tone shifting, filled with a fierce determination. "That's why I'm so passionate about our band. We're not only making music—we're trying to change this damn world."

He looks at the sky, and I follow his gaze. A beam of sunlight breaks through the clouds, casting a warm golden glow directly over the campground. It feels like God himself is reaching out, offering a ray of hope. I hold my breath, the moment feeling sacred.

"Camp, I … I don't even know what to say," I finally whisper.

He smiles. "You don't need to say anything. I'm happy you're here with me."

Before I can think twice, I throw myself into his arms, burying my face in his shoulder. Tears spill over as I cling to him, and he pulls me in tighter, his embrace strong and reassuring. For a moment, the world fades away, and all that matters is the steady rhythm of his heartbeat against mine.

He pulls back. "Your mom's coming this way," he whispers.

I reluctantly loosen my grip and slide off Camp's lap, standing up as she approaches. Her brow furrows, eyes full of concern. "Lavender, have you heard from Kalendar?" she asks, much too breathless for the small walk it took her to get here.

"No, why?" I grab my phone from the chair. *Six o'clock.* Kalendar's been gone for nearly two hours, and it takes forty-five minutes to get to town and back. "I'm sure he ran into someone. Have you tried calling him?" My fingers tremble as I search for Kalendar's number; it rings several times before going to voicemail.

"Yes, he's not answering." She puts one hand on her hip and the other on her forehead. "I'm sure it's nothing, but…I don't know. Something doesn't feel right."

A rush of anxiety pulses through me as the horrific dreams flood my mind.

Jake strides over, a hint of urgency in his step. "Mom, I'm going to drive into town. Maybe he's stuck with the Bronco or something."

"I'll drive you," Camp says, standing up and giving my arm a squeeze. I watch them until they round the corner of the house and vanish from view.

Mom sinks into Camp's empty chair, rubbing her hands together. "Lavender, I just have this feeling …"

"Mom, I'm sure he's fine," I say, though doubt lingers in my voice.

Anna and Nate join us, their faces shadowed with concern as they settle in beside us.

"Your dad went with them," Anna says, her tone steady. "I'm sure Kalendar is fine. A handsome guy like him? He probably picked up a cutie at the supermarket." She flashes a reassuring smile, but the crease between her brows betrays the worry in her eyes.

I nod, appreciating her attempt to lighten the mood, but the knot in my stomach tightens.

Thirty agonizing minutes crawl by with no word. I'm redialing every fifteen seconds, my thumb aching from the relentless tapping, desperate to hear Kalendar answer with his usual "Ender!" But all I get is his voicemail on repeat. Anger bubbles up, irrational but fierce.

I swear, if Kal is fine, I'm NEVER talking to him again. How could he do this to us?

Mom paces the yard, her deep breathing techniques failing to calm her.

Nate's phone buzzes, and he glances at it before saying, "I'll be right back." I watch him walk toward the house, running a hand through his long hair as he answers.

"That's it. Let's go to town. I can't understand why we haven't heard anything," Mom announces, frustrated.

Just then, her phone rings on the side table next to me. Dad's name flashes on the screen. I snatch it up and pass it to her, and she grabs it with trembling hands.

"Hun? Please tell me you found him," she pleads, her voice breaking.

Her fingers grip the phone tight as her face collapses. A piercing scream rips through the air, and she sinks to her knees, the phone slipping from her hand and landing with a soft thud in the grass.

TWENTY-FOUR

I LUNGE FOR Mom's phone, my heart racing. "Dad? Dad, it's me!" My voice cracks as I press it to my ear.

"Lavender? Listen." Dad's tone is strained. "Kalendar's been shot. He's in the emergency room in Mason." He pauses, his breath shaky. "You guys need to go to the hospital. Camp is driving us now."

"What happened?" The trees spin around me. I collapse onto my back, struggling to breathe as my eyes squeeze shut.

Dad's silence stretches painfully before he responds, his voice breaking. "Someone shot him in the parking lot of the market. I don't know more than that. Please get here with Mom. Have Nate or Anna drive you."

The phone feels impossibly heavy in my hand. Tears spill down my cheeks, disappearing into the grass beneath me. "Okay," I whisper.

Mom crumples against Anna, her sobs shaking both of them. I crawl over to them, taking fistfuls of grass along with me. Gently, we lower Mom to the ground. I kneel in front of her, cradling her tear-streaked face in my hands. "Mom, we need to go to the hospital. We have to—" The earth drops beneath me as words escape me. I can't think, I can't move, I can't … I can't …

Mom's grip tightens around my hand, yanking me from the abyss. "Let's go," she says, her soggy eyes burning with an unexpected resolve.

Nate rushes over, breathless. "I talked to Camp. Can we take one of your cars? He has ours."

"Take mine," Mom says, helping me to my feet.

"Where are your keys?" Anna shouts as she dashes toward the house.

"In the kitchen drawer, next to the oven."

The car's suddenly in front of us, though I don't even remember the walk here. Nate slides into the driver's seat as Mom and I tumble into the rear.

The silence is thick, suffocating.

"Nate, can you put on music?" My voice trembles.

"Sure, what do you want to—"

"Anything. I just need something."

Zach Bryan's voice fills the car, and as the first lyric hits, I realize I'll never be able to listen to him again without thinking of this moment. My mind spirals as we drive into town. Who could've done this to Kalendar? He's loved by everyone—he doesn't have enemies. Could it have been a random robbery? No, not here in Rosewood.

Then, a memory flashes—Camp and Kalendar whispering the other day. I distinctly remember hearing the words, *get him*.

Billy.

Is this *my* fault? My stomach twists, bile burning in my throat.

The town center appears as if it's been ripped from the set of a crime drama—police cars and flashing lights bathe the streets in an eerie red glow. Police have cordoned off the grocery store with yellow tape and a fire truck and squad cars block the entrance. I glimpse our Bronco, its driver's door hangs open, and two ketchup containers lie on the ground.

I'm gonna be sick.

"Nate, pull over!" I gasp.

The car maneuvers to the side of the road, and I throw myself out, doubling over as I retch into the grass. Mom is behind me, silently holding my hair back, while Anna rushes over with tissues.

"Thanks," I mumble, wiping my mouth, the acidic taste clinging to my throat. "I'm okay," I say, though the words feel hollow as I slide into the car, the stench of vomit thick around me.

The car moves on as I press my nails into my arm, hoping the sharp sting will snap me out of this nightmare, but the crescent marks left on my skin tell me it's all too real.

Nate glances over his shoulder. "You two head inside. I'll park and meet you in a minute."

Mom nods next to me.

A siren wails faintly as I look out the window, my eyes landing on the emergency room entrance. *How are we here already?*

Anna is at my door, reaching in to help. My body feels like it's weighed down with sand. I force my legs to move, dragging them out of the car and leaning against the side while I wait for Mom.

The twenty feet to the automatic doors stretch out like an endless mile. I shuffle behind Mom and Anna, my eyes locked on Anna's pink Converses as they blur in and out of focus with each step. Sweat clings to my skin, and a high-pitched ringing fills my ears. The world around me begins to fade, slipping away …

Suddenly, muscular arms steady my wobbling frame.

"Hey, just breathe," Camp murmurs.

"Where is he?" I whisper.

"Kalendar's in the emergency room. Jake and your dad are with him. Let's see if we can get you back there, too."

I lean into Camp, letting him be my legs, eyes, and ears as we navigate the waiting area. He lowers me into a seat beside Mom and heads straight for the reception desk.

Anna hovers protectively over us.

"Mom, Lavender!" Jake's voice slices through the fog. He jogs over, his eyes swollen but dry.

"Jake! Where's Kalendar?" Mom throws herself into his arms.

"He's in critical condition," Jake says, holding Mom close as his eyes meet mine.

"What happened?" I barely recognize the sound of my own voice.

"Someone shot him twice in the abdomen. The police are investigating. They have a suspect in custody, but they're not releasing any names or motives yet."

"Can we see him?" Mom and I ask at the same time.

"Not yet," Jake replies. "He's in surgery. The doctor said it could be a couple of hours."

"Why surgery?" Panic surges in my chest.

"They need to remove the bullets and make sure they didn't hit any major organs," Jake says, his eyes glistening.

"Where's Dad?" I scan the room.

"Talking to the police. He'll be out soon."

Time crawls—hours or maybe just minutes pass; it's impossible to tell. I clasp Mom's clammy, trembling hand in mine.

Camp sits on my other side, his hand resting on my thigh. I lock my gaze on the ER entrance, tracking the steady stream of people coming and going. None of them seem to be dying. Why are they here and taking up precious resources? Don't they understand my brother IS FIGHTING FOR HIS LIFE?

The ER doors creak open, and Dad steps through, his gaze searching.

"Dad!" I rise to my feet, my hands trembling as he meets my eyes with a tired, but grateful, smile.

"Hey," he says as I hug him tight.

"Any news?" My voice is barely above a whisper.

"No." He glances at his watch. "But we should hear from the doc soon."

"Were you with the police?"

"Yeah." He rubs a hand through his blonde hair. "They were asking questions about Kalendar. I get the sense they're close to identifying the shooter."

"What makes you say that?"

"I just think they know more than they're letting on." He kisses my forehead before crouching beside Mom.

I plop in my seat and lean in toward Camp. "When you visited the other day, I overheard you talking to Kal. You weren't planning on getting back at Billy, were you?"

He exhales slowly. "Kalendar wanted to have *a talk* with him, but I convinced him it wasn't worth it."

My heart races.

Camp's jaw tightens. "You don't think Kalendar confronted him, do you? We promised each other we'd let it go."

I stare at the ER doors. "Kal doesn't let things go, especially when it comes to protecting me." I cross my arms tightly over my chest, feeling a guilt spiral pulling me under.

TWENTY-FIVE

THE GLOSSY PAGES of *Rolling Stone* flip by, untouched by my gaze, each turn feeding my frustration. My leg bounces uncontrollably, my crossed foot a blur that intensifies with each impatient shake. *Why the ef is this taking so long?*

Camp, Anna, and Nate left to pick up dinner, insisting we eat something.

Jake sits next to me. One earbud in; arms folded.

Dad clears his throat, and I look up to see two doctors in white coats and surgical caps approaching. My heart lurches as I grab Jake's hand, and we exchange a tense glance before standing, my legs shaky beneath me. Mom and Dad stay seated, their expressions a weary mix of hope and dread.

"Hello," one doctor starts, his gaze kind as he looks at us. "I'm Dr. Larson, Chief of General Surgery and this is Dr. Jeffries, Chief of Neuro."

Neuro?

"We finished surgery on Kalendar." Dr. Larson clasps his hands together. "We removed a bullet from Kalendar's abdomen successfully. The other passed right through. Fortunately, his organs are intact, though he lost a lot of blood. We had to give him a transfusion, but we expect him to make a full recovery from the gunshot wounds."

"Thank you, God!" I squeal, bouncing with relief. I turn to Jake, my excitement bubbling over, but his eyes are downcast, his brows furrowed. My stomach drops as I look at the doctor, who now wears a heavy expression.

Oh no, there's more.

"I'll let Dr. Jeffries take over from here," Dr. Larson says softly.

Dr. Jeffries removes his cap and folds it in his hands as he steps forward. His warm brown eyes shift between us before he clears his throat. "Unfortunately, when Kalendar collapsed from the gunshot wounds, he struck his head on the edge of a parking curb, resulting in a traumatic brain injury. A CT scan revealed intracranial bleeding. We performed an emergency craniectomy to relieve the pressure on his brain, but… he has yet to regain consciousness."

He pauses, letting the words settle.

"At this point, Kalendar is in a coma. The next few weeks will be crucial."

A piercing ring fills my ears as I try to speak to Dad. The sound sharpens, growing louder until it drowns everything else out.

And then—

Nothing.

Just black.

When I come to, my eyelids flutter open, squinting against a harsh, unforgiving brightness. Blurry shapes hover above me—familiar faces. My family. The light stabs at my eyes, and I squeeze them shut again.

Mom's soft voice pulls me back. "Lavender, babe? You fainted. You're okay, we're here."

I force my eyes open again. Worry lines and furrowed brows stare down at me.

"Huh?" I mumble, trying to sit up.

"No, hold on. A nurse went to get you a gurney." Jake rests his hand on my shoulder.

"A gurney? No. I'm fine. Cancel it," I say, swatting at the air.

Dad brushes his finger along my cheek. "I'm sure you are, love. They want to make certain since you're still healing from the accident."

I roll my eyes but stay put on the ground, trying *really* hard not to think of all the bodily fluids cemented into the carpet beneath me.

"Can we see Kalendar?" I ask, the nightmare of this situation crashing back down on me.

"Yes, they're moving him to his room now," Dad says, his eyes shifting to somewhere beyond me.

"Did the doctor say anything else? You know, after my dramatic fainting episode?" I stammer, hoping for good news.

"He said the best thing we can do is talk to Kal," Jake replies. "Apparently, people in comas wake up more often when their family talks to them and plays their favorite music." His eyes brighten. "We should take shifts, so someone's always with him."

I smile at Jake's enthusiasm.

The squeak of rickety wheels grates against my ears, growing louder as a gurney glides closer. From my miserable position on the floor, I can do nothing but watch.

"Do I have to do this? I want to see Kalendar." I groan.

"Let's make sure you're okay," Dad says, taking my elbow to help me up. "I'll come with you."

"No, Dad. You need to be with Kalendar," I insist.

"Mom and Jake will go first. I'm not leaving you alone." Dad's voice has that unmistakable tone that means there's no arguing.

With a heavy sigh, I allow Dad and two male nurses to guide me onto the gurney, and for the first time since my fainting spell, I see beyond the waiting room lights and my family's concerned expressions. Naturally, the space is full of people and *everyone* is staring at me. *Wonderful.* One nurse adjusts the arms of the stretcher, and we roll toward the elevator. Dad's holding my hand tight as he walks next to me.

My heart pounds as I try to keep my anxiety in check. *Come on, Kal, please wake up.* I whisper the words like a mantra, hoping it'll reach him.

The ceiling foam tiles of my hospital room are yellowing at the corners. *Ugh, this place.*

Thankfully, after a battery of tests and scans, the verdict is clear: I am totally and completely fine. They'd kept me overnight to double-check that my fainting spell wasn't a sequel to my recent head injury. Spoiler alert: it wasn't. Check done. Now get me the heck outta here.

Jake's asleep on a chair in the corner. His trucker hat covers his face, his arms cross over his chest, and his long legs sprawl out in front of him. He's my ticket out.

I shimmy up to a sitting position, cautiously avoiding the wires sprouting from my arms. I'm even more careful to avoid looking at the IV needle embedded in my hand—no need for a repeat fainting spell.

"Pst, Jake!" I loud-whisper, not entirely sure why. It's not as if a swarm of nurses will burst in if I wake my brother. But still, they'll ask a million questions, make me fill out endless discharge papers, and honestly, all I want is to be with Kalendar. Right. Freaking. Now.

Jake turns his head, causing his hat to fall to the floor, and settles back into sleep. *Ugh.*

The door opens, and in pops Mom. "Oh, thank goodness. Can you please get me out of here, Mom?" She doesn't look great—her clothes are crumpled, and her eyes are sunken—but she manages a smile for my sake.

"Hi, hun. How are you feeling this morning?"

"I'm fine. I *need* to see Kal. Please?"

"Actually, yes. The nurses are getting your discharge papers ready, but they said you can visit Kalendar in the meantime. Let me unclip your IV here." She wrestles with my octopus wires as I turn my head and hum the theme to *The Office* as a distraction.

"Done. Let's get you up." Mom takes my arm and helps me stand. Her eyes catch the five brown bags on my side table. "What's that from?" She nods to them.

"Oh, Camp. Anna and Nate came by with an eighteen-course meal late last night. The nurse wouldn't let them in, but she brought the food. Jake ate most of it, though I have no idea how he fits it all in that skinny body of his."

She laughs. "That was nice of them."

"It was. Sorry, Jake tried to call you, but I think you guys might have been sleeping."

Her face falls slightly before she forces a smile. "We attempted to; it was a long night. Kalendar's room isn't the most comfortable." She glances at Jake. "Then again, I guess no hospital room is."

"Anyway, are you ready?" Her tone is gentle.

A lump the size of a golf ball forms in my throat. Nodding, I head toward the door but pause, turning back to Jake. "Should we wake him?"

"Let's let him sleep for a bit longer."

We ride the elevator up to the ICU, each floor passing like a countdown. After a few minutes of walking, Mom stops in front of room 242. I take a deep breath and step inside. Dad is sitting beside Kalendar, his face breaking into a smile as he rises and gestures for me to take the chair.

I ease into it and reach for Kalendar's hand. It's cool and unresponsive.

"We'll give you some time," Mom whispers as she and Dad close the door behind them.

Kalendar's tethered to a web of medical devices, his head swathed in bandages, but he looks as though he's just asleep. I squeeze his hand three times. "I love you, Kal. Please wake up." My voice trembles as tears blur my vision.

I place my other hand on his chest, feeling the slow, fragile rise and fall beneath my palm. If love and hope could transfer through skin, I'd be blasting him with enough of it to light up all of Colorado right now. "Kal, I need you. I can't do this life without you." My voice breaks.

Time dissolves around me; I don't know how long I sit there, clinging to his stillness, desperately willing him back.

Eventually, the door creaks open, and I barely register the sound until Dad walks in. He moves quietly, crossing the room with heavy, slow steps. Without a word, he rests his hands on my shoulders, his touch gentle but grounding, trying to offer comfort where words fail.

"Has Dr. Jeffries given any updates?" I ask, my eyes fixed on Kalendar.

"No, there's nothing new yet. We're just waiting," he replies, walking to the other side of the bed and taking Kalendar's free hand in his own. "Come on, bud. Wake up, son," he whispers.

"Dad, we *just* lost Grandpa. How is this fair?" My voice shakes, frustration bubbling beneath my grief.

Dad exhales, his shoulders heavy. "I know, sweetheart. Sometimes life doesn't make sense." He looks at me, his eyes rimmed with red. "But you know what? It gives me some comfort knowing Grandpa's up there. He won't let Kalendar leave us—not yet." A small, weary chuckle escapes him. "I can just picture him arguing with the angels, refusing to take no for an answer."

A tear slips down my cheek, but I smile. "Yeah. That sounds like him."

We both glance up at the sound of a quiet knock. Jake's face appears in the window, and Dad motions for him to come in.

Jake opens the door, holding his phone. "Dad, we need to get to the police station. They have news for us."

TWENTY-SIX

HOW DID IT COME to this? Is the world so broken that my brother can't go to the grocery store WITHOUT GETTING FREAKING SHOT?

My fists clench so hard that a tremor runs through my arms, but I keep them at my sides, trying to appear in control.

Passing under the rustic wooden Rosewood Police Department sign, I march straight to the reception desk with Dad and Jake close behind.

An older lady with gray hair and round glasses greets me; her expression softens when her eyes meet mine as if she's been awaiting our arrival.

"We're the Flynn family. Sheriff Ludlow wanted to see us." I'm trying to sound confident, but it comes out way too harsh. "Uh, sorry." I tug at my necklace. "We came as soon as he called."

"Of course, dear. Let me get him for you." The older woman rises, reaching for a cane beside her desk. *Great. A-hole of the year, right here.*

She hobbles over to us, her eyes glistening. "I'm so sorry about your brother," she says, extending her wrinkled hand to mine. Her skin is soft, fragile, and her handshake is air. "I'll pray for him," she adds, her voice shaky.

"Thank you," I reply faintly.

"Can I help?" Jake offers from behind me.

"No, dear. Thank you. The doctor says I need to move every hour, anyway." She winks at us and then slowly moves through the hallway.

Moments later, Sheriff Ludlow steps into view, his expression soft and his movements unhurried. He offers a small, sympathetic smile. "Please follow me," he says, leading us through a short hallway into a small conference room.

The room smells of stale coffee and dry-erase markers. My eyes drift to the whiteboard, where someone hastily erased writing, leaving ghostly smudges of Kalendar's name. Six black roller chairs look comically huge against a tiny rectangular table.

Dad and Jake sit, clasping their hands together and resting them on the faux wood surface. Jake's jaw tightens, and Dad taps his foot steadily. I catch myself picking at my cuticles. One begins to bleed. I press it against my jeans before taking a seat beside them.

Sheriff Ludlow clicks the door shut behind him, the sound echoing. He sits across from us, tenting his fingers on the table. His eyes meet ours, somber and steady.

Mom stayed with Kalendar. Considering the look on Sheriff Ludlow's face, it's probably for the best that she's not here.

"We have identified Billy Beauford as the man who shot Kalendar," he begins, his voice even. "He confessed last night. Frankly, he didn't have much of a choice. We have nine witnesses who saw him."

The room swirls, and a high-pitched ring fills my ears. *Not again.* I drop my head between my knees to steady my breathing. Dad's hand rubs slow circles on my back. "Are you okay, sweetheart?"

No.

Sweat trickles down my forehead onto the threadbare carpet inches below me.

"We know Billy." Dad clears his throat. "But why? Why would he shoot my son?"

Shoot my son. The words make me sick. My skin burns, my chest clenches. Blood rushes to my head as I stare at Dad's brown boots—solid, still.

"The shooter claims it was self-defense. He says Kalendar was about to attack him."

"No way!" I exclaim, jolting upright. "Sorry, Sheriff, but that's ridiculous. Kalendar wouldn't hurt a fly." The room spins around me and I grip the table to steady myself.

Dad places a hand on my shoulder. "Yes, Sheriff, that's simply not in Kalendar's nature. He'd never attack anyone."

Jake clears his throat. "Well ..."

We turn toward him.

"Jake? Do you know something we don't?" Dad's words come fast, his blue eyes narrow.

Jake rubs a hand down his face but says nothing. He looks up at the sheriff and then fixes his eyes on the table.

"Jake?" I whisper, leaning in closer.

He raises his hands in surrender. "It's just… I wouldn't blame him if he did. Billy could've killed Lavender at the rodeo. What if she snapped her neck?"

I stare at him, incredulous. "And so what? Kal throws his life away for me? When I'm totally *fine*?"

Jake shakes his head. "No. There's no way Kalendar would've known Billy had a gun. And he wouldn't have, like, killed Billy or anything—just roughed him up a little."

"Excuse me," I whisper, as I push to my feet. Stumbling out of the conference room, I make it halfway down the hall before the dizziness hits again. I press a palm to the wall, breathing deeply.

The familiar drag of Jake's boots syncs with the rise and fall of my breath.

I rest my forehead against the wall beside my hand, the surface cool against my skin. "Jake, please leave me alone."

"Lavender, this isn't your fault. I know you're blaming yourself, but it's not." He steps closer and wraps his arms around me. I collapse into him, letting the tears flow.

It is, though. It's my *fucking* fault.

The drive home from the police station is quiet. Dad, Jake, and I each lost in our own spirals. My particular spiral consists of all the what-ifs.

What if I'd gone to get popcorn with the guys?

What if we'd never gone to the rodeo?

What if I'd never met the band?

Exhaustion hangs on me, heavier than ever as we pull into our driveway, yet all I want—*need*—is to get back to the hospital. Back to Kalendar.

Jake drops Dad and me off at the house before circling to the garage.

The warm scent of a home-cooked meal wraps around us as we step inside.

I stop in the doorway, unblinking at the scene before me.

Flowers spill over every surface of the kitchen—pinks, reds, whites—so many, they blur together against the white marble. It's suffocating and beautiful at the same time. On the counter, a card the size of a movie poster waits, like the centerpiece of this vigil.

Dad's eyes glisten as he passes the card to me. It's heavier than I expect, almost slipping through my hands. My knees buckle as I kneel, trying to steady it. On the front, a hand-painted heart, wrapped in a white bandage. Lacey's work. My throat tightens as I open it to a flood of handwritten notes, but the words swim and fat, hot tears spill over, blurring the ink. I pass it to Dad. I can't read any of this. Not yet.

I shuffle over to the refrigerator and swing open the door. Rows of neatly stacked containers greet me, each labeled with ingredients and reheat instructions.

The mudroom door creaks and Jake steps in, his eyes widening before he lets out a low whistle. "Wow."

"You can say that again," Dad agrees.

Emma's ringtone pierces through the kitchen, startling me. I mutter a curse under my breath—guess I'm a girl who swears now. How have I not called her yet? My hands fumble through my bag, desperate, until my fingers close around my phone.

"Hey, Em."

"Lavender!" Her voice is frantic. "How's he doing? Any updates?"

"What have you heard? I'm sorry I didn't call you."

"It's okay," she whispers. "I can't imagine what you're going through. I heard Kalendar was … shot and that he's in a coma."

"Yeah. We just got back from the police station, but I'm headed to the hospital soon. Want to come?"

A hesitation then, "Yes. I'll drive. You must be exhausted."

"That'd be amazing," I say, the words coming out on an exhale. "Thanks. See you soon."

"Is Emma going with you?" Jake asks after I hang up.

"She is."

"Kalendar would love that you two are friends again," he says, a faint smile on his lips.

"He would," I say, then clear my throat. "I mean… he will."

I climb the stairs to my bedroom. As I undress, a slip of paper flutters from my jeans pocket. Camp's note. The nurse had given it to me last night when she delivered the food and I'd forgotten all about it. I pick it up and smooth out the crumpled edges: *Call me for anything. XO Camp.* His number, scrawled in boyish handwriting, stares up at me. I hover over my phone, torn between needing him and not wanting to talk to anyone other than Emma and my family. With a sigh, I drop the note beside the bracelets and the crystal heart on my dresser.

TWENTY-SEVEN

THE DAYS BLEND into each other, two weeks passing in an indistinct haze. I spend nearly all my time in the hospital, at Kalendar's bedside. He remains unconscious. Each day, the doctors seem less hopeful.

Camp and Anna call often, checking in. Nate even tried once. I've yet to call them back. They've tried to visit a few times, but I always get Dad or Jake to turn them away. They do it reluctantly, making excuses and whispering apologies. I know I'm being a jerk, but I'm in such a dark place that I can't bring myself to face them.

Mom keeps pushing me to reach out to Josephine, suggesting I go to one of her meditation classes to clear my head. She's tried to get in touch, but I've ignored her messages as well.

Jake missed his first week at UCLA. Mom and Dad tried persuading him to return to school, but we all know it's pointless. California might as well be another planet—he's not leaving. Not until Kalendar wakes up.

It's Friday. Or Sunday. Whatever. The wind is fierce as I sit on the back porch, watching a storm roll in. Rain falls in ghostly sheets miles away, dark clouds flash with light, and the rumble of thunder grows louder. I pull my hoodie over my head and loop my thumbs through the holes for warmth. One of Mom's hundred thousand throw pillows flies off the porch and lands on the lawn below. I watch it twirl across the grass like a tumbleweed, heading toward the cliff.

"*Ahem.*" Mom's frustrated voice cuts through from behind me. I don't bother turning around. She lets Bruce out, and he hurries down the stairs, rescuing the pillow from its death.

Her lavender scent fills the air as she plops in the cushioned deck chair beside me, her hair pulled in a tight bun. She's dressed in her yoga clothes.

Unbelievably, Mom and Dad are holding it together. They visit Kalendar daily, but still stick to their regular routines. I don't get it. All I'm capable of doing is sitting with Kalendar and mourning his situation. I guess everyone handles grief differently, but it makes me want TO SCREAM.

"I'm taking a trip to Sedona," she states matter-of-factly.

I look at her. "What?"

She crosses her arms. "You heard me. I'm going to Sedona, and I think you should come with me."

I raise an eyebrow and stare at her, my eyes wide in disbelief. Thunder rumbles in the distance.

"Mom, how could you possibly go on vacation right now? With Kalendar ..."

"It's not a vacation," she interrupts me. "I need healing and spiritual guidance. Sedona is the only place that will do that for me."

Mom visited Sedona after her mom died years ago. She was gone for nearly a month and returned a new person, refreshed and at peace.

"I can't go. I can't leave Kalendar," I mutter, the frustration simmering.

"I'm leaving on Monday. That gives you two days to decide. I really think this would be good for you, Lavender." She uncrosses her arms and leans in closer. "Honestly, I'm having trouble recognizing who you are these days. You're so angry. I know how scared you are. We're *all* scared. But I don't want you to lose sight of the beautiful person you are inside and out."

"And also, I'd miss my first week of school ..." I add, ignoring her. Even though I have no intention of actually going.

She stands up and plants a firm kiss on my head. "You have two days to decide," she repeats, then walks away. "And please come inside soon. The storm looks pretty bad." She slides the door shut behind her with a solid click.

A lightning bolt strikes one of the mountain peaks, its jagged line illuminating the sky. Suddenly, torrential rain pounds the metal roof above me. My hair is whipping around, getting tangled and slapping me in the face.

Had I changed that much? And so what if I have? MY BROTHER IS IN A COMA. Also, how can she leave Kalendar, even for a few days? She's lost her mind. I can't go to Sedona. I can't leave him.

The lanterns swing wildly in the trees above the campsite, their light flickering bright against the stormy sky. All at once, I want to be with the band. I want to laugh with Anna, be in Camp's calming presence, and even hang with Nate. I miss them. I miss when life was simple, when the most annoying part of my day was Kalendar's dramatic eye roll whenever I left to hang with them. Lord, I miss that eye roll.

As if reading my mind, Camp's guitar chords drift out of the forest, filling my ears. It's "The Night We Met" by Lord Huron. My breath catches at the hauntingly beautiful melody. It's been weeks since I last heard his music, and my heart aches at realizing how much I miss it.

Another sound joins the storm's cacophony, loud and rhythmic. It's not thunder. *What is—*

A gasp sounds from behind me. I turn to see Mom in the doorframe. Following her gaze back to the mountains, my jaw drops—hundreds of crows soar toward us from the forest. They glide serenely through the airwaves as if dancing to the rhythm of Camp's guitar.

As they near, they elegantly settle among the aspen trees encircling our home. Their feathers shake with the wind gusts.

I face Mom. "What's happening?" I shout over the noise.

She smiles and shrugs, completely unfazed by the mob of birds.

Camp's guitar riff intensifies, becoming impossibly loud. I glance back toward the campsite. The lanterns appear brighter now, like little suns strung from the trees, swaying in sync with the wind.

"Can you hear any music?" I yell into the electric air.

"Music?" she shouts back, a wide grin on her face. "No."

I look at the crows above, and to my surprise, every one of them is staring at me, with impossible but unmistakable smiles.

The next morning, I leave for the hospital right after sunrise, the sky still painted in shades of pink and gray. On the way, I stop at the coffee shop and pick up a box of blueberry muffins for the nurses—something small, but it makes me feel useful. The halls of the ICU are quieter than usual. I've grown to hate the quiet—it gives my thoughts too much room to roam, and they never wander anywhere good. Shame, doubt, what-ifs—they all come rushing in when there's nothing to drown them out.

I slip into Kalendar's room and sink into the chair beside him, my fingers finding his without thinking. I start talking like always, filling the room with words meant for both of us. He would've gotten such a kick out of last night's crow spectacle.

A few minutes later, Emma steps in. She doesn't say anything right away—just comes behind me and gives my shoulders a gentle squeeze.

"Morning, Em," I say with a small smile. Emma's been my rock these past two weeks. She's the only person I talk to, the only one who gets what I'm going through outside of my family. Though after last night's conversation with Mom, I'm not even sure they get me anymore.

She settles on the other side of Kalendar and pulls out her phone, cuing up his Spotify playlist.

"I brought muffins." I nod toward the pastry box on the counter.

"Yum, thanks."

The music fills the room. Kalendar's favorite band, Dispatch, sings of wild ones. Emma nervously adjusts her shirt, her gaze flitting between me and the floor. She opens her mouth like she's about to say something, then shuts it, biting her lip.

"What is it, Em?"

She coughs. "So I spoke to your mom last night."

Great, here it is.

"She told me about the crows. Incredible. Have you ever seen anything like that before?"

Smiling, I shake my head, relieved it's not about Sedona. "No. Isn't it wild? I was just telling Kal about them. I wish you could've seen it. It's like they were trying to tell us something," I reply, my voice escalating.

"Maybe they were," Emma responds.

My thoughts drift back to last night. The experience felt unreal. The crows hung around for several minutes before leaving; their eyes were fixed on me the whole time. At first, I panicked, thinking they were a bad omen. But later, I searched online and found that yes, they can symbolize death, but also rebirth. I'm counting on the latter.

Emma clears her throat. "Also," she begins, "your mom mentioned she's taking a trip to Sedona. I think that's really great." She pauses, her eyes meeting mine.

"Yup. She told me that too. You should go with her. I'm sure she'd love the company," I reply stubbornly.

A V forms in Emma's forehead. "Well, actually, I was thinking it might be nice for you to get away," she says carefully.

ARGH! Do they think I'm that dumb? Obviously, Mom put her up to this. I open my mouth, ready to share my not-so-kind feelings when—

"Listen, Lavender. It's simply not healthy for you to sit here, day after day, next to Kalendar, while he's in this state. He wouldn't want this for you—you know that." Her tone is borderline bossy, the Emma I once knew flickering to life. Not the one who's been walking on eggshells since the whole mess with the love affair, but the fiery, unfiltered friend from before. And actually, I'm glad about it. I rest my chin in my hand to cover a smile.

"I promise you, I'll visit with Kalendar every day while you're gone, and if anything at all happens, I'll call you." She sits straight, shoulders no longer hunched.

My gaze falls on Kalendar. His breathing tubes remain the same, just as they'd been during my previous visit and every time before that. The steady beeping of his heart monitor echoes in the background, a constant reassurance that I haven't lost him—not yet.

"Ender, get outta here," Kalendar would say if he were awake. I smile at the thought.

"I'll think about it." I say with a side-eye.

She smiles, clearly happy with my answer, then suddenly gasps. "Kalendar!" she yells.

"What? What happened?"

"His eyes! They moved!"

"Like he opened his eyes?"

"No, but I saw them move under his eyelids! Have you seen that before?"

"No!" I squeeze his hand harder. "Do it again, Kal," I plead.

I stare at his eyes, and in an instant, they shift. My heart explodes as I ring the bell for the nurses.

Three of them come rushing in. "What's wrong?" they ask, gently moving us aside to get to Kalendar.

"His eyes, they moved!" I say, catching my breath.

"Twice!" Emma adds.

The nurses manually open Kalendar's eyes and shine a small flashlight on his eyeballs. While Emma and I hold hands in the corner of the room, they murmur to each other, running through a quiet checklist of tests.

Nurse Kate makes her way over; her kind eyes meet ours. "It's not uncommon," she says. "Involuntary movements like this can occur in a coma. It doesn't mean he's waking up—not yet—but I'll call the doctor to check, just to be sure."

"It's got to be a good sign, though. Right?"

"It's certainly not a bad sign," she answers warmly.

Dr. Jeffries arrives minutes later and performs the same tests as the nurses. He comes to the same conclusion. Nevertheless, I'm re-energized with hope.

I call Mom, Dad, and Jake to fill them in. They arrive within the hour, and we all gather around Kalendar, holding hands as we say a quiet prayer. The doctors might not think the eye movement means much, but to us, it's everything—a small sign that he's still fighting.

Dad insists I get fresh air and promises he'll call if Kalendar moves again. I'm hesitant at first, but eventually agree. Emma says she'll come with me.

We decide on the lake, though apparently, everyone within a ten-mile radius had the same idea. After my tenth lap around the parking lot, I'm about ready to give up when someone backs out of a spot right by the entrance. "Thanks, Kal," I whisper.

Paddleboards and kayaks glide across the calm water while families barbecue and play games on the lawn. I spot a dark cloud not far in the distance and lean into the back seat to grab an umbrella, just in case.

"I can't believe tomorrow is September 1," Emma says as we hop out of Betty.

"Yeah, I know. We're heading into Kal's favorite time of year."

The gravel crunches under our sandals as we walk toward the path leading to the beach.

A wave of nostalgia sneaks up on me, bringing back autumn adventures with Kalendar. He'd always plan fun road trips across Colorado on weekends, on a hunt for the brightest, most colorful leaves. He was obsessed with the golden aspens. Some of my best memories are from those trips—camping, getting lost, building fires, and talking for hours.

One October, Mom surprised him with a trip east to visit family in New England. After seeing the foliage there, I didn't think he'd ever leave.

"Remember that Halloween where he dressed up as Santa Claus and had to spend the entire evening listening to little kids' Christmas lists?" Emma giggles. "He handled it so well."

"Oh my gosh, yes! We were his elves! How did he talk us into that one?"

"Kalendar is great at getting what he wants." Emma sighs.

"He sure is."

"Shoot," Emma says, lifting her hand as rain drizzles. "Should we head to the car?"

The sky is darkening, with clouds swirling and thickening into a bruised purple. My hair swirls with the breeze, and nearby families rush to gather up their chairs and picnic blankets as the drizzle turns into fat raindrops.

"Yeah, let's go."

Emma turns toward the car, then gasps and quickly spins me so I'm facing her.

"What is—"

"Camp's here!" She loud-whispers, gripping my arms.

My stomach somersaults. "What's he doing?"

I haven't spoken about Camp in a long time. Whenever Emma brought him up, I deflected or changed the subject. Eventually, she stopped asking.

"He's sitting on the grass with his guitar."

"Does he know we're here?"

"Definitely. He's staring at you."

Shit.

I've decided over the last two weeks that I need to quit Midnight Peace Runners. It wasn't an easy decision, but I'm too much of a wreck to talk to anyone outside my tiny bubble, let alone sing in front of thousands. And the Red Rocks concert on October 5th is approaching quickly; there's no way I'll be able to pull myself together by then, even if Kalendar wakes up. *When.* When Kalendar wakes up.

The other thing is guilt. None of this would've happened if I hadn't met the band. I've been selfish—spending all my free time with them, letting my other relationships fall to the wayside. And if I'm being honest, it wasn't just about the music. Most of it was Camp. My stupid crush on Camp. I mean, I care about what they're trying to do—I really do—but I still don't know how I'm supposed to fit into any of it. My voice is... fine. Maybe even good. But not "change-the-course-of-humanity" good. And we hadn't even started writing a song yet. Maybe this Maggie person got it wrong. Maybe she meant some other violet-eyed girl with more to offer.

Of course, I've been too nervous to actually tell them. I keep waiting for the right moment—a day I'll wake up and not want to crawl under a rock. Maybe this is as good as it's going to get. I take a breath, brace myself, and start walking toward him.

The rain picks up, and I hand my umbrella to Emma before continuing, the cool drops splashing on my skin.

Camp stands as I get closer and takes off his cowboy hat. A smile spreads across his face, his dimples deepening. Already, I feel my carefully built wall crack.

"Hey, Camp," I say casually, trying to keep my distance so I don't end up jumping into his arms.

"How are you, Lavender?" He speaks with genuine concern and opens his arms. "Can I give you a hug?"

"Uh, sure." I step forward, feeling a mix of hesitation and longing as I let him embrace me. His strong arms are familiar now, and his scent instantly transports me to happier days. I feel myself softening, sinking into him. *No. Stay strong.*

I pull back, forcing myself to break the connection. "Camp, I ..."

"Look, Lavender. I know we've been coming on strong with the phone calls and visiting the house, but we ... *I* really care about you." His eyes hold mine, vulnerable in a way I've never seen before.

My strength wavers and I fix my gaze on the lake behind him.

"Camp… I can't be part of Midnight Peace Runners anymore." I pause, trying to steady the tremble in my voice. "You all deserve someone who can actually *be there*. Who's not living in hospital hallways or waiting rooms. Kalendar is my priority right now." I return my gaze to him.

Camp's eyes lock on mine, his voice low, thick with his Southern drawl. "Please, don't do this." His gaze is full of silent desperation. "We'll wait for you."

He extends a hand to me. I stare at it, my chest heaving, but I can't take it. I want to. Lord, I want to. I can't.

"Camp, no. The world needs you. I mean, geez, look at Kalendar. If there's even a slight chance you all can make a difference, then you need to start. Like, now." My voice is rising and tears are falling freely. It's pouring now and they mix with the rainwater, salty and fresh.

"We'll keep it going. Don't worry. Come back when you're ready." He places his hand on his heart, hair soaked.

I rest a hand on his arm and fix my eyes on his. "Please, forget about me. I gave up my other life for you guys and now Kalendar is in a coma and it's my fault. I can't do this. I'm done, Camp." Turning, I storm toward Emma, unable to look back.

"Are you okay?" Emma asks, her eyes darting from me to Camp.

"Can we please go?"

"Of course."

Emma jogs to keep up with me. I slide into the driver's seat, then steal a glance at Camp. He's sitting on the lawn, head in his hands, his clothes soaked through. His guitar rests on his lap, likely ruined. He's the last one left out in the rain.

"Let me drive, please." Emma stands by the passenger door, rain dripping from the umbrella.

"I'm fine, just get in." I snap.

She reluctantly climbs in and drops the umbrella by her feet. My hands are trembling as I grip the wheel, tears smudging my vision. I back out and turn onto the main road, trying to blink the blur away. When I swerve to avoid a puddle, the car jerks too hard—fishtailing into the other lane. My heart slams against my ribs as I wrestle it under control.

"Lavender, pull off the road. You're not okay," Emma shouts.

I steer Betty to the shoulder, and the moment I shift into park, everything inside me unravels. The air is gone from my lungs, and I hyperventilate.

Emma unbuckles her seat belt and scoots closer, wrapping her arms around me. "It's okay," she whispers. "It's going to be okay."

Minutes pass in silence, broken only by the ticking of the hazard lights and the steady patter of rain on the windshield. My breathing finally evens out. Emma shifts, pulling back enough to look at me. Her hand stays on my arm. "What happened back there? Camp looked shattered, and you're *clearly* not okay. What did you say to him?"

"I told him I couldn't see them anymore," I whisper.

"Why on earth would you do that?"

"Because when I was with them, I turned my back on everything—my friends, my family. I got so wrapped up in being with the band that I abandoned my old life. I lied; I snuck out. That's not who I am." I throw my hands up in frustration. "What happened to Kal was Karma. He was at the store to grab ketchup for Mom's barbecue—*for the band.* Billy shot him because of that night at the rodeo, and the only reason we were even there was so my brothers could spend time with *the band.* Don't you see, Em? God, the universe, whatever, is screaming at me to let them go."

I bury my face in my hands. My eyes feel heavy, and there's a dull ache starting in the back of my head.

The drumming of the rain lets up, and I can sense the sky brightening. I crack open one eye, then the other, and glance over at Emma, who has been suspiciously quiet. She rests her chin on her hands, which prop up on the dashboard, and the corners of her mouth turn up as a ray of sunshine breaks through the clouds and lights up the world. She clears her throat.

"I get that you're trying to make sense of what happened to Kalendar, but you're so wrapped up in blaming yourself that you're not seeing things clearly. I've never seen you this torn up. I mean, Brandon *cheated* on you and you hardly batted an eye. You clearly care about them. The universe isn't telling you to stay away from them. See that rainbow?" She gestures toward the windshield, where a brilliant rainbow arches over the lake. "*That* is a sign from the universe that everything will be okay. That you're *meant* to be with the band." She lifts my chin so I have to look at her. "I think Kalendar's shooting happened for a reason we don't understand yet. It doesn't mean you aren't meant to be in the band. They're counting on you."

"That's a huge part of it, too. I can't even imagine singing right now, and I don't think I'll ever get back to that headspace, at least not until Kalendar is better." I run a hand through my damp hair, my fingers snagging on a knot.

Emma stares at me, her brow furrowed and her eyes steady. "I love you, Lavender," she says, her voice firm but gentle. "And because I care about you so much, I need to tell you, you're making a mistake."

I sigh and lean my head against the window, feeling like I've just returned from battle.

"So, can I drive?" Emma asks.

I nod, unbuckling my seat belt and stepping out of the car. I close my eyes and take a deep breath, savoring the damp mountain air—it's sweet and calming. I walk around the car and slide into the passenger seat.

Emma is already seated, her fingers drumming lightly on the steering wheel. "Where to?"

"Home. I need to pack."

"Pack? Where are you going?"

"Sedona."

TWENTY-EIGHT

MY BREATH FOGS up the rear window as we descend into Sedona, and I swipe a quick smiley face onto the glass. It vanishes almost instantly—figures.

The vintage pines thin out to reveal towering red cliffs, glowing under the unrelenting sun. AC pours from the vents above me and I mentally high-five the genius who invented air conditioning as my weather app boasts a high of 110. Why anyone chooses to live in this inferno is beyond me.

"My GPS says we're twenty minutes from the hotel," our driver Jason announces, his big brown eyes glancing at us through the rearview mirror.

For the record, we're not a family that hires a driver, but with everything that's been happening, Dad insisted, probably for his peace of mind.

"Thanks, Jason." Mom's voice is quieter than usual.

Mom has said *maybe* four words during this endless eight-hour ride. Her lap is a graveyard of shredded tissues and now she's moved on to twisting the hem of her shirt. Perhaps this wasn't a good idea.

I glance at my phone, knowing full well there won't be any messages because the volume is up so high it's deafening. Dad swore he'd call at the first sign of change—if Kalendar so much as twitched a pinky. That promise is the only reason I got in the car.

As we pull into the wellness center, my eyes catch on a sprawling labyrinth in the front yard. Women in billowy pants and fitted tank tops move through it in slow, deliberate steps. Before I can take it all in, a bellhop swoops in for our bags, and Jason politely says, "See you Saturday."

"Ladies, please follow me," the bellhop says, steering our luggage cart toward the entrance.

"Thank you. What's your name?" Mom asks.

Great. That's five words. Maybe she's back to being a human.

"Nate."

My heart stutters. Nate might be a common name, but the timing feels uncanny. I miss *my* Nate. I wonder what he thinks about me leaving the band. He's probably pissed. Definitely. He's definitely pissed. And the fact that I just called him "my" Nate would for sure annoy him. I can't help but giggle at the thought.

"What's funny?" Mom asks as she reaches the check-in counter.

"Oh, nothing."

We get our room keys and Nate leads us to our suite. As soon as we step inside, a peony floral arrangement on a side table catches my eye, with a note clipped to the top. Mom puts a hand on her heart and reads it aloud, "*My Girls, try to enjoy this time away. I love you, Dad.*"

"Your father is the best. I'm going to call him and let him know we got here okay," she says, stepping onto the patio.

I nod, rummage in Mom's handbag for cash to tip Nate, then explore the suite. In the kitchen, fresh fruit piles high on the countertop. Bottled water, freshly squeezed juice, and a rainbow of vegetables stock the fridge. I grab a water then return to the living room. There's no TV, just meditation pillows and blankets neatly arranged in a corner.

Sinking into an oversized chair, I settle in while Mom wraps up her call. She's smiling, which is a good sign. I reach for a stack of magazines on the coffee table, flipping through them absentmindedly until one headline stops me cold: "Midnight Runners." I scan the photos of several runners, about my age, wearing shirts with peace signs, their smiles bright under the moonlight. Goosebumps prick my skin as I slam the magazine shut, tossing it on the table. It's only a coincidence.

Mom steps in from the patio, bringing a wave of heat with her. "Dad says hi. Emma's with Kalendar at the hospital. There's no news."

"Thanks."

Her eyes narrow. "What's wrong? You look like you've seen a ghost."

"Oh, it's nothing." I say, standing and reaching for my suitcase. "Should we get dinner?"

She puts her hand on her stomach. "I could eat."

"Great, I'll get changed."

I roll my suitcase to the bedroom on the left. As I pass the coffee table, the magazine cover with "Midnight Runners" jumps off the page. I turn it over. *Yup, a coincidence.*

I wake up the next morning and immediately reach for my phone, but there are no missed calls or new messages. My shoulders sink with relief. For the first time in weeks, I'm somewhat rested. I throw on the hotel's waffle-patterned robe over my nightgown and wander around the suite in search of Mom.

She's on the patio, lounging in pink silk pajamas with a steaming cup of tea beside her, a magazine spread across her lap. She looks almost peaceful. If it weren't for the blue half-moons under her eyes, I'd even say normal.

"Morning, babe. How did you sleep?" she asks, glancing up with a soft smile.

"Um, good, actually," I mumble.

"That's great to hear. I slept fine too. Sedona's magic must be working already." Her voice is bright, too cheerful. Forced cheerful. She holds up the magazine. "I'm reading this article about a group of friends who run at midnight for charity. Isn't that inspiring?"

My stomach tightens as I recognize the cover. "Y-yeah, I saw that yesterday." I force a smile.

"It's heartwarming to see young people making a positive impact." Her eyes twinkle.

"Uh-huh," I reply, my head bobbing like one of those dashboard toys. "So, any news from home?"

"I spoke to Dad this morning—he was at the hospital. Kalendar's condition hasn't changed," she replies, her voice dropping to a more serious tone.

She sets the magazine down with a sigh, her cheerfulness dimming. "So, what's the plan for today?"

I took the lead in planning our spiritual healing activities for the trip—mostly to keep busy and distract myself from worrying about Kalendar. It didn't completely work, but at least it gave me something to do.

"Today's our free day. I thought we could explore on our own. I rented a car, which should be here at ten."

Mom glances at her watch. "That sounds lovely. Should we head to a vortex? They're pretty incredible."

"Sure," I say, eager to check one out for myself. Before coming to Sedona, I went down a rabbit hole reading about these energy vortexes—places where the earth's energy supposedly spirals, boosting spirituality and self-discovery. Native Americans considered them sacred gateways for spiritual transformation. I'll take all the transformation I can get. Bring it on.

After what feels like a mini pilgrimage, I finally see it—a sun-warmed slab of rock where people sit in silence, faces tilted to the sky. The air hums, or maybe that's my imagination. "It's here," I loud-whisper, turning back to Mom as she catches up.

"Oh, thank goodness," she says, sinking onto the smooth stone to catch her breath. "I had no idea this hike would be so long. And my gosh, it's hot here." She wipes her forehead with a bandana.

"Well, we got lost a few times," I remind her, earning a side-eye.

"It's been a while since I've been here, and I definitely came at a cooler time of year," she admits, hugging her legs as her eyes flutter shut. "Can you feel it, though?"

I take a swig of water from my Stanley and settle cross-legged, inhaling deeply, and there it is—a faint, pulsing vibration, like the earth itself is breathing. It hums beneath my skin, grounding yet weightless, strange yet familiar; as if I've tapped into something ancient that's been waiting for me. It's the strangest, most comforting feeling in the world.

It's easy to slip into meditation here. A deep sense of relief washes over me, quieting my mind, softening the edges of my thoughts—until a flicker of light interrupts the darkness behind my eyelids.

Kalendar appears, his image projected on a massive movie screen. I look at my surroundings, expecting to be in a theater, but no, I'm alone in the empty bleachers of an old rodeo arena. He stands perfectly still, his eyes on mine. He doesn't speak, just smiles, and there's so much love in his gaze that it feels like a warm blanket wrapping around me. I don't say anything or move closer; I watch him, letting his presence calm me.

The scene shifts, and now I'm watching Anna at the campsite. She's behind her drums, her face lit up with laughter as she playfully shouts at someone out of view. Her joy is infectious, and I laugh along. Suddenly, I see myself, twirling in circles with a microphone, my hair wild in the wind. It's a carefree joy I haven't felt since the shooting.

"Excuse me?" A small voice jolts me from my meditation. I open my eyes to see a little girl with green eyes staring at me. "What are you doing?" she asks.

I smile, but before I can answer, her mom rushes over. "I'm so sorry! Violet, you can't interrupt people like that. This is a special place." She gives me an apologetic look and ushers her daughter away.

"She reminds me of you at that age," Mom says, her voice soft and reflective. She remains in her meditation pose, legs crossed, palms resting on her thighs.

"Really?" I glance over at the little girl skipping away. "She's adorable."

"Oh, you were too. People would stop me all the time to comment on how special you were," she reminisces.

I point to my eyes with a flourish. "That's because of these."

"No, sweetheart. It's because you *are* special. People can sense that." She watches the little girl and her mom walk away. "Did her mom call her Violet?"

"Yeah, I think so."

"Interesting," Mom mutters.

On our way to the car, we stop at a creek to cool off. I lower onto a stump next to an old tree and notice names etched into the bark. One catches my eye: *Kal was here.*

"Mom!" I yell. She's in the creek, water up to her ankles.

"What is it, love?"

"Did Kalendar ever come to Sedona?"

"I don't think so. Why?"

"Come look at this."

She slips her sandals on and walks to me. When her eyes rest on the faded inscription, her expression shifts—worry clouding her features. "Huh. Isn't that something?"

The next morning, we grab breakfast on the way to a sound healing session. Mom and I both order smoothies and settle by the window, looking out at Sedona.

Mom seems a million miles away, her gaze distant as she drums her fingers on the table.

"How's this trip going for you? Is it helping?" I ask, studying her.

She stops drumming and lifts her eyes. A flicker of … confusion? pain? … crossing her features before she offers a small smile. "It's a nice change of scenery. Thanks for coming, babe." She hesitates, and I stay quiet, sensing she has more to say. "I just … really miss him." She looks at her white sneakers, her voice catching.

"Oh, Mom!" I stand and wrap her in a hug, my chest tight.

She touches my arm lightly. "I've been praying, looking for any sign that things will be okay, but…" Her eyes fill with tears as she searches mine. "Have you received any signs?"

I glance away, unsure if the vision of Kalendar means anything. "Well, there was the tree with his name."

"That worries me—it says 'Kal was here,' in the past tense. It feels like a message, like maybe he's not coming back." She dabs at her eyes with a tissue. "Have you noticed any other signs? When I came here after Mom died, I saw signs everywhere, nudging me toward yoga. That's why I signed up for teacher training when I got home, and it turned out to be one of the best decisions I ever made."

YES. Our bellhop named Nate. The Midnight Runners article. The vision with Anna and Kalendar. "No, not really."

She takes a deep breath and straightens. "Keep your eyes open, Lavender. Ignoring signs can be dangerous." Mom warns, tucking the tissue in her palm.

I pull back and sit, resting my chin on my hand. "What do you mean?"

Her eyes search mine. "They say if you ignore signs from the universe, it can lead you down the wrong path—or worse, force you to relearn the same lesson in another life."

"Hmm," I mutter, not entirely convinced by the whole reincarnation idea.

Just then, a woman sets our smoothies on the table. Her name tag reads *Anna.*

"Thank you, Anna," Mom says warmly. "That's a beautiful name. My daughter's close friend has the same one." She gestures toward me.

I smile politely at the woman, then quickly look away, taking a long, desperate gulp of my smoothie.

After breakfast, we arrive at the sound healing center. Mom's a pro at these classes and swears by them, but it's my first time, so I booked us a private session, not knowing what to expect. The instructor, a kind woman named Claire *(thank goodness),* has a bunch of glass bowls set up. She begins the class by explaining how each bowl resonates differently based on her client's energy, making the sound unpredictable for any day. I pray my energy won't give off ominous tones. I say so to Claire, and she laughs. Little does she know what we're going through.

As the class starts, the bowls' intense sounds catch me off guard. My body vibrates along with them. A quick glance at Mom shows she's already deep in meditation, her face slack and serene. I lie on my mat, pulling a blanket up to my shoulders and adjusting my eye mask. The vibrations blur the edges of reality, and suddenly, I'm sitting across from Camp.

His hand rests on my shoulder, his eyes warm as he smiles and whispers, "Ready?" Heat floods my cheeks as his breath brushes my ear. Gently, he takes my chin and turns my head. Hundreds, maybe thousands, of people fill the Red Rocks venue, their voices echoing as they chant, "Midnight Peace Runners." I look down—there's a microphone in my hand. My heart races as I scan the faces in the crowd, searching desperately for Kalendar. He's nowhere in sight, but his voice is as clear as day: "Ender, you got this."

I look at Camp, confused. Where's Kalendar's voice coming from?

Instantly, I'm back in the empty arena, staring at Kalendar again. He's silent, smiling.

"Lavender, honey?" Is Mom here too? I scan the stadium, but there's no sign of her—just the gentle shake of my arm. I crack open an eye to find her hovering over me.

"Hey there," she says.

I sit up, rubbing the lingering fog from my eyes. Shadows dance across the room, cast by the soft flicker of several candles glowing nearby. The space is eerily quiet. I blink, trying to ground myself. "Is it … over?" I ask, disoriented.

Mom laughs. "Yes, you were certainly somewhere else. Who are the Midnight Peace Runners? Is it from that magazine?"

"Er, I don't know," I stammer, quickly averting my eyes. "Should we leave?" I ask, hurrying to get up.

"Claire said we can stay as long as we want. We were her last session of the day."

"That's nice of her. Let's get going, though. I need sunlight."

She laughs. "Okay."

The sun is blinding as we step outside, so I dig through my bag for sunglasses. An old bench with chipped green paint is on the sidewalk, weathered but inviting. I nod toward it. "Mom, can we sit? There's something I need to tell you."

It's time to tell her the truth. I can't keep hiding the band from her any longer. Maybe it's because of her warning about ignoring the signs, or these recurring dreams, or maybe it's simply that the weight of all these secrets is too much for me to carry. Either way, it ends now.

Mom's brows knit together, concern spreading like wildfire across her features. "Okay," she says as we settle on the warm bench, the Arizona heat radiating off the wood. She shifts uncomfortably, waiting for whatever's coming next.

I waver, my mind swirling with the reasons I've kept this secret for so long—the fear of disappointing her, of being misunderstood, and mostly, the guilt that's been eating at me since Kalendar got shot. But hiding hasn't made anything better. If I want any chance of relief, I need to be honest.

"I should have told you this a long time ago," I say, my voice a mix of nerves and determination.

And then I tell her *everything,* hesitating when I get to the midnight gatherings, but there's no turning back now—I lay it all out.

Mom listens in silence, her expression unreadable as I recount every detail. When I talk about the signs I've seen in Sedona, a small smile grows on her lips, as if she's been waiting for me to share this part of myself all along.

When I finish, she holds me close, giving me a hug that lasts a couple of minutes. I feel lighter. A *million* times lighter.

As she pulls away, she tucks a few stray hairs behind my ear. "So, where do we go from here?"

"What do you mean?"

"The universe is practically shouting that you belong with that band, love. Remember what I said about ignoring signs? It could be dangerous."

I bury my face in my hands. "I think it's the opposite. The trouble started when I tried to mix my two worlds. I obviously won't leave my family, so I feel like I need to leave the band. I don't want to hold them back. They're doing something important, and waiting for me isn't fair."

Mom lifts my chin so our eyes meet. Her gaze is steady, unwavering. "You don't have to choose one world or the other. You can live in both."

I'm deep in an Instagram doom scroll the next morning, catching up on everyone's carefree summer, when Mom's voice cuts through—soft, but edged with urgency. It's the tone that snaps me out of it.

The soft glow of the morning light seeps through the blinds and I quickly rise from bed, throwing a robe around my shoulders.

Mom has her phone to her ear. She notices me entering the living room and forces a smile.

"Yes, tomorrow," she says into the phone, nodding.

My stomach drops. Tomorrow? What's tomorrow? She has to be on the phone with Dad; her voice is too familiar for it to be a stranger, but we aren't supposed to leave here until Saturday. What could she be talking about?

"Is everything okay?" I ask when she hangs up.

"Fine," she replies, but then she adds, "I was thinking, would it be all right if we leave tomorrow instead of Saturday? Dad's checking with Jason to see if he can pick us up a day early."

"Of course, but why?"

"I miss Kalendar," she says softly.

I press, "Are you sure there's nothing else?"

Mom's voice snags, and she brings her hands to her face, rubbing her eyes. After a deep breath, she finally admits, "Honestly, Kalendar's been in a coma for over three weeks now, and well … I don't know … I just want to get home."

"Should we leave now?" I ask, my voice tight.

Mom pauses, her eyes shimmering with unshed tears. "Not yet, sweetheart. Let's give Sedona one more day to work its magic on you." She winks, trying to keep her tone light. "So, what do we have on the schedule for today?"

"Chakra balancing at one and a hot stone massage at three. But we can do something different."

"Would you mind, babe? I'd love to walk around Sedona and keep physically busy. I doubt I can relax enough for the chakra reading and massage."

I reach for my phone. "Of course. I'll cancel the appointments."

As we drive into town, Mom's mention of the three-week mark lingers in my mind, tightening into a knot in my chest. *Has it been too long?* No. I shake my head, forcing the thought away. *I can't let myself go there.*

Soon, we pull up to a charming shopping village, a maze of adobe-style buildings filled with unique art galleries. After winding our way through what must be the fifth or sixth gallery—and watching Mom strike up conversations with every owner—we decide it's time for lunch. But as we turn toward the courtyard, something in a window display stops me.

I try to steady my breath, tapping Mom's arm. "Hey, can we check out one last gallery?"

She peers through the window, thankfully not noticing what has caught my attention. "Sure, hun. Looks cute. Let's go inside."

Mom heads straight to the register and starts chatting with the gallery owner. While she and the owner, Jose, hit it off, I make a beeline for the display.

A crystal heart sits in the middle. It's the same size and color as the one Anna gave me. What really shakes me is the painted musical note in the center—it's identical to the design I asked Lacey to create for our bracelets.

"Jose, do you have a restroom I could use?" Mom asks.

Jose points at a door in the corner.

This is my chance.

Clearing my throat, I ask, "Um, Jose? Which artist created this?" I tuck a strand of hair behind my ear as I hover above the heart.

Jose walks over. "Isn't that beautiful? An artist named Maggie brought that in yesterday."

Maggie?

"Sure is." I slouch my shoulders, trying to appear as casual as possible while my heart is running the NYC Marathon. "Does she have any more artwork here?"

"No, only the one. I hope she submits more. There's been a lot of interest in the piece already."

I rub my elbow. "Do you have her contact information, by any chance?"

"Afraid not. She was quite private and mentioned she'd be back later this month to check if it sold."

Mom steps up beside us. "What are you looking at?"

"Oh, nothing." I turn around abruptly.

"Jose, thanks for showing us your beautiful gallery. You should certainly be proud." I smile at him and then turn to Mom. "Ready for lunch?"

"Uh, sure, honey. I'd love to see what you were admiring before we go, though."

"It's really nothing." Taking her hand, I steer her out of the gallery.

So much for keeping secrets. Despite Mom's approval, I've already decided to leave the band. Kalendar needs me. Besides, if Mom sees the crystal, she'll take it as another sign, 1,000 percent. I respect her beliefs, but I see it differently. If the universe—or God or whoever— wanted me with the band, they wouldn't have put me in this position in the first place. If this was all meant to be, Kalendar would be fine, and living his best life at Montana State, while I would be the next Taylor Swift.

Still, something doesn't add up. This artist, Maggie—she *has* to be the same mysterious Maggie who brought the band together, right? It's way too crazy to be a coincidence. But how would she know about my design? I haven't even handed out the bracelets yet. And why would it show up here, in Sedona, of all places? My mind races as I glance around, half expecting to spot someone watching me from the shadows.

We slide into a booth at a Mexican restaurant, and I take slow sips of ice water, focusing on my surroundings to stop my mind from spinning around Maggie.

Vines entwined with delicate string lights hang above us, and the floor is covered in gorgeous Mexican tile. The aroma of sauteed peppers and Mexican spice hangs in the air.

"This place is perfect—great choice," I say, smiling at Mom.

She looks around and nods. "It's quite charming, isn't it?"

A *very* good-looking guy approaches our table. "Good afternoon, ladies. I'll be your server today. My name's Campion. Can I get you started with something to drink?"

For fuck's sake.

Mom's eyes are the size of cantaloupes as she looks at me, then turns her attention to the waiter. "Campion? What a unique name," she says, smiling at him while giving me a side-eye.

"It is, yes. I haven't met another yet." The waiter grins.

Just then, Mom's phone rings. She glances at it. "It's Dad," she says to me. "Campion, can you give us a moment?"

"Of course, ladies."

"Hun?" Mom answers.

She catches her breath. Tears well in her eyes.

I'm gonna be sick.

"Okay, we'll see you soon. Drive safe." She drops her phone and stands up. "We have to go. Dad's on his way to get us. He's a few hours away."

"What happened?"

"Dr. Jeffries wants to see all of us tomorrow morning to talk about Kalendar."

TWENTY-NINE

THIS OLD BRICK building has become too familiar, a second home I never asked for.

Mom and Dad walk ahead, holding hands, with Jake and me trailing behind. As they step into the hospital, I double over, grabbing my knees.

"You okay?" Jake crouches beside me.

Vomit creeps up my throat, and I gulp it back, grimacing as I straighten. The sour taste threatens to make me bend over again. I manage a nod and let Jake guide me through the entrance.

The elevator doors slide shut, and my hands turn clammy as we ascend to the ICU. Mom's knuckles are bone-white, her grip on Dad's hand unrelenting. The air in the small space feels tight, suffocating.

When the doors finally open, my anxiety subsides a bit at the sight of my favorite nurse, Kate, standing outside Kalendar's room. Her eyes soften with a familiar warmth. With a gentle nod, she leads us into the room where the doctor is waiting.

"Good morning, Flynn family." Dr. Jeffries smiles, extending his hand to Dad.

"Morning, Dr.," Dad replies.

Mom walks over to Kalendar and takes his hand in hers. I stand by the door, leaning against the wall for support.

"Thank you for coming," Dr. Jeffries begins, dragging his words out with deliberate slowness. "We need to talk about the next steps for Kalendar. He's been in a coma for three weeks and two days. We were hoping to see increased brain activity by now, but it's still largely unchanged." He is speaking so damn slow, he must win an award for the slowest speaker EVER IN THE HISTORY OF THE WORLD.

This is unbearable.

"Doc, just give it to us straight. What are you proposing?" I demand, my hands trembling.

He glances at me briefly, then shifts his gaze to the rest of the family. He clasps his hands tightly in front of him, his eyes revealing a deep mix of compassion and sorrow. It's obvious he's delivered devastating news before.

"At this point," he begins carefully, "I'm not confident Kalendar will regain consciousness. With each passing day, the chances grow slimmer. I suggest you start to consider his quality of life."

"What does that mean? Is there no chance he could wake?" Mom's voice cracks.

"There's a chance," Dr. Jeffries says. "But if Kalendar remains in this state for another week, even if he wakes up, he'll likely face severe disabilities and won't be able to lead a normal life."

"What difference does another week make?" Jake interjects, his voice rough with frustration.

"The damage to Kalendar's brain from the fall is extensive. The longer his brain remains inactive, the more likely he'll wake up in a vegetative state," the doctor explains.

"Meaning?" Mom whispers.

"Meaning he might not be able to talk or even recognize you." His words hit like a hammer to my heart.

Mom's sobs fill the small room as I make my way to Kalendar's bed. I lay one hand on his chest and the other on his cheek, feeling the warmth beneath my fingertips. He looks so peaceful.

"I know this is incredibly hard," Dr. Jeffries says quietly. "I don't expect you to decide now. I only wanted to start the conversation. We will support whatever decision you make. I'll give you some time and space. If you have questions, please reach out." He nods at each of us, then reaches for the door handle.

"Thank you, Doc," Dad says, his tone heavy.

"Of course." He smiles, the door clicking shut behind him.

"This can't be happening," Jake mutters, running a hand over his face.

"Dad, what are we going to do? I can't lose Kal." I say, turning to him and collapsing into his chest. His arms wrap around me, and his chest rises and falls with silent tears.

"We don't have to decide right now," Dad says. "Let's pray."

He takes my hand, then places his other hand on Kalendar's. I reach for Jake, who grasps Mom's hand, and we bow our heads together.

Dad's voice trembles as he prays, raw and unsteady. "Dear Lord, please bring Kalendar back to us. We're lost without him. We love him more than words can say. Please..." His breath hitches on the last line.

Mom crumples to the ground.

Emma's white Subaru rolls into the hospital entrance precisely at noon.

As I watch her pull up, a knot tightens in my stomach. I did my best to cover up the fact that I'd been crying in the bathroom, but I know Emma will see right through my attempts to appear normal the moment she looks at me. She thinks we're grabbing lunch, thanks to my hurried call thirty minutes ago, but I doubt she buys it.

Her tires crunch as she pulls alongside the curb. I open the passenger door and plaster a smile. "Hey, Em."

"Hey," she says, her smile falling short of reaching her eyes as they search mine.

I climb into the car and pull my sunglasses from the top of my head. "Could we go to the park first? I'm not starving at the moment, unless you are."

Emma shifts in her seat. "I'm not hungry either. The park sounds great."

The occasional click of the turn signal breaks the quiet in the car as we drive.

Emma pulls into a parking spot and shuts off the engine. Silence stretches between us.

"It's bad news, isn't it?" she asks, her voice barely above a whisper.

I focus on the dirt path leading to the river. "Can we take a walk?"

She nods, and we step out of the Subaru.

The path is soft underfoot and magpies flit between the trees as we walk among them, their blue and white feathers flashing in the sunlight. When we reach the river, I stop, gazing at the gentle current. The peacefulness of it settles over me, soothing the frustration that's been building ever since Dr. Jeffries spoke to us this morning, bringing a strange kind of peace, kind of like the vortex.

Emma crosses her arms, her voice urgent. "Lavender, what are we doing here? Just tell me."

I kick at a rock with my Converse.

"Dr. Jeffries called us in this morning," I begin, feeling tears well up.

Her face crumples, and she gasps. "No, no, no, please no."

"Oh wait, no!" I blurt, realizing my mistake. "It's not what you think—he's not … he isn't dead. I'm so sorry. I didn't mean…" I stumble over my words, taking a deep breath to steady myself before trying again.

"Dr. Jeffries asked our family to come in this morning to discuss Kal's condition."

Emma stays silent as her almond eyes lock onto mine. Tears leave shimmering trails down her bronze skin, vanishing into the fabric of her T-shirt.

"They're losing hope. He's been in a coma for too long, and they want us to prepare for the next steps." I rush to get the words out, as if I can't keep them in any longer.

"What do you mean, 'the next steps'?" she asks, her voice trembling.

"They say that if Kalendar stays in a coma for much longer, it's unlikely he'll live a normal life if he were to wake."

Emma's face tightens, and she whips around, facing the river. She has her back to me. "So what? You're just going to pull the plug?"

Her angry outburst takes me by surprise, and I recoil, unsure of what to say.

"I'm sorry, Lavender. I … we … we can't lose him," Emma says after a few minutes, sinking to the ground. Silent sobs shake her shoulders.

Kneeling beside her, I wrap her in my arms. "I know, Em. I know."

THIRTY

I'M LYING IN THE hammock just outside our barn. The silence around me feels heavy; the usual breeze is absent. Aspen leaves hang limp above me, as if they're mirroring my sadness. The sun dips lower in the sky, casting long golden shadows that signal the start of evening. Emma dropped me here right after our talk in the park, which means I've been in this cocoon for hours. That's the strange thing about grief—it warps time, making it feel like it's both frozen and racing by at once.

Since coming back from Sedona yesterday, Camp's music hasn't surfaced. Maybe that's why the silence feels so suffocating. They must be gone by now. Left to find my replacement. A single tear escapes at the thought. But my mind always returns to Kalendar, the doctor's warning echoing relentlessly: *If he stays in a coma much longer, even if he wakes, he may never lead a normal life.*

"Kal, please come back to me," I whisper into the quiet.

A sudden, sharp sniffle breaks through the stillness.

With a jolt, I sit up, my hands clutching the sides of the hammock to steady myself. The sniffle turns into sobs which echo, so close it's as if they're right next to me.

But there's no one here.

"Hello?" My voice wavers. "Who's there?"

A car engine rumbles in the distance, growing louder, drowning out the crying. I lean back into the hammock. The tires crunch to a stop, a door slams, and then soft, graceful footsteps approach.

"Hello, Lavender." *Josephine.*

I'm not sure if I'm annoyed or grateful she's here. Either way, I lift my head.

"Hey, Josephine," I reply faintly before settling back into the cocoon.

She crosses her arms, her gaze filled with concern as she looks at me. Her braids fall over one shoulder, and her cropped T-shirt and loose-fitting harem pants are cute. I peek at my stained hoodie and old running shorts. *Wonderful.*

Josephine glances around, then heads to the barn and grabs a camping chair. She returns, unfolds it, and sits, her hands resting in her lap, radiating calm. The chair creaks slightly as she shifts.

"Suzy, at the yoga studio, mentioned you went to the hospital this morning. Any update on Kalendar?" Her voice is steady.

"They want us to consider taking Kalendar off life support." I reply flatly.

I wait for Josephine to respond, to offer some kind of comfort, but the silence stretches between us. Frowning, I shimmy to my elbows. Did she not hear me?

Her eyes are closed, her breathing deep and even.

"Josephine?"

She opens her eyes and meets my gaze. "I'm so sorry to hear that."

I wait for her to say more, but she remains silent. *O-o-okay.*

Crossing my arms behind my head, I lay back on the hammock, and the crying starts again. I shift to look at Josephine, but it's not coming from her. *What the hell?*

"Do you hear that?"

"Hear what?"

"Crying. I can hear someone crying, but I don't see anyone."

Josephine tilts her head, listening intently. After a few seconds, she says, "I don't hear anything."

She fixes her gaze on me, her expression serious. "Lavender, how was your trip to Sedona?"

Seriously? THAT's what's on her mind?

"Fine," I mutter, refusing to elaborate.

"Yeah? Sedona is a very spiritual place. Did you see any signs when you were there?" Her brows lift.

"The universe has always spoken to me profoundly when I visit Sedona."

"Nope, not really," I reply curtly, my shoulders tensing.

Josephine nods and gazes up at the mountains, her expression thoughtful.

The crying is louder now. "Do you really not hear that?" I ask her again.

"I want to tell you something," Josephine begins, brushing past my question. "When we first met, I didn't tell you the whole story about how I came to meditation. It was... kind of forced on me."

I narrow my eyes but stay quiet.

"A few weeks before my brother died, I was in Sedona, fresh out of an abusive relationship and looking for a change. I met an older man in the park, with gray hair and a long robe. He resembled a wizard, like from a children's book or something, so I assumed he wasn't all there."

She twirls a finger near her temple. "You know, *a little out there.*"

"He told me I'd become a meditation guru traveling the world. I thought he was nuts and walked away."

Her voice lowers. "That night, I dreamed of my brother falling from a building. I brushed it off as a nightmare."

My body stiffens, a chill running down my spine. Did I ever tell her about the visions of Kalendar falling? No, I'm almost sure I didn't.

"The next day, a girl bumped into me, spilling my coffee. It turns out she was a meditation teacher and invited me to a class as an apology. Her name was Josephine. I thought it was a weird coincidence. I didn't go to the class, and that night, I had the same dream about my brother."

She pauses, tears forming. "I left Sedona after that. As I was leaving, I saw a bumper sticker that said 'Meditate' next to a New York license plate reading 'Josefin.' With an *F*, not a *P-H*. But, still. I thought it was just another coincidence. The signs kept coming until the day my brother died—a drug overdose—along with that recurring dream. I ignored them, even though they were impossible to miss."

She wipes her eyes. "It wasn't until his death that I began taking these signs seriously. I've lived a very fulfilling life ever since. My practice has helped hundreds, maybe even thousands, of people. But it can never bring him back."

Her red eyes meet mine. "I'm not saying it was my fault he died. Maybe it would've happened anyway; he was involved with some dangerous people. But sometimes I wonder if things could've been different if I'd discovered meditation sooner. Maybe I could've helped him."

Her words linger, the story about her brother strangling my airways. What does this mean? Am I really meant to be a part of the band? Would that somehow save Kalendar?

She stands and hands me a small gift-wrapped box. I hesitate for a moment before accepting it. "What's this?"

"It might help explain some things," she says. "Open it later when you're in a better headspace."

I nod and set it on the ground beneath my hammock. "Thanks," I mumble.

She looks at the box and then back at me. "Please don't forget about your gift, Lavender. You have one, and the world needs it. Kalendar needs it." She squeezes my shoulder and walks to her car.

I watch her leave, noticing she's driving a Jeep Wrangler with Tennessee plates. *Wait, isn't that Camp's Jeep?*

My heart slams as she pulls out of our driveway. I reach for the box on the ground and unwrap it with trembling fingers. The top has a musical note etched into the smooth cardboard. Slowly, I lift the lid. Inside is a crystal heart with a music symbol painted in the middle—the same piece of art I saw at the gallery in Sedona, the same design I used for the bracelets.

My breath catches. I grab my phone and frantically type *Josephine Dutton Maggie artist and meditation guru,* into the search bar.

The first result pops up with Josephine's photo, accompanied by a caption that reads, *Josephine "Maggie" Dutton leads a meditation and art workshop in …* My eyes lock on the name Maggie. Could Josephine be *THE* Maggie? The same Maggie who started the band?

I navigate to Mom's number, and she answers on the first ring. "Everything okay, Lavender?"

"Mom, does Josephine go by another name?"

"Josephine, our meditation friend?"

"Yeah."

"She does, actually … Maggie. But I think only her close friends call her that. Why?"

"No reason. Thanks." I end the call and get up from the hammock, my mind racing.

Rubbing my sweaty palms on my shorts, I pace in front of the barn. Why would Josephine hide she was Maggie all this time? I walk toward the house, trying to figure out what to do next, when the crying starts again.

"Who's there?" I scream, frustrated.

I follow the sound to a large aspen tree, the one my hammock is tied to. The bark feels smooth against my ear as I press into it, straining to hear. The faint whisper, *"Kalendar,"* drifts from deep within, causing goosebumps to prickle my skin. Sap glistens like a golden tear, winding its way down the bark's white face.

Am I losing my mind? My mind flashes back to my first conversation with Camp. He talked about how some humans vibrate at the same frequency as animals, insects, and plants, allowing us to communicate with them. It sounded crazy then, but now I can't deny it. I'm hearing the tree cry. Of course, this tree misses Kalendar; it watched him grow up.

I slump against the tree and slide to the ground. Closing my eyes, I press my hands into the dirt, desperate to ground myself. I focus on the crying, letting it swell and fill my mind. The sound multiplies, as if the sorrow isn't coming from just one tree but from all the surrounding trees.

When I open my eyes, the world is different. Sharper. Every blade of grass, every flower petal, every tiny insect crawling past—crystal clear, like I'm seeing through a new set of eyes. My heart pounds.

The unmistakable caw of a seagull cuts through the quiet. That can't be right. Seagulls? In Colorado? I look up, finding the bird sitting on a branch overhead, unblinking. A single feather drifts down, landing delicately in my lap.

"Grandpa?"

The seagull caws again, then circles once, twice—and disappears into the trees.

And suddenly, everything clicks. The visions. The signs. They've been there all along, waiting for me to understand. How could I have misinterpreted them for so long?

I'm *meant* to be part of this band.

They need me. The world needs me.

And most importantly—Kalendar needs me.

I've been focusing on the wrong thing for too long.

I wipe the single line of sap from the tree and pull my phone from my pocket, ready to call Camp. Before I can dial, the haunting chords of his guitar drift from the forest.

THIRTY-ONE

MY EYES STRUGGLE TO adjust to the inky night as I race through the forest. Branches claw at my arms and I'm suddenly grateful I wore a hoodie today instead of a T-shirt. The flashlight on my phone refuses to turn on, leaving me to navigate by instinct and the half moon. Where are the fireflies when I need them?

Relief floods me when I finally spot the warm glow of lanterns ahead. I'm close.

Anna is waiting for me at the entrance of the campsite. The moment she sees me, she pulls me into a bone-crushing hug.

"I've missed you so much," she whispers.

"I've missed you too," I squeak, my breath nearly knocked out of me.

She lets go, and I gulp in air.

"Ah, sorry." She laughs. "I'm just so excited to see you."

I straighten, laughing with her and rubbing my sides where she'd almost squeezed the life out of me. "It's exactly what I needed."

Nate steps up next, initiating a hug. It's stiff and awkward, but weirdly comforting. "Really glad you're here," he says as he pulls away.

My eyebrows raise in surprise. "Did I hear you right?"

He laughs and nudges my arm. "You've grown on me."

I smile at him, feeling a mix of gratitude and guilt as my heart swells at the welcome I'm not sure I deserve.

My gaze drifts past Nate and lands on Camp. He's leaning against a tree, one foot planted firmly while the other rests against the trunk. A smirk flickers across his face.

"I knew you'd come back," he says, pushing off the tree and sauntering toward me.

"You're awfully confident. What if I didn't?" I challenge.

His eyes lock onto mine, crinkling at the corners. "You were always coming back." He sweeps me off the ground and spins me before gently setting me down. "I've missed you," he breathes.

My heart stumbles, and I squeeze my eyes shut to steady the rush of emotions.

"Camp, I'm so sorry …"

"Nothing to be sorry for," he interrupts, smiling as he takes my hand. He leads me to the campfire, and there's another silhouette in the flickering shadows, one that I recognize immediately.

Josephine glows in the campfire's light. She gazes at me like a proud mother with her hands over her heart.

"Lavender, this is Maggie. Or rather, you know her as Josephine." Camp chuckles, then adds warmly, "Your guardian angel."

She walks over, cradles my face, and looks deep into my eyes. "You've embraced your gift," she whispers. It isn't a question.

My throat tightens, and I blink rapidly to keep the tears at bay. "Thanks for helping me see clearly," I whisper.

She hugs me tightly.

I reach into my pocket and retrieve the two crystal hearts—the one she gave me and the one from Anna—and hold them up so they catch the firelight. "I imagine you're behind these?"

She wraps her long fingers around them, a soft smile playing on her lips. "These stones were sitting just off a path I was hiking in Sedona, near an ancient Native American ruin. I hired an artist to smooth them into hearts." She leans in closer and whispers, "I believe they have special powers. What do you think?"

I laugh. "That's an understatement."

She hands them to me, her eyes twinkling. "Keep them. I have a few at home and one in Sedona, though you already know that." She laughs. "I added a musical note in the center of a couple to match your bracelets." She winks.

"Thanks." I tuck them into my pocket. "So, what do I call you now?" I ask, half joking.

"Whatever you want, my dear."

"I think I'll stick with Josephine." I grin.

"That's perfect," she says, her hand tightening briefly on my arm. "Ya know, I almost told you that day on the lake."

"Really?"

She nods slowly. "When you mentioned the band. But something told me the timing wasn't right."

"You made a good call. I probably would've panicked and floated off into the sunset. I wasn't in the best state of mind that day."

She laughs.

I set my eyes on her, a thousand questions circling. She must sense it, because she nudges my shoulder with hers.

"What are you thinking?"

"Why me? What's so special about me that you went through all this trouble?"

She smiles and takes my hands in hers. "You came to me in a dream a few years ago. And since then, the feeling of you—your presence—it never left. It took time to find you, but then the mountains, Snettles, kept appearing in signs. That's when I knew."

I nod, letting it settle in my chest. "I guess I'm just still struggling to see what I actually bring to all of this."

"You haven't started writing lyrics yet, have you?" There's a playful glint in her eye.

I shake my head.

"Just wait," she says with a smile.

She beckons Camp, Anna, and Nate over, and the five of us fold into a messy, warm hug. I want to disappear into it—to let their closeness quiet the buzzing in my chest—but all I can think about are the lyrics.

I've never written a single line of a song. What if I can't do this? What if her visions were wrong?

As if reading my mind, Josephine pulls back and looks at me. "Are you up for spending a few hours with us? Now that the band is together, we should start working on your songs. The concert at Red Rocks is a few weeks away." Her eyes smile at me. "You can do this."

I give a hesitant nod.

"Great. How about you call your mom and let her know? Let's keep everything transparent from here on out. What do you think?"

I smile, feeling a weight lift off my shoulders. "I couldn't agree more."

Stepping away from the group, I call Mom. She answers again on the first ring. "Hi, sweetheart. Everything okay?" This has become her default greeting lately, and I can't blame her.

"I'm good. How are you guys? Anything different with Kalendar?"

"Well, I wasn't going to call since it's happened before, but he moved his eyes a few times about ten minutes ago." There's a spark of hope in her voice.

"He's in there, Mom. I really think he'll be okay," I say confidently. This time, I actually believe it.

"I hope so, babe." Mom says, her tone weary. "What are you up to?"

"I have news," I begin, suddenly anxious about her reaction. "I've rejoined the band. Something happened tonight—I'll explain later—and it made me realize the band needs me. And, honestly, I need them too."

"Finally!" She sings. "I was hoping you'd come to your senses. Are you with them now?"

"Yeah. Would it be all right if I spend time with them tonight? Unless you need me at the hospital—I can come and take over if you and Dad want to head home."

"No, but thanks, babe. You hang with your band. Jake's on his way here now, and I'm not ready to leave anyhow."

"Are you sure?"

"Definitely. Have fun."

"Thanks, Mom."

"And Lavender?"

"Yeah?"

"You sound happy. It's been a while since I've heard that in your voice."

I let that sink in for a moment. "As happy as I can be, given everything. Thanks, Mom. Love you."

"I love you too. Say hi to Campion for me," she adds mischievously.

"I will," I say, rolling my eyes.

I make my way back to the group, and Camp's the first to notice—a deep V forms on his forehead.

"Everything's fine. Mom's happy I'm here and says hi."

Camp's grin spreads wide. "Glad to hear it. Tell her I said hi next time you chat."

"Will do," I reply, feeling a mix of giddy and anxious. "So, where should we start?" I ask, turning to everyone.

"I think we should write a new song," Nate suggests. "We've got great ones already, but we need a new one from the whole band—our single." His eyes flash to mine.

I gulp.

"That's a great idea," Anna agrees. She dashes into her tent and returns with a journal and pencil. "I'll handle the writing."

We gather around the band equipment, and my nerves are throwing a full-blown rager. "Okay, full disclosure—I have zero clue how to write a song," I admit, my face going up in flames.

"Don't worry about it," Camp says, placing his hand on my lower back, sending my body into an electric spiral. "We'll work on the lyrics together, and Nate and I will take care of the music."

Nate nods in agreement. "That's how we usually do it."

As Camp's hand leaves my back to grab his guitar, my mind snaps into focus.

Okay, this is it. I hope Josephine's visions were right.

I search for a spark of inspiration, and suddenly Kalendar's voice drifts in like a quiet whisper. *"Just bring 'em peace, Ender."* A smile tugs at my lips as his words settle, lighting a flame of creativity I didn't know I was capable of.

"Anna, could I borrow that journal and pencil for a minute? I've got an idea I want to work out."

"Of course," she replies, passing them to me.

"What's brewing in that head of yours?" Camp asks, his hazel eyes twinkling in the firelight.

"You'll see." I smirk, turning to a blank page and channeling Kalendar as I write.

Minutes tick by as I scribble, erase, and rewrite. Kalendar's voice steers me through each messy line. Josephine and Anna stay close, their quiet support keeping me focused. Camp and Nate huddle nearby, whispering about beats.

Finally, I slam my pencil, drawing everyone's attention. Not usually one to brag, I hand the journal to Anna. "There's our chorus," I say proudly.

Camp turns to me with a smirk. "That was awfully fast for someone who claims they can't write a song."

"I had a little help." I shrug, my smile easy.

Anna's eyes dart over the lyrics, and her face lights up excitedly. "Yes! Yes! Yes! Yes!" she squeals.

"Well, read them out loud for the rest of us." Nate says as he paces across the forest floor, hands clasped behind him.

"Lavender should read them," Anna says, handing it to me.

I accept it with my free hand and then pass it to Josephine. "Actually, would you, Josephine?"

Her eyes sparkle as she takes the paper from me. "I'm honored."

I drop my eyes to the fire, its flickering flames the only thing I can focus on as a sudden wave of vulnerability washes over me.

Josephine clears her throat.

"Not a simple wish upon a star tonight
But a pleading for the world to hold hands and unite
The runners hold their pace till twilight
Singin' and chantin' with sweet release
Bring 'em peace

Oh please, bring 'em peace."

Doubt creeps in as the silence stretches.

Did they not like it? Was Anna just being nice? Ugh. So much for those visions, Mags.

I swallow hard, then glance up and notice Nate staring at the fire, his eyes brimming with tears. Josephine's eyes are misty, her lips pressed into a tight smile.

"It's perfect," Camp says, his Southern accent thick with emotion.

"Well, dang, Lavender. You got us crying," Anna says, laughing as she wipes her eyes.

I let out a breath. "I'm not sure what happened. It felt like Kalendar was whispering the lyrics in my ear. Is that crazy?" I glance at Josephine.

"Not at all," she replies with a smile. "Now that you're embracing your gift, you'll see this world runs far deeper than you ever imagined. The spiritual realm has more to offer than we could ever dream."

"So, you're saying it might've been Kalendar communicating with me?"

"Absolutely. Kalendar's caught between worlds right now. He can't reach out physically, so he's reaching you spiritually." She must notice the skepticism in my eyes. "I know it sounds strange, especially if you're new to this, but the more you experience it, the more you'll understand."

It sounds pretty wild, but honestly, this is the closest I've felt to Kalendar since the shooting.

"How about we tackle the rest of the lyrics? Lavender's got us on a roll," Anna suggests, taking the notebook from Josephine.

"Why don't you ladies handle that?" Camp says, nodding at us, dimples deep. "Nate and I can start working on the music to go with the chorus."

"Sounds good," I say, my voice steadier than I feel. I hope Kalendar's ready for round two.

Anna, Josephine, and I gather in a circle, and for a second, I swear Kalendar's voice is in my ear: *"Gave you a start; can't write the whole thing for you,"* before it fades away.

Still, the words move through me like a current—clear, honest, and unexpectedly easy. Anna and Josephine share a glance, quiet and knowing.

I'm so lost in the songwriting that I don't even notice Camp until his words break through my focus. "Hey," he whispers, and I jump.

"Camp, you scared me." I smile, bumping my shoulder against his.

His dimples deepen. "It's nearly midnight. Time to get you home," he says, his eyes reflecting the soft glow of the campfire. "Can I walk you?"

Fumbling with the pencil, I glance at him. "Is it already that late? I should go; tomorrow is my first day back at school." After handing the pencil and notebook to Anna, I return Camp's smile. "And yeah, I'd like that. Thanks, Camp." I stand, though my legs wobble beneath me at the thought of being alone with him for the first time in weeks.

Josephine and Anna wrap me in a tight hug.

"We'll see you tomorrow. Come by when you get home?" Anna asks.

"Yup, I'll be here."

"Good luck at school," Josephine adds.

"Thanks, guys."

"Bye, Nate!" I wave at him. He's lost in his bass, strumming thoughtfully.

"Bye, Lavender. See you tomorrow," he replies, giving a quick wave before returning to his music.

Camp steps closer. "Ready?"

"Ready," I reply, my fingers tingling with anticipation.

He loops my arm through his and reaches for a lantern hanging from a branch.

"I've been meaning to ask," I say, nodding at the lantern as we leave the campsite. "Is that safe? Ya know, wildfires and all that."

Camp chuckles and lifts the glass lid to reveal a flameless candle.

"They look so real!" I gasp.

"I think that's the point." He smirks, then his expression turns serious. "How are you? I've been worried about you."

I pause, realizing I haven't truly confronted my feelings since that awful day. Anger was easier—it drowned out everything else.

"Honestly, not okay," I admit, my voice shaking. "I miss him so much, and I've felt so alone. I…" My throat constricts, the weight of the last month crashing over me all at once.

Camp pulls me into his arms, my head resting against his warm chest as I melt into him.

"You're never alone. I'm here for you," he murmurs into my hair. "However you need me."

I pull back, meeting his eyes with a smile as I wipe away a tear. He brushes one from my other cheek, his smile soft.

He resumes his stride, and I stay close, looping my arm back through his.

After a silent stretch of walking, I ask, "Did you know I was friends with Josephine—er, Maggie?" I'm still wrapping my head around the fact that Josephine is the Maggie everyone's been talking about.

"I knew," Camp admits, hesitant. "Not right away, but Maggie told me after Kalendar's accident. When we first got to Rosewood, she mentioned she'd be reaching out to you, but I didn't think it would happen like that." He chuckles, rubbing his chin thoughtfully. "She's got more layers than an onion, that one." He shifts his gaze to me, brow furrowing in thought. "Are you mad at her? I mean, I'd probably feel betrayed if it were me."

"Not really." I shrug. "She knew what she was doing. If she'd come to me saying I was destined to join the band, I probably would've bolted in the opposite direction."

Camp smirks. "Well, that's pretty much what I did, and you didn't run."

"Maybe I didn't run, but I definitely thought you guys were nuts at first. Actually, I thought *I* was nuts—I was convinced I had imagined you guys." I shake my head. "Anyway, her meditation sessions helped a lot, and having her as a friend meant everything. Especially in bonding over our shared eye color. And did you know she's the one who gave me the confidence to sing?"

Camp's grin grows wider. "I didn't know that, but it doesn't surprise me. You'd have figured it out on your own, though—your talent was clear from the start."

I laugh. "I'm not sure about that, but thanks."

We reach the entrance of my driveway, and he hesitates, his hand brushing my hip as he motions toward the house. A spark ignites my lower stomach at this touch.

"Mind if I walk you to the door?"

I swallow. "Sure."

He grins, his gaze flicking to my lips for the briefest second, lighting up my insides.

A rush of warmth floods me, and before I realize what's happening, my eyes are closed and I'm tilting my head up toward his, drawn by his intoxicating sandalwood scent. Our lips meet in a soft, fleeting kiss, there and gone in a heartbeat. When I open my eyes,

Camp's gaze locks with mine, his brows furrowing as if searching my face for answers, concern clouding his expression.

"I'm sorry, Lavender. I can't."

Heat rushes to my cheeks. Had I completely misunderstood his feelings? I avert my gaze toward the house, wishing I could teleport inside.

I allow my eyes to sweep him once more before my lips twitch into a small smile. "Actually, I can walk by myself." I smooth my hair and turn away from him, my steps clumsy as I navigate the uneven driveway in the dark.

"Lavender, wait. I—"

I spin to face him, cutting him off. "Camp, you *really* don't have to explain. It's been an emotional month and I guess I was looking for comfort or whatever. I don't know what I was thinking. It was a mistake." My stomach knots around the lie.

He drags a hand down his cheek, his eyes on mine, searching. His lips part like he's about to say something—but then he closes them and takes a few steps to meet me. He holds out the lantern. "Here, take this. Don't want you falling on your way up the driveway."

He turns and disappears into the night, his footsteps scuffing against the dirt until they fade, swallowed by the whispering trees.

The second I step inside the house and shut the door behind me, my legs buckle, and I sink to the floor. My face burns with embarrassment, my pulse thrumming in my ears. The kitchen is eerily still, but it's the emptiness of Kalendar's absence that presses down on me the hardest.

THIRTY-TWO

THIS ISN'T HOW I pictured my first day of senior year.

The girl in the mirror looks wrecked.

Dark circles bruise the skin beneath her eyes, making her face appear even paler than usual—ghastly white, where there should be a hint of summer tan by now. Her pink floral mini-dress hangs awkwardly on her too-thin frame.

And is my hair… thinner?

Lord.

How did I let it get this bad?

And, of course, all eyes will be on me. At least Billy's out of the picture for now, locked away in a detention center in Grand Junction. If he were here, I wouldn't even set foot inside the school.

Emma's Subaru bounces along our driveway, kicking up a cloud of dust.

Thankfully, I don't need to show up alone.

I throw my Herschel pink backpack over my shoulder and head downstairs.

"Morning, sweetheart. Are you sure you're up for this today?" Mom asks as I step into the kitchen.

I grab the to-go coffee she's left on the counter.

"Yeah. I need to try, at least. Hopefully, the attention will fade after today."

I give her my best smile.

"Well, you know, everyone just cares about you. But I get it. Call me if you want me to pick you up early."

She kisses me on the cheek.

"Thanks, but I'll be fine." I grab a peanut butter granola bar from the pantry. "Emma and I are going to visit Kal after school. Will I see you there?"

"Probably. Dad wants me to rest this morning. I didn't get home until five a.m."

"Mom! I thought Jake was staying with him last night."

"He was. But I couldn't leave Kalendar," she confesses, her voice catching.

"Has anything changed since we last spoke?" I ask, scanning her face. "Did you and Dad talk more about what the doctor said?"

"He's the same." She sighs. "And no, we haven't. I can't even bring myself to—" Her jaw tenses, cutting off the thought.

I take her hand, giving it a reassuring squeeze. She clutches back with surprising strength and tilts her chin up, glistening eyes tracing invisible patterns on the ceiling.

"On second thought, maybe I should stay home. I can always start tomorrow."

Mom shakes her head. "No, babe. You go. I'll be fine."

"You sure?" I try reading past her brave front, watching as she takes a slow breath that quivers.

"Absolutely. Tell your friends I say hello." She manages a smile.

"Okay. I'll see you later. Love you."

"Love you too." Mom plays with an invisible necklace at the base of her throat as she watches me leave.

Emma's face lights up when she sees me.

"Hey, Em. Thanks for picking me up," I say, tossing my backpack in the back with a thud and sliding into the passenger seat.

"Course." Her smile widens. "You seem happier today. What's up?"

I raise my eyebrows and grin. "I think Kal's going to pull through this."

"Seriously? What happened?"

"Let's go. I'll tell you everything."

As we drive to school, I talk through the events of yesterday, sidestepping any mention of the failed kiss.

We pull up just as I finish. Emma unbuckles her seat belt and looks at me with wide eyes, a flicker of disbelief crossing her face. "Wait, so Josephine is Maggie?"

I nod and thump my head against the headrest. "Can you believe it?"

"I mean," she gives me a sidelong glance, "I'm not surprised, actually. Nothing surprises me anymore." We both laugh.

I look at her, really seeing her for the first time in a while. She's noticeably thinner, her collarbone more prominent under the fabric of her shirt. Her thick dark hair, usually shiny, hangs flat and lifeless. Tired eyes meet mine, still full of warmth but edged with something fragile. A pang of guilt twists in my chest for not noticing it sooner.

"Em, thanks for being here through all of this. I know it's been hard on you, too."

"Of course. I love you guys so much. You're my second family." Her voice wavers, and a soft grin lifts on her lips, though her eyes glisten with unshed tears.

I hug her tightly, hoping she can feel all my unspoken gratitude and love. "We love you too," I whisper.

She wipes her eyes as she pulls away. "Okay, are you ready for this?" She grabs the door handle.

Nope. "Yup."

The morning went as expected—a constant flow of hugs and sympathetic glances. Our school counselor and Principal Simmons hovered around me, as if I might break down at any moment. I wanted to tell everyone I'm fine and actually, *PLEASE LEAVE ME ALONE CAUSE YOU'RE MAKING IT WORSE*. But no one knows how to act in these situations, so I accepted the hugs and offered thankful smiles at the sad glances.

Emma, my angel, asked to switch her schedule so she could shadow me for the day. She was always ready to change the subject if it veered into weighty territory with well-meaning friends or teachers.

Then it hit me.

All these people are grieving too. Kalendar was … *IS* … such a big presence in this community. The sorrow isn't just mine and my family's; it's everyone's. And so, the hugs became deeper, and the smiles more genuine.

As I sit in math class, trying impossibly hard to pay attention, I glimpse Camp's Jeep pulling up through the window. I glance at the clock—*noon*. Why is he here? My heart races. Did something happen to Kalendar? My hands instinctively grip the desk, ready to bolt, but then Nate hops out of the passenger seat, grinning.

My gaze drifts to the back of the Jeep, where Camp leans, arms crossed, waiting. Ripped jeans, a faded T-shirt, and that damn cowboy hat—always wakes the butterflies in my stomach. But last night's memories crash down like bricks. Shame curls in my chest, and I sink lower into the hard plastic chair, willing myself to disappear. And yet, I keep one eye on him.

He pulls off his hat and runs a hand through his unruly hair, saying something to Nate that I can't make out. Nate scratches his head, then points to the entrance as Camp opens the trunk.

What are they—

Before I can process what's unfolding outside, my hand flies to my mouth to stifle a laugh. Nate and Camp are trying—and failing spectacularly—to balance at least twenty pizza boxes between them while wrestling with closing the trunk door. Nate's leg swings out repeatedly in wild, ridiculous kicks that miss the door by a mile, each miss more pathetic than the last. Meanwhile, Camp's shoulders shake with uncontrollable laughter as he clings desperately to the teetering stack of pizzas while he shouts something at Nate … *instructions?*

I can't help but laugh, drawing the attention of the entire class. One by one, giggles ripple through the room as everyone turns to watch. The trunk door stays stubbornly open as Nate and Camp, looking every bit like circus clowns juggling pizzas, stagger toward the front door, miraculously keeping every box intact. Tears of laughter blur my vision, and I swipe at them repeatedly, unable to keep up.

"Who are they?" someone asks.

"Lavender's friends," Emma answers proudly.

Sitting next to me, Meg leans over and whispers, "That guy with the cowboy hat is gorgeous."

My smile fades as my humiliation returns to haunt me. "Mm-hmm," I reply.

Moments later, the intercom crackles, and Camp's drawl fills the room. "Hey, everyone. Sorry to interrupt your learning, but we've got pizzas for everyone to celebrate our girl Lavender. So, when you see her, give her a high-five—or better yet, a big hug." I can practically hear his mischievous grin through the intercom. "Okay, have a great day." There's some rustling, and then, "Oh, and Lavender, I got you pepperoni—your favorite." The intercom clicks off.

My face is on fire. How on earth did Camp get the admin to let him do that?

Before I know it, my class is surrounding me, offering hugs and high fives. The day's mood shifts instantly, from somber to celebratory. I'm touched by their kindness. Maybe this is Camp's way of extending an olive branch. I know he didn't mean to humiliate me. I was the one who got it all wrong.

I glance out the window and see him leaving. He catches my eye, flashes a huge grin, and tips his hat before hopping into the Jeep.

"He must really like you," Meg says as we head to lunch.

I shake my head. "He's just a nice guy." The Jeep glides out of the parking lot and slips from view.

Emma and I get to the hospital after school. Jake stands from the chair beside Kalendar and greets us.

"Hey, Jake. Any updates?" I ask, glancing at Kalendar.

He follows my gaze and shakes his head. "None." He shifts uncomfortably. "So, how was your first day back? Mom mentioned you seem better. We've all been real worried about you."

"I'm doing better, thanks." I give him a side-eye. "Actually, how much did Mom tell you?"

He shrugs. "Not much. Just that you were in good spirits and hanging out with Camp and the crew again."

"Did she say anything about a band?"

"A band? No, why?"

"Do you have time to talk?"

"I've got all the time in the world for you." He smiles.

So, I fill Jake in on everything from the beginning. He listens intently while I keep glancing at Kalendar, hoping he's catching it, too. Though I have a hunch, he already knows.

When I finish, Jake runs a hand down his face and says, "So, the fireflies are your friends now?"

The absurdity of it all sends Emma and me into fits of giggles, the sound breaking the tension in the room. Jake's laughter joins ours, filling the sterile hospital space with a momentary warmth. But as the laughter fades, the weight of where we are settles back in.

"You guys need to record that song, Lavender," Jake says, a spark of urgency lighting his eyes as he rubs his hands together. "I honestly think you heard Kalendar's voice when you came up with the lyrics. It feels right. Kalendar might be trying to reach us through this."

"That's what Josephine said!" I exclaim.

Jake nods, his eyes landing on Kalendar's still form. "Kalendar's still in there; I'm sure of it. Maybe if we record the song and play it for him, it'll wake him." Jake grips Kalendar's hand. "We have to try everything."

THIRTY-THREE

EMMA DROPS ME OFF around six, and I get ready to meet the band. I change into jeans and a sweater, then head downstairs. A bowl of noodles is on the counter with a note: *Please eat, Lavender. You're getting too thin. I'm headed to the hospital. I'm sure you're meeting the band. Be safe and home before midnight. Love you. xx Mom.*

I scarf down the noodles, grab a seltzer, and head out.

I'm halfway down the driveway when it hits me—I completely forgot about the bracelets I made for everyone. I whirl around and dash inside to grab them.

Bruce follows me back outside, his tail wagging in excitement. I almost tell him to stay, but catch myself, remembering how much he adores Camp.

"All right, boy, come on," I say, rubbing his ears.

We head into the forest, where the air smells of pine and earth. The daylight is just beginning to fade, so I don't need my flashlight yet, but I keep it ready in my hand.

When we reach the campsite, Anna greets me with a playful smile. "So, I hear you had a special pizza delivery today," she says, eyebrows dancing.

My face heats as I wonder if Camp mentioned the failed kiss to her, but she doesn't give any sign that she knows.

"Yup," I say, throwing a mock-serious look her way. "And I must say, those delivery guys were *very* good. Five stars."

Anna laughs as I face the guys. "Thanks for the pizza!" I call, a grin spreading across my face.

Nate's smile widens as he sets down his bass, while Camp is already petting Bruce behind the ears.

"It was fun," Nate says as he stands.

Camp jogs over, Bruce trotting beside him. "We wanted to make your day a little brighter," he says, his eyes crinkling with an easy smile. They linger on mine a bit too long, like he's checking to make sure I'm okay.

I run a hand through my hair. "Well, mission accomplished."

"How's Kalendar?" Anna asks, rubbing my arm.

"Um, the same," I reply, my throat suddenly tight.

"Oh! I almost forgot—I have something for you guys." I push up my sleeve to reveal the bracelets, the colorful threads catching the fading light.

"Lavender, these are gorgeous!" Anna exclaims, taking my wrist in her hands and inspecting them.

"Thanks! I thought the heart could be our band logo. No pressure if you guys don't like it, though."

"Are you kidding? I love it! Is it based on the heart I gave you?" Anna asks.

"Yeah, and I added the music symbol in the center for obvious reasons." I slip off the bracelets and pass them around.

"These are great," Camp says, admiring his. "Thanks."

"Yeah, thanks," Nate adds, turning his wrist. "I've never worn a bracelet before. Does this mean we're all Swifties now? Don't they wear bracelets?"

I giggle. "That hadn't even crossed my mind! Guess we are."

Camp chuckles but shakes his head. "Don't get me wrong—I love Taylor, but this isn't about that. This is ours," he says, his eyes meeting mine. "This symbol means something bigger. It's the start of our peace revolution."

Anna extends her arm, showing off her bracelet. "All right, guys, get over here," she says.

I follow her lead, and Camp and Nate join in, forming a small circle with our wrists.

Anna grins. "On three, let's say, Midnight Peace Runners."

We all share a quick look, rolling our eyes, but go along with it.

"One, two, three … Midnight Peace Runners!" we shout together.

"All right, all right," I say, covering my face, embarrassed but smiling. "Let's get to work." I take a breath before continuing. "I spoke to Jake today about the new song. and how Kalendar helped with the chorus. He thinks if we record it and play it for him, maybe he'll respond somehow. Even wake up? I know it's a long shot, but …"

"Then let's do it. Let's bring Kalendar back," Anna interrupts.

God, I love her.

Camp nods. "Nate and I have the music for the chorus done. How are you guys doing with the rest of the lyrics? Need help?"

"Are you kidding?" Anna's laugh sparkles. "Lavender's got this down. I've never seen anyone write such amazing lyrics so fast. She's a natural."

Heat rises to my cheeks. "Thanks, Anna."

I scan the area, a frown forming. "Wait, where's Josephine?"

"She's in Denver, working on promoting the concert," Nate replies.

"Oh. Are people, like, buying tickets now?" My heart skips—this is really happening.

"Well, it's first-come, first-served. No pre-sales. Adds to the hype, but we need to get the word out," Nate explains. "We're gaining traction, but people don't know who we are, for the most part."

"Don't worry. Maggie's on it," Camp says confidently.

I scratch my nose. "Wow, we're getting close, huh?" My stomach twists.

"Less than four weeks!" Anna chimes, spinning in the grass with a carefree laugh.

Camp gives my shoulder a reassuring squeeze.

"Let's not worry about that now. Can we hear the finished song?"

Swallowing the knot of nerves, I take the worn notebook from Anna and read our lyrics aloud. As we take turns sharing them with Camp and Nate, a wave of relief washes over me when their faces light up.

We spend the next few hours blending the lyrics and melody by verse, the night growing darker around us. It's nearly eleven, and reluctance settles in, knowing I'll have to leave soon. Camp must sense it because he leans in.

"Lavender, how about we run through the song before you head out? It'll be good to hear it all together," Camp suggests, his breath warm against my neck.

A shiver races down my spine, but I try to shake it off. "Sure, but I'm still learning the melody."

"Just follow my lead," he says with a smile, nodding toward the microphones.

I stand behind one while Nate picks up his bass and Anna settles behind the drum set, her fingers tapping the snare.

Camp slings his guitar over his shoulder, adjusting the strap before positioning his mic near me. His hazel eyes meet mine.

"You ready?" he drawls.

I nod, my nerves fluttering wildly, but I take a deep breath and remind myself, this is for Kalendar.

Camp sets our handwritten lyrics on the stand in front of us and leans into the mic. "Drummer, count us in."

The sharp, rhythmic clicks of Anna's drumsticks match the thrumming of my heart. *Here we go.*

I shouldn't have been nervous; the song came together perfectly. Following Camp's lead, I even pushed my vocal range, hitting a high note I didn't think I was capable of. The melody he and Nate crafted is so emotionally charged, every note brimming with raw energy.

Silence wraps around us as the last of Camp's guitar chord fades into the night, heavy with emotion. Tears sting my eyes, and I blink them away before they fall.

I lean into the mic, my voice barely more than a whisper. "Thanks, guys."

Without hesitation, Anna, Camp, and Nate wrap me in a tight group hug. As I glance up, a shooting star streaks across the sky, slicing through the velvet night. *Kalendar.*

Camp insists on walking me home, but the déjà vu is unbearable. I keep my distance, dragging my feet and pretending the endless stretch of darkness is so fascinating that I must look anywhere but at him.

As we reach my front steps, he hesitates, pulling off his hat. The porch light casts a glow over half his face, his eyes fixed on mine.

"Well, thanks for walking me, Camp." I start up the stairs, but his hand on my arm stops me.

"Lavender, wait."

I turn, raising a brow.

"Did you mean what you said yesterday? About the kiss being a mistake?" His voice is careful as his eyes search mine.

I force a light laugh, waving my hand as if brushing away a meaningless thought. "Definitely. Like I said, it was just… a weird moment. I'm sorry." A lie. The truth is, I can't stop thinking about it. About him.

A flicker of something—hurt?—crosses his face, gone almost as quickly as it came. He offers a small, unreadable smile.

"Okay, then." He steps back, putting on his hat. "See you tomorrow. Goodnight, Lavender."

"Good night, Camp," I whisper, watching him disappear into the night.

Inside, Mom sits alone on a kitchen stool, her back turned to me. Her shoulders tremble.

No, no, no.

"Mom, what's wrong?" My voice is panic.

She lets out a broken sob. "I miss him so damn much," she whispers, her voice splintering as the sobs take over, wracking her entire body.

I rush to her side and pull her into my arms, holding her tight.

As her cries subside into shaky breaths, I lift her chin, searching her tear-streaked face.

"I thought you were staying at the hospital tonight. Did something happen?"

"No," she whispers, shaking her head. "But that's just it. He's not getting better. Your dad wants us to have a family meeting on Friday if there's no change. I know what he's thinking. He doesn't want

Kalendar to suffer, but I can't lose him. My baby boy … " Her voice fractures, and she breaks down again.

It feels like the floor is giving way beneath me.

Friday. Only four days away. We have to move fast.

THIRTY-FOUR

THE NEXT DAY, I drift through school, unable to focus on anything. I'm beginning to think I should take a break from it altogether, but Kalendar is always in the back of my mind. *"Don't you dare, Ender. You're college bound soon,"* he'd say.

As the final bell rings, I'm already texting Camp. We need to record this song *now*—I'm not totally convinced it'll help Kalendar, but we've got to try.

"Are you guys around?"

The bubbles bounce instantly.

Camp: We're at the campsite. Do you want us to meet you somewhere?

"The lake?"

Camp: Be there in twenty.

I arrive before them and recognize Charlie's truck in the parking lot. He's a freshman at the University of Boulder, so I can't imagine why he's here; it's nearly a six-hour drive.

Hopping down from Betty, I scan the area until I spot Charlie on a bench by the lake. A worn baseball hat is pulled low over his eyes and his trusty Helly Hansen windbreaker shields him from the wind that's picked up significantly since this morning. One arm is casually draped across the back of the bench as he gazes out at the water.

"Hey there," I say, walking over.

Charlie looks up, and his face brightens when he sees me. "Lavender! You're a sight for sore eyes."

I lean in for a hug, and his big, teddy bear frame brings back memories of happier days. I choke down the lump in my throat.

"What are you doing home?"

"Jake called me, actually," Charlie says, his gaze shifting to the lake. "Sounds like you guys are making a big decision on Friday." When he turns back to me, his eyes are shining.

I take a deep breath and sit down next to him. The sky is mostly overcast, but there's a small break where a patch of blue peeks through. A strong gust of wind sweeps my hair, and for a moment, it feels like Kalendar is here with us.

Charlie rubs his neck. "I came to say goodbye, ya know, just in case."

His Adam's apple bobs as he wipes a tear from his eye with his thumb. My own tears spill over, and without a word, I lean my head against his shoulder.

"I know I'm in the minority with this thought, but I think Kal's coming back to us," I whisper.

Charlie drapes his arm around me, his jacket rustling. He stays silent for a moment, simply resting his head against mine. Then he breaks the silence with a chuckle.

"Remember that time Kalendar mooned the entire lake?"

I groan. "Oh my gosh, yes! He claimed he lost the string to his bathing suit. I was sitting right over there—" I nod toward the slight stretch of sand by the water "—completely mortified."

Charlie laughs, shaking his head. "He really gave the lake a show, wiggling his bare ass without a care in the world."

I can't help but laugh, too.

"Oh my goodness, and his dance moves? The best and the worst."

"Definitely the worst. He moved like one of those air dancers on 'shrooms." Charlie says with a laugh. "You know, the ones always flailing in front of car dealerships?"

"Yes!" I giggle, the image of Kalendar's wild moves flashing through my mind.

A voice clears behind me. Camp is standing there; a faint smile tugs at his lips, though his brows knit together in confusion.

"Camp, hey! This is Charlie, Kalendar's best friend," I say, gesturing between them.

Camp's confusion melts away, replaced by a warm smile. He steps forward, extending his hand to Charlie. "Hey, Charlie, nice to meet you."

Charlie shakes Camp's hand with a knowing grin.

"Ah, Kalendar's told me about you. Said you were pretty cool. Thought you and Lavender might be, you know, an item," he adds, his eyes twinkling with mischief.

"What? That's ridiculous." I giggle-snort AGAIN. What is *wrong* with me? My face burns.

Camp chuckles, his eyes flick to mine. "Did he now?"

I scramble for a change of subject.

"We were just reminiscing about the good old days." I laugh nervously.

"That's cool. We can catch up later if you need more time," Camp offers.

I glance past him and spot Anna and Nate approaching.

"Thanks, but I was about to head to the hospital," Charlie says. "How about we all grab dinner later?"

"I'd love to," I reply, avoiding Camp's gaze.

"Yes, count us in," Camp says.

"Perfect. I'll text you around five thirty," Charlie says to me, getting to his feet.

"Sounds good. See you later, Charlie."

I watch Charlie head to his car, throwing a dramatic bow as he passes Anna and Nate.

Anna bursts into giggles, giving him a curtsy in return.

"Who was that?" she asks as she joins us, casting a glance over her shoulder.

"That's Charlie, Kalendar's best friend."

"Well, he's quite the looker. If only I were straight…" She raises an eyebrow.

I laugh and shake my head.

"Why aren't you dating him? Or have you already?" Her eyes narrow, as if trying to read me.

Camp coughs, cutting in. "Okay, settle down, Anna." He forces a laugh before turning to me, his gaze softening. "So, what's on your mind, Lavender?"

I clear my throat. "Last night, when I got home, I had a talk with my mom," I say, my eyes dropping to the ground as I try to keep my voice steady. "She was really upset. She told me my dad has hit his breaking point. He doesn't want to see Kal suffer anymore, so he's scheduled a family meeting for Friday. And I know what that means—they're thinking about taking Kal off life support."

With a soft gasp, Anna draws me in, her arm around my shoulders like a protective wing.

I lean into her. "How fast can we get our song recorded? I want to play it for Kal by Thursday or Friday morning at the latest. Do you think that's possible?"

"Nate and I fine-tuned the outro last night, so we're solid there," Camp says. "But we need a recording studio. I called around this morning and the local studio can't fit us in until Monday. The other option is to head to Denver. I know a couple people there, and they might be able to squeeze us in before Friday."

I think for a moment. "Let's ask Charlie tonight if he can help. I think he knows the owner of the studio here. Henry, maybe? If that doesn't work, a road trip to Denver tomorrow?"

"Sounds like a plan," Nate says, with Anna and Camp nodding in agreement.

"Thanks, guys," I say, my voice catching.

Camp takes my hand, squeezing it. "We'll make it happen. By Friday, Kalendar will hear this song. Promise."

"This might sound dumb, but what if we just played it for him live right now?" Nate asks.

I shake my head. "That's not dumb at all. I asked the hospital staff, but they said we can't play live in the ICU. It could disturb other patients. They suggested we put headphones on Kal instead, which is why I'm eager to record it."

Nate nods. "Makes sense. But hey, if it comes to it, I'm all in for bending some hospital rules."

"We could even pull a Beatles move and sing from the rooftop." Camp grins.

I laugh. "Thanks, guys. Let's keep that in our back pocket."

A warm glow spreads through me as I look at the three of them, my heart brimming with gratitude. How did I get so lucky—for strangers to become family?

"Coffee run?" Camp yawns, rubbing his eyes. "Didn't get much sleep last night."

"Please," Nate replies, stifling a yawn of his own.

I laugh. "All right, sleepyheads. Let's get you some caffeine."

Anna rides with me in Betty as we follow Camp into town. The dirt roads are quiet this afternoon, and dust swirls around us as Camp's Jeep leads the way, leaving a light brown layer on Josephine's license plate.

The aroma of cinnamon and butter greets us as we pull open the coffee shop door. Aly's mom looks up from behind the counter and gives me a warm smile. I wave before heading to the corner table.

After our coffee orders are placed, Camp gets a call from Josephine. He puts it on speaker and sets it in the center of the table.

"Hey, Maggie. You're on speaker. Gang's all here."

"Oh wonderful!" She exclaims. "I'm on my way back from Denver and have some exciting news. I spent yesterday visiting Denver's local radio stations and colleges. They're all on board to promote the concert, and everyone seemed genuinely excited about Midnight Peace Runners and our mission."

Camp and Nate exchange high-fives over the phone as Aly's mom brings over our coffees. I give her a quick side-hug before returning my attention to the conversation.

"That's fantastic, Mags. Do you think we'll draw enough people to fill the venue?" Anna asks.

"It's hard to say, but it's a great start," Josephine replies. "I'll keep spreading the word. In the meantime, you guys focus on the music. I heard you've finished the first song."

"Sure did," Camp says with a grin. "I doubt there will be a dry eye in the house. Even Nate here shed a few tears." He nudges Nate playfully.

Nate chuckles. "Guilty as charged."

"Awesome! I can't wait to hear it," Josephine says, her voice breaking up.

"Mags, I think we're losing you." Anna says.

The call cuts off suddenly. "She's probably going through the Eisenhower tunnel," Camp says, reaching for his phone. "This is great news, guys, but the most important thing is Kalendar." He swings his gaze to me. "Do you think Charlie will come through with the studio space? If not, I'm game to head to Denver right now."

My phone buzzes.

Charlie: See you at 5:30 at that new Mexican place. Gato something?

I meet Camp's eyes. "Only one way to find out."

THIRTY-FIVE

THE FLOOR-TO-CEILING windows of the recording studio glint in the September sun, with the *Motts Recording Studio* sign prominent among the neatly arranged boulders. It's a strange mix of modern and rustic, yet somehow, it works.

As Camp eases the Jeep into a parking spot, my nerves spike.

Henry Motts shakes his cane at us from the entrance. Not the warmest of greetings, though Charlie did mention he's a bit of a curmudgeon. His broad, squat frame fills the width of the doorway, and on his head sits a top hat, its base wrapped in a colorful ribbon. I can't tell if his cane is for support or just for flair. He looks like the Beatles' Mr. Kite come to life, eccentric and theatrical, but like, the cranky version.

Last night, I had to start from the beginning to catch Charlie up on everything, especially since he hardly knew about the band—apart from Mom's quick rundown at the hospital. He listened intently, nodding as Camp and Anna chimed in with extra details now and then.

His eyes widened when I told Charlie how Kalendar had "spoken" to me while I was writing our latest song. It turns out that Charlie's had visits from Kalendar too, mostly when he's half asleep or zoning out in class. He wasn't sure if they were real until he found out I'd had the same thing happen to me.

"There's no doubt; he's communicating with us!" Charlie said, his voice full of excitement.

When Charlie reached out to Henry and explained everything, Henry reluctantly squeezed us into his studio schedule—not without making sure Charlie knew just how much of an inconvenience it was. The only reason he agreed at all was because he owed Charlie's parents a favor. Though, when asked, Charlie's parents had no recollection of any such debt.

Charlie was invited to watch the recording, but Henry made it crystal clear: "Absolutely no other visitors, except the band." *Yes, sir.*

And now, here we are.

I step out of the Jeep and give Henry a small wave. He frowns and swats at the air with his cane again before turning on his heel and marching inside. Great. As if I wasn't anxious enough already.

Camp must sense my nerves because he catches my hand, pulling me toward him. When I meet his gaze, his eyes smile. "This will be fun," he says. "You're going to be amazing." His touch sends a low, electric hum up my arm.

Anna links my free arm with hers. "Yes, so much fun!" she echoes.

"Um, yeah." I slip my hand from Camp's and tuck a stray hair behind my ear.

"You coming or what?" *Henry.*

Camp glances at him, standing by the door again, and laughs. "We'd better get moving." He grabs his guitar from the trunk. "Did Charlie say when he'd be here?"

Before I can answer, Bob Dylan's "Rainy Day Women #12 & 35" spills through the air. I grin. "Right now," I say as Charlie's red truck rolls into the lot. He hops down, flashing a smile.

"Charlie! I'm not getting any younger. Get your friends up here!" Henry calls in a surprisingly high-pitched voice, like a toddler in the midst of a tantrum.

I glance at my watch—we're ten minutes early.

"We're coming, Henry!" Charlie calls back, turning to us with a wink. "Told you." He holds out a hand, and Anna immediately abandons me, placing her hand in his as they ascend the stone steps together.

"Well, I've been replaced," I say with a laugh, watching Anna giggle at something Charlie said.

Camp smirks, his drawl easy. "He's a charmer."

Nate strides up beside me, bass in one hand, and offers his other arm with an exaggerated flourish.

"Why, Nate, I never pegged you for a gentleman," I tease, looping my arm through his.

He smirks. "I have my moments."

We step into the studio behind Charlie and Anna, and my breath catches. I'm not sure what I was expecting, but definitely not this. The place is like a dream—plush leather couches rest on even plusher white shag carpets, sleek wood floors shine under the warm lights, and abstract paintings of aspen trees and mountains pulse with the energy of the room.

The air is sharp and fresh, like after a thunderstorm when everything feels new and alive. Whether it's the studio itself or my nerves, I can't tell—but the whole place is buzzing, and so am I.

"This way," Henry shouts, guiding us down a narrow hallway and proving that his cane, indeed, is a prop. The walls are painted deep red and lined with framed albums, their glass surfaces gleaming in the dim light. I squint, trying to make out the names, but the shadows make it impossible to read.

Henry swings open a thick door, his massive hand holding it wide as we step inside. "Your workspace for the day," he mutters.

Inside, the room splits into two distinct areas. On one side, three stools are positioned in front of a platform holding a sleek drum set, each paired with a microphone stand. Speakers and cables are meticulously arranged around the space.

On the other side, the control room holds an array of professional-grade control boards and several computers. A large glass window separates the two spaces, allowing a clear view from the control room into the recording area. The air smells of burning incense—pine, maybe?

"Would you prefer to use your equipment or ours?" Henry asks, looking somewhere beyond us. I turn around expecting to see someone else, but apparently he talks to walls.

"Nate and I brought ours," Camp replies, his gaze flicking to Anna, "but Anna was planning to use your drum set, if that's cool."

Henry gives a single, gruff nod. "Fine," he mutters, and without another word, he turns toward the control panel. "Charlie, you're here with me." He swings out a roller seat that rolls half-way to where we're standing.

"I would love nothing more!" Charlie booms in a terrible British accent. He gives us a thumbs up before plopping in the seat and rolling over to Henry. He puts his arm around Henry's shoulders. "So, what do we have here?" His British accent is somehow worse.

Henry's voice drops low as he starts explaining something to Charlie, his hands gesturing wildly, clearly caught up in the details. Charlie, ever the attentive listener, rests his chin between two fingers, nodding along as if Henry's the most interesting man in the world.

I can't help but laugh.

"Come with me," Camp whispers, slipping his hand into mine. He opens the door to the recording studio, and I trail behind him, my nerves instantly kicking back in.

As Anna and Nate set up their equipment, Camp walks me through everything. I'm relieved that this isn't their first time in a studio—knowing they've done this before takes a bit of the pressure off.

"So, are we performing live? Like singing the song straight through and then we're done?" I ask, my nerves slipping into my voice.

"I wish it were that easy, but recording is done in multiple takes," Camp explains. "There are two ways to do it: live and all together, or in parts."

"Which one are we going with? I really want us to perform as a full band." I shoot him my best puppy-dog eyes, hoping he'll understand. The thought of singing alone sends my stomach into a series of somersaults.

"We can try it that way first," Camp says, laughing. "But I've got a feeling Henry will want us to record in parts. Still, let's give it a shot." He glances through the window at Henry. "I'm going to let him know our plan. I'll be right back."

Camp leaves the room to talk with Henry, and I watch them through the glass, their conversation silent on this side of the studio. Henry shakes his head, his gestures sharp, frustration clear in his body language. My stomach twists; this doesn't look promising. He follows Camp to the door, leans against the frame, and watches as Camp returns to my side.

"Sorry, I really tried," he whispers, his voice low but filled with regret.

"All right, guys. Time's ticking. Let's give it one go-around, then we'll record in parts." Henry's eyes narrow on me for whatever reason. "You all ready?"

I swallow hard and glance at Nate and Anna.

"Ready!" they both chime in. I wish I had even half of their confidence.

"Ready," I say, but it comes out in a whisper.

Camp leans in close, smiling. "Just pretend it's you and me, okay?"

I nod, feeling the nerves settle a bit.

Camp hands me a pair of headphones, and I slide them over my ears.

"Let's go!" Henry's high voice shouts, shutting the door behind him. I watch through the glass as he takes his spot behind the control boards.

He flicks on the "Recording" light and points at us. My heart does a backflip.

I lock eyes with Camp. Everything else blurs. It's just us.

THIRTY-SIX

MY VOICE CRACKS in the first chorus.

Henry presses the intercom. "Go again." His voice has somehow deepened in the last thirty seconds. He frowns at me from his seat, a mixture of impatience and something else I can't read.

Already on edge, my entire body feels hot with sweat, and I suddenly wish I could vanish into thin air.

Camp brushes my arm; his gaze locks on mine. "Just like we practiced."

I inhale deeply and fix my gaze on the concrete floor while I try to channel Kalendar, but I can't feel his presence at all.

Anna claps her sticks together three times, and the music starts up again. My body moves in tune to the beat and I grip the microphone tight. Camp's voice kicks in and my cue to join him is in three, two, one.

"The runners hold their pace until—" My voice cracks again, like an actual boy going through puberty. "Shit," I mutter, slapping my hand to my face, feeling the heat flood my cheeks. I can't look Camp in the eyes, I can't look anyone in the eyes. I squeeze them shut instead.

"AGAIN," the intercom crackles, and someone squeezes my arm.

Three breaths in, four breaths out.

I nod, eyes still closed, my throat tight.

Anna's sticks clap again.

Music.

Camp.

Now…me.

But I can't.

"I'm sorry," I whisper, my hands shaking as I fumble with the microphone. It slips from my grasp and clatters to the floor—the harsh screech of metal on concrete echoing through the studio. I tear the headphones from my ears and stumble into the hallway, leaving the door swinging behind me. My legs give out just as I shove the front door open, and I tumble to the ground. I bury my head between my knees.

Breathe. Breathe. Breathe.

The door creaks open and shut.

Footsteps.

A hand is drawing circles on my back. *Charlie.*

"I can't do it, Charlie," I whimper. My breathing steadies and my body begins to feel again. The stone is cold and seeping through my jeans. My head feels heavy, hanging between my knees. I crack open an eye and watch a lone ant scurry across the ground beneath me, weaving in and out of the cracks in the rock. Charlie's khaki knee is next to my foot, and the sound of him humming that Dylan song from earlier fills the silence. My fingers instinctively tap out the rhythm on my arm.

Charlie sings in his best Dylan impression, "… I would not feel so all alone."

"Everybody must get stoned." I finish.

We smile.

I sniffle.

"Kal's favorite Dylan song," I say as I lift my gaze.

Charlie grins down at me; his familiar droopy eyes bring me back to safety. "Look, this is all maybe too much, too fast." He begins, hesitating for a moment as he tries to find the right words. "And I know you've never exactly been... confident in, well, anything." He chuckles softly, nudging me with his elbow. "But, I've known you forever, Ender."

The sound of my nickname—Kalendar's nickname for me—sends a chill down my spine, both comforting and painful at the same time. Charlie falters, maybe realizing his slip, but he keeps going, his tone reassuring. "One thing you should definitely be confident about, besides everything," he adds with a crooked smile, "is your musical abilities."

I roll my eyes.

"Don't do that," he says. "If anyone knows music, it's you. Well, and me, of course." He smirks. "I've heard you sing over the years— you're not just good, you're amazing. I mean, watch out, Taylor, there's a new girl in town."

I snort and swat his shoulder. "Yeah, okay."

His expression softens but stays serious. "I mean it. You have talent, Lavender. You just need to believe it."

The door opens behind us, and I look up as Camp's head pops out. His eyes find mine; worry settles in his features. "Are you okay?"

I nod, a small smile tugging at my lips. "Thanks, Camp. I'll be right in."

He hesitates, eyes searching mine. "Are you sure? If you need more time, we can reschedule."

I exhale, straightening my shoulders. "No, I'm ready."

When I turn back to Charlie, he's squinting at the sky. "Is that a seagull?" He points at the evergreens above us, where a seagull circles.

I laugh. "Yup."

He whips his head toward me, eyes wide. "A seagull? In Colorado? My, my the times, they are a-changin.'" He says again in a Dylan impression.

I giggle and stand, offering him my hand.

He takes it with an exaggerated groan. "Oh, my poor, aching bones. They just aren't what they used to be."

"Okay, Grandpa."

The bird swoops low, right over our heads and caws as it flies away.

Back in the studio, Henry is lying on the floor, spread eagle.

"Um, did we kill him?" Charlie asks the room, eyebrows raised.

"Yes. From boredom," Henry mutters, coughing as he sits up. He exhales an exasperated sigh, flicking his gaze between me and Charlie. "Well? Are we doing this or not?"

"We're doing this," I say, squaring my shoulders.

I resume my place besides Camp and slip on the headphones. Without a word, he lifts his cowboy hat and settles it on my head. It's warm, carrying the scent of him. He gives me a small nod.

"Ready, girl?" *Anna.*

I nod and straighten Camp's hat, relieved to find the tremble in my hands is gone.

"You got this, Lavender." *Nate.*

The recording light comes on.

Anna's drumsticks.

Music.

Camp.

Me.

The lyrics flow effortlessly, each note landing exactly where it should. My soprano voice harmonizes perfectly with Camp's soulful, raspy twang. Charlie nods from behind the control board, a proud smile spreading across his face. For a moment, his features blur—becoming Kalendar's. My heart stumbles, but I keep singing, as if he's right there in the room with me.

As the final note fades, I steal a glance at Camp. His eyes are set on me, a loving intensity in them.

The intercom crackles to life. Henry clears his throat. "Well, okay. Nice job. Let's move on and record in parts."

My eyes grow wide at the compliment.

"And the grinch's heart grew five sizes…er, wait. *Three* sizes that day…" Anna stage-whispers behind me.

Laughing, I pull the microphone back to my lips. "Let's finish what we started."

"Yeehaw!" Nate shouts.

After three hours of recording, I've come to realize this whole process is far more exhausting than I'd expected. Don't get me wrong, I'm so grateful to be here, but I never imagined how painstakingly detailed it would be. So much starting, stopping, and fine-tuning—re-recording a single line ten times, adjusting mic levels, trying a different vocal range, then doing it all over again just in case. My brain's buzzing, my throat's dry, and my back aches from sitting on the stool for so long, but weirdly, I love it.

I'm perched on Charlie's lap while Camp, Nate, and Anna wrap up the instrumental. The studio lights cast a soft glow over us, reflecting off the glass windows and giving the room a warm golden hue. The colorful waveforms pulse across the monitors as the song's final notes fade out.

"And that's a wrap," Henry announces through the microphone into the recording room.

I let out a deep breath and jump up from Charlie; clapping soundlessly as Camp, Nate, and Anna share high fives. The studio hums with a quiet, contented energy. Henry *actually* smiles and gives a thumbs-up.

Camp returns to the control room, sweeping me into his arms and twirling me around. "You were amazing," he murmurs, setting me down gently.

Smiling, I place his cowboy hat on his head. "Thanks for letting me borrow this. Must be magic or something," I tease.

Camp adjusts his hat and winks. "Must be."

Henry exhales sharply. "Honestly, I thought this would be a disaster." His high-pitched voice cuts through the room. "And trust me, I've seen a lot of disasters. But that? That was damn good."

Charlie smirks, bumping Henry's shoulder. "Told you they'd be great."

Henry waves his cane dismissively. "Yeah, yeah. Alright, help me mix this now."

Charlie cracks his knuckles. "I have no idea what that means, but okay."

Nate chuckles, rolling a spare chair over to Henry. "I can help with that."

Henry's bushy brows lift. "Where'd you learn how to mix?"

Nate ties his long hair into a ponytail. "My uncle, actually. He's a musician too. Was. He was a musician." He glances at Henry. "Never quite hit the big time, but music was his passion. Taught me everything I know."

I lean toward Anna, keeping my voice low. "What happened to his uncle?"

Her brows knit together. "He was murdered a few years ago. I'm sure Nate will share the details with you when he's ready," she whispers.

"Oh my gosh, that's awful."

Nate's fingers dance across the keyboard, his head nodding in rhythm with the music streaming through his headphones. No wonder he's so passionate about this band; he's doing this for his uncle. Tears sting my eyes as the realization sinks in and I immediately feel guilty about judging his overall cranky demeanor so strongly. Camp's right; everyone's carrying something.

Camp taps Nate on the shoulder.

Nate pulls back one headphone and looks up.

"I'm going to drop the girls off," he says. "I'll be back to help."

Nate nods. "Cool." He replaces the headphone and resumes typing.

I walk over to Henry and wrap my arms around his shoulders. He stiffens.

"Thank you," I say.

His shoulders relax and he rolls around to face me. "It's fine," he says, his thick lips lifting into a smile. "After listening to this song, I'm impressed. And that doesn't happen often." He laughs. "Charlie filled me in on your brother. If any song could wake a person from a coma, this would be it." His large brown eyes meet mine. "We'll have it ready by morning."

THIRTY-SEVEN

KALENDAR'S CEILING is covered in glow-in-the-dark stars.

I remember the night he tacked them up there. He was thirteen, maybe; I think Charlie had given them to him as a birthday present. Or someone else. Not important. But it's pretty incredible that they've stuck around all these years.

Turning on my side, I clutch Kalendar's pillow tight. God, I miss him. The crystal heart is warm and smooth in my palm as sleep comes.

"Ender. Hey, Ender." Kalendar's voice fills the room. My eyes snap open, and I bolt upright. Kalendar's sitting at the foot of his bed with a wide smile. "Morning."

This can't be real. I rub my eyes. It's him, but a faded version of him. Ghostly. He's wearing the outfit he wore the night he was shot. Old jeans and a Montana State hoodie.

"Kal?"

"Yeah, it's me. Sort of." He laughs, and I lose it.

I'm crying so hard I can barely see. I throw myself toward him, but he vanishes.

"It's me, just not physically," he says.

I spin around, and he's by the door now.

"What's going on? Why can't I touch you?" I try to get up, but it's like I'm stuck in bed. I keep struggling, but I'm getting nowhere, and the tears keep coming.

"Hold on, Ender," Kalendar says, his playful grin fading into something serious.

"Kal, what is this? Is this real?"

"As real as we can make it," he says, leaning against the doorframe. "But listen, there's something you need to hear." His eyes lock onto mine. "Keep writing songs. You're going to change the world." A lone tear slips down his cheek. "I'm so damn proud of you."

"Thanks, but—" He's gone before I can finish.

"Kalendar! Kalendar!" I scream, my voice cracking. "Kalendaaaaar!!!"

A gentle shake pulls me back. Jake's voice, distant at first, gradually cuts through the haze.

"Lavender, wake up! It's a dream."

My eyes flutter open to find Jake leaning over me, his brows pinched.

"Oh, Jake." I sob into his shoulder. "It felt so real. I saw him."

Jake holds me close, rubbing my back. I must fall asleep against him because when I wake again, morning light is creeping into the room. Jake's curled up on the floor beside Kalendar's bed, asleep.

The crystal heart lies next to my thigh. I pick it up, clutching it tight.

"Today's the day," I whisper to myself, the words trembling in the quiet.

I carefully drape Kalendar's blanket over Jake and slip out of the room.

In the kitchen, Mom greets me with a warm, "Good morning, babe," but her half-smile fades as soon as she sees my face. "What's wrong?" Her voice sharpens with concern.

"I had a dream about Kal last night," I say, the words heavy.

"What happened?" She quickly puts her tea down and rushes over, her eyes searching mine.

"He said he was proud of me, and then … he was just gone." I try to keep my voice steady, replaying the dream in my head.

Her arms wrap around me tightly. "He *is* proud of you. I know he is."

"I know, but it felt like he was saying goodbye …" My voice cracks and my eyes burn with unshed tears. I think I'm officially out of tears.

Mom sniffles and grabs a tissue to dab her eyes. She doesn't say anything, just pulls me closer. What's left to say anymore?

THIRTY-EIGHT

RAIN HAMMERS THE metal roof, spraying my face through the open window. I sit at my desk, watching the water soak everything—paper, pens, picture frames, candles. It drips off my chin like sweat, darkening the lap of my light jeans.

"Hun? Campion's on the phone. You left it in the kitchen." Mom's voice echoes through the house as her footsteps pad up the stairs. "What are you doing? Everything's soaked!" She rushes in, slams the window shut, and hands me my phone. "Here." She crosses my room, grabs a towel hanging from my headboard, and wipes the rain from the desk.

"Camp? Hey," I breathe.

"Song's ready. Do you want us to meet you at the hospital?" Camp's voice is hurried.

His words pull me from my trance. "Yes. I'll get everyone ready, and we'll meet you there."

Mom's eyebrows are floating. "Go time?"

"Yup," I say, standing. "I'll get Dad and Jake. Can you call Emma, Charlie and Josephine?"

"Of course," she says, reaching for her phone from her pocket.

The ride to the hospital is quiet; a nervous energy pulses through the car. Emma's grip on my hand tightens as we enter the parking lot. We picked her up from school on the way in. I was too anxious to pretend I was interested in learning today.

Dad parks next to Camp's Jeep, which is in serious need of a wash. The once bright white has turned into a dusty brown. I don't see him or the others, so they must already be inside. A wave of nausea comes over me, and I swing open the door and make it to the curb just in time. Mom's hand sweeps across my back as I retch for twenty years. When I can finally breathe, I sit on the pavement and hang my head between my knees.

"You okay, hun?"

I shake my head.

"Why don't you all go inside? We'll be right there," she says, her palm still steady on my back.

Dad's concerned voice cuts in. "You sure? Want me to get a nurse?"

There's a beat then, "No, she'll be okay. Go on," Mom reassures him.

I can sense hesitation before their footsteps crunch on the asphalt as they walk away.

"Mom," I whisper, my voice almost lost in the air between us. "Why did I think this was a good idea? There's so much riding on this song. I'm so stupid; to pretend like this is going to fix him."

Mom sighs before pressing a tissue into my palm. "You're not stupid." She pats my arm, and I lift my face to meet her eyes. "All we can do is try, babe."

I nod, closing my eyes for a moment before standing. I wipe my mouth and shove the crumpled tissue into my pocket before looping my arm through hers.

"Okay," I say as we head to the hospital entrance together.

After a quick cleanup in the restroom and the longest elevator ride of my life, Mom and I reach the ICU. A crowd is gathered outside Kalendar's door. Camp strides over without hesitation.

"It's damn good," he says, falling in step beside us.

"I've got the song queued up on my phone," Nate says as we reach the room, holding up a Bluetooth speaker and Bose headphones. "We can play it however you want."

"Thanks, Nate." I glance at Mom, Dad, and Jake. "Ready?"

Dad pulls me close, his arm firmly around my shoulders, and reaches for Mom's hand. She clasps Jake's, and together, we step through the door.

Wires snake across Kalendar's body. Machines breathe beside him, and he sleeps on—unchanged, unmoving.

Nate hands me the speaker and headphones, his cold fingers brushing mine. I stare down at them, my hands trembling slightly.

"Which one?" I ask no one in particular.

"Headphones," Jake says after a moment. "Might get through to him faster."

I nod and carefully slip the headphones over Kalendar's ears, avoiding the bandages around his head. The beep of the heart monitor fills the room, mingling with the soft rustle of Mom's jacket as she shifts beside me. Once the headphones are snug, I glance at Nate and give him a shaky thumbs-up.

Emma's arms wrap around my waist, grounding me as I try to breathe normally. My eyes lock onto Kalendar's peaceful face.

"Okay, it's playing," Nate says, his voice tense.

We all watch Kalendar, searching for the slightest twitch, a flutter of his eyelids, the flick of a finger—anything. Seconds stretch into minutes, but nothing changes.

"The song's over. Should I play it again?" Nate asks, his voice cutting through the quiet.

"Yes, please," Mom answers quickly. She steps closer to Kalendar, settling into the chair by his bed, and takes his hand. "Come back to us, baby," she whispers, her voice trembling.

Nate plays the song again, but Kalendar doesn't stir.

Suddenly, I'm nauseous and extremely dizzy. *Not again.*

"Excuse me," I mutter, bolting from the room. The door slams shut behind me as I stumble into the hallway, collapsing against the wall. My lungs tighten, like they're bound in Saran wrap.

"I'll go," comes Camp's muffled voice from behind the door.

It opens, then clicks shut, and I sense Camp settle beside me. He gathers my hair back, his breath cool on my neck as he blows. The dizziness fades. I sit up straighter and manage a small smile. "Thanks. That helps, actually."

"My mom used to do it whenever I got dizzy or sick; it always helped me feel better," he says, releasing my hair and swinging an arm around my shoulders.

"Your Mom knew what she was doing." I rest my head against his shoulder.

Camp strokes my hair, humming our new song. After a while, he clears his throat. "Can I suggest something?"

"Of course."

"Let's all listen to the song together on the speaker. Kalendar might want to share it with us."

A tear breaks free and slides down my cheek. A nod is all I can manage.

Camp stands and offers me his hand. I take it, letting him pull me to my feet. I draw a deep breath, then turn the handle to Kalendar's room. Everyone turns when we walk in. One glance at their faces tells me everything—no change.

"Camp has a good idea," I say, my voice shaky but hopeful. "Let's play the song out loud. Maybe Kalendar wants us all to hear it together." I fidget with the sleeves of Kalendar's oversized sweatshirt—the one I threw on this morning.

"That's a great idea," Anna says, taking the speaker from Nate. She switches on the Bluetooth, glancing at him with a nod.

"Connected," Nate confirms, checking his phone. "All right, here we go." With a tap, he presses *play*.

I take a deep breath, my gaze settling on Kalendar. *C'mon, Kal.*

Camp's guitar melody fills the room, each note achingly beautiful. I hold my breath; the lyrics are coming.

When my voice flows from the speaker, it sounds different from in the studio—stronger, confident, like someone who's done this a thousand times before. The song reverberates through the room, filling every corner with a hope I cling to with everything I've got.

"A world where I used to belong,
Seems as if it were an age-old song.
Nostalgia rears its head tonight
While thoughts of memories delight

I miss those days of cheer and joy
When love felt like a brand-new toy
When I felt like I could soar
Now kindness is gone, and hope a chore

Not a simple wish upon a star tonight
But a plead for the world to hold hands and unite
The runners hold pace until twilight
Singin' and chantin' with sweet release
Bring 'em peace

Oh please, bring 'em peace

Violence fills our streets
People throw fire and then retreat
Bullies, enemies, frenemies, foes
These are the new times we know

Music can save your soul
And bring you back up from that hole
Listen for the magic within
That's where our new world will begin

Not a simple wish upon a star tonight
But a plead for the world to hold hands and unite
The runners hold pace until twilight
Singin' and chantin' with sweet release
Bring 'em peace
Oh please, bring 'em peace

We can do better if we try
The world is made for you and I
Where fireflies 'neath velvet skies
Dance and sway till mornin' goodbyes

Where we run free and hope returns
The world will once again be firm
With friends and family in joy and love
Let's bring peace just like a dove

And so we wish upon a star tonight
A plead for the world to hold hands and unite

We, runners, hold pace until twilight
Singin' and chantin' with sweet release
Bring 'em peace
Oh please, bring 'em peace"

Tears fall down my cheeks despite my best efforts to hold them in. It is *damn* good.

A profound silence fills the room. Mom rushes over, pulling me into a tight hug.

"That was beautiful," she breathes, her voice thick with emotion. She cradles my face in her hands, her eyes shimmering with tears. "Just beautiful."

She moves to Camp next, hugging him with the same intensity.

"It's perfect," Dad says, his voice steady as he walks over to me. He kisses my forehead and wraps me in his arms.

I glance at Jake, Emma, and Charlie. Tears run down their faces, mirroring the emotion that's overcome me. Jake has his arm around Emma, who holds Charlie's hand. They all look at me with expressions of love and admiration. My heart's on fire.

"Midnight Peace Runners. You're going to change the world," Josephine says. A single tear slips down her cheek—something I've never seen from her before. She moves to Kalendar's side, placing her hand over his. Her eyes close and she stands silently for a few moments.

I watch Kalendar, hoping for any sign of change, but my heart sinks as he remains still.

"Please play it again," Josephine requests, her voice soft as she clings to Kalendar's hand.

Nate presses *play*, and the song begins once more.

Jake walks over and wraps his arm around my shoulder. "No matter what happens, I'm so proud of you," he murmurs.

"Thanks, Jake," I reply, giving him a grateful smile and squeezing his side.

Josephine whispers something under her breath, still holding Kalendar's hand.

When the song ends for the second time, she kisses Kalendar's forehead before stepping away. She leans in to whisper something to Camp, who nods in response. Clearing his throat, he addresses everyone.

"We're going to give you all some time alone," he says, his narrowed eyes meeting mine.

I nod, assuring him that I'm okay.

"I'll send you the song now, Lavender, and I'll leave the headphones and speaker here if you need them," Nate says.

"Thanks, Nate." I address the rest of the group, my voice catching. "And thank you all … for everything. I … I don't even have the words to say how much this means…" My voice trails off, overwhelmed by the gratitude and love I feel for these incredible people.

Dad steps in, his voice warm. "Yes, thank you. You've all been so supportive of our family. We can't thank you enough."

Amid the goodbyes and hugs, Josephine weaves her way over to me.

"Don't lose hope just yet," she whispers, her eyes holding a spark that makes me wonder if she knows something I don't.

Camp is the last to say goodbye. He steps close, his hand brushing a stray hair from my face. "If you need anything, call me. I'll be here," he promises.

"Thanks." I rest my face against his chest, feeling it rise.

The rest of us linger at the hospital; Charlie shares stories about Kalendar that we'd never heard before. Our emotions fluctuate between laughter and tears, a bittersweet dance of memories and hope. *Dwindling* hope.

As time passes, my confidence struggles. The room grows quieter, with longer, more frequent pauses that echo our collective anxiety. Each of us steals glances at Kalendar, silently begging for a sign, a miracle.

"Let's play your song again," Dad says eventually.

I place the speaker on the over-bed table and pull up Nate's text on my phone. With a deep breath, I hit play.

We watch Kalendar as the song plays through. When it ends, the room remains still. Kalendar unchanged.

"Would anyone like to get some fresh air?" Mom's voice trembles with emotion.

"That sounds like a good idea," Emma replies, her tone reflective.

"Yeah, why don't we step outside for a bit? We could grab some food or just walk around town," Dad suggests.

Everyone nods in agreement, and we quietly make our way toward the door. I walk with Dad at the back of our group as we head to the elevator.

"We don't need to make any decisions tomorrow. Let's take a little more time," Dad says, reaching for my hand.

I turn to him with a grateful smile. "Thanks, Dad," I reply, leaning on his shoulder.

"Should we bring the speaker? Maybe we can listen to the song again outside." Dad says. "I quite like it." He squeezes my hand.

"Sure, I'll grab it." I squeeze his hand in return. "I'll catch up with you downstairs."

He nods. "Thanks, sweetheart."

A chill runs through me as I step into Kalendar's room and reach for the speaker resting on the counter. Shivering, I tug the hoodie over my head, ready to leave—when something stops me. An invisible pull urges me to turn back to Kalendar. Slowly, I pivot, my gaze settling on him. I dig into my bag, pull out my AirPods, and make my way to his bedside. Gently, I place one earbud in my ear and the other in his. With a steadying breath, I pull out my phone, scroll to our song, and press *play*.

I close my eyes, letting the song seep into my soul. Suddenly, a warm glow spreads across my thigh. Startled, I reach into my pocket and pull out the crystal heart—it's almost too hot to hold. Confused, I open my eyes and my heart stops.

Kalendar is looking at me.

His eyes are open.

I blink rapidly, trying to shake off the disbelief—this isn't a dream. He's still staring right at me. "Mom! Dad! Jake!" I shout, bolting to the door and yelling down the hallway.

Through my tears, everything blurs, but when I glance back, I swear Kalendar is smiling.

THIRTY-NINE

THE COOL, CRISP AIR carries the scent of campfire smoke as I cradle my coffee mug in both hands.

The mountains are alive with strikes of gold as the aspens begin their autumn transformation. Beside me, Camp's munching on the sourdough Mom baked this morning. Anna and Nate are playing cards on the table behind us.

I relax into the rocking chair, surrounded by a million pillows—naturally. This past week has been a whirlwind of hospital visits and band practice. Kalendar wasn't unconscious long enough to cause any permanent brain damage, thank God. And just as the doctor predicted, since that miraculous afternoon, he's become more alert each day. He's regained movement in his neck, fingers and toes, and although he hasn't spoken yet, his eyes are full of life, brimming with words he can't yet say. Every morning, I still wake up in a haze, half-convinced it was all a dream. Then I remember—and it hits me like a sunrise: he's still here. I don't have the words for how grateful I am. It feels like I've been born again, right along with him.

I've decided to take a brief break from school. After talking it over with Principal Simmons, we agreed that focusing on family should come first. We set October 9 as the target date for my return. With my solid grades and extracurriculars, Principal Simmons assured me that this break wouldn't jeopardize my college prospects—if I decide to go.

Making music has consumed most of my time. The messages in the songs we create move me to actual tears. And yes, I said "songs" because I've written three more in the last eight days. Yup, three. Songwriting has become my second nature; the lyrics just flow like I'm channeling something greater. It's hard to explain, but it feels like magic.

A car engine hums in the distance as Josephine's 4Runner emerges on the dirt road leading to our driveway.

I set my mug on the side table, my stomach tightening. "Did you know Josephine was stopping by?" Not that I mind, but it's unlike her to show up without calling.

Camp looks at his phone, then shakes his head, squinting at the driveway. "Anna, Nate, did you know Josephine was coming?"

"No," they say in unison, standing to join us.

"Let's go, I have a feeling something's up," Anna says.

As we reach the bottom of the front steps, Josephine emerges from her SUV, and it looks like she hasn't slept in a while. Her hair is frizzy, and the whites of her eyes have taken on a reddish tint. Still, her warm smile remains as she spots us.

"I'm sorry to drop by unannounced, but we've hit a bit of a snag," she says, her voice full of exhaustion.

"What's wrong?" Camp and Nate ask at the same time.

"Red Rocks threw us a curveball," Josephine says, frustration in her words. "They're suddenly against selling tickets only on the day of the concert. I was just on the phone with my contact, and it sounds like their board is putting on the pressure."

Anna scratches her eyebrow thoughtfully. "Well, can't we start selling them now?"

Josephine sighs and shakes her head. "It's not that simple. The ticket agency needs at least a couple of weeks' notice to set everything up online, and we don't have that time. The concert's in two weeks. They're threatening to cancel unless we can guarantee a big turnout."

"Well, looks like we've got our work cut out for us," Camp says, rubbing his hands together.

I raise an eyebrow. "What are you thinking?"

"I've got a few ideas brewing. Don't you worry about it," he says, his mind clearly already racing ahead. "Anna, Nate, let's go."

"But I want to help. What can I do?"

Camp places his hand on my shoulder. "Spend time with Kalendar for a few days. If we need you, I'll call, I promise."

I reluctantly nod.

Josephine begins to speak, but Camp raises his hand and shakes his head. "Before you offer to dive in, let me remind you that you've already done so much for us. Besides, I know you've got that meditation retreat starting tomorrow. You focus on that, and I'll reach out if we need anything."

Josephine's expression softens. "Thanks, guys. Please keep me posted. We need this concert to happen."

"It will," he says confidently, tipping his hat before heading toward the Jeep. "Oh, and thanks for letting us keep the Jeep." He smirks.

"Of course, it's for the band." She smiles.

"Thanks, guys. Don't forget to check in." I say with a small wave, turning toward the house. I reach for Josephine's hand when I'm startled by a sudden rush of movement behind me. Camp takes my free hand and spins me around. His eyes lock onto mine, and his dimples flash as he grins.

"Just needed one last look to keep me going." He winks before walking away.

"He's head over heels for you, dear." Josephine chuckles as we both watch the Jeep bounce down the driveway.

Laughing, I shake my head. "He's the most confusing man in the world."

The first (very obvious) thing I notice when I enter Kalendar's hospital room is that his bed is missing, which, of course, means *he* is missing.

Emma rises from a chair in the corner, her smile lighting up the room.

"Where's Kal?" I ask, a mix of curiosity and concern in my voice.

"Oh, they took him for some tests," she replies, her eyes sparkling. "But guess what?!"

"What?"

"Kalendar spoke! Right before they took him away!"

"Really? What did he say?" My pulse speeds.

"Hi."

"Are you sure?"

"Absolutely, sure!" Emma's enthusiasm is infectious.

A fleeting pang of jealousy crosses my mind. I wish I'd been here, but I quickly push it aside. Emma's been a constant presence, and her love for Kalendar is so freakin obvious; I hate that it took me this long to realize it.

"Tell me more! Did he say anything else?"

"Nope, just that. It was a whisper, but still, he spoke! I told the nurses as they were taking him for his tests, and they said it's a fantastic sign. We should start seeing more activity from him soon. Oh, Lavender! I can't believe he's come back to us!" Emma wraps me in a hug, her head resting on my shoulder.

She pulls back and grabs her jacket from the chair. "I'll leave you to have some time with him. I'm sorry you weren't here; I'm sure you're feeling a bit sad about it. But with you here now, I know he'll want to say even more!"

Of course, she knows *everything* that goes through my mind. "Thanks, Em. How did I get so lucky to have you as a friend?"

She shrugs. "Just won the friend lottery, I guess." She winks. "Okay, so let me know if he says anything else." She reaches for the door handle.

"I will. Thanks," I reply, blowing her a kiss as she leaves.

I call Mom to share the good news, and before I can even finish my sentence, she, Dad, and Jake are on their way.

As I wait for Kalendar's return, my mind spirals about this concert situation. If the show at Red Rocks falls through, we'll need to find a new venue, but it's hard to imagine finding a place as perfect as Red Rocks. Then I remember Jake's newfound connection. Jim Baker. I make a mental note to see if he can help.

The door opens, and Kate wheels Kalendar back into the room.

"How's he doing?" I ask.

"He's doing great, sweetheart. We took him in for some routine tests. Did Emma tell you he said 'hi' earlier?"

"She did! Has he said anything else?" I ask eagerly.

"No, but he keeps winking at me." She laughs. "He certainly has a sense of humor."

"He sure does," I reply just as Kalendar gives us a wink. Laughing, I roll my eyes.

"I'll leave you two alone. Holler if you need anything," Kate says as she heads for the door.

There's more color in Kalendar's face today, and he's only hooked up to a couple of wires. His hair, longer now, peeks out from under his bandage, and a hint of stubble has grown on his chin. He smiles and motions for me to come closer.

I walk over and sit on the edge of his bed, crossing my arms and raising an eyebrow. "So, I hear you spoke for Emma?" I tease, nudging his leg lightly with my knee. "I see how it is."

His blue eyes brighten, lighting up with a spark I haven't seen in months. In a soft, husky whisper, he says, "Ender."

"Oh, Kal!" I gasp, my voice breaking as I throw my arms around him, pulling him close and burying my face in his shoulder. When I finally pull back, a single tear slips down his cheek, mirroring my own.

FORTY

JAKE AND I CRUISE down I-70, the open road stretching before us. The windows are down, and the mountain air sweeps through the car, a refreshing rush against our skin. I close my eyes, feeling the cool breeze tangle in my hair.

I know Camp's got the concert crisis under control, but if he thinks I'm just going to kick back and let him handle everything, he clearly doesn't know me well.

Opening my eyes, I peek over at Jake. His hands grip the steering wheel, and he sings along to "Dancing Nancies" by Dave Matthews Band (obviously). His Patagonia jacket ripples in the breeze.

"Hey, thanks for doing this," I shout over Dave's raspy voice.

Jake lowers the volume and shoots me a quick smile. "No problem. Jim was happy to meet with us. Besides, it's a good chance for me to catch up with him before my position starts."

My eyes go wide. "Wait. You *got* the position?"

Jake glances at me, his eyes sparkling. "Yup, he offered it to me a couple of weeks ago. With everything going on, I forgot to mention it." He nods toward the windshield, a proud grin tugging at his lips.

"You're looking at the new assistant for the County of Denver's Arts and Venues Division beginning in the spring."

"Jake! I'm so proud of you! Only one way to celebrate." I give his arm a squeeze before turning up the volume and humming along to Dave.

Outside the window, the landscape is a gold, green, and white blur, with the towering mountains as a steady backdrop. This highway can be a mess in winter, but in September, it's like driving through a postcard. I bop along to the beat, a smile lighting up my face.

"What's on your mind?" Jake shouts, squinting against the wind.

"Honestly, everything." I laugh. "I'm just so grateful. Kalendar's turning a corner, I get to spend time with you, and this state is so *freaking* pretty." As "Ants Marching" starts playing, I grin. "And yeah, I totally see why you're obsessed with Dave."

Jake chuckles and nods. "Windows down, perfect weather, and Dave on the speakers—can't beat it." He cranks up the volume, letting the music fill the air.

We're winding our way up to Red Rocks Amphitheater the next morning.

"It's just up ahead," Jake says as we drive through a tunnel that looks like it was carved by a million tiny elves.

"This is gorgeous."

I slide down my window and pop my head out to better see the smooth and perfectly sculpted iron-red rock. My hand reaches for my phone to capture it for Instagram, but I stop myself—choosing, instead, to just enjoy the moment.

We pull into a parking spot and climb what feels like a thousand stairs, finally reaching the venue. The natural beauty takes my breath away—well, what's left of it. I'm pretty sure you need to be an athlete just to visit this place. I glance back at the never-ending steps, bent over to catch my breath.

We move closer to the seating area, and I watch as hundreds of people jog up and down the endless stairs leading to the stage. Sweat drips from their sculpted bodies despite the lack of humidity. Others are in the midst of their yoga practice. I glance down at my Converses, jean shorts, and long-sleeve sweater. Clearly, I didn't get the memo.

Jake chuckles. "I might've forgotten to mention this is a morning workout hotspot."

A ridiculously good-looking guy jogs past us, his ebony skin gleaming with sweat, and I can't help but stare.

"Yeah, that detail would've been nice to know."

The rocks around us rise up like giant guardians, making me feel tiny in comparison. From up here, Denver sprawls below like a painting, the skyline sharp and clear against the horizon.

"There's Jim!" Jake points to the far right of the stage. I follow his finger and spot a guy in jeans and a black blazer waving at us.

I wave back as my heart stumbles. *Ugh.* Why didn't I invite Camp? He'd have no trouble sweet-talking our way into performing here. What am I even going to say to this guy? How have I not prepared for this?

"Ready?" Jake says.

Nope. "Yup."

We hop down the stairs together, dodging runners along the way. Jim approaches with a welcoming smile as we get closer to the stage.

"Hey, Jake," Jim says, his voice warm.

"Hi, Jim. Thanks for meeting us," Jake replies, his voice sounding oddly professional.

"Of course. I appreciate you both coming out," Jim says, turning his attention to me. He extends his hand with a confident smile. "And you must be Lavender. I'm Jim Baker."

"Nice to meet you, Jim," I say, matching his handshake with a firm one.

Jim is one of those cool music guys. His graying hair is pulled back into a tight bun, and he wears a gray hoodie under a black blazer, striking a perfect balance between laid-back and stylish. His blue Ray-Bans catch the sunlight before he takes them off, revealing kind eyes that put me at ease.

"So, tell me about your band. Midnight Peace Runners, right?" he says, diving in.

"Uh, yeah." I push my sunglasses up onto my head.

Here we go.

"Our mission is to spark a peace revolution. Our songs speak about what's going on today. We want people to feel they're not alo—"

Jim interrupts, "I'm so sorry, but your eyes are unique. I've never seen that color before. Are they contacts?"

"Er, thanks," I say, caught off guard. "They're real." Behind him, Jake gestures for me to slow down.

Jim crosses his arms, his expression apologetic. "I'm sorry; please go on."

I take a deep breath, feeling my shoulders relax a bit. "Anyway, we're just a group of friends trying to make a difference in this crazy world through our music. I know I'm biased, but our songs are *really* special. It even woke my brother from—" I pause, smoothing my ponytail as I decide to skip that part. "Nevermind. I just know we've got something good here, and if you give us a shot, I promise you won't regret it."

Jim presses his lips together in a smile, a mix of amusement and something I can't quite read—maybe he's impressed, or maybe he thinks I'm naïve.

Jake nods for me to keep going.

"Look, I know it sounds far-fetched. We're not naïve—how can one band possibly change the world, right?" I say, gesturing across the sky. "But let me ask you this: What reaction do you get when you hear an amazing song? Especially a new one that inspires you?"

Jim hesitates, his gaze drifting off into the distance. *Great, I've lost him.* But then his expression changes, as if he's a kid on Christmas morning. His voice starts soft, but with each word, his excitement builds.

"When I hear a song like that, I'm completely in the moment. Everything feels right, and all my problems… disappear," he says, his eyes lighting up. "Next thing, I'm texting everyone I know, telling them they've got to hear it, too. And then it's on repeat—in my car, my house, my head, everywhere."

Yes, yes, yes, yes!

"Exactly," I say, feeling a surge of pride. "That's the impact our songs will have. Once they're out there, they'll spread like wildfire. I'm sure of it."

Jim nods but places his hands on his hips, his eyes narrowing. "I get what you're saying, but how will you draw an audience? That's what the board is worried about. You're a new band, and few people even know you exist. How do you plan on selling out our venue on the concert day when you're still under the radar? You have to see where we're coming from."

I freeze for a moment, searching for a clever reply. But before I can come up with anything, Jake steps in.

He clears his throat and gestures toward the seats. "Maybe this will answer your question?"

Jim and I turn to see a crowd gathering at the top of the stairs. Front and center are Camp, Anna, and Nate. Camp has his guitar slung around his neck, and Anna and Nate are each holding speakers high above their heads.

Air leaves my lungs. Who are these people? How did they pull together such an enormous crowd? I glance at Jake, and he meets my gaze with a knowing smile, giving me a quick wink before turning back to the scene unfolding before us.

Camp strums his guitar; the familiar chords of our first song—the one we played for Kalendar—echoing off the stone walls.

The yogis and runners pause their work outs and turn their attention to the gathering mob.

"We are the Midnight Peace Runners!" Camp's voice booms from the speakers.

Goosebumps crawl up my arms.

"We're about to play the recording of our very first song. Who's ready to hear it?"

The audience behind him erupts, chanting and cheering like they've been waiting for this moment their whole lives.

I can't believe this is happening.

"All right then, geez, y'all. Give me a moment." Camp chuckles into the microphone.

Beside me, Jim laughs, his eyes bright.

"Before we kick things off, I need y'all to do me a favor," Camp says, his voice full of mischief. "Take a look down at that beautiful lady standing on the stage. Can y'all say, 'Hi, Lavender'?"

"Hi, Lavender!" echoes through the venue. My cheeks are burning.

"Perfect, well done," Camp says, laughing. "You're not mad at me for that, right, Lavender?" He grins.

I cover my face with my hand in an attempt to hide.

He chuckles. "Okay, okay, here we go. Nate, please play our song for these fine folks."

Nate gives a thumbs-up, and within seconds, our song fills the venue, reverberating off the ancient rocks. At this volume, I can almost see every word and note weaving its way through the audience, wrapping them into the fabric of the song.

When the song ends, I exhale, gathering the courage to glance at Jim. When I do, I'm startled to see his eyes glistening with tears.

"Well, what'd y'all think?" Camp calls out, his voice brimming with enthusiasm.

The response is immediate—cheers and excited shouts erupt.

"Are you planning to come to our concert on October 5?"

The crowd goes wild, whistling and shouting for more, their excitement contagious.

"We're only selling tickets on the day of the show, so make sure you get here early," Camp continues, his grin widening. "Bring everyone you care about. Heck, even bring the people you don't care about. This concert is going to change how you see the world. That's a promise."

Another thunderous cheer erupts, echoing through the stadium.

Camp descends the stairs to us and the crowd moves with him. I gasp at the sheer scale of the audience; it's even larger than I imagined.

When he reaches me, he sweeps me up into his arms and twirls me around.

"Kiss her, kiss her!" the crowd chants, making my face flush a second time.

Camp just laughs as he sets me down and turns to Jim.

"Hi, I'm Campion, but everyone calls me Camp," he says, extending his hand.

"Well, hello, Camp. I'm Jim Baker, the booking agent for Red Rocks," Jim replies, shaking his hand. "After today's performance, I'm confident the board will have no problem keeping your concert on October 5th."

"I sure do appreciate that," Camp says. "I'm sure Lavender here sweet-talked her way into it." He squeezes me closer.

"She did, actually. I was already convinced, and then you guys showed up and … Wow," Jim replies, looking at the crowd. "There must be five hundred people here." He says, astounded.

"Five hundred and fifty-four, to be exact," Camp says with a confident grin. "Nate did a head count before we came in. And that was after *one* day of hitting the Denver streets. Just wait until the concert."

Jim's smile widens. "Well, all right then."

FORTY-ONE

"HAPPY BIRTHDAY, BABE!" Mom bursts into my room, her energy filling the space. "We've got a big day ahead!" She shivers as she hurries to shut the window.

Groaning, I pull the covers over my head.

"I told Kalendar we'd visit him this morning, then we're getting our nails done this afternoon, and I've invited Emma and the band over for dinner, a little party of sorts. I can't believe you're eighteen! My baby's all grown up!"

I lower the covers and glare at her.

She ignores my glare and rubs her arms. "How did you sleep in here? It's freezing!"

A sigh escapes my lips as I massage the sleep from my eyes and sit up, squinting at her. She's wearing a *Happy Birthday* headband and holding a *Birthday Girl* sash in her hand.

"So, what do you think of the plans?" she asks, watching me with wide, sparkling eyes.

"It's wonderful, Mom. Thanks," I say, managing a sleepy smile.

"Of course, love. Take your time getting up. I told Kalendar we'd be there around eleven, so we've got time," she replies, kissing my forehead before leaving.

As I stretch my arms overhead and yawn, my gaze drifts to the campsite outside the window. I do a double take—the lanterns glow a vibrant purple instead of their usual white. I reach for my phone and call Camp.

"Morning, birthday girl," he answers; his southern twang makes his greeting sound like a melody.

"Hey. So, I'm looking at the campsite right now. Are the lanterns purple, or have I gone colorblind at eighteen?"

He chuckles. "Yep, purple for my Lavender girl. Happy birthday."

MY Lavender girl?

"Thank you," I say, my voice embarrassingly soft.

"Your mom filled me in on your plans for today. Sounds like you've got a busy morning ahead. Enjoy it, and I'll see you tonight."

"Can't wait," I reply, my voice a tad stronger this time.

I slip into my robe and head downstairs to the kitchen, where an enormous spread of flowers, fresh fruit, and pastries sits on the counter. Dad stands by the refrigerator, sipping his coffee.

"What's all this?" I ask, my mouth watering as I take in the feast.

"Camp dropped everything off early this morning," he says. "Said it's from the band."

"Wow." I exhale.

"Happy Birthday, hun." He walks over to hug me. "I love you."

"Thanks, Dad. I love you too." I melt into his hug, savoring the softness of his flannel shirt against my cheek.

After loading my plate with fruit and a pumpkin muffin, then pouring myself a cup of coffee, I find Mom on the porch and take a seat beside her.

"There you are, birthday girl," she says with a twinkle in her eye. "So, how about Campion's gift?"

"It's from the band," I reply, my eyes probably giving away the dreamy look I'm trying to hide.

"Mm-hmm," Mom grins. "I have a feeling this is just the start of many more gifts."

"Maybe." I smile, glancing at the campsite.

"Are those lights purple?" she asks, following my gaze.

"Sure are." I grin and clutch my mug tighter, letting the warmth enhance this perfect moment.

"Well, I'll be." Mom laughs, adjusting in her seat. She clears her throat. "Lavender, I know you're eighteen now, and I know that you and Brandon were never … intimate in *that* way," she says. "At least, I don't think so …" Her eyebrows take flight as she fixes her eyes on mine.

I roll my eyes and groan. "Mom, where is this going?"

"It's just that I see how much you like Campion—and with good reason. That young man is handsome and charming," Mom fans herself with her napkin. "So, I can understand if you want to take your relationship to the next level," she continues, her eyes softening. "Please, make sure you're safe."

My face burns with embarrassment. "What relationship? He's never actually told me he likes me. And," I gesture wildly at my lips, "I *tried* to kiss him once, and he pulled away. He literally *pulled away*, Mom. It was mortifying."

She clicks her tongue, her gaze drifting into the distance. "How old is Campion, do you know?"

I frown. "He just turned twenty. Why?"

She crosses her legs, her foot bouncing in the air. "And before today, how old were you?"

"Seventeen, obviousl—" The realization slams into me. "Oh."

A knowing smile tugs at her lips. "That Campion… he's a gentleman."

Is *that* why he pulled away? Because I wasn't eighteen yet? It all clicks into place—the flirting, the touches, the lingering glances. Could he…does he…is it true he *actually* likes me?

I clear my throat, forcing my voice to calm. "So… should we head out soon to see Kalendar?"

"Yes. Jake's going to meet us there."

"Where is he?"

"Oh, he had some things to do this morning. He didn't want to wake you but told me to give you this." Mom gets up from her chair and sits on my lap, covering my cheeks in a thousand kisses.

"I doubt this is what Jake meant." I laugh, pushing her away.

"Sure it is." She smiles.

A couple of hours later, we walk into Kalendar's hospital room, and it's as if someone threw a pink party grenade. Shiny balloons bounce along the ceiling, and glittery banners stretch across the walls. Kalendar, Jake, and Emma wear birthday hats and blow noisemakers as if attempting a world record. In the corner sits a giant cake that looks like it could feed an army.

"You guys!" I exclaim, my voice full of surprise.

"Happy birthday!" Jake sings as he approaches me.

"Thank you!" I reply, hugging him tightly before turning to Kalendar's bed.

"Happy birthday, Ender," Kalendar says quietly, a warm smile lighting up his face.

Over the past week, Kalendar's made incredible progress with his speech—so much that Dr. Jeffries said he's never seen anything like it. He still can't project well, though, so he whispers most of the time.

"Thanks, Kal. My birthday wish has come true." I hug him carefully.

"Happy birthday, Lavender," Emma wraps her arms around me.

"Thanks, Em."

Kate strolls in with a huge grin. "There's the birthday girl! Kalendar's been buzzing about today. Has he given you his gift yet?" she asks, glancing at Kalendar.

"No," I say, squinting at him curiously.

Kalendar sits up straighter, his blue eyes locking on mine. "I'm coming home in a week. They're releasing me."

I look over at Kate, who nods in agreement. Tears fill my eyes as I look back at Kalendar.

"What? My word isn't good enough?" he teases.

I pull him into a hug, squeezing a bit too hard.

"Ender, I can't breathe," he squeaks.

I let go, my face flushing. "Oh my gosh, sorry! I'm just so happy …" My voice fades as tears of joy stream down my cheeks.

Kalendar hands me a tissue from his bedside table. "I know, Ender."

Once I manage to stop crying, I turn to Kate. "So, what day exactly?"

"Next Saturday, October 5," she replies.

My heart sinks.

Kalendar catches the look on my face. "I know you've got the concert that day, and I don't want you feeling guilty. I'll see you on Sunday."

"No, Kal, I need to be here." I protest.

"No chance," he cuts me off. "You're going to that concert. The world needs a band like yours now more than ever. This is only the beginning for you guys." His eyes fix on mine, and I know there's no use arguing.

"Thanks," I whisper.

For the rest of the afternoon, I'm walking on air after hearing Kalendar's news. At the nail salon, Mom, Emma, Anna, Josephine, and I can't stop talking about him. Turns out, Mom knew about his release for a few days, but kept it a secret to surprise me on my birthday.

I bombard her with questions: Are they sure he's ready to come home? What will recovery look like? When can he start college? She answers patiently—he's ready, but recovery will involve six months of physical therapy, and he'll take this year off from college to start fresh next year.

I insist she and Dad miss my concert to bring Kalendar home. She reluctantly agrees, but only if I let Jake come.

"We've talked about this as a family. Kalendar wants all of us to go to the concert. Then Jake and I spoke about it separately, and he wants to support you if Dad and I don't go. I know Kalendar would want that too," she says. I can't argue with that.

It's early evening, and I'm home in my room, getting ready for the party. Mom gifted me a new Free People dress for my birthday—a flowy white spaghetti strap with delicate floral details that makes me feel beautiful. With Emma's help, I curl my hair, letting it fall in soft waves around my shoulders.

"Wait, is that Camp?" Emma says, peering out the window.

I follow her gaze and spot the Jeep climbing up the driveway, a trail of dust swirling behind it.

The clock on my bedside table shows it's four o'clock.

"Shoot, he's an hour early!" Navigating the fabric of my dress, I rush downstairs, then to the front door, opening it just as Camp steps out of the Jeep.

His eyes take me in, crinkling at the corners. He removes his cowboy hat and lets out a slow whistle. "You look beautiful."

"Thanks," I reply sheepishly as I admire his outfit—dark blue jeans and a light denim shirt.

"I know I'm early, but I'm hoping we can take a quick ride. There's something I want to give you."

"S–s–sure," I stammer. "Let me ask Mom."

"Of course." He smiles.

I step inside and find Mom on the back porch, prepping for the party. Her cheeks are flushed, and there's a smudge of flour dusting one of her cheeks.

"Mom, why are there so many plates?" I ask, eyeing the basket overflowing with paper dishes.

She pauses and glances at me. "Oh, I may have gone a bit overboard. We'll use them for another event," she says quickly. "Did I see Campion's Jeep coming up the driveway?"

"Yeah, he wants to take me for a quick ride before the party."

"Of course. Have fun." She kisses me on the cheek.

I hesitate. "Aren't you going to remind me to come back in time for the party?"

She straightens the floral arrangement on the outdoor table. "It's Campion. He knows when the party starts. I trust he'll get you here in time."

"Okay, thanks." I head inside, but pause. "Are you all right? You seem flustered. I hope you're not stressing about dinner."

She shakes her head. "I'm fine. I'm just feeling emotional today." Her lips press together in a smile. "You go have fun with Campion."

"Okay." I scratch my nose. "Be back soon."

She blows me a kiss.

"Oh, and Em will be down in a minute to help you," I shout over my shoulder.

"Wonderful! Tell Campion I say hello."

I slip on my sandals and grab my purse before heading outside. Camp is leaning against the Jeep, gazing at the mountains.

He turns as I approach. "All set?"

"Yes, but my mom seems a little weird. I'm surprised she's okay with us leaving with the party starting so soon."

"She trusts me to bring you back on time. I'd never let you be late for your own party." His hazel eyes sparkle in the sunlight.

"That's exactly what she said." I laugh.

"See?" He grins and opens the passenger door for me.

"Thanks," I say, sliding inside. Butterflies flutter in my stomach as he shuts my door and heads to the driver's side.

Camp navigates the Jeep down the driveway, and when we reach the end, he turns left, leading us up into the forest.

"Are we going to the campsite?" I ask.

He smiles and shakes his head.

The Jeep continues its climb up the mountain, bouncing over dips in the dirt road. I grip the grab bar tightly; my smile is so wide that a bug flies into my mouth. I spit it out, laughing.

Camp slows the Jeep, concern clouding his perfect face. "You okay?"

I laugh. "Yes! Just maybe swallowed a bug."

He chuckles. "Do you want me to put the windows up?"

"Heck no." I grab the handle again, ready to go.

He shakes his head, an easy smile crossing his face. "All right, then." He presses on the gas.

Golden aspen leaves dance around us, some finding their way into the Jeep. The towering trees line the dirt road, their trunks stretching high into the sky. Sunlight filters through the leaves, casting a warm, enchanting glow in the forest.

We eventually stop in a clearing several miles from my house. Camp parks and gives me a quick smile before reaching for his door handle. "Wait here," he says, his voice low. A thrill of anticipation stirs in my stomach.

There's rustling in the trunk, and I glance at the side-view mirror. Camp is pulling out a blanket with one arm and holding a small box wrapped in kraft paper with the other; a twine bow sits on top.

A few moments later, he opens my door and extends his hand with a soft smile.

I slip my hand into his, feeling like I'm floating out of my skin as he guides me out of the SUV. A short distance away, the blanket lies on the grass on a small hill. As we reach it, a gasp escapes my lips—the view from this hill is breathtaking. Mason sits clear on the horizon. How have I never been here before?

"Beautiful, isn't it?"

"It really is," I reply, still amazed.

"I have something for you." He holds out the small box. "Would you like to sit?" He motions to the blanket.

"Sure." I settle onto the blanket, smoothing the folds of my dress.

Camp sits beside me, handing me the box. "Happy birthday, Lavender."

"Camp, you didn't have to …"

"I wanted to," he interrupts.

I peel off the wrapping, revealing a jewelry box. Inside is the most stunning necklace I've ever seen—a delicate gold chain with a music note pendant encrusted in tiny diamonds. It shimmers in the fading light.

"Camp, I don't even know what to say," I breathe.

He takes the box from my hands, lifting the necklace out. He drapes it around my neck, his fingers brushing against my skin. "It looks beautiful on you." His eyes brim with affection.

"Lavender, listen." His voice is soft, almost hesitant. "I need you to know—I'm so sorry about that night, when you kissed me." His eyes search mine. "God, I wanted to kiss you back. With *everything* in me." He exhales, shaking his head. "But my mom raised me right, and you were seventeen. I just couldn't."

His fingers brush a stray hair behind my ear, lingering for a moment. "But I've thought about that moment every day since."

Without a second thought, I lean in and press my lips to his. The taste of berries and mint hits me, a sweet burst of flavor that sends shivers down my spine. My whole body is buzzing with a thrill I've never felt before. Camp's hands cup my face as he leans into the kiss, and everything else fades away. It's as if we're connected on a level beyond just being together—something magical and deeply intimate. He parts my lips with his tongue and searches for mine; I eagerly let him find it.

Camp's lips trail down my neck. My breath quickens, a soft moan escaping as I lean into his touch. His kisses travel toward the edge of my dress, and then he pauses, lifting his head to meet my eyes.

"You're perfect," he whispers.

I cradle his face and pull him back to meet my lips. Time stands still until a sudden snort breaks the moment. I pull away, laughing as I glance around. Camp follows my gaze, and we both chuckle. A herd of elk surrounds us, their curious eyes watching.

"Can't look away, huh, guys?" Camp laughs. He checks his watch. "We should probably head back, anyway. Time to celebrate the birthday girl."

"This is all the celebration I need," I murmur, pulling him into another kiss.

Camp kisses me back, then chuckles against my lips. "I promised your mom I'd get you home on time, remember?"

I groan as he stands, reluctantly letting go. He extends his hand, and as I rise, everything around me seems to come alive. The leaves seem more vibrant, and the breeze caresses my body in a way it hasn't before. It's like when I first realized Josephine was Maggie, and the world shifted most unexpectedly.

The elk surround us. As a kid, I was terrified of them and was always told to keep my distance. But right now, I'm not afraid at all. A massive bull walks toward me, and Camp steps between us.

"It's okay, Camp," I reassure him, squeezing his arm.

He hesitates but shifts to stand beside me, staying close.

The bull inches closer, its presence surprisingly calm. I reach out and place my hand on his nose, surprised by the softness of his fur. He leans into my touch, nuzzling his head against my palm.

Camp gathers the blanket with a playful grin. "Looks like you've made a new friend," he teases. "But we'd better get going."

"One sec," I reply, returning to the bull. I lean in and kiss his nose. It lets out a playful, throaty sound—almost like a cheerful grunt—as it bounds across the valley.

"What's he doing?" I gasp in amazement.

"You made that bull's day." Camp chuckles. "He's playing!"

I can't help but laugh as I watch the bull nudge his elk friends with playful enthusiasm, dancing around them.

As we descend the mountain, a wave of joy washes over me, so different from how I felt just weeks ago. I gaze up at the sky and whisper a heartfelt, "Thank you." I'm unsure who I'm thanking, but this day feels like proof that someone is watching over me—maybe Grandpa, teaming up with the universe. I smile at the thought. Camp's laughter fills the Jeep; he's looking in his rearview mirror.

Turning around, I spot the elk trotting behind us, their presence making me laugh so hard I snort. "What are they doing?"

"They can't get enough of you." Camp chuckles. "I know the feeling." He winks and my cheeks flush with warmth.

A strange energy shift fills the Jeep as we approach the house. Camp seems suddenly nervous.

"Everything okay?" I ask.

He clears his throat. "Yeah, more than okay," he replies with a smile.

As we emerge from the forest, my house comes into view and air rushes from my lungs—at least a hundred cars fill our front yard.

"Camp! What's going on?" I exclaim, turning to him in disbelief.

He laughs, shaking his head. "Don't look at me. It's all your mom and dad's doing. I was just here to keep you distracted."

"You knew about this? No wonder Mom was so casual about me leaving."

Camp chuckles as he pulls into the driveway.

My heart pounds so hard it beats in my fingertips—Camp picks up on it, because his hand closes over mine in a steadying grip.

"These people care about you, Lavender. You and your family have built something beautiful here—so enjoy every minute. And if you ever need to step away, find me, okay?"

I tilt my head up to him and nod, a slow calm settling in my chest.

As we round the bend in the driveway, tears well up in my eyes at the sight before me. My friends and family line the entrance, shouting, "Surprise!" They're holding balloons, gifts, flowers, and banners, their overwhelming love and excitement making my heart swell.

"I'll get the door for you," Camp says, his voice steady and warm.

As I wait for Camp to open my door, my gaze sweeps over the crowd. At the front, Anna has her arm wrapped around Charlie's waist, while Emma and Josephine hold hands nearby. Sophia and Aly wave enthusiastically. Dad rests his arm across Nate's shoulders, and

Mom stands beside Jake, their fingers intertwined. Jake lifts his phone, and Kalendar's smiling face beams from the screen. All of my worlds have come together, and they sync so beautifully.

FORTY-TWO

PEEKING OUT AT THE crowd is definitely one of the most idiotic things I've ever done.

I can't believe we sold out Red Rocks. Jim Baker just shared the news. Not only that, but they had to turn *hundreds* away.

All these people—here to see us. They look so cool and there's *So. Many. Of. Them.*

I start to hyperventilate.

Josephine spots me in distress.

"Deep breaths," she says, her calm voice immediately working its magic. She grabs my hands and matches her breaths to mine, and I slowly feel better.

I give her a grateful smile.

"Remember why you're here," she advises. "The way you four play—it sparks love, connection, and vulnerability. If you start to panic, close your eyes and picture that spark. That's what they came for." Her lips twist. "And if that doesn't work, pretend everyone in the audience has spinach caught in their teeth."

I laugh and nudge her with my shoulder. "Thanks."

She smiles, and my anxiety fades, replaced by a warm, euphoric buzz.

For years, I wondered if I'd ever be anything more than a weirdo with purple eyes. But tonight, standing here, feeling the crowd's energy like they already know us—like they already *feel* the music—I know I'm part of something bigger. Something that matters. And somehow, all those years of feeling lost brought me right here.

"Better?" Josephine asks, holding my arms.

"Yes," I exhale, then study her. "Can I ask you something?"

"Of course, love. What's on your mind?"

I hesitate for a beat. "Why do all this? Start the band, put in all this effort? I mean, I know the universe talks to you." She narrows her eyes. "Which I really *do* believe in," I quickly add. "But this is *a lot*. And you don't even take credit for it."

Her expression softens, and her gaze drifts toward the stage. "It's a way of honoring my brother." A pause, a flicker of something unreadable in her eyes. "And… Well, there's more to it than that. But that's a story for another time." She winks.

"All right, guys, ten minutes until showtime!" Anna announces, excitement bubbling in her voice. "How about we take a pre-show photo? We're about to make history!"

"That's a great idea!" Josephine chimes in, clapping her hands.

"I'll take it. Get together," Jake offers, reaching for his phone.

I walk over to where Anna, Nate, and Camp stand.

Camp wraps his arms around my waist, and his warm breath tickles my ear. "You okay?" he whispers, his voice sending a shiver down my spine.

"Just a little nervous."

"You're going to be amazing," he breathes, and I squeeze his arms, finding comfort in them.

"All right, everyone ready?" Jake announces, pointing his phone at us.

Camp's arm slides over my shoulders, and I nuzzle my cheek into his jacket, smiling shyly at the lens. Nate stands next to us, with his hands in his pockets, and Anna loops her arm through his; one big, happy pile.

"Josephine, get in here!" I motion for her to join us.

"Yeah, c'mon, Mags. You're part of this band too," Camp says.

Josephine flashes a smile and moves in, settling beside Camp.

"One, two, three." Jake's camera lingers for a while.

"Thanks, Jake," I say, walking over to him. "Any news from Mom or Dad?"

I'm still feeling guilty for not being home to welcome Kalendar. He was supposed to get out of the hospital a few hours ago; they should be home by now.

Jake shakes his head. "Nothing yet, but you know how hospitals are; discharges always drag on longer than they say."

I twist my lips. "Okay. Promise me you'll tell me if you hear anything, right?"

"I mean, I won't stop the concert or anything but, yeah." He smirks, then pulls me into a quick hug. "You go out there and give it everything you've got. Sing for Kalendar."

I nod and stay wrapped in Jake's hug a little longer, soaking in the warmth and safety I always find in his arms. A wave of gratitude hits me hard, and tears well in my eyes.

Jake pulls back slightly, meeting my eyes. "What's wrong?"

"I'm so grateful for you, Jake," I say, my voice trembling. "You're an amazing brother. Thanks for always being there for me."

He smiles and wipes a tear from my cheek. "Of course."

"Okay, guys, it's almost show time. How about a huddle?" Nate says.

We form a tight circle, wrapping our arms around each other and lowering our heads like we're gearing up for a big football play. We stand there for a moment, soaking in each other's energy.

Nate clears his throat, digging a crumpled piece of paper from his pocket. He unfolds it, bringing it close to his face.

"We are the Midnight Peace Runners. Our mission is to stop hate and spread love. Let's bring back connection; get our generation to unplug from the feeds and actually talk to each other. Face-to-face. Imagine that." He glances up from the paper and wiggles his brows.

Camp and I laugh.

Anna claps slowly, mock-serious. "Preach."

"Let's drown out negativity and turn up the volume on peace, love, and connecting with nature. *That's* why we're here."

Nate's eyes shine as he adds with a grin, "Oh—and to make some damn good music."

"Amen," Camp drawls.

"Hallelujah!" Anna and I chime in together.

"That was awesome, Nate," I bump his shoulder with mine.

"Thanks, Lavender." He grins.

"Ready to do this?!" Anna shouts.

The whole band erupts in a loud "Whoop!"

Anna loops her arm through mine, and we move toward the stage with Nate and Camp close behind. My heart is hammering.

Josephine strides ahead of us, then suddenly whirls around, her smile so big it's contagious. "Let's start a peace revolution," she declares with a wink, then spins on her heel and heads for the stage. Her long, flowy kimono billows out behind her as she gracefully walks to the microphone.

I lift my eyes to the sky, watching the clouds glow peach and rose as evening settles in. The air is surprisingly warm—almost like summer snuck back for a night—and it makes me want to freeze time; stay in this perfect moment a while longer.

Josephine's voice, steady and sweet, floats through the venue. "Thank you all so much for coming tonight."

The crowd bursts into loud cheers. She lets the applause die down before continuing.

"I especially want to thank you for taking a chance on a new band. Some of you might have heard their music before, but I know many haven't. Maybe you're here because a friend brought you, or maybe you just stumbled upon this event. Well, lucky you." There's laughter. Josephine chuckles and tilts her head, thinking. "It's amazing, isn't it? That we're all here together, sharing this moment. We put down our phones, stepped away from our screens, and we're simply present in this incredible space. The power of music is divine."

The whoops grow louder; the air is electric.

"The world has been a sad and lonely place lately. I think you can all agree with me on that."

The crowd shouts in agreement.

"Well, the band you're about to see is here to change all that. They're on a mission to spread peace, community, and love, and I know you'll feel every bit of that tonight!"

The cheers get even louder.

"So, please join me in giving a huge welcome to the Midnight Peace Runners!"

The roar of the crowd thunders in my ears. I steal a glance at Camp—he's focused on the stage, but finds my hand and tightens his grip around it.

"No turning back now." He grins, swinging his guitar over his shoulder and leading me onto the stage.

My breath catches at the sight of the crowd. They're incredible— thousands of smiling faces beaming down at us.

Camp strums his guitar, and instantly, the crowd goes quiet.

"Good evening, Red Rocks!" he shouts into the microphone.

The crowd erupts in another wave of cheers, whistles, and applause.

"Thank you for spending the night with us," he continues.

The crowd goes wild, cheering and catcalling, especially the ladies. I roll my eyes and chuckle.

He laughs into the mic. "Seriously, though, we're so damn glad you're here. Since this is our first time playing live together as a complete band, let me introduce you to everyone."

He gestures to Nate. "This here is Nate on bass."

Nate throws up a peace sign and then waves at the crowd.

"On drums, we've got the insanely talented Anna."

Anna hits a quick solo and then waves her drumsticks at the audience.

"And standing next to me is the lovely Lavender on vocals. I have to confess, I'm quite smitten with her, y'all," Camp adds, grinning.

The crowd screams in response and I can't help but turn beet red, covering my face with my hand.

Camp catches my eye and winks, making me blush even more. I lower my hand, smile, and give a shy wave to the crowd.

"And, well, I'm Camp," he announces before breaking into his signature pterodactyl dance. It's the same hilariously awkward move I saw once before in the woods, and it's as ridiculously awesome as I remember. I laugh and glance at Anna. She's shaking her head, grinning from ear to ear. The crowd is into it—laughing, and some even join in.

Camp's goofy intro instantly puts me at ease, and I wonder if he planned it to make me feel more comfortable.

"Our first song is one we literally wrapped up last night," he says, flashing a grin. "So, if it's a bit rough around the edges, don't throw bottles at us or anything." More laughter. "We might be a little crazy for debuting it so soon, but I think it's good. It's called *And Onward We Go.*"

As Camp and Nate strum the opening chords, my excitement skyrockets. All my nerves have vanished, replaced by a rush of adrenaline.

Camp wasn't kidding about finishing this song last night. I wrote it during our drive to Denver, which turned into an adventure thanks to a wild hailstorm on I-70. We stopped at every accident to make sure people were okay, called for help, and handed out snacks and water. It slowed us down, but it felt amazing—like we were really making a difference.

Camp gives me a quick nod, and I tighten my grip on the microphone, ready.

"In the heart of a storm, when hail starts to fall,
A call to unite can be answered by all.
Braving the tempest, we stand side by side,
To protect our friends, we won't let you slide."

Camp's raw twang joins in for the chorus.

"In a hailstorm's rage, we'll shelter the weak,
A symphony of kindness, the love that we seek.
Umbrellas of compassion, we'll hold them high
Together we'll weather, under the same sky."

The crowd's energy is electric. We pour everything into the song, giving it our all as if it's our last. The response is overwhelming when the final notes fade—cheers, tears, and thunderous applause.

Before I know it, hours have flown by like mere seconds. It's hard to believe we're already in our last song. The crowd has been fantastic—so warm and energetic.

"This final song is our first single," Camp announces. "It came out of a really hard time for us, but it became something extraordinary. We want to dedicate it to Kalendar Flynn."

I can't help but tear up as I clutch the mic, feeling the weight of the dedication.

"But before we dive in, we've got a little surprise for Lavender," Camp adds, his grin widening.

My heart races.

"There is a special guest in the crowd tonight. Where are ya, friend?" Camp shields his eyes from the spotlights and focuses on the area at the foot of the stage. I follow his gaze, eagerly searching for …

Kalendar.

Sitting in a wheelchair just beyond the barricade.

Mom, Dad, Jake, Charlie, and Emma are all there with him. Tears blur my vision as I rush to the edge of the stage.

With help from the security officers, I jump down and sprint to Kalendar, throwing myself into his arms.

"How long have you been here?" I ask, my voice cracking as I wipe my tears.

"The whole time," Kalendar says with a grin. "I'm so proud of you, Ender. And hey, stop crying, or you'll mess up that pretty makeup of yours."

I chuckle and swipe at my eyes again, then quickly hug everyone and rush back to the stage, trying to rein in my ugly crying.

Camp hands me a handkerchief.

"Was it a good surprise?" he asks into the microphone.

I take the handkerchief, dabbing at my eyes. "It was the best surprise I could've imagined," I half-cry into the mic.

Our audience cheers and cries along with me.

Camp leans close to me, covering the mic with his hand. "You ready?"

I nod, glowing from the inside out.

Camp strums the opening chords of "Kalendar's Song." We named it after him the day he woke up in the hospital—Nate's idea. "It's only fitting," he'd said, and it felt like the perfect tribute.

Camp moves from his mic to stand beside me, and we sing together, our voices blending in perfect harmony.

As the song fades, the crowd gasps in awe. I blink my eyes open, having shut them briefly to soak in the final notes.

"Well, I'll be," Camp says, his voice full of surprise.

I follow his gaze skyward. Thousands of fireflies light up the sky, their glow creating a magical canopy above the venue. It's the most beautiful sight I've ever seen.

Camp regains his composure and leans into the microphone.

"A big thanks to our firefly friends for showing up tonight." He chuckles. "And thank you, Red Rocks. You've given us an experience we'll never forget." Camp raises his arm triumphantly, and the bracelet I made for him sparkles in the stage lights.

"Can you guys shine some light on our amazing audience?" Camp speaks into the mic, addressing the lighting crew.

As the lights scan the crowd, a collective movement catches my eye—every hand thrust into the air, each wrist bearing the bracelets I made.

Thousands of bracelets.

Emotion wells up inside me, rendering me speechless. The crowd's unified cheer is overwhelming.

I glance at Camp and cover the mic with my hand. "How is this possible? Did you do this?"

"We all did," he says, glancing behind me at Anna, Nate, and Josephine. "And the proceeds from the bracelets are buying your neighbor, Hoosier, a new tractor. I know that's important to you."

I turn around as they make their way over. "Guys …" I can't hold back my tears anymore.

"We love you, Lavender!" Anna shouts, her voice full of warmth.

"Eh, guess we'll keep you." Nate winks.

"A love that extends beyond this physical world," Josephine says.

They form a circle around me. My gaze drifts to the sky, the fireflies flickering in time with the stars and I swear I can hear Camp's magical guitar chords floating through the air; the same chords that helped me find my way here.

Home.

EPILOGUE

"*THE MIDNIGHT PEACE RUNNERS are taking the state by storm. Their concerts are consistently selling out across Colorado. A spokesperson for the band announced that they'll be adding shows in Montana and Idaho to their summer concert series. Their distinctive bracelets, symbolizing love, peace, and unity, are regularly sold out online, indicating a readiness for change in the world.*"

"Ender, this is crazy! Can you even believe you guys are *this* big?" Kalendar grins as he looks up from the *Denver Post* article he just read aloud.

"It's wild, definitely." I laugh. "But honestly, I'm not surprised—people are ready for a change. I can feel it happening already." I meet Camp's eyes. "Can you?"

Camp rubs my back. "Absolutely," he says, leaning in for a kiss.

"You guys are like celebrities!" Emma exclaims.

She's helping Kalendar with his PT stretches on the lawn when she snatches the article he was reading and scans the page.

"Okay, listen," she says, bringing the newspaper closer to her face. "People are literally organizing Midnight Peace Runners meetups in California. Like, actual people meeting up to spread your message."

She flips the page and beams.

"Look at this—fans hosting a forest clean up day in Breckenridge. This is incredible." She turns the magazine to show me the photo.

"Lavender, Sweetheart? Ivy's on the phone for you," Mom shouts from the porch.

"Thanks. Be there in a sec!" I call back.

I turn to Emma, my heart glowing. "It's amazing," I admit. "Actually, a Cali tour sounds pretty awesome." I catch Camp's eye with a mischievous grin.

He laughs. "I'm totally up for it, but I don't want you burning out before college starts."

"College? Boston is so far away, I'm still kind of on the fence about it …"

"You're going to college!" Camp and Kalendar say at the same time.

"All right, all right." I laugh. "Be right back."

I rise from Camp's lap, feeling the coolness of the early spring air. The sun is setting here, so it must be late in Rhode Island.

"Tell your cousin I said hi." Camp grins.

"I will." I wink at him.

"And tell her to come visit us!" Kalendar adds.

"Yup," I reply with a grin.

The kitchen air is thick with the aroma of tomato sauce and garlic. Mom walks over from the stove and hands me her phone.

"Hey, Ivy!" I sing.

"Lavender? Hey. Sorry I called your mom's phone, but yours kept going to voicemail. Are you by yourself?" Her voice is quiet.

I glance toward the stove—Mom's humming softly as she stirs a bubbling pot.

"Uh, give me a sec," I say, heading into the living room. I plop down on the leather couch, grabbing one of the bajillion throw pillows to hug.

"All right, I'm alone now. What's up?"

"I've been hearing music," Ivy blurts. "Like... music no one else can hear. The same thing that happened to you. Do you think that's even possible? I mean—there's only one Camp, right?"

Her words tumble out fast.

I shift the pillow behind me and cross my legs, trying to absorb her words.

Maybe she's imagining it. But I remember how disoriented *I* felt when the music first started. I can't just brush her off.

And if it *is* real... how is that even possible?

There *is* just one Camp. But…

"It could be possible, Ives. When did you last hear it? And how often?"

"Just now," she replies, nerves leaking into her voice. "I called you right away. I've been hearing it for about a week. At first, I thought my mind was messing with me, like I was dreaming it or something, but now I'm sure it's real."

I glance out the window, watching Camp and Kalendar laughing together. Emma's sprawled out on the lawn, flipping through the newspaper, completely absorbed.

"Okay," I say, thinking it over. "Keep track of when you hear it. Also, try to figure out where it's coming from."

"I think I already know where," Ivy says, her voice suddenly urgent.

"Oh yeah?"

"This might sound totally bananas, but I think it's coming from Harborside Island. That little island across the ocean from us."

"That's far," I murmur, "but not impossible." My mind is already racing. "Let me talk with Camp, and I'll call you soon."

"Thanks, Lavender. Would you mind keeping this between the three of us for now?"

"Of course. Bye, Ives."

I wrap a blanket around my shoulders before heading back outside.

Camp lifts his gaze as I approach him.

"How's Ivy?" he asks.

"She's good." I scratch my nose. "Hey, have you heard from Josephine this week?"

He nods. "Yeah. She's on vacation for a bit."

"Oh, where'd she go?"

"Rhode Island."

Upstairs on my nightstand, the crystal heart glows.

ABOUT THE AUTHOR

Christina King once roamed the world of luxury fashion in high heels and blazers. These days, she's more likely to be found in muddy boots chasing chickens or writing in her cozy nook with the San Juan mountains as her backdrop. She lives off the grid in Colorado with her husband and their three wild-hearted kids. *Lavender* is her debut novel. Discover more at ChristinaKingBooks.com.

Author photograph by Jennifer Morrissey